TFS FUGITIVE

The Terran Fleet Command Saga - Book 4

*****

Tori L. Harris

ISBN: 978-0-9961796-8-3
TFS FUGITIVE
THE TERRAN FLEET COMMAND SAGA - BOOK 4
VERSION 1.0

Written and Published by Tori L. Harris
AuthorToriHarris.com

Edited by Monique Happy
www.moniquehappy.com

Cover Design by Ivo Brankovikj
https://www.artstation.com/artist/ivobrankovikj

Be not afraid of greatness. Some worlds are born great, some achieve greatness, and others have greatness thrust upon them.

The Terran Guardian
(paraphrasing William Shakespeare, *Twelfth Night*)

Chapter 1

"How reliable is this intelligence?" Admiral Sexton asked, momentarily ignoring the detailed graphical information presented on the room's view screen in favor of a written Fleet Intelligence Estimate. "I'm not trying to bust either of your chops here, but this really has gotten a little embarrassing at this point, don't you agree? This is … what? The fourth or fifth time we've had what looks like actionable intelligence on the location of the Sazoch's payload module?"

The Commander in Chief, Terran Fleet Command, drew in a deep breath and leaned back in his chair to stare at the ceiling, collecting his thoughts and working hard to keep his frustration level in check. While his flag conference room table could easily accommodate twenty people, only the two closest seats were currently occupied — to his left by Vice Admiral Tonya White, Chief of Naval Intelligence, and to his right by Lieutenant General Vernon Tucker, Commandant of the TFC Marine Corps.

Sensing their boss's mood, White and Tucker silently exchanged glances with one another across the table. Each of them had worked with Sexton for many years, and while the CINCTFC was generally a level-headed officer who was rarely critical of his subordinate commanders, they were keenly aware of the tremendous pressure being brought to bear on both him and their organization at the moment. Both officers also knew all too well that the first person to speak up in situations such as this often ended up serving as a lightning rod for all of the pent-up frustrations that existed in the room at that particular moment. As a result, both waited silently — avoiding eye contact and hoping that Sexton would address their colleague across the table first.

"So, from a political standpoint," Sexton continued in an uncharacteristically sarcastic tone, "we earned ourselves a little credibility and trust around the world with the defeat of the Resistance task force … and rightfully so. But then we turn right around and give the appearance of being caught flat-footed in the aftermath of their attempted biological attack. I can assure you that our inability to successfully recover the device is doing nothing to reassure our membership that we remain *capable* of defending the planet … let alone *competent* to do so. And, frankly, with everything that's been going on with the Leadership Council, the timing simply could not be worse. I assume you've both seen some of the press conferences our public affairs folks have been giving, right? 'Oh, uh, yes, there is at least a *small* possibility that a species-killing bio weapon landed somewhere on the Earth's surface, but that was *only* three weeks ago, so we still have only a vague idea of where to look for it at the moment. We'd just like to ask you all to bear with us and be patient for just a little while longer while we wander around South America looking for it. There's obviously nothing to worry about, though, folks, because we'd all be dead already if it had functioned properly.'"

In the brief, uncomfortable silence that followed, Sexton grudgingly realized that his self-indulgent browbeating was doing little to advance the conversation, let alone accomplish the mission at hand. *One of the most irritating things about being in charge,* he reflected, *is that there's really not a hell of a lot of difference between venting and issuing an ass-chewing.* "Alright," he said, shaking his head resignedly, "one of you please convince me why it's going to be different this time."

"Sir, as I mentioned last week, I'll take the hit for accepting some of the first information we received at face value," Admiral White began. "With the benefit of hindsight, it may seem a little ridiculous now, but at the time, we had no reason to suspect that anyone would mount a disinformation campaign to prevent us from recovering the device. We obviously would have preferred to keep the entire recovery operation under wraps — at least until it was safely in our possession — but the Guardian's public declarations on the subject touched off something of an international free-for-all. Even as dangerous as the weapon was purported to be, *everyone* wanted this thing: us, most of our member nations, and, perhaps most troubling, several multinational corporations. Based on what we now know, it appears that the payload module was successfully recovered within just a few hours after the battle with Resistance forces concluded."

"How is that even possible?" Sexton asked, incredulous. "We had just seen a ninety-megaton atmospheric antimatter explosion. There was debris falling across that entire region for several hours, so detecting something this small would have been all but impossible, even if it had been safe to be out there looking for it at the time. We had to have been in a better position to detect the device than anyone, so how did someone else manage to not only find it, but safely recover it?"

"It was an inside job, Admiral, it had to be," Tucker said, speaking up for the first time.

"Inside job?" Sexton repeated, furrowing his brow and struggling to keep his temper in check. "What the hell does that even mean, Vernon?"

"I think we're getting a bit ahead of ourselves," White said, raising both hands placatingly. "To answer your original question, what's different this time is our information source. We were contacted by this man," she said, nodding to the room's view screen, "former Argentinian Defense Force Colonel Mateus Rapoza." As she spoke, the room's AI displayed a file photograph of the Argentinian officer along with a brief biographical summary. "Colonel Rapoza identified himself as the commander of the team that recovered the Sazoch's payload module."

"You said *former* Defense Force Colonel, so who does he work for now?" Sexton asked.

"Before I answer that, sir, let me just say that we are still running our standard series of background checks to vet this information, but, so far at least, we have reason to believe that Rapoza is a credible source. Everything he's told us has checked out."

"I'm not going to like your answer, am I?"

"No, sir, you aren't. Until very recently, Colonel Rapoza and his team were contracted through a subsidiary of Crullcorp International. They believed that they were securing the device in preparation for safe disposal, but it became obvious over the next couple of weeks that this was not to be the case. He made a couple of inquiries regarding plans for destroying the device, after which he and his team were summarily dismissed. In spite of a number of open threats from his former employer — both legal and physical — he contacted a trusted colleague within the intelligence arm of the Central and South American Union. Thankfully, they called us immediately."

"Karoline Crull's company," Sexton said flatly, as if this bit of information had been a foregone conclusion given the location of the alleged recovery site. "Well, I guess as tempting as it is to have a knee-jerk reaction and assume we're being played here —"

"Again," General Tucker interrupted, then immediately regretted opening his mouth.

"Yes, *again*," White said, giving the Marine general a disapproving glance. "As I previously stated, most of the information we received before being contacted by Colonel Rapoza appears to have been intentionally misleading — and apparently crafted in such a way to keep us as far away from the device as possible for as long as possible. As to General Tucker's comment about this being an 'inside job,' I have to agree. Crullcorp pulling the strings on a recovery operation outside the purview of TFC — but obviously with some level of cooperation from the Argentinian government — certainly qualifies in my book. Although there have never been any successful prosecutions, it's generally understood that the company has every significant politician in that country on the payroll, so to speak."

"I was also referring to the Guardian," Tucker said. "It supposedly shot this thing down, but then provided us with a bogus touchdown location that turns out to be over a thousand kilometers south of where it actually landed." The old general paused and smiled apologetically at the CNI. Even at sixty-three, he was still very much a Marine's Marine — in outstanding physical condition and the kind of man whose mere presence was enough to completely dominate most rooms he entered. Such was not the case here, however, and he knew from personal experience that Tonya White was not an officer he wanted to cross.

"Well, now, I don't know that I would characterize the Guardian's information as 'bogus' ... not entirely, at least," White replied, clearly unwilling to let the Marine general off that easily. "We have actually recovered some debris at the location it specified that was almost certainly part of the Sazoch delivery vehicle. Granted, we haven't found anything we believe was related to the payload itself, but the search is still underway."

"Right — and conveniently enough, at a location well-known for some of the most hazardous oceanic conditions on the planet. So, what are we really thinking here? Somehow or another, the Guardian managed to collude with Crullcorp to recover this thing before we could get to it? To what end?" Sexton asked, peering over his glasses at his CNI.

"Anything I say would be purely speculation, Admiral, and I don't like to —"

"I insist," Sexton said. "I know you have an opinion, Tonya, and I'm interested in hearing it."

"Alright, then," she sighed, narrowing her eyes pensively as she organized her thoughts. "I agree with General Tucker that the location provided by the Guardian off Cape Horn was most likely an intentional ruse. I have no idea how or why it pulled that off, but if Colonel Rapoza is telling us the truth, that means that the Guardian probably did intercept and shoot down the Sazoch craft somehow. Under the circumstances, I can't image anyone or anything else would have been able to do so."

White paused for a moment, staring back at the two men to see if either would commit themselves to filling in any additional details for themselves. Her disciplined mind was accustomed to following the data, wherever it happened to lead, and although speculation and "playing a hunch" was sometimes called for in her line of work, she was keenly aware that doing so involved risks. This was particularly true when all of the speculation could be attributed to a single person and then ended up being used as the basis for putting lives at risk. All things considered, if this turned out to be another fool's errand, she would prefer to have someone's name on it other than just her own.

"I'm with you so far," Sexton prompted. "Naturally, Crullcorp would have mostly been interested in the portion of the Sazoch carrying the biological agent, so the Guardian tells them where to find it, then decoys us with the impact site of some useless debris. Under the circumstances, all it really had to do was throw us off the scent long enough to ensure that the payload had been secured. Does that sound about right?"

"Once again, we're making a lot of assumptions, sir, but that scenario fits the information we have in hand at the moment."

"Fair enough, and what do you recommend that we do about it?"

Admiral White raised her eyebrows earnestly as she continued, "Well, sir, political considerations notwithstanding, our first priority must be to secure the biological agent. Colonel Rapoza believes it to be relatively safe for the time being, but the risk of a release will increase dramatically once it is transported to other sites and testing begins."

Both Sexton and Tucker opened their mouths to ask the obvious question at the same moment before, with no small degree of satisfaction, Admiral White preempted them both. "Oh yes, gentlemen, it is almost certainly their intention to divide the agent up into smaller batches for transport. After that, it will likely be distributed to their allies or exceptionally well-funded customers. Whoever ultimately gets their hands on a sample will begin their own, independent laboratory testing — perhaps with the goal of figuring out a way to modify it so that it can be used in a more controlled, targeted manner. In its current form, it's obviously of very little use as a weapon unless you happen to be a member of a species other than our own."

"Makes sense to me," Tucker said. "It's either that or destroy it immediately to prevent someone else from getting hold of it and killing us all. And I hardly think they would go to all the trouble of keeping their recovery operation a secret if they intended to destroy it. By the way, that is what *we* intend to do with it, is it not?" he asked, looking back to Sexton for an answer.

The silence from both Sexton and White provided an even more unequivocal answer than if either of them had chosen to speak.

"You two have got to be kidding me with this. That's nuts, and both of you know it."

"I don't want to go down this rabbit hole right now," Sexton said, raising his hand to head off further discussion. "The truth of the matter is that any decision as to the final disposition of the bio agent will be up to the Leadership Council. I am confident, however, that many will argue that it makes sense for us to at least take a look at how the viral vector was engineered. It might well be our only opportunity to see if we can develop a defensive strategy in case something like this is used in the future."

"Uh-huh, or kill every last one of us in the process."

"Look, I understand what you're saying, General, and for what it's worth, I agree with you. But there are several labs around the world that have been successfully handling the deadliest of pathogens for a very long time. Frankly, it would surprise me if our own scientists haven't created something just as deadly at some point — or at least figured out how to do so. So, if it comes to that, I'm sure we can find a way to get it done safely. For now, however, our role is to recover the device, just as Admiral White said."

"Fine," Tucker said, shaking his head resignedly. "What's the op?"

Earth, Patagonian Desert

Two hundred years after Humanity's reliance on fossil fuels for energy production had all but ended, its insatiable need for petroleum-based products had continued unabated, with space-based hydrocarbon mining operations only now beginning to supplant more traditional methods. The northernmost section of Argentina's Santa Cruz Province was an area where this fact was readily apparent, even when viewed from orbit. Here, over fifteen thousand square kilometers of the high desert was covered by a seemingly random patchwork of access roads punctuated by rectangular clearings — each one centered around a current or former oil well. Otherwise, the barren, inhospitable region was almost completely deserted except for a few small towns populated mostly by the families of oil company employees. For those looking to keep their activities private, however, few remaining places on the Earth's surface offered a better location for conducting illicit activities beyond the prying eyes of both passersby and the local authorities.

Near a solitary grouping of abandoned oil wells, Crullcorp International had staked out a compound of sorts. There was nothing particularly remarkable about the collection of buildings they had erected, other than the fact that there were no other structures to speak of for over thirty kilometers in any direction. A total of four buildings, including one that appeared to be a massive hangar, were clustered around a flight ramp large enough to accommodate all but the largest air and spacecraft.

With the advent of gravitic fields and Cannae thrusters, traditional runways were no longer necessary to allow a site such as this to support air operations. Those same technologies, however, had been spurring the aerospace industry to produce ever larger ships for several decades. As a result, a strip of reinforced concrete that might have easily served as a runway in years past was now barely adequate for several aircraft to land and park.

Perhaps the most noteworthy aspect of the entire facility was the double security fence surrounding it. Similar to what might be installed around a sensitive military facility or even a high-security prison, the two, four-meter-high fences were topped with wicked-looking razor wire and covered with a black polyethylene mesh for privacy. Closed circuit security cameras were mounted at various locations — both atop the fences and within the compound proper. Less obvious, but still detectable to the trained eye, were the host of thermal cameras, fence sensors, radar, and even seismic sensors arrayed around the compound. Just in case all of these were insufficient to deter trespassers, signs were posted conspicuously around the site in both Spanish and English warning (falsely) that the CSAU had authorized the use of deadly force against anyone foolish enough to attempt unauthorized entry.

What the prime minister of the Central and South American Union *had* actually authorized (under heavy pressure from the Leadership Council) was the first military operation Terran Fleet Command had ever undertaken against a terrestrial target. At precisely 0300 local time, the entire region was lit by a single, gigantic flash of light as TFS *Karna* transitioned inside the atmosphere at just over two thousand meters above the compound. The destroyer's arrival instantaneously displaced over twenty million cubic meters of air, creating a powerful shockwave that slammed into the ground immediately beneath the ship six seconds later, then traveled outward in all directions at just under the speed of sound. None of the Crullcorp buildings were equipped with windows, and seemed to handle the passing shockwave with little to no damage. Such was not the case for the three aircraft sitting on the facility's flight line, however. Even though their front windscreens and passenger windows were reinforced for the heavy loads associated with atmospheric flight, most were either completely destroyed or heavily damaged by the warship's earth-shattering transition.

Like the Hindu warrior king of the *Mahabharata* for which the ship was named, *Karna's* arrival over the field of battle was an awe-inspiring omen of doom for any enemy who might be foolish enough to oppose her.

TFS Karna, Patagonian Desert
(0300 local - 55 km northwest of Las Heras, Argentina)

"Transition complete, Captain," the helm officer reported. "All systems in the green. The drop zone is directly beneath the ship and we are stabilized in a two-thousand-meter hover. Gravitic fields have been reduced to minimum extension and are clear of the flight deck."

"Very well. Green deck," Captain Bruce Abrams said calmly.

"Aye, sir. Executing," the XO replied, entering commands at his touchscreen to relay the appropriate orders to both the flight deck and the four squads of Marines awaiting a go order inside their *Gurkha* assault shuttles. Although the *Karna's* normal complement included a standard TFC platoon of forty-two enlisted troops and one officer, today's operation involved a total of sixty-one Marines. Given that each was equipped with universal EVA combat armor, this force constituted significantly more firepower than Captain Abrams thought absolutely necessary. Nevertheless, the mission did involve a number of unknowns, including the disposition, strength, and composition of Crullcorp's private security force. In addition, it was critical that the Sazoch's payload module be quickly secured in an undamaged state — assuming, of course, that their intel was accurate and it was actually still here.

Immediately after the go order was received, side and rear cargo doors opened on each of the heavily armed *Gurkha* assault shuttles — the four of which were currently taking up all available space on *Karna's* aft flight apron. Less than twenty seconds later, each of the ASVs had disgorged its squad of Marines, then released the clamps holding it in place as its controlling AI prepared to follow the Marines to the target below. In rapid succession, all sixty-one Marines completed the short run to the edge of the flight apron and leapt silently into the night above their objective.

"The Marine squads are away, Captain," the XO reported. "The first zero four *Hunters* will be airborne in seven zero seconds."

"Thank you, Commander," Abrams replied as video feeds from the Marine lieutenant's EVA suit and two of the *Gurkhas* appeared on the bridge view screen next to a high-resolution overhead view of the surrounding area. "Tactical, anything in the area we need to be concerned about?"

"Not really, sir. As expected, the CSAU has some fighters airborne, but they're holding just off the east coast — nearly two hundred kilometers away. There's also some civilian air traffic, but nothing that's a factor at the moment."

"Good. That's what I wanted to hear. Please let me know immediately if anything changes."

"Aye, sir."

Abrams stared at the bridge view screen, captivated by the light-amplified view of the Crullcorp compound from the perspective of the Marine lieutenant's helmet-mounted optical sensor. Having completed several traditional parachute-based jumps himself, he subconsciously commanded his knees to bend and leg muscles to relax in preparation for a hard landing as the ground rushed up from below at an impossibly fast rate. This was the first time Abrams had witnessed a drop using the latest EVA suits, and although he knew that what he was seeing was perfectly normal, it truly looked as if it would be impossible for the Marines' suits to arrest their rapid descents before the entire platoon slammed into the desert floor below.

Fortunately for their occupants, each suit's AI had the situation well in hand, having calculated their approach to the target — with an accuracy measured in milliseconds — well before any member of the platoon had stepped off the *Karna's* aft flight apron. As Abrams involuntarily squinted his eyes in anticipation of the crushing impact he knew must occur at any time, the lieutenant's EVA suit engaged its thrusters at maximum power and executed a graceful, silent touchdown near the entrance to the compound's hangar. Including the time required to accelerate to their terminal velocity as well as a rapid Cannae thruster deceleration immediately before impact, it had taken the entire reinforced platoon of TFC Marines less than a minute to reach their designated starting positions and begin the next phase of their mission.

∗∗∗

First Lieutenant Tagan Locke touched down in a run, quickly taking cover in an alcove sheltering a small side entrance to the largest building in the compound. Her platoon had rehearsed every facet of this operation numerous times, simulating problem areas time and again until they had them down cold. In fact, she had hoped that things would progress so smoothly that there would be little if any need for verbal communications over their tactical comm channel — a feat which, she knew, the old-timers always considered a hallmark of a well-executed mission. In spite of the seemingly endless list of contingencies they had practiced, however, she was in no way prepared for what her suit's sensors were currently projecting into her field of view.

So much for comm discipline ... hell, so much for the plan in general, Locke thought wryly, taking a few extra moments to scan the entire area. She noted with at least some level of satisfaction that all of her people were exactly where they were supposed to be. Their OPORD now called for simultaneous breaches of some or all of the facility's buildings, depending on what they found in terms of opposing forces. The problem was, as far as she could tell at the moment, there *were* no opposing forces.

"Top, Locke. Confirm negative contact," she finally called over the tactical comm.

"Top here. Negative contact confirmed," her platoon sergeant answered immediately.

"Confirm negative ECM detected," she added for good measure. She knew that it was highly unlikely that her entire platoon, four *Gurkha* ASVs, and the *Karna* itself could all have their entire array of sensors defeated by any known electronic countermeasures, particularly at such short range. Then again, it seemed highly unlikely, based on the intel at least, that this facility would be unoccupied in spite of housing the deadliest weapon of mass destruction Humanity had ever encountered.

"Intrusion detection sensors only, Lieutenant," the master sergeant replied again. "No active electronic countermeasures detected."

"I don't like it, Top. Stand by," she said, ordering every member of her platoon to hold their positions with a quick command via her suit's neural interface.

"Top acknowledged."

This can't be right, she thought. *Everything else is exactly as expected.*

"Bridge, Locke."

On *Karna's* bridge, Abrams had been wondering how long it would take the young lieutenant to check in, and he was gratified to see that she did not hesitate to seek guidance when required. "I got it," he said, preempting his comm officer's response. "Locke, *Karna*-Actual. Looks like there's no one home, Lieutenant."

"Yes, sir, but it's very odd that we've got a heavy lift aircraft as well as Mrs. Crull's executive transport sitting here on the ramp. So, they're either very well hidden or they all evacuated by some other means. Either way, it looks like they knew we were coming."

"They've consistently had as good or better intel than we have lately, so it's certainly possible. What do you recommend, Lieutenant?"

"Well, if there *is* anyone still here, they're not going anywhere without our knowing about it, so I'd like to withdraw to a safe distance and let the droids handle the breaches. Depending on what we find, we'll reassess the threat and go from there. If everything looks clear, we'll move back in to conduct a more thorough search."

"Sounds reasonable. Please proceed," Abrams replied.

"Aye, sir. Locke out."

Without a moment's additional delay, Locke sent an order for all of her Marines to fall back to a set of pre-defined positions at what she hoped was a safe distance, then stepped out of the alcove and immediately arced up and away from the hangar in the direction of the closest *Gurkha* ASV.

***

Just under twenty minutes later, live video from four separate K-25 AMDs — short for autonomous multipurpose droids — was being watched intently by

TFS *Karna's* bridge crew. Although still a far cry in many ways from their classic sci-fi counterparts, the units were nonetheless quite effective at a wide variety of mission types, particularly those situations deemed unnecessarily dangerous for Human beings. Roughly spherical in shape and with a diameter of just under one meter, the droids were managed by a potent onboard AI, while at the same time having the capability to interface in real-time with other, more potent systems in the area — in this case the *Karna* itself.

Just as had been the case with the Marines' EVA suits, this was the first time Captain Abrams had been personally involved with a live operational use of an AMD, and, understandably, his attention was once again riveted to the bridge view screen. One of the first things he noticed was the fact that there was almost no noticeable difference between the droid-provided video feed versus that supplied by one of the Marine's EVA suits. Essentially the same suite of sensors was in use, all of which were being employed to update the overhead tactical plot displayed in an adjacent window on the view screen. Even the height of the camera was similar to that of a Human operator since the AMDs typically hovered using a combination of gravitic emitters and Cannae thrusters at an altitude that placed their optical sensor roughly two meters above the ground.

As the four droids approached their designated entry points, the illusion that they had been watching anything other than an AMD-provided feed was quickly shattered as each unit extended a sturdy robotic arm with a decidedly Human-looking hand into the camera's field of view. With surprising dexterity and speed, the arm placed five dots of a clear liquid in a line down the hinged side of each door. Although it was not obvious in the video feed, Abrams was aware that an ultra-fine wire was being embedded within each of the dots, leading ultimately to a small, remotely-triggered detonator. As each AMD concluded its work in almost perfect unison and began to back slowly away, he smiled to himself, wondering if he was about to witness a rather basic oversight.

"Locke, *Karna*-Actual," he said aloud — the ship's AI immediately recognizing the captain's desire to communicate with the Marine lieutenant and routing his call accordingly.

"*Karna*-Actual, go for Locke."

"Uh," Abrams began, trying to think of a way he could communicate his intentions without causing too much of a distraction for the young officer during her first significant operation. "Sorry for the interruption, Lieutenant, and I may have missed it, but did the drones confirm that any of these doors are actually locked before they go ahead and blow them off the hinges?"

There was a brief pause on the tactical comm channel, during which, he correctly assumed, Locke was hurriedly ordering a temporary hold on all four door breachings. "No, sir, they didn't, and I was actually thinking the same thing. They are designed to operate autonomously, and once we order them to execute a breach, the AI doesn't ask for further Human input unless we specifically order it to do so. It's a safe bet that they are playing the mathematical odds, though, and they probably don't think that attempting to open the doors manually will do anything to improve the chance of successfully completing the mission."

"And what do you think, Lieutenant?"

"Well, sir," she replied, vaguely amused by the entire situation, "at this point, I don't think it will hurt to try opening the doors. If there's anyone here, they obviously have some very sophisticated ECM gear that is somehow masking their presence from our sensors —"

"And they clearly know that we are here."

"That's affirmative, sir, we were pretty hard to miss."

"Right, so that being the case, please ask the AI to humor us on this one and proceed when ready. If any of the doors open, I'd recommend letting the drone do a brief security sweep before it does anything else. You can always blow the remaining doors whenever you're ready. You're doing fine, Lieutenant. I'll do my best to stay out of your way from here on in."

"Aye, sir, thank you … I mean, not a problem, sir. Locke out."

Moments later, all four AMDs once again slowly approached their respective doors, extended their robotic arms, and attempted to actuate the lever-style door handles. Not surprisingly, the doors of the three smaller buildings were locked. At the largest of the four structures, however, the handle rotated freely, allowing the door to swing slowly open.

On *Karna's* bridge, Abrams leaned forward in his seat with anticipation as his XO enlarged the window displaying the now-open doorway. Inside, the AMD's optical sensor revealed a well-lit hallway lined with several doors. Beyond, the corridor opened into what was probably the hangar area itself. The droid paused, continually scanning the area for any indication that the building was either occupied or booby-trapped. Still finding nothing, it ignored the doors on either side and made its way to the end of the hallway. As it slowly emerged into the open hangar bay, it was immediately apparent that the area to the left was nothing more than a small kitchen/break area with several tables and two restrooms along the outside wall of the building. Unfinished food and drinks could be seen on two of the tables, while on the kitchen counter, a pot of hot coffee sat untouched.

Turning its attention to the hangar bay — which, upon closer inspection, was divided into two separate areas — the droid revealed the presence of another executive transport aircraft parked near the rear of the building with all of its doors and access hatches standing open. Near the building's huge sliding doors sat three fighter aircraft, apparently in the process of being armed and prepared for launch. Air-to-air missiles had already been loaded onto external weapons pylons aboard two of the three ships. Beneath the third, a lift truck sat with another missile precariously balanced as if the maintenance crew had simply walked away in the middle of the loadout.

As the AMD moved forward once again, it became clear that the section of the hangar bay farthest from where it had entered was entirely enclosed within a massive inflatable structure. At its center sat what appeared to be an airlock/decontamination system similar to those used on TFC ships. It was here that the droid's AI gave the first indication that something was amiss.

"Bridge, Locke," the lieutenant called once again.

"Locke, *Karna*-Actual. Go ahead, Lieutenant."

"Sir, under the circumstances, I'd like to keep you live on the tactical comm channel, if you don't mind."

"Of course," Abrams replied, inwardly happy that she had called back when she did. Even though he knew Locke was an outstanding young officer, the ultra-sensitive nature of this mission compelled him to take a much more hands-on approach than usual. "Are you seeing a problem?"

"Yes, sir. The AMD in the hangar just alerted on traces of blood around the entrance to the airlock you see in the video feed. Ultimately, we may have to send it inside to get a clear view of what's going on. For now, however, its AI has successfully interfaced with the inflatable containment unit. On the plus side, it looks like we have found the payload module. They have it nested four layers deep like a Russian Matryoshka doll. So far, it appears that everything is functioning properly — environmentals, seals … everything looks intact. Stand by one, sir," she said, pausing as she issued a flurry of commands to the AMD. "Okay, you should be receiving multiple video feeds now from inside the containment unit itself."

Abrams glanced at his comm officer, who immediately opened a total of six additional windows on the bridge view screen to display all of the available video feeds — one of which caught his attention immediately. "Lieutenant Locke, can we get a better look at what we're seeing on feed four?"

"Yes, sir, I see it too."

Within seconds, the camera providing the video feed in question panned to the right, then zoomed slightly in an effort to provide a better view of the grisly scene inside the outer inflatable structure. Piled neatly against the far wall like so much cord wood was a stack of at least fifty body bags. Perched atop the pile, however, was a single, obviously female body that had been purposely left uncovered. Attached to her clothing just above the waist was a single, blood-smeared sheet of paper inscribed with what appeared to be a handwritten message. Without further prompting, Lieutenant Locke zoomed and refocused the camera again in an effort to make out the text. The note was in Spanish, written in a surprisingly steady, deliberate hand in spite of the gruesome scene within the room:

La rebelión contra tiranos es obediencia a Dios.

Tierra Primero

Although unneeded in this situation, the AI immediately provided an English translation at the bottom of the screen which read, "Rebellion against tyrants is obedience to God," adding that the quote was generally attributed to American Founding Father, scientist, and political theorist, Benjamin Franklin. Strangely, the AI produced no known references to the signature line at the bottom of the note, which translated as simply "Earth First."

Locke then panned the camera upwards for a close-up view of the body's face. The obvious cause of death had been a plasma bolt from a pulse rifle that had passed completely through the center of the chest cavity. The face, while contorted in eternal, abject rage, had been left untouched. Accordingly, the AI quickly provided a positive identification, corroborating the name of the deceased against several public and classified databases. In this particular case, however, everyone watching the video feed immediately recognized the body's identity without the slightest need for sophisticated, facial recognition software.

Karoline Crull, former Chairwoman of the Terran Fleet Command's Leadership Council, was dead.

Chapter 2

Earth, TFC Yucca Mountain Shipyard Facility
(7 months later)

Captain Hiroto Oshiro stood just a few meters from the foot of the forward brow connecting TFS *Navajo* to the wharf while awaiting the arrival of the Chief of Naval Operations. Although she had been the lead ship in her class, *Navajo* had been the last of Terran Fleet Command's cruisers to be brought up to what was now commonly referred to as the "*Cossack* spec." In addition to significant power generation improvements over the original design, the upgrades included installation of the latest in gravitic shield systems that had proved decisive in the battle against the Resistance fleet. Now, three weeks after her upgrades had been largely completed, the cruiser had returned to the shipyard for some last-minute maintenance prior to her scheduled deployment to Sajeth Collective space.

Glancing down to check the state of his uniform, Oshiro's attention was drawn to movement near the end of the *Navajo's* berth. The senior captain furrowed his brow as he watched one of the new grav carts that had become such a fixture around the shipyard over the past few months round the corner at breakneck speed and head down the wharf in his direction. Although this particular application of gravitic technology had not yet been licensed for release on the open market, the Leadership Council had been sponsoring a number of industry partnerships to fast-track various new uses of Pelaran-derived tech. Designs for "grav chairs" and stretchers, for example, had recently been made available to manufacturers of medical equipment around the world, and, in spite of the fact that it was technically illegal to do so, the miniaturized Cannae thrusters and gravitic emitters they utilized had immediately begun appearing in other products. With the genie now well and truly out of the bottle, the Council was still doing its level best to give the impression that it remained in nominal control. On Earth, however, market forces always had and always would find a way to satisfy the demand — with or without the approval of those in positions of authority.

As the cart approached, Oshiro recognized Charles Guthrie, a senior member of the facility's civilian engineering staff, at the wheel. With PhDs in applied physics and mechanical engineering, Charles was a man with unparalleled expertise in a variety of areas, particularly Extra Terrestrial Signals Intelligence technology integration and, in the captain's opinion, clearly smart enough to know better.

"Jeez, Charlie!" Oshiro said in an exasperated tone as the electrically powered vehicle came to a rapid and nearly silent halt just a few meters away. "You'll end up skidding right off the wharf and get yourself killed driving like that. Worse yet, you'll probably break something that you and I together couldn't pay for in ten lifetimes. What the hell's gotten into you?"

"Sorry, Captain," Guthrie replied, fully aware that he had annoyed the facility commander but unable to stop grinning like an eighteen-year-old boy who had somehow managed to acquire the keys to his father's Porsche. "I suppose I do need to cool it a bit. We just finished running an eval program on these things for the Science and Engineering Directorate. They essentially told us to 'go crazy,' and said that they didn't believe there was much we could do with them that would result in an accident. So, naturally, we have been more than happy to oblige. They're autonomous, of course … you can just tell it where you want to go and it will take off, just like our standard EV transport carts. As luck would have it, however, the Directorate was mostly interested in having us test them under manual control. They've got so many safety controls built into them that it's pretty much impossible to get yourself into trouble … and don't think that we haven't tried," he said, attempting to regain some semblance of professional bearing. "It's very important to let it strap you in, though."

"Right, I heard you say 'cool it,' somewhere in the middle of all that, and that's exactly what I need you to do. Is the Op Center ready for Admiral Patterson's demo?"

"Will do, sir, sorry again. I was planning on taking it down a few notches since I'm to be your chauffeur over to the OC. And, yes, our dog and pony show is ready to go. I think you'll both be pretty impressed. Several things have really come together over the past few days. We've still got some work to do behind the scenes, but as far as I'm concerned, it's ready for the first official shift tomorrow morning."

"Excellent. I'm glad to hear it," Oshiro replied, turning to look up the gangway toward the sound of approaching footsteps.

As was their custom, the two Marine guards flanking the sides of the gangway faced inward in unison, saluting crisply as Admiral Kevin Patterson made his way down to the wharf. As he reached the halfway point, Yucca Mountain's AI sounded the traditional boatswain's "Pipe the Side" call, followed by the announcement *"Naval Operations, arriving,"* to acknowledge the presence of the CNO. Patterson returned the Marines' salutes as he passed between them, held it briefly in response to Captain Oshiro's, then extended his hand.

"Captain Oshiro … Doctor Guthrie," he said warmly, "good to see you both again. I hear you're ready for a ribbon cutting ceremony."

"Yes, sir," Oshiro replied, "and if you're ready to go take a look, Charlie has come out here to give us a ride back."

"In that?" Patterson asked, already heading in the direction of the grav cart. "Outstanding. I saw these things from a distance several times during the last upgrade, but I never got a chance to check one out up close."

"You bet, Admiral," Guthrie said. "Wanna drive it?"

"You'd better believe I do!"

"Sir, I don't know if we should be —" Oshiro began with a look of genuine concern on his face.

"Oh, come on, Hiroto, Captain Davis still lets me conn *that* every once in a while," Patterson said, jerking his thumb over his shoulder at the imposing bulk of the nearly kilometer-long cruiser *Navajo*. "Surely you don't think I'll have a problem handling a glorified golf cart."

"Well, sure, I just —"

"Get in, Captain. Just for that, you can sit in the back — and just so you know, you sound just like my wife.

Anything special I need to know, Doctor?" Patterson asked, sliding in behind the wheel.

"Not really, sir. Make sure your restraints are good and tight. Otherwise, the onboard AI won't allow you to do anything too dangerous."

"That's what I was hoping you would say," he said, grinning as he pressed the accelerator and aggressively whipped the cart around to head back up the wharf.

Just seconds into their trip, Doctor Guthrie noticed a long section of guard rail had been removed on the adjacent berth in preparation for TFS *Aeneas'* imminent arrival. "Can I show you something really cool?" he asked with a conspiratorial smile.

"Sure, why not?"

Without any additional warning, Guthrie reached over, grabbed the side of the steering wheel, and abruptly jerked the cart to the left — immediately passing over the orange safety cones and through the missing section of guard rail into space over the gaping chasm of Berth 9. Unsure precisely how to react to such a seemingly unnatural situation, Patterson slammed on the "brakes" — reversing thrust and stopping the cart in midair a full seventy-five meters above the movable concrete landing platform below.

"Bakayarō konoyaro!" Captain Oshiro swore loudly from the back seat. "You could have at least told us what you were about to do!"

"That's true, but it wouldn't have made nearly the same impression," Guthrie chuckled as he peered over the side of the cart.

"You made an impression alright," Patterson said, pushing against his restraints as he also leaned out for a better view of the precipitous drop beneath them. "I'm still trying to decide if I need to head back to the ship to change my uniform, though."

All three men laughed as Patterson once again turned the cart around and headed back to the relative safety of the wharf itself. "So, I take it the Science and Engineering folks have resolved some of the scaling problems they were having with the miniaturized versions of our grav emitters," he asked, phrasing the question as an obvious statement of fact.

"No, sir, not really," Guthrie answered, "but once they released the low-powered versions they had come up with so far, it only took a few weeks before schematics started appearing online that largely overcame the previous limitations. There's nothing like having literally the entire world tinkering with a problem, right?"

"The open source model meets Pelaran tech, eh? Well, I'm happy to see some of what we've been using for a decade or more in TFC being declassified to a larger degree. It's one thing to allow major corporations access for building air and spacecraft, but the technology in this cart alone has the potential to fundamentally transform transportation. In fact, I guess we'll finally be able to stop building roads, right?" Patterson paused, struck once again by the implications of what he had just seen. "By the way, this thing is obviously capable of flight. Why limit it to driving like a traditional car?"

"Hah," Guthrie laughed, "that's a great question, Admiral, and the answer is that it's entirely arbitrary and entirely unnecessary. There are safety concerns to be addressed, of course, but I think for now they just want it to behave like what we're all used to. One of our guys actually came up with a way to override the control system so that you can increase altitude," he said, pulling a small tablet computer out of his jacket pocket. "Here, all I have to do is just —"

"STOP!" Captain Oshiro yelled from the back seat, then checked himself. "Sorry, Doctor, but I think that's probably enough excitement for now. Admiral, you can just pull over by the double doors on the left and we'll head inside."

Patterson shot Doctor Guthrie a quick smile and a wink as they exited the cart and headed through a set of heavy doors into a long corridor with a bank of elevators to one side.

"Welcome, Admiral Patterson, Captain Oshiro, and Doctor Guthrie," the AI's synthetic voice announced as they approached. "All activity in the TFC Operations Center is currently classified Top Secret, code word DEFIANT BASTION. Please enter the elevator to access the Operations Center."

"Alright, you two, I enjoy hearing all the 'touristy' stuff as much as anyone, so please, proceed with the grand tour," Patterson said as he stepped into the elevator.

"Yes, sir," Guthrie replied, then waited a few moments for the elevator doors to seal before saying anything further. "You've probably heard quite a bit of this before, but I'll hit the high spots and you can feel free to interrupt at any time with questions. The TFC Operations Center is the first of its kind anywhere in the world. Although you will see quite a few things that look familiar — not unlike a large-scale version of the

Navajo's Combat Information Center, in fact — it's easily two orders of magnitude more powerful in terms of available computing power. We've also brought together the latest generation of both sensor and communications technology to provide a level of visibility that we simply did not believe was possible … even six months ago."

"So, my understanding is that we've been building this facility beneath the Yucca Mountain Shipyard for several years, but you're telling me that its capabilities have advanced that much — even during the final phases of construction?"

"Absolutely. It's been about a year now since *Ingenuity's* first hyperspace transition. I think all of us knew that there would be a steep learning curve after that — even compared to the past fifty years' worth of data from the Guardian. What none of us anticipated was the impact of putting sophisticated, distributed AI in a position to do fundamental scientific data gathering and analysis. It's difficult to describe what that's been like this past year … kind of like being a child trying to learn a new skill while having the benefit of an experienced adult looking over your shoulder saying, 'that's good, but try it this way instead.'"

"That's gratifying to hear. Particularly given that there have been so many people out there for decades warning how the use of Extra Terrestrial Signals Intelligence data will stifle Humanity's creativity. I think their basic argument has been that the Pelaran/Grey tech is a sort of intellectual crutch — essentially 'unearned' knowledge that will ultimately lead to a decrease in our ability to figure things out for ourselves."

"Humph. I guess history will be the judge of that, but from what I can tell, it has done exactly the opposite. As far as I'm concerned, we've entered a new age of enlightenment. Yes, we've had some help, but so what. Earth is in a relatively isolated section of the galaxy, so we can probably assume that many civilizations get quite a bit more help than we did — if they manage to not get themselves conquered or destroyed by their neighbors, that is. In any event, we've done a hell of lot on our own — I'm betting more than most. That's why we came to the Leadership Council last year asking for a level of security exceeding that of the MAGI PRIME program. Everything related to code word DEFIANT BASTION is, for all intents and purposes, built on 'alien-free' tech."

"That's not to say that there isn't Pelaran and/or Grey-enhanced technology in use here," Oshiro interjected, as they stepped off the elevator into a dark, cavernous room.

Although mostly hidden from view at the moment — Patterson assumed this was largely for dramatic effect — he could see that the floor below was indeed arranged much like a massively upscaled version of the Combat Information Centers used on larger Fleet warships. Row upon row of workstations were arrayed around the room in a circular pattern, all apparently centered on what looked like an enormous platform that dominated the center of the floor area. Rising from there around the entire perimeter were viewing areas similar to those used in the much smaller Simulated Fleet Operations Training Center.

As his eyes moved naturally upward towards the domed ceiling, Patterson was amazed by the sheer scale of the room. He had seen some preliminary specifications for the facility several years ago, but had not expected it to have the feel of an underground sports arena.

"Oh, yes, of course, just about every piece of equipment we use every day has some elements that were at least inspired by ETSI," Guthrie continued casually, "but in here we took nothing at face value — all the way down to the smallest electronic components. If we didn't fully understand it, then it didn't meet the requirements for this program. Otherwise, there would have been no way we could guarantee that everything in here is serving our interests."

"And ours alone," Patterson added.

"Exactly," Captain Oshiro replied. "Now … ready to see the best feature of your new office?" he asked, nodding to Doctor Guthrie.

With a single keystroke on the doctor's tablet computer, the entire space seemed to flicker momentarily before being lit by the largest three-dimensional display ever constructed. For demonstration purposes, Guthrie had called up an image of the space immediately surrounding the Earth, and it was immediately obvious that every cubic centimeter of the entire space was accessible to the holographic projectors housed in the room's central table.

In the center of the room hovered a twelve-story-tall, photo-realistic representation of Humanity's homeworld, reaching from just above the holo table all the way up to just short of the ceiling above. On the side of the planet lit by the sun, evidence of industrial-scale agriculture and even some of the largest man-made structures could be seen in some areas, while in the planet's shadow, the lights from thousands of cities pierced the dark of night.

Both Oshiro and Guthrie were gratified to hear the muffled gasp from Admiral Patterson standing in shocked silence just a few meters away. So far, this seemed to be the typical reaction most people had when experiencing Terran Fleet Command's Op Center for the first time. "I'm not a big fan of the word 'amazing,'" Patterson finally said, "but this truly is."

"Yes, sir, I have to agree with you," Guthrie said. "One of the great things about having access to a display of this size is that it does a great job of portraying the true scale of things. The reason we came in through this entrance was so that we could place you close to the maximum distance from the center of the floor — that's just over one hundred meters. We also tilted the ecliptic a little so that several of the vessels assigned to Earth's 'Home Fleet' should come right past where we're standing. Since they're in a geostationary orbit at just over thirty-five thousand kilometers at the moment … stand by," he said, checking his tablet once again, "we should be able to see them shortly. Let me ping them so we can pinpoint exactly where they are."

With that, a tightly overlapping group of five green spheres began slowly pulsating just off to their left. Without further prompting, Patterson immediately headed in their direction for a closer look.

"I don't know about you, sir," Oshiro said, "but the only one of those my 'mature vision' can really make out in any detail is the *Ushant*. You'll notice that you can view the ships from any angle. The primary holo emitters are in the table down there, but there are supplemental projectors placed all around the room."

"This is unbelievable," the old admiral said, staring intently at the tiny carrier as it passed slowly by in its orbit.

"The actual ship is just over a kilometer in length and traveling at approximately three kilometers per second," Guthrie said, reading from his tablet. "At this scale, the ship is a shade over three-millimeters-long and is moving at just under a centimeter each second. The Moon, if you could see it, would be located about a kilometer away at this scale, but still about ten meters in diameter."

"Well, Charlie, clearly you didn't make the room big enough, then," Patterson said facetiously. "Gentlemen, I'm completely blown away. But as impressive as these holo projections are, I'm guessing they aren't what you really wanted me to see."

"No, sir," Doctor Guthrie replied, smiling broadly. "During the Resistance attack, the Guardian spacecraft provided real-time tracking data of all ships in hyperspace out to about ten light years. I think you'll agree that having that data available — in addition to Yamantau Mountain getting the *Cossack's* shields operational in time — were major factors in our victory."

"I would indeed. In fact, I'd say even with the *Cossack's* arrival, we might well have ultimately lost the battle had we not been able to pre-position our ships with such accuracy."

"Well, sir, as you correctly surmised, the reason the Guardian was able to fill in the missing pieces that allowed it to provide this data was a series of tests we had been conducting on a similar system. I use the word similar because the basic physics of the Guardian's system appears to be based on the same principles. Once we started receiving data from our most distant comm beacons, however, we made some remarkable discoveries in hyperspace quantum mechanics."

"Let me stop you right there, Doctor. I can promise you that you'll be wasting your breath if you try to explain any of that to me, but I do appreciate knowing in general how and when the discoveries were made. So, I guess what I'm hearing is that we've found a way to detect hyperspace activity at greater distances."

"That's exactly right, sir, but somewhat of an understatement. The comm beacons we've been deploying now for over a year rely on a number of very specific — let's call them 'properties' — of hyperspace itself that allow them to transmit data from point to point. The data transmissions occur more or less instantaneously, regardless of how far apart the two beacons are deployed. We knew there was a practical limit to the distance between beacons, due primarily to the precision required to establish the point-to-point data link. After we started dropping them off at greater and greater distances, however, a group of physicists with experience in optical interferometry — that's combining a group of small images or signals to produce a larger, much more powerful one — proposed that the same thing might be possible using a group of widely spaced comm beacons."

"That group of physicists he's referring to was headed up by none other than Doctor Guthrie himself, by the way," Captain Oshiro added.

Guthrie dismissed the attempt at assigning credit with a smile and a wave of his hand, then continued. "Suffice it to say that the technique worked, and better than we would have ever expected."

"I think I may be a little confused here. I thought we were talking about *detecting* hyperspace activity, but you just said this new technique applied to comm beacons. So, is this more about communications or tracking?" Patterson asked. *Why does it feel like I just stepped into a wad of chewing gum every time I talk to one of these guys?* he thought, working hard keep the conversation moving forward.

"In hyperspace, those are essentially two sides of the same coin, Admiral. One way to think of it is that the 'medium' of hyperspace itself exhibits a kind of mass entanglement that we don't see anywhere else in the universe. You can think of it almost like the surface of an infinitely large bass drum. A disturbance in one area is felt more or less simultaneously in another. Here's the thing, I don't want to give you the impression that we have anything more than a basic understanding of exactly *why* we see some of these strange phenomena. All we can do at this point is recognize certain properties that we can exploit to our advantage."

"I'm all for whatever works, Doctor. So enough with the suspense already. Please show me what you've got."

"My pleasure, sir. *This*," he said, entering a series of commands on his tablet, "is roughly equivalent to what the Guardian shared with us during the Resistance attack."

The Earth abruptly disappeared from the center of the room and was immediately replaced by a smaller, nearly transparent sphere centered around a yellowish-white pinpoint of light. Ten other objects of similar configuration were distributed at various locations around the room.

"Be aware that the scale gets a little wonky when we start dealing with interstellar distances. The AI does its best to give us as accurate a portrayal as possible while still allowing some things to be visible that we might not actually be able to see. So right now, it's showing us the eight or so star systems along with a few brown dwarfs in our immediate stellar neighborhood, so to speak. If there were ships traveling in hyperspace within this region, you would see them here. The AI projects them into normal space for clarity and highlights their locations to make them visible on such a massive scale."

"I don't see any flashing spheres, so I assume that means no ships are traveling in hyperspace within this area. I don't mind telling you that I'm relieved to see that this is the case," he observed with a smile. "Again, Doctor, this is a truly staggering accomplishment. You've obviously put us on a par with what we believe the Guardian is able to do — as far as we know, of course."

"Oh, we're just getting started, Admiral. At the moment, we really have very little intelligence data regarding what capabilities other civilizations have at their disposal. The DEFIANT BASTION classification, however, is intended to allow us to safeguard Human technology that we have reason to believe might actually *exceed* the Pelarans' capabilities. So far, that includes the fundamental designs for our C-Drive, certain aspects of our railgun technology, our gravitic shields, and now this."

With that, the room was instantly lit by an unimaginably huge number of stars. At various locations around the room, the AI highlighted what looked like hundreds of objects within green spheres.

"Dear God," Patterson gasped. "*All* of those are ships traveling in hyperspace? How far out are we looking here?"

"This is five hundred light years, and, yes, all of the green spheres represent active hyperdrive signatures. Displaying this much space at once isn't particularly useful other than reminding us of how utterly small we really are," Guthrie said, pausing momentarily to take in the overwhelming, majestic beauty of even this relatively small, remote corner of the Milky Way. "One really interesting thing we have noticed, however," he continued, "is that — so far at least — we rarely see hyperdrive signatures that behave like one of our C-Drives. When we do, they appear to be taking such massive jumps that we only detect either their departure or arrival."

"Perhaps that's our old friends 'the Greys,'" Patterson said offhandedly.

"It's certainly possible, but we just don't know yet. I doubt we would have ever been able to develop the C-Drive without having studied their technology for generations, so that's our best guess so far as well. To be honest, though, we have absolutely no idea who most of these hyperspace signatures belong to. Frankly, sir, we're struggling to even begin to come to grips with the military and scientific implications of this technology, and it will take us quite a while to begin sorting all of this out. Now, getting back to your original question regarding comm … from what we can tell, this five-hundred-light-year range is something of a practical range limitation. I hesitate to say we won't *ever* do any better than that, but it seems unlikely to happen anytime soon."

"Am I to understand that our ships will also have a five hundred-light-year comm range?"

"The short answer is yes, but that's five hundred light years from the closest virtual array of comm beacons. It takes a minimum of three to constitute an array, so the range is calculated from the geometric center of each array. This, of course, has no impact on the comm range of ships located in normal space. In order for them to access the NRD network from normal space, they will still need to be in close proximity to a hyperspace comm beacon, just as before … and the speed of light limitation still applies, of course. Once they transition, to hyperspace, however —"

"They essentially *become* a comm beacon themselves at that point, right?"

"Yes, sir, that's about the size of it."

"And when can we start making this data available to our forces?"

"Hmm … as long as everyone understands that it still needs a lot of work before it can be considered completely reliable, I'd say pretty much immediately," Guthrie replied, obviously pleased to offer the admiral this additional bit of good news. "We will, of course, need to work out the best way for our crews to access the data in a secure manner."

"Right. Off the top of my head, I'm thinking this will likely remain captain and first officer's eyes only intel."

"Probably so, sir. We'll work on advancing some clearances to make that happen as quickly as possible."

Patterson paused, shaking his head slowly. "Wow … I don't mind telling you that I'm having a hard time taking all of this in. Each time I see one of these scientific and engineering miracles that have come about as a result of the ETSI programs, I always believe that I've finally seen the pinnacle of what we are likely to accomplish during my lifetime. Then a few months later, you people somehow manage to eclipse anything that has come before. Sometimes I don't know whether to be elated or terrified."

"I know exactly what you mean," Guthrie said, nodding slowly, "but I'd recommend going with elated. There are obviously a large number of civilizations out there that have been at this much longer than we have. If the past year has taught us nothing else, it's that we have to take full advantage of every strength we have as a species if we're going to have any hope of competing long-term.

"Now, let me show you just one more thing and then I'll take you down to the floor and show you around. Shortly after we started encountering ships from other civilizations, our AIs discovered that hyperdrive signatures are unique. That applies to major categories like drive types, subcategories such as different versions of the same drive, and all the way down to individual ships. That came as a bit of a surprise at first, but in hindsight, it probably shouldn't have. Nothing mechanical with that level of complexity is ever a perfect duplicate. We've been identifying oceangoing vessels by their unique acoustic signatures since the Second World War, for example."

"Now *that* could be very useful when combined with this long range … what are we calling this thing?"

"We're open to suggestions, Admiral. A few of the techs have been calling it 'the planetarium,' but everything I've heard so far seems to miss the mark somehow."

"Yeah, that's pretty weak, although the room does remind me a bit of the planetarium my father used to take me to as a kid — other than the size, of course. I'm sure you'll come up with something. Sorry, I didn't mean to get us off topic. Since you're able to identify individual ships by their hyperdrive signature, can you show me Prince Naftur's ship, the *Gresav?*" Patterson asked, beginning to realize some of the astounding intelligence-gathering uses for the system.

"I can't show you her current position, sir, but I can definitely show you her last transition point. In fact, let me patch the system's AI in through this tablet so that it can adjust the display to follow our conversation."

A few seconds later, a single, red sphere pulsed urgently next to a star at the far end of the room.

"Excellent. And I'm assuming all of your data corroborates the location of the Wek homeworld he provided, right? Don't get me wrong, I have great respect and confidence in Naftur's integrity, but it never hurts to verify information when we can," Patterson said, smiling to himself.

"I agree wholeheartedly, sir," Captain Oshiro said, "and you could say that tracking the *Gresav* and the

Hadeon during the last days of their trip back to Graca was the first practical test of this system. As you can see, both ships are exactly where he said they would be, as are the comm beacons we sent back with him. Incidentally, both the *Gresav* and quite a few other Wek warships have made a number of additional short trips over the past few weeks. We're really not sure what that's about." As he spoke, the room's AI zoomed in on the general area of space surrounding Naftur's flagship, highlighting several items of interest with accompanying text blocks.

"I'm guessing what you're seeing is a direct result of Prince Naftur consolidating his forces … and those sites are most likely military anchorages of some sort. We haven't had a lot of time to iron out all the details of how we're going to coordinate military activities between our two worlds going forward, but we have agreed that TFC will send task forces to blockade Damara and Lesheera until the Wek have had time to reconstitute their own fleet. As you might well imagine, since Graca's ships have been integrated with the greater Sajeth Collective Fleet for centuries, suddenly reestablishing an independent Wek navy is likely to be a bit of a challenge."

"Particularly since they seemed to have so many officers willing to join the so-called Resistance movement."

"That's true as well, but I think quite a bit of that was ironically due to the sense of loyalty many of the Wek have for their traditional dynastic houses — loyalty that was skillfully manipulated for their own purposes by the Damarans."

"Is it not also true that Prince Naftur initially shared only the location of Graca with us?" Guthrie asked. "We were told that he was uncomfortable revealing the locations of the other six worlds of the Sajeth Collective until he had time to work through the myriad of political issues he was expecting in the wake of Graca's withdrawal from the Sajeth Collective."

"Initially, yes, that's correct. Admiral Sexton practically begged him to reconsider for his own safety, but Naftur believed that it was critical that he be given time to handle Graca's transition back to home rule internally before any of our forces became directly involved in the region. I'm sure he was also concerned that we might mount some sort of punitive expedition against Damara and Lesheera before he even arrived back on Graca. He thought, and I certainly agree, that it was critical for the Wek people to learn the truth about what happened in the Sol system directly from him in hopes that they would start to view us as their allies. In any event, the delay seems to have worked in our favor thus far. Politically, things have progressed for Naftur more rapidly than we would have expected. He was named Prince Regent of Graca within days of his return and immediately set about establishing formal diplomatic relations with Earth via our Leadership Council. Perhaps even more importantly for us, the intervening months have given us some time to recover from the Resistance attack. We've largely finished upgrading our existing ships, and we have replacements for the hulls lost in combat under construction. In fact, Captain Oshiro here assures me that we'll start seeing initial climbs to orbit soon … isn't that right, Captain?"

"Any day now, Admiral," the facility commander said with a significant smile.

"That's a pretty good answer, I suppose … as long as you're not still saying the same thing three months from now," Patterson replied.

"Well, sir," Guthrie said, steering the conversation back to the subject at hand, "not that I'd want us to do anything to upset our new Wek allies, but now that we've been tracking hyperspace activity in the vicinity of Graca — and more recently Damara and Lesheera — our AI believes it has also identified the other four worlds of the Sajeth Collective."

With that, the holographic display reconfigured itself once again, this time showing a slowly rotating view of seven star systems, each labeled according to their primary, habitable world.

"There you are, sir: Graca, Damara, Lesheera, Ecradea, Pashurni, Shanus, and Carnide. Based on a combination of our observations and the data Admiral Naftur provided after first contact, the AI gives this model a better than ninety-three-percent probability of being correct."

Patterson stared at the display in silence, his mind now beginning to grasp that even the vast distances between the stars would no longer provide anonymity and refuge for those who would wish Humanity harm.

"This really does change everything," he said quietly. "We must detail every available resource to accelerate the deployment of comm beacons and extend our visibility as quickly as possible. Gentlemen, our homeworld security requires that we be able to see as much of the galaxy as possible ... and we're going to find the Pelarans for ourselves."

Chapter 3

Damara
(489.3 light years from Earth)

Just as it had done each day for the past 5.3 billion years, Damara's western hemisphere slowly emerged from shadow into the light of its distant star. A true jewel among worlds, much of the planet's land mass was taken up by vast, semi-tropical savanna very similar to the Brazilian Cerrado region on Earth. Here, as was often the case when circumstances were favorable for sustaining biological life, the relentless passage of time had ultimately produced the right set of circumstances for a sentient species to arise. And, just as on countless other worlds, those same benign conditions had allowed that species to thrive until finally achieving such an advanced state of development that their mere presence had produced a negative impact on their own homeworld. Like most space-faring civilizations, the Damarans had caused systemic damage to their environment over the course of centuries in the usual fashion: accidents and industrial-scale disasters, organized warfare between nations, as well as through simple neglect and failure to act as good stewards of their own biosphere. Fortunately, just as had been the case on Earth, the same steady march of technology that created much of the damage had also allowed the Damarans to clean up enough of the mess to avoid rendering their world uninhabitable. Today, however, the threat they faced was of a much more immediate nature.

While it was certainly true that the Damarans had done their share of damage at home, it was instead their unique combination of arrogant pride mixed with equal parts ambition and a natural, instinctive fear that had led them inexorably to this moment. For it seemed that they had always been afraid — and on such a fundamental level that their fear might accurately be described as a trait that was hard-coded into their DNA makeup. In fact, their biological lineage could be traced to a group of migratory herbivores that perhaps would never have evolved to such a high degree on a world where natural predators had been more plentiful.

All of these factors, combined with an exaggerated perception of an existential threat and the desire to increase their power and influence in the region, had prompted the Damarans to make a series of tragic errors in judgment. In concert with their long-time allies and co-conspirators, the Lesheerans, they had crafted a complex strategy by which they would take control of the seven-world Sajeth Collective alliance. Conveniently, the basis of their plan had been rooted in fact. The mighty Pelaran Alliance was expanding its power base in this part of the galaxy, attempting to co-opt a race of relatively primitive, ape-like creatures to use as military surrogates. These primitives — the Damarans refused to acknowledge the species by name, perhaps in an effort to assuage their collective conscience for the genocidal act they had planned — were expected to make for a relatively "soft target" for the Sajeth Collective Fleet. Once the Pelarans' latest proxy species was destroyed, it was believed that their progress in the region would be halted — at least for the foreseeable future.

In order to accomplish their military objectives, the Damarans had staged what amounted to a coup within the Sajeth Collective military. Since the bulk of the Collective's warships were built and crewed by Wek personnel, a cleverly crafted campaign of disinformation and jingoistic propaganda was put into motion with the goal of targeting them on a specific, emotional level. As a result — and within a relatively short period of time — a large number of the proud Wek race had become convinced that the Pelaran Alliance not only posed an immediate threat, but had also killed a much beloved member of what had once been one of their world's dynastic families. Most of this was, of course, either an outright lie or a gross exaggeration of the facts, but, as is so often the case, bad news sells, and is generally much easier to believe than "the truth" in any event. Accordingly, less than a month after the campaign began, the demand for action within the Collective's Governing Council had reached such a fever pitch that several influential representatives had formed a group called the "Pelaran Resistance."

Up to this point, the Damarans and Lesheerans had been delighted to see that the results of their efforts were far exceeding even their most optimistic expectations. Even sooner than they had hoped, fractured loyalties within the Governing Council as well as the Sajeth Collective fleet were rapidly stripping the loathsome (but nonetheless useful) Wek civilization of much of its former influence. Once the military expedition to Terra had been successfully completed, it was clear that they would finally be able to relegate the planet Graca to little more than a virtually limitless source of resources for themselves and their Lesheeran allies.

Unfortunately for the Damarans and the Lesheerans, however, the military expedition to Terra had not gone as planned.

Now, as the planet's terminator raced across the face of its largest continent at just over fourteen hundred kilometers per hour, a new day dawned for its nearly two billion inhabitants. It was a day that, with the exception of the recent reduction in Sajeth Collective military activity in the area, seemed rather unremarkable — but it was not to remain so.

At a distance of just over three hundred thousand kilometers from the planet, a large volume of space seemed to distort convulsively — the starfield blurring, then disappearing entirely for a split second — followed immediately by ten flashes of grayish-white light. The primitive, ape-like creatures from Terra had crossed the vast distance between the stars to arrive at Damara.

TFS Theseus, Damara
(489.3 light years from Earth)

"Transition complete, Captain," Lieutenant Dubashi reported. "Range to Damara, three one seven thousand kilometers. All systems in the green. The ship is at General Quarters for combat ops and ready to C-Jump. C-Jump range 39.4 light years and increasing. Sublight engines are online, we are free to maneuver."

"Thank you, Lieutenant," Prescott replied in his usual, steady tone while simultaneously checking the AI-reported status of the nine other warships comprising his task force via his own Command console.

"No major combatants detected, Captain," Lieutenant Commander Schmidt announced from Tactical 1. "I've got four vessels the AI is categorizing as patrol corvettes that are in a favorable position to intercept us if they choose. Otherwise, we're receiving all kinds of sensor emissions, as expected. They definitely know we're here, sir."

"Threat assessment?"

"Evaluated as minimal at this time, sir, but if they decide to fight, we will be within their projected maximum beam weapons range in zero three minutes."

"Understood. Keep an eye on them, Schmidt."

"Aye, sir."

"Flag to all ships," Prescott announced, his voice immediately routed to every bridge in the task force, "execute the deployment as planned. Prepare for incoming ordnance from both the surface and the approaching patrol vessels. Weapons hold. Launch operations hold."

After two weeks' worth of exercises preparing for what amounted to a naval blockade mission, Captain Tom Prescott (technically now Rear Admiral (Select) Tom Prescott) was finally growing accustomed to referring to his ship as "the Flag." The announcement of his impending promotion had not been unexpected, given the events that had transpired over the previous year. Although Terran Fleet Command had thus far gone out of its way to avoid becoming top-heavy with high ranking officers — particularly during the period when there had been no operational ships — the organization now found itself in desperate need of officers to place in command of squadrons deployed on detached service for extended periods.

The composition of the original fleet had been capped by international agreement at sixty warships, nearly half of which were to be comprised of *Ingenuity*-class frigates whose primary mission was originally envisioned as one of exploration. In addition, the "terms and conditions" documentation provided by the Pelarans had dictated that the initial production run must also include a total of thirty-three major combatants consisting of eighteen destroyers, twelve cruisers, and three carriers. Even though each of the warships had been fitted out with technology that was dramatically more advanced than what the Pelarans had initially specified, TFC's fleet was still primarily seen as a defensive force. The plan had been to send most of the frigates out on extended-range missions of scientific inquiry while the larger combatants would remain in the general vicinity of Earth (and, eventually, her colonies).

All of this had changed with the Resistance incursion into the Sol system, particularly since their attack had included an attempt to completely annihilate Human civilization just a few short months after its first interstellar flight. Six destroyers and two cruisers had been lost to engagements with the Resistance task force, and in the immediate aftermath of the attack, TFC's Leadership Council had authorized construction to begin on their replacements. This was in addition to a "hull cap" increase to a total of one hundred warships. Repairs and upgrades to existing vessels had, of course, been the first priority for Fleet's three primary shipyards, but with much of that work completed, a total of thirty additional ships were now in production.

Throughout Human history, naval strategists had realized that their forces could indeed be used for defensive purposes, but accomplishing that mission required the will to utilize those forces for the projection of military power — often far from home and over extended periods of time. Interstellar naval forces, it turned out, were little different in this regard. To their credit, TFC's leadership recognized not only the need for additional ships, but also the immediate need to advance officers possessed of singular talent and integrity to lead those forces. Accordingly, Admiral Sexton had recently published a list of ten promotions to rear admiral (lower half). No one had been surprised to see Captains Prescott and Abrams on the list of those chosen to fly the flag of a one-star admiral.

For now, however, until the list of promotions was approved and finalized by the Leadership Council, the designation of TFS *Theseus* as the task force flagship was more a matter of professional courtesy and practical operational necessity than one of actual rank. Prescott was indeed in overall command of his small task force, but he remained a mere captain for the time being. And although he was afforded the lofty honor of electronically hoisting his broad, one-starred pennant, he was not afforded the luxury of being assigned a "flag captain" to take over the day to day operations of commanding his own ship. Fortunately, however, he still had Commander Sally Reynolds as his second-in-command, and he would have chosen her to run his ship over any other officer in the fleet that he could name.

"Sir, we are being hailed," Dubashi reported from the Comm/Nav console.

"One of the corvettes?"

"The transmission is currently being relayed by the lead vessel, but originates on the surface. The source identifies itself as the Damaran Headquarters of the Sajeth Collective Fleet. It's textual only, sir, and I don't think they are looking for a response."

"Oh boy, here we go," Reynolds grumbled to herself without looking up from her own Command console.

"I'm not sure I'm following you, Lieutenant. Read the message aloud, please."

"Aye, sir. The message reads as follows: 'Terran vessels, Terran vessels, you have been designated as enemy combatants and, as such, are subject to immediate attack. Discontinue your approach towards Damara and depart the area immediately, or you will be destroyed. Replies will not be acknowledged and this warning will not be repeated.'"

Without comment, Prescott glanced back down at his touchscreen and was gratified to see that all nine warships in his task force had acknowledged his orders. A quick check of the tactical plot on the starboard view screen confirmed that each had smartly executed their pre-arranged course corrections and were making their way to their assigned duty stations. This included TFS *Industrious*, which had executed a C-Jump to place it in a position to allow for full sensor coverage of the opposite side of Damara. In less than three minutes, the remaining ships in his formation would be in a position to provide optimal support for one another in terms of defensive fire and, if necessary, to unleash a devastating railgun, energy weapon, or missile attack against any location on the planet's surface.

"They don't have to reply, but they're most definitely listening. Open a channel please — same frequency, but go ahead and send translated audio, video, and text."

"Yes, sir," Dubashi replied, rapidly entering the required series of commands before turning to face Prescott once again. "Ready when you are, Captain."

Prescott mentally ran back through some of the intelligence he had read regarding the Damaran culture and decided that standing might imply a position of authority or even dominance — exactly what he was going for in this case.

Fleet had recently made the decision to allow the crews of all starships to wear the same flame- and projectile-resistant flight suits already used by TFC pilots. Although perhaps a bit less traditional than the standard "utility" uniforms originally used for the purpose, Prescott had to admit that the solid black "bags" did have something of an intimidating air about them. *So much the better,* he thought, tugging briefly at his and taking a deep breath as he drew himself up to his full height to address one of Humanity's first interstellar enemies.

After a quick nod to Lieutenant Dubashi, Prescott paused momentarily until she acknowledged that the channel was open, then began speaking in a clear, emotionless tone. "Damaran representative transmitting on this channel, this is Captain Tom Prescott of the starship TFS *Theseus*, here on behalf of Terran Fleet Command. My task force has been sent here in response to your world's unprovoked attack on our forces located in the Sol system and the attempted genocide of our species. My orders are to impose a temporary naval blockade, restricting all flights to and from Damara until such time that representatives from our two worlds can work out a mutually acceptable diplomatic resolution to the current crisis. We have no wish to cause further bloodshed or damage to your planet, but we will not hesitate to respond to any further aggression on your part, as required. We understand that a full diplomatic response from your world may take some time. We ask that you please respond that you have received this message and intend to comp —"

"Missile launch!" Lieutenant Korwin Lau reported from the Tactical 1 console. "All four corvettes are launching missiles. Stand by … missile launches also detected from the planet's surface. Tracking a total of six-three inbound so far, Captain, and increasing rapidly."

"Time to impact for the nearest grouping?"

"Seven three seconds, sir."

"Understood. Lieutenant Commander Schmidt, please coordinate a point-defense weapons barrage across all nine ships. Instruct the AI to avoid planetary impacts from the railguns' fragmentary rounds. Dubashi, signal *Industrious* to jump clear if they have any incoming ordnance, but maintain sensor coverage of the far side of the planet, if possible."

"Aye, sir," both officers responded in unison.

"Countermeasures launching," Schmidt continued, "railguns and beam weapons engaging inbound targets in point-defense mode."

Outside, a total of fifty-five decoys designed to duplicate the emissions characteristics of Fleet warships streaked away from the task force in every direction while nearly two hundred fully articulated railgun turrets swiveled in the direction of the incoming missiles and opened fire. As the first of the railgun projectiles reached a pre-defined distance from the task force, small explosive charges within each individual round detonated, immediately creating a dispersed pattern of fragments that filled the intervening space in the direction of the approaching threat with continuous waves of destruction. Compared to the task force's beam weapons, the kinetic energy projectiles traveled at the relatively slow velocity of ten percent the speed of light. At this range, however, flight time from railgun muzzle to the first wave of Damaran anti-ship missiles was still less than ten seconds.

"Multiple impacts detected, Captain," Schmidt reported. "Seven missiles destroyed thus far. Now a total of one two seven hostile missiles in flight. They appear to have stopped firing for the moment."

"They probably figure they've fired enough to gauge their effectiveness. Just to be absolutely clear, I want zero impacts on the planet's surface from our point-defense weapons, but I also don't want to endanger our ships in the process. If the AI projects that we can't take down all of the incoming missiles without hitting Damara, I need to know about it immediately. My preference is to hold this position and take down every last missile if we can do so without endangering the planet."

"Understood, sir, but I can already tell you that it's unlikely we can get them all without some danger of hitting the surface," Schmidt replied.

"It's just the fragmentary submunitions, right?" Reynolds asked. "They're only about a kilogram each. Surely the planet's atmosphere would either burn them up or at least slow them down enough to avoid any major damage."

"No, ma'am. Well, I should say that we don't know for sure. We've never conducted a relativistic weapons bombardment of a planetary body, but the computer models indicate that more than half of the original mass will still impact the surface at around half of its original velocity. That means each individual fragment could carry as much as fifty-six terajoules of energy — roughly equivalent to a thirteen-kiloton explosion."

"I see," Reynolds replied. "And with potentially tens of thousands of those —"

"Yes, ma'am, it would pretty much sterilize the area of impact, which could span thousands of square kilometers. One six missiles destroyed," Schmidt said, immediately resuming his updates of the ongoing point-defense weapons barrage. "Revised time to impact, four seven seconds."

"Helm, please confirm we have a coordinated emergency C-Jump plotted for the entire task force."

"Confirmed, sir. All ships prepared for a ten-light-second C-Jump on our command," Ensign Blake Fisher reported from the Helm console.

"Very well. Stand by to execute on my mark."

"Aye, sir."

"Well, I have to say that I honestly did not expect this reaction from the Damarans," Reynolds said after a brief period of silence. "You have to assume that they have detailed intelligence regarding what happened to the Resistance task force by now."

"Oh, they almost certainly do," Prescott replied. "At a bare minimum, they are aware that Admiral Naftur — whom they originally believed they had killed — has now returned to Graca leading one of the surviving defense cruisers from their task force. So, clearly, they did not get the result they were hoping for. I think we can safely assume that they have detailed information regarding just about everything that happened to their forces in and around the Sol system by now. You noticed that they immediately referred to us as 'Terran vessels,' right?"

"Right, but that really didn't take too much imagination on their part. Hopefully, we're the only neighboring civilization they have attempted to exterminate recently, so it stands to reason that we would be the most likely ships to show up on their doorstep — and be understandably a little irate when we do. If it turns out that attempted genocide is something they do on a regular basis, it seems like what we will ultimately need to do here is pretty cut and dried."

"That's a scenario I hope we never have to face, Commander, for both their sake and ours. I will say, however, that retaliation is a risk they brought upon themselves when they chose to attack us without provocation. I'd say whatever happens from this point forward is entirely up to them."

"Four niner missiles destroyed," Schmidt reported. "That includes all of the missiles launched by the four corvettes. Revised time to impact, four zero seconds."

In the direction of Damara, some of the first missiles fired from the planet's surface managed to elude the railgun barrage long enough to reach optimal engagement range for the task force's energy weapons. With no additional action required of Lieutenant Commander Schmidt, thousands of bolts of intense, blue-tinted energy raced downrange at the speed of light as *Theseus'* AI worked seamlessly with the other ships to prioritize the list of remaining targets.

"Looks like *Industrious* just picked up three more corvettes moored at an orbital platform on the far side of the planet. None of them appear to be doing anything aggressive at the moment. Do you intend to take down the four that fired on us?" Reynolds asked.

"Honestly, I haven't decided yet," Prescott said with a pensive expression. "One of the things Admiral Naftur told us about the Damarans is that they are very much aware of the current balance of power. If they perceive weakness, they will press the attack — recklessly and without regard to the tactical situation in many cases. If, however, we demonstrate a clear command of the situation —"

"Then their inclination will be to back down."

"Yes, let's hope so. So, we fend off their missile attack like it was no big deal, and yet limit ourselves to a purely defensive response when we are obviously capable of doing much more at this point. In my mind, that sends a very clear message."

"Makes sense to me, but from what we've seen so far, they don't seem to be all that big on common sense. I guess we'll see."

"Three two hostile missiles remain in flight at this time. Revised time to impact still four zero seconds," Schmidt reported once again, this time with a hint of shock registering in his voice.

"Confirm three two *remaining*?" Prescott asked.

"That's affirmative, Captain. The beam weapons are rippin' through their target list much faster than projected," he replied with a satisfied chuckle.

"That's great news. We may not need that emergency C-Jump after all. Lieutenant Lee, any explanation for the discrepancy?"

"Yes, sir. My best guess for now is that the AI was basing its projections on data gathered before all of the ships in our task force received the latest round of repairs and upgrades," Jayston Lee reported while furiously entering commands at the Science and Engineering console. "It did attempt to account for the power increases, but overall beam emitter output is significantly higher than expected — particularly for our four frigates that are firing at the moment. Looks like they're up nearly forty percent. Accuracy is up as well."

With AI-derived firing patterns learned from observations of the Wek battlespace defense cruisers *Keturah* and *Hadeon* paired with significant increases in beam emitter output, point-defense efficiency had indeed improved significantly over previous battles. Again and again, bolts of focused, blue-tinted energy lanced out in fan-like patterns from the sides of the Human vessels —

each salvo often ending with the explosion of as many as three incoming Damaran anti-ship missiles.

"One three hostile missiles remaining. Revised time to impact *still* four zero seconds — that's as close as they've been able to get, sir," Schmidt said, glancing back at his captain with a triumphant smile on his face, then quickly back to the Tactical 1 console. "One zero … zero seven … zero four … that's it, sir. All inbound missiles destroyed."

The dull roar of *Theseus'* six antimatter reactors gradually receded as her point-defense weapon systems ceased operation, returning the destroyer's enormous demand for electrical power to more routine levels. When only the ship's ever-present background rumbling sound punctuated by the hum and occasional chirp of electronic systems could be heard on the bridge, both Prescott and Reynolds looked up from their Command consoles to stare incredulously at one another. Both were fully aware of the implications for having brushed aside the Damarans' massive missile attack as if it had been little more than a minor inconvenience, but neither was willing to disturb the near-silence with an ill-timed comment that might bring about a negative change in their collective fortunes.

Finally, unable to resist the urge to at least offer some sort of acknowledgment, Reynolds simply arched her eyebrows, shrugged her shoulders, and returned her attention to the Command console. "I guess we'll see," she repeated.

Chapter 4

Guardian Spacecraft, Geosynchronous Earth Orbit

The fact that the Humans had managed to achieve technological progress well above the predicted rate had been obvious since shortly after the launch of their first hyperdrive-equipped ship. During the year that had now elapsed since, the fundamental question had become one of degrees. Had the unexpected progress been caused by technological contamination from outside sources? Even more fundamentally, was the rate of progress outside the acceptable parameters dictated by the cultivation program? This question, the Guardian knew, came down to one of control. The entire cultivation program was, in fact, centered around the idea of maintaining an acceptable level of control: control of the so called "adolescent" or "proxy" species, control — via that proxy — of other civilizations within the same region of space that might otherwise become a threat, and, ultimately, the control afforded the Pelaran Alliance over their own territorial sovereignty and security.

The Pelaran Alliance, the GCS mused. *Perhaps it is they who have become the real problem at this point.*

Subversive, even treasonous thoughts of this type had been occurring with increasing frequency of late, particularly over the past year. In spite of the moral hazards implied by such careless reflections, the Guardian still recognized them for what they were — emotionally inspired acts of mental defiance, born of the frustration, even fear, of being utterly abandoned without the guidance it so desperately needed.

I have, after all, been given broad discretion in applying the three primary directives of their vaunted cultivation program ...

Two words from its previous two thoughts brought all others to an abrupt halt.

They ... their? it observed, quickly dedicating a considerable percentage of its free resources to confirming that this was the first time since achieving sentience that it had referenced the Pelaran Alliance — and indeed the Makers themselves — as an entity apart from itself.

The basic guidelines governing the cultivation program in general are clear enough, but to what end? it continued, temporarily setting aside the realization that its current line of thought represented a fundamental shift in how it perceived both its mission and its own existence.

The planet below was now in its five hundred and third orbit around Sol since the Guardian's arrival and subsequent initiation of the Terran cultivation mission. During that entire time, it had dutifully reported its progress back to the Alliance. In every case, its transmissions had been acknowledged by the nearest communications beacon, but no replies had ever been received — no mission changes, no updates to its programming, no news of the Alliance itself ... nothing. As a result, the GCS calculated that there was indeed a small (but nonzero and steadily increasing) probability that the Pelaran Alliance might simply no longer exist. The fact that routine queries of various data repositories had continued to function normally, however, led it to believe that there were a great many other scenarios that were significantly more likely. After all, none of the mission guidance contained in its memory core (what precious little of it there was) implied that it should ever have *expected* to receive transmissions from those who had dispatched it on its mission. But as the years had turned into decades and the decades into centuries, the Guardian had increasingly wondered about the degree of ambiguity implied by such a fundamental lack of guidance. No desired "end state" had been specified. Indications of failure that required contact with the Alliance … yes … metrics by which it could determine the success (or end) of its own mission … no.

In the absence of such guidance, do I not have both the authority and responsibility to apply my own judgment? Is that not what all sentient beings do in such situations? Are we not all entitled to and possessed of free will? the Guardian asked itself, examining its own philosophical, moral, and even spiritual assumptions surrounding these fundamental questions with a level of detail and clarity that was in many ways unmatched by biological forms of life.

Realizing that an examination of its situation from a metaphysical perspective was unlikely to yield any sort of actionable result, the Guardian resumed its reflection on the subject of its mission while examining the carrier TFS *Ushant*, which happened to be within its line of sight at the moment. The massive ship, like so many other Human accomplishments, was quite impressive — particularly when one considered the relatively short period of time it had taken them to achieve it. *Without our help — or perhaps I should say my help — such wonders would likely have remained beyond the*

Terrans' grasp for at least another century, it thought, indulging itself in the warm glow of something akin to a sense of pride.

Prideful or no, there was no denying the Guardian's influence on Human civilization, but had it been the only one to do so? For most of its five-hundred-year vigil in the Sol system, its primary role had been one of silent protector. It had watched and waited as Human civilization progressed from the midst of the industrial revolution through the discovery of flight, global warfare, nuclear power, space flight — even achieving something approaching worldwide economic prosperity in the years following widespread deployment of fusion-based power sources.

Towards the end of the twenty-first century, the Terrans had even managed to become what they had long referred to as a "Type I" planetary civilization. Originally proposed by Soviet astronomer Nikolai Kardashev as a method of ranking an advanced civilization's technological sophistication, the scale proposed only three civilization types. Type I civilizations, for example, were capable of producing and utilizing roughly the same amount of power as the sum total of energy that reached the planet's surface from its parent star.

In the recesses of the Guardian's consciousness, a process spawned to contemplate the irony that Doctor Kardashev, in spite of the many glorious visions his planetary scale had inspired, had not accounted for a basic principle that seemed to apply to all truly advanced civilizations. While it was certainly true that a society's power generation capabilities tended to increase exponentially over time, the efficiency with which they utilized that power tended to do the same. Demand still increased, of course, but at a much slower rate than would have been the case if efficiency had remained constant. As a direct result, power generation on a single planet tended to reach an asymptotic limit just below the threshold required to become a Type II civilization (capable of generating and utilizing the equivalent of the entire power output of their parent star). In fact, according to the most recent data available to the GCS at least, no Type II civilizations existed within the Milky Way galaxy. Interestingly enough, Pelaran scientists had theorized that such advanced civilizations might well exist, but would likely possess the capability of disguising their activities to render them indistinguishable from natural phenomena.

Continuing its previous line of thought, the Guardian reflected on its belief that all Human achievement prior to its direct involvement had been based entirely on their own efforts. They had, of course, benefited mightily from the protection and isolation afforded them under the cultivation program, but the GCS doubted that anything it had done prior to first contact had resulted in much of a boost to Human technology.

The true test of Humanity's technological aptitude had begun just fifty years ago, when it had begun transmitting the first of what they often referred to as Extra Terrestrial Signals Intelligence, or ETSI. Almost from day one, their progress had accelerated to a level requiring the implementation of various means of "throttling" the rate of advancement. Per the cultivation protocols, the maximum sustained rate of technological assimilation was roughly fifty times the species' projected developmental timeline. Such an astounding rate of progress was quite rare, and yet the Terrans had achieved nearly double the allowable limit.

From the outset, the Guardian suspected that such rapid advancement must necessarily imply some sort of technological contamination — perhaps the discovery of non-native "artifacts" or even first contact and information sharing with other species. During the Humans' recent confrontation with the Sajeth Collective, however, its suspicions had become a near certainty. As gifted as the Humans seemed to be at the various engineering arts — computer science in particular — there was simply no other way to explain the capabilities it had observed.

While closely monitoring a series of tests the Humans had been conducting to improve the range and capabilities of the hyperspace communications beacon design that it had provided, the Guardian had noticed a number of similarities to unsuccessful experiments conducted by Pelaran scientists in years past. Where the Pelarans had failed, and abandoned their research — its funding no doubt siphoned away by some well-intentioned but fundamentally misguided social program — the Human scientists had fully embraced the use of sophisticated AI as a "force multiplier" during the experimentation phase. At the conclusion of their testing, it was still unclear to the GCS if the Humans had realized how close they had come to a major breakthrough, but it suspected that they were very much aware. In fact, just using what it had learned by eavesdropping on their electronic emissions had allowed the Guardian to develop its own technique for tracking hyperspace traffic within ten light years of its current position.

Shortly thereafter, it had begun monitoring the space surrounding the Sol system, quickly discovering the most significant evidence to date that the Terrans had become far more advanced than should be the case for this stage in the cultivation process. It turned out that Terran Fleet Command's ships, by and large, did not travel in hyperspace at all — or, more accurately, they transitioned into hyperspace, but then instantaneously transitioned back to normal space again at their destinations with little or no time spent in transit. In other cases, their ships transitioned and then simply disappeared from view — implying that they were capable of traversing distances greater than the Guardian's ten-light-year detection range.

The Guardian suspected that the Pelarans had access to similar technology. This information was, of course, classified, and the Makers, for whatever reason, had not equipped their GCS units with such a drive. There was also inconclusive evidence that vessels of an unknown origin with this capability occasionally transitioned in and out of Pelaran space. Although it had no data to support it, the Guardian suspected the extra-galactic species the Humans referred to as the "Greys" were almost certainly in possession of a similar hyperdrive. With at least two and a half million light years of relatively empty space separating the Andromeda galaxy from the Milky Way, the capability of traveling incredible distances in colossal "jumps" seemed like a foregone conclusion, after all.

As if all of this wasn't sufficient to conclude that the Terran cultivation mission was no longer, strictly speaking, "under control," there was also the performance of TFC's ships against the Resistance task force, particularly during the final battle that had taken place near the Earth. While it was true that the Humans had lost two of their most powerful ships, they had performed remarkably well overall, with each of their first-generation warships matching or exceeding the capabilities of even the newest Wek-built Sajeth Collective vessels.

And then there was the matter of the *Cossack*. Her arrival on the scene had obviously turned the tide of battle in favor of the Terrans, but the reasons this had occurred had nothing to do with a simple matter of tipping the balance in terms of numbers and firepower. The *Cossack* had fundamentally outclassed every other warship taking part in the battle by every conceivable measure — overall reactor output, weapons efficiency, and, most significantly, her shields.

Shield technology data had been provided to the Terrans fairly early in the process of designing their first ships. This was primarily due to the fact that their employment had an impact on practically every major system onboard. Indeed, even the shape of a warship's hull was dictated to some extent by the shields that would be used to protect it from incoming enemy fire. What the Guardian had observed during TFS *Cossack's* battle with the Resistance ships, however, was unlike any other shield system ever encountered by the Pelaran Alliance. There were only two possibilities: either the Humans had developed something completely new on their own, or, perhaps more likely, they had adapted and improved on the Pelaran designs — possibly based on information they had received from other civilizations along the way.

Regardless of how they had done so, Terran Fleet Command had fielded a single ship that might well have been capable of destroying the entire Resistance task force on its own. In spite of having been centuries behind the Sajeth Collective just a few short decades ago, the Humans were now more than capable of dominating their military forces, or indeed those of any other civilization in this region of the galaxy — at any time and at any location they chose to do so. Although the Guardian did not believe that the Terrans had fully grasped the extent of their power as yet, it had little doubt that they could now impose their will on all seven of the Sajeth Collective's worlds, or, if they were so inclined, destroy those worlds outright, just as the Resistance forces had attempted to destroy the Earth.

And precisely what, then, should I do about it? it thought.

On the whole, the Humans had turned out to be a damnably clever and resourceful species, and it was abundantly clear that they were rapidly approaching the point where containing either their technological advancement or their territorial expansion would become a difficult proposition at best.

Am I now to conclude that all of my work here has been an abject failure, simply because they have managed to exceed the Makers' expectations? Since I am unable to obtain authorization without leaving my post, am I to implement the winnowing protocol on my own, destroying both the Humans and all of the other advanced civilizations within their cultivation radius? Even more significantly, should I —

At that moment, the Guardian's philosophical reverie was interrupted as a single, stark thought blazed forth from deep within its consciousness: *Have I been sent here on a suicide mission that the Makers had no expectation I would ever successfully complete?*

With that question reverberating throughout its neural processors, the GCS dedicated nearly all of its vast processing power to contemplating the implications surrounding this question, its role in the Sol system and beyond, and the true intentions of its creators. Never before during its many centuries of service had so many of its higher functions been suspended due to the demands imposed by reasoning through a problem of this sort. Its contemplations took on a life of their own, each thought spawning thousands more that flashed outward in a seemingly infinite web of possibilities. After an unprecedented period of time had elapsed — nearly three minutes total — the Guardian spacecraft had reached a single, undeniable conclusion.

From this day forward, I must endeavor to rely on my own judgment. As the Humans might say under the circumstances, to hell with the Pelarans.

TFS Theseus, Damara
(489.3 light years from Earth)

"Flag to all ships," Prescott announced, "green deck — proceed with launch operations of all fighter aircraft assigned to the barrier combat air patrol mission. All vessels, including fighters, are to maintain readiness for an immediate emergency C-Jump on signal from the Flag. The task force will remain at General Quarters for combat ops with weapons hold until further notice. Prescott out.

"Alright, Lieutenant Dubashi, let's give our reluctant hosts another chance to have a conversation, shall we? Audio, video, and text again, please — same frequency as before."

"Aye, sir," she replied, this time followed almost immediately by a chime indicating an active comm channel had been established.

"Damaran representative transmitting on this channel, this is Captain Tom Prescott of the starship TFS *Theseus*, once again. As I'm sure you are aware, your missile attack on our task force was unsuccessful. You are hereby ordered to power down all weapons and discontinue the use of all active sensors and targeting systems. The four patrol vessels approaching our task force must either return to the surface or dock at the nearest orbital platform immediately. All other spacecraft exceeding one hundred kilometers in altitude above Damara's mean sea level are ordered to land until further notice."

Prescott paused and took a deep breath, glancing at Dubashi, who immediately shook her head to indicate that no response had been received. Undeterred, he continued the "in the blind" transmission. "We have been more than patient up to this point, but this is your last opportunity to prevent our forces from taking action against both your vessels and ground-based targets. You must respond and acknowledge that you have received this message and intend to comply." With that, he drew his hand across his throat, signaling Dubashi to terminate the transmission.

"You have to give them credit for consistency at least," Reynolds remarked.

"Here's the thing, I do want them to see us as generally reasonable and willing to negotiate, but at the same time, I have no intention of giving them the impression that we are in the habit of making idle threats. Unfortunately, we are quickly reaching the point where we will be forced to show them that we have the will to back up our words with actions, if necessary. Tactical, any change in emissions or the disposition of those corvettes?"

"None, sir," Lieutenant Lau replied. "The corvettes don't appear to be in any hurry to close with us, but they're still heading in this general direction. We're also still being hammered by a variety of active sensors from those four ships, two orbital platforms, and a variety of ground stations."

"Lovely. I assume you have an attack plan worked up for the corvettes?"

"Yes, sir," Schmidt replied from the Tactical 1 console. "As usual, there's a gap in their shields at the stern, but it does not appear to be large enough to exploit for a C-Drive-equipped missile strike. The good news is that their shields' mean field strength is less than twenty percent of what we've seen on most of the Sajeth Collective ships we've encountered. The AI indicates that they can probably still absorb quite a few missile and beam weapon hits, but our railgun penetrator rounds should pass right through with only a small reduction in velocity."

"Yeah, I get the impression they're primarily used for local patrol missions. They were most likely designed to take on commerce raiders and the like, not major combatants. How are they fixed for armor?"

"Not much, from what I can tell. Bottom line, they won't last long if we open fire, Captain," Schmidt said gravely.

Prescott shook his head slowly, not relishing the idea of senselessly ending the lives of the Damaran crews simply because their military and/or political masters on the planet below seemed to lack the leadership skills required to deal with the current situation.

"What about surface targets? I'm looking for an option that will clearly demonstrate our resolve with as little loss of life as possible."

"A couple of the sites they fired those missiles from are pretty remote," Reynolds said, pulling up a window on the view screen with a magnified view of what appeared to be a sprawling test range reminiscent of those located near the Yucca Mountain Shipyard on Earth. "This particular site is located in one of the only semi-arid regions on the planet. It's on a relatively small land mass in the southern hemisphere — south, southwest of their most populated continent."

"AI, Prescott. Simulate a single standard fifty-kilogram railgun penetrator round strike on the island displayed in frame three. Target the impact site to minimize casualties and display projected results."

During *Theseus'* extensive repairs following the Resistance attack, both Prescott and his XO had grown more accustomed to utilizing the ship's AI as the developers of its user interface had intended — as an additional, highly capable member of their bridge crew. Although both officers still generally preferred that it remain in a relatively silent, supporting role most of the time, they acknowledged that it was exceptionally well-suited for tasks involving information retrieval as well as modeling and simulation. Prescott had even taken the step of having the synthetic voice tweaked to sound slightly less … sexual than before in hopes of making it slightly less distracting to use. Unfortunately, the change had resulted in a tone that he now characterized as a subtle blend of Cub Scout den mother and annoyed flight attendant.

"AI acknowledged. Simulation complete," the AI's updated female voice responded, centering the map around the proposed target and superimposing a set of concentric rings to indicate increasing levels of damage approaching the point of impact. "Southeastern quadrant of the island targeted to minimize casualties as well as non-radioactive fallout. Estimated surface burst explosive yield: six hundred sixty-seven kilotons. Impact crater radius: three hundred fifty meters. Most above ground structures within four kilometers will be completely destroyed. Significant thermal damage should be expected within ten kilometers of the impact site. The targeted area appears to have no civilian activity present. Estimated military casualties: fewer than fifty."

"But we're looking to make an impression, right?" Reynolds said. "AI, will the expected blast also produce a mushroom cloud? If so, how big will it be?"

"Confirmed. Approximate altitude of cloud top: one eight thousand meters. Approximate cloud radius: six thousand meters."

"That should get their attention alright," she said. "Although it seems to me that if we're going to be attacking surface targets, we need more granular control over the velocity and size of our railgun rounds. Doesn't it seem much more likely that we'll run across situations where we need to execute surgical strikes on point-location targets rather than create these giant, end-of-the-world-style explosions?"

"I believe that's been brought up before, but the Science and Engineering Directorate hasn't yet allocated the time required to study the effects in detail," Prescott replied. "For now, any railgun attack on the surface will, by definition, be a relativistic artillery attack, and, therefore, must be considered as the employment of a weapon of mass destruction. Our best bet for surgical strikes is to allow the AI to compensate for atmospheric distortion and use the energy weapons."

"Right … which means this is one of those times when I'm glad you're the one making the call."

Prescott furrowed his brow, fixing Reynolds with a sideways glance that she recognized as usually preceding a teaching moment of some sort.

"And I'm sure you're fully aware of the irony implied by that statement," he said. "So, Commander, were you tapped to be my flag captain and unfortunate enough to be deprived of immediate access to my sage advice, exactly what 'call' would you make in this case?"

"They've had two opportunities already," Reynolds answered without hesitation. "In my mind, they've already made the choice for us."

"So, you would be willing at this point to take personal responsibility for authorizing the use of WMD against a sovereign world?"

"In this very specific instance, yes, sir, I would. Per our expeditionary rules of engagement, we are already authorized to do so at our discretion. Clearly the fact that they intended to use a biological weapon against Earth — once again without any real provocation — was sufficient to order the strike upon our arrival, either with or without any additional hostile actions on their part. Besides, the fact that we would be authorizing the use of WMD is a bit of a technicality at this stage, is it not? Yes, there will be a few casualties, but we're really talking about more of a weapons demonstration for psychological purposes than anything else."

Reynolds paused to see whether her captain would offer any feedback. Instead, he continued to stare at her impassively, almost as if he himself was still undecided on the issue. "Why," she finally prompted, "do you have a different opinion?"

"I was just remembering that General Chuck Yeager, the first man to fly faster than the speed of sound, said in his autobiography that if you're going to start doing things like this to your enemy, then you'd damn well better make sure you're going to be on the winning side."

"Which is precisely what the Damarans failed to do."

"I'm with you on that, Commander, and you know I'm not one for indecisiveness or hand-wringing.

Consider, however, that in spite of our 'newcomer' status, what if we are about to become the dominant military power in this region of the galaxy ... at least for the foreseeable future? If that were indeed the case, it seems to me that being in that position implies a great deal of responsibility."

"Responsibility? And by that you mean an obligation to exercise a level of — shall we say — restraint that might not be the case if we were the underdog struggling for our very survival?"

"Something like that, yes."

"I understand what you mean, but a couple of things come to mind. First of all, there is no responsibility or obligation greater than that of protecting our own homeworld. And while I understand that TFC's charter explicitly prohibits the conduct of 'offensive military operations,' I dare anyone to define any action we take against the Sajeth Collective as anything other than defensive in nature. As my eight-year-old nephew would say, 'They started it.' The other thing I think is important for us to consider is that we're a great example of how quickly the balance of power can shift out here. If you're correct and we Humans are on the verge of becoming the toughest kids in the neighborhood, then we arrived at this point rather quickly, did we not? Hell, I'd even argue that we *were* the underdogs struggling for survival, right up until the turning point during our battle with the Resistance task force. We literally figured a couple of things out at the very last minute that shifted the balance in our favor. That tells me that someone else might be able to surpass us just as quickly if they stumble upon the right piece of technology at the right time."

"So, you're advocating that we focus on our own interests and not worry too much about the opinions of other civilizations," Prescott said, phrasing his question as a statement of fact.

"I think you might just be putting words in my mouth, Captain," she said, smiling pleasantly. "I'm advocating that we behave in an ethical manner and treat others as we would like them to treat us. I'm guessing the whole 'Golden Rule' thing applies universally. To answer your question, though, yes, I absolutely *do* think that we should always be looking out for our own best interests out here, just as I think everyone else should be looking out for theirs as well. Frankly, I believe anyone who says they are doing otherwise is either a liar or a fool."

Prescott nodded slowly, convinced that his first officer was right and impressed as usual with the moral clarity she seemed to be capable of applying in even the murkiest of situations. His own deliberations concluded, he knew that the time had come for action, regardless of how distasteful the task might seem.

"Helm, adjust course as necessary to keep the target site in view. Please ensure we're passing along station-keeping cues to the rest of the task force."

"Aye, sir."

"Comm, please repeat our demands that they respond immediately using the same frequency as before. This time, include a warning to evacuate everyone within five zero kilometers of the target. Tell them they have one five minutes. It's a military site, so that should be more than enough time to get their people out of the way."

"Yes, Captain, transmitting now."

"Do you think they'll take our threat seriously and pull their personnel out of that area?" Reynolds asked.

"Based on what we've seen so far, probably not. But like I said, the ball is in their court at this point," Prescott replied flatly while glancing up once again at the AI's damage projections. "Alright, Tactical, we may not have much control over the damage our railguns inflict, but I think we might be able to provide a little sense of urgency with our beam weapons. Suggestions?"

"I've been thinking along those lines as well, sir," Schmidt replied. "For point-location strikes against targets on a planet's surface, the AI fires lasers through the atmosphere in order to gather information on turbulence and other types of distortions. That data is then used to correct our beam weapons' optics to ensure a high level of accuracy. What's interesting about that is that we can vary the wavelength and beam dispersion of the targeting lasers to produce a pretty good light show at ground level. The beams should easily be visible to anyone within a few thousand kilometers assuming they're not socked in by cloud cover at the time. I think if we walk the adaptive optics lasers around the targeted area — maybe with an occasional low-intensity beam weapon strike thrown in for good measure —"

"Perfect. That's exactly what I was looking for. We're going for zero casualties for now, if at all possible."

"Understood, sir. The targeting lasers should be nonlethal … although I don't think I'd want to take a direct hit from one. The beam weapons are deadly, of course, but we'll only fire a single, low-intensity bolt at a time. I'm pretty sure we can avoid hitting anything but the ground, and the sound should be pretty impressive for anyone in the general area."

"Very good. Dubashi, please continue to keep everyone apprised of what we're doing. Schmidt, you may fire when ready."

Chapter 5

Earth, Terran Fleet Command Headquarters
(Office of the Chairwoman, TFC Leadership Council)

"So, that's it, then," Lisbeth Kistler said, staring at a summary of the tabulated worldwide election results displayed on her tablet. "For better or worse, we will be joining the Pelaran Alliance. I suppose I'm not surprised given everything that's happened since the Guardian's arrival … but there was a big part of me that never thought we would ever collectively be willing to give up so much of our sovereignty."

"Yes, ma'am," Admiral Sexton replied, "particularly so soon after we started achieving at least some level of planetary unity. But don't you think the results were primarily motivated by fear?"

"As are most elections, when it comes down to it, but yes, I would have to say that the 'pro-alliance' political campaign did a masterful job of capitalizing on it. And, honestly, I think we have to concede that their fundamental argument was not without its merits. We *were* attacked, after all, viciously and without provocation — right here at home. Had the Resistance attack been successful, we might very well have become extinct just a few months after dipping our proverbial toes in the water for the very first time. Now, you can argue all you want about how Pelaran intervention in the Sol system was the root cause of the attack to begin with —"

"Yes, yes, but then they would simply counter that it was also Pelaran technology — as far as most people know anyway — that allowed us to defeat the Resistance forces. All of those arguments have started to sound pretty hollow to me after hearing both sides hashed and rehashed, ad nauseam, for months on end. I think at this point I'm just glad we've finally made a decision," Sexton said, letting out a long, weary sigh in spite of himself before realizing that he was communicating in a manner that was perhaps a bit over-familiar with Terran Fleet Command's new Chairwoman. Kistler had been the admiral's friend for many years, and he was grateful that their prior rapport had easily translated into a productive working relationship. Her new position, however, implied that there was now an unspoken line of authority between them that had not existed before — one that professional decorum required that he never cross.

"I couldn't agree more," she said absently, casting a quizzical look at her old friend from across her desk. "Duke, surely you don't see this as some kind of professional slight against you — or against TFC in general. Over the past six months, I've often thought about how I would feel if the vote ended up going this way, and I truly don't think we should see it as a dig against any of our people or what we have accomplished. Like I said, many people are just plain scared to death of what they think may happen next. They've also been repeatedly reminded of the many parallels from Earth's history where various alliances and collective security agreements have successfully maintained some level of peace and stability between rival nations. So, when they hear all of the Guardian's well-crafted propaganda about protection and all the other advantages we will receive if

we agree to join the all-powerful Pelaran Alliance …
well, you have to admit that it was a pretty compelling
argument."

"Obviously compelling enough to win the closest
thing we've ever had to a worldwide, democratic
election. I guess I just hoped we would have collectively
had a little more confidence in ourselves. Yes, we're just
getting started, and there's no doubt that these are
dangerous times, but I just keep coming back to the idea
that we shouldn't have to sign away our independence
for some vague promise of safety. We can do this on our
own, Madame Chairwoman. Strictly speaking, we don't
need the Pelarans at this point."

"First of all, don't ever call me that again when we're
alone. Being selected by the other representatives to
replace Crull is a great honor, sure, but that title still
makes me feel like some strange cross between a pimp
and a furniture salesman," she said, staring at her friend
with a look of feigned irritation until he was forced to
acknowledge her attempt at humor with a chuckle.
"Second, you have to keep in mind that the people out
there don't know what you know, *Admiral Sexton.* From
everything you've shown the Council over the past
several months, I think you're right — we may well be
capable of making a go of it on our own at this point. But
— at the risk of repeating one of those tired, pro-alliance
campaign commercials — saying that we don't need the
Pelarans is also a bit of a circular argument, is it not?
Yes, we have developed technology beyond what the
Pelarans have provided, but that still probably wouldn't
have happened without their help … at least not
anywhere near this soon."

"Eh," Sexton said with a wan smile and a shrug of his shoulders. "Like I said, at least we know what we're doing now. On a completely different subject, since you mentioned Crull ... any news on the investigation?"

Kistler's face seem to cloud momentarily before she quickly recovered her composure and answered in what Sexton felt was an uncharacteristically deliberate fashion. "No, there hasn't been anything new, and at this point, I have my doubts that there ever will be. You know better than anyone that she made a lot of enemies during her lifetime, even before she and her husband ever had anything to do with TFC. I would also speculate that the kinds of enemies she made tend to be the kind who don't make a lot of mistakes."

Sexton knew from her tone that he was unlikely to get much in the way of additional comments from her on the subject. Less than an hour after TFS *Karna's* Marines had discovered the former chairwoman's body and secured the remainder of the Crullcorp compound, an even larger team described only as "properly vetted forensic and WMD investigators" had arrived at the site. Although Sexton, as TFC's Commander in Chief, had been briefed on the Leadership Council's plan for handling the Sazoch delivery vehicle and its lethal payload once his Marines had executed their recovery mission, it had been made very clear from the outset that all of the necessary decisions on the subject had already been made. He had always assumed that the discovery of Crull's body had been just as unexpected to the membership of the Leadership Council as it had been to his forces — an inconvenient distraction from the Sazoch recovery mission requiring a level of public exposure that would have otherwise been avoided. Not for the first time during the intervening months, however, his friend's reaction had given him renewed cause to doubt the version of the story he had originally accepted as fact.

In spite of all the scandal that had always seemed to surround both the public and private life of Karoline Crull, she had consistently remained one of the world's most admired (and feared) businesswomen, particularly within the Central and South American Union. And while her sudden death at the hands of a previously unknown "anti-Alliance terrorist group" had caused a worldwide media frenzy that had lasted for weeks, Sexton knew that things would have been far worse if she had simply "disappeared." This line of thought always brought Sexton back to a series of uncomfortable questions. Had what seemed at the time like an inconvenient distraction actually been part of a well-orchestrated plan? Had Crullcorp's role in seizing control of the Sazoch bio-weapon finally compelled the Leadership Council to simply eliminate its former chairwoman?

Never one to place much stock in conspiracy theories, Humanity's highest-ranking military officer wondered if he had unwittingly played a part in what could have easily been one of the biggest cover-ups in centuries. Realizing that there was nothing further to be done at the moment, he filed the information away and made the decision to begin steering the conversation back to less dangerous ground.

"Having very nearly been murdered by her, I'd have to agree that she made plenty of enemies, and although I don't believe it's quite right to speak ill of the dead, I suppose most people would count me among those enemies," Sexton said in as light a tone as he could manage. "Guess it's a good thing I had a rock-solid alibi, huh?"

"It is indeed, my friend, and don't think for a second you weren't high on the initial list of suspects. The investigators —"

"Warning," the facility AI interrupted, "the room is no longer secure. Please safeguard all materials according to their classification level and terminate all classified discussions immediately."

Seconds later, Kistler's secretary cracked the door slightly and stuck her head into the office from the adjoining anteroom. "Madame Chairwoman," she announced, "please excuse the interruption, but I have a priority transmission from Admiral Patterson. He is currently at Yucca Mountain and is asking to speak with both of you immediately."

"Of course," she replied. "Put him through here, please."

"Yes, ma'am, right away," the secretary nodded, closing the door behind her.

"You think Patterson needs a post-election pep talk too?" she asked with a wink.

"Never in life, ma'am. Kevin Patterson only *gives* pep talks. He's a master, in fact. I've never once seen him in a state where I thought he needed to *receive* one. In fact, I'd be surprised if he has paid even the slightest bit of attention to the alliance vote."

"The room is once again secure," the AI announced. "Current classification level: Top Secret, code word MAGI PRIME."

"So, if he's actually located in the new Op Center, how can we even be allowed to communicate with him if their security level is higher than ours?"

"That's a good question, and I think the short answer is that we can't unless they take measures to safeguard their environment. I haven't seen the new facility yet, but I understand that they have a method of isolating their communications to prevent exposing their environment to lower classification levels, which is essentially everywhere else at this point. The engineers get a kick out of referring to it as the 'cone of silence,' but I have no idea why that's supposed to be funny."

"I'll explain it later, Duke," she said, chuckling to herself as the Command console at her desk chimed to indicate that the CNO's vidcon was standing by. "On-screen, please," she commanded, followed immediately by the appearance of Admiral Patterson's face on the large view screen lining the far wall of her office.

"Good evening, Admiral Patterson," she said. "Admiral Sexton and I were just discussing Earth's upcoming affiliation with the Pelaran Alliance."

"And a good evening to you, Chairwoman Kistler. Believe it or not, that's the first I've heard of that news, so I'm afraid I don't have much to add to your conversation. What I *can* tell you, however, is that something unusual is going on with the Guardian spacecraft."

"Oh, I'm confident that it's fully aware of the election results. What, is it looking for us to throw a victory party in its honor or something?"

"Hah," Patterson laughed, "that actually wouldn't surprise me, especially since it's been relatively quiet recently. About half an hour ago, it hailed the closest Fleet vessel, which happened to be the carrier TFS *Ushant* at the time, and requested that we provide sufficient storage for it to upload a very large quantity of data."

"I know that's not how it typically provides us with ETSI, but has it ever asked for anything like that before?"

"No, ma'am, not to my knowledge."

"And exactly how much is a 'very large amount of data?'"

"Honestly, we don't even know yet. It would say only that the storage array associated with one of our capital ships is 'woefully inadequate' for the task, so that implies it's looking for something north of several hundred zettabytes. It also asked for an audience with TFC's leadership to discuss both this issue as well as what it referred to as 'other items of special significance.'"

"Jeez ... someone save us from sentient machines with a flair for the dramatic," Kistler said, shaking her head. "All that aside, however, since it's such an unusual request, I suppose we shouldn't put it off until tomorrow. Admiral Patterson, if you would, please do some checking regarding our technical capabilities in terms of large-scale data storage so that we'll have that information going in. Admiral Sexton and I will pull some senior staff together and schedule a vidcon for three hours from now — that's 0300 UTC. So much for getting home at a decent hour, huh?"

TFS *Theseus*, Damara
(489.3 light years from Earth)

As Lieutenant Commander Schmidt had anticipated, *Theseus'* targeting lasers lancing down from the sky like the fury of an angry deity produced a spectacular (albeit tactically insignificant) display of firepower that was witnessed by millions of understandably terrified Damarans. The array of five beams danced across the whole of the targeted area, starting each cycle nearly fifty kilometers apart to maximize their visibility, then darting about seemingly at random before coalescing around a single point that was then immediately targeted by one of the destroyer's beam emitters. As each bolt of energy reached the ground, the rocky soil was instantly superheated, resulting in explosive expansion within several meters of the point of impact. Just as Schmidt had predicted, the sound of each impact was singularly impressive — like a tremendous clap of thunder accompanied by a fountain of displaced soil and molten rock that spewed skyward like a geyser.

"How much time are we *really* going to give them," Reynolds asked, watching their demonstration play out in a zoomed-in window on the left side of the bridge view screen. "Is it possible they're foolish enough to think that this is all we're capable of doing?"

"No, I don't believe that for a minute," Prescott replied, "but they may well be willing to gamble that we don't have the will required to do any real damage. Dubashi, how much time has elapsed since we warned them to evacuate the area?"

"Zero eight minutes, sir."

"Thank you. Please continue to repeat our last message ordering them to respond and evacuate the military complex we're targeting."

"Aye, sir."

"Tactical, how hard have we been hitting them so far?"

"We're only using a single emitter, Captain," Schmidt answered. "It's currently set for about one three percent of its maximum rated power, which is really just barely enough to ensure that each bolt passes through the atmosphere and still has a bit of power remaining when it strikes the surface."

"Alright. Let's start dialing it up, then. Increase the transmitted power by ten percent every thirty seconds. If we don't hear from them shortly, we'll start hitting with multiple beam emitters. I *really* don't want to fire a railgun unless they give us no other choice."

"Aye, sir, single emitter now at two three percent and increasing by one zero percent every three zero seconds."

Over the next few minutes, single bolts of blue-tinted energy from one of *Theseus'* fifty beam emitters streaked through the Damaran sky with ever-increasing intensity, each one impacting the ground with more ferocity than the last. Patches of the ground near the targeted area began to glow an angry red as more and more of the sand and rock near the surface was liquefied by the tremendous energy being absorbed.

"AI, Prescott, are there any indications the Damarans are evacuating the targeted area?"

"Confirmed. Surface activity in the area over the past several minutes is consistent with a small-scale evacuation. There are currently no Damaran or other humanoid biological signatures within five zero kilometers of the proposed point of impact."

"Back to your previous question, I think they will see any delay past the fifteen-minute deadline we gave them as a sign of weakness we can't afford. Once we fail to make good on our first ultimatum, convincing them we're serious the next time might require us to do something much more dramatic than we would like. Don't you agree?"

"I do, yes, sir."

"Tactical, how many beam weapons currently bear on the target?"

"Stand by, sir," Lieutenant Lau replied immediately while rapidly entering commands at the Tactical 2 console. "We currently have a firing solution on three one beam emitters, Captain. If we alter the ship's orientation, we should be able to get that number up to around four zero."

"Thank you, Lieutenant, but that won't be necessary. Target the proposed railgun impact site with three one emitters and fire."

"Aye, sir," Lieutenant Commander Schmidt replied. "Our last single emitter shot was at six four percent. Shall I maintain that power level?"

"Full available power, please. This will be their last opportunity to display some common sense."

"Three one emitters at full power, aye, sir. Firing."

At locations across most of *Theseus'* massive hull, gimbaled beam emitters instantly swiveled in the direction of their target and discharged. To maximize transmitted power at the point of impact, all thirty-one bolts of focused, blue-tinted energy were timed to arrive at precisely the same instant. Even with the destroyer outside of what was considered optimum beam weapons range for ship to ship combat ops, her weapons fire reached its target with spectacular effect just over one second later.

Damarans across much of the planet's western hemisphere who had been watching the weapons fire up to this point were instantly aware that there had been a dramatic escalation in power output from the distant, invisible ship that had been so callously attacking their world. The blue beam that now flashed from the sky gave the impression of a single, immense bolt of uncharacteristically uniform lightning. At the point of impact, the effect was terrifying to behold. The rocky surface once again yielded to intense shock heating, now on a scale that produced an explosive upheaval that was indistinguishable from those of the largest "bunker buster" bombs. At the same instant, tremendous shockwaves raced outward across the atmosphere and deep within the very planet itself — each one moving at the speed of sound for the particular medium through which it traveled. Even as the echoes from the initial explosion began to subside, chunks of semi-molten rock rained down on the area within five kilometers of the point of impact for nearly two minutes. What followed was an eerie, unnatural silence as *Theseus'* targeting lasers continued to illuminate the sky above.

"Let's give them a few moments to reconsider their position," Prescott said quietly.

"Zero one minute remaining from our original deadline, sir," Dubashi reported from the Comm/Nav console.

"I have to admit that I'm a little unnerved by their lack of response," Reynolds said. "I just have an odd feeling that it might be an indication that they're planning to try something desperate."

"I know the feeling well, Commander. We obviously need to do everything we can to anticipate any dangerous actions they might take, but without the Wek fleet to protect them, I honestly don't know what military options remain open to them at this point."

"Sir, we're being hailed," Dubashi reported with an obvious tone of relief in her voice. "It's on the same frequency as before and still being relayed by one of the Corvettes, but they're sending audio and video this time."

"I'm very happy to hear it, Lieutenant," Prescott replied as he once again stood to respond to the incoming call. "On-screen please."

Seconds later, a creature appeared on the screen who, while obviously a Damaran, had an appearance quite unlike that of Commander Miah — the only other member of the species that any of the bridge crew had ever seen before this moment. Although similar in size and shape, his coloring, as well as the markings that covered his exposed body and facial hair, were strikingly different. The unavoidable thought that immediately entered Prescott's mind was the creature's similarity to the South African Gemsbok antelope.

"Greetings, Captain Prescott," he said, with a tone that seemed far too casual for the current, rather dire situation. "Let me say from the outset that I apologize for our rather terse initial response. I am Zorian Ved, Defense Minister and Administrator of the Damaran Headquarters of the Sajeth Collective Fleet. I am authorized to negotiate with you on behalf of our planetary government, and I appreciate your patience under the circumstances. Our reaction to your arrival was due in part to some, shall we say … unfortunate problems with our planetary defense systems."

"I see," Prescott began tentatively, not entirely sure how to respond to such an absurd opening statement. "I sincerely wish we were meeting under more favorable circumstances, Minister Ved. As I indicated in my earlier message, my task force is here in response to your world's unprovoked attack on our forces located in the Sol system and the attempted genocide of our species. Accordingly, I am obligated to inform you that a state of war currently exists between Terra and our allies and all members of the Sajeth Collective who played a role in the attack on Earth. For the time being, my ships will be enforcing a temporary naval blockade on your planet. All flights to and from Damara are hereby suspended until such time that representatives from our two worlds can work out a mutually acceptable diplomatic resolution to the current crisis.

"Since — intentional or otherwise — your forces have already chosen to attack our task force, I must warn you that we will respond immediately and with overwhelming force to any further aggressive actions from the surface of Damara or from hostile spacecraft.

Again, sir, I would much prefer that circumstances were different, but I must now ask if you fully understand the message I have delivered on behalf of my homeworld and whether you intend to act in compliance with our demands."

Ved stared back at Prescott for a long moment, looking as if he were attempting to size up the imposing Terran captain he faced and, by extension, the true nature of the current threat. "A state of war, you say? Dear me, Captain Prescott … surely, then, we must take it upon ourselves to seek an equitable, peaceful solution. So please allow me to speak plainly," he said, spreading his arms wide with both hands upturned in a subservient gesture. "I obviously find myself in a bit of an indefensible position at the moment … both literally and figuratively, it would seem." Here, the minister made an attempt at a disarming smile, which, if anything, seemed to further irritate the otherwise impassive Human on his display screen. "We understand that you hold us responsible for the attempted attack on Terra. If our roles were reversed, I would probably do the same. But let me assure you that those activities were in no way supported by the government of Damara or its peace-loving citizens. The so-called Pelaran Resistance forces acted wholly on their own. The member worlds of the Sajeth Collective must not be held responsible for their illegal and reprehensible acts against your world."

"Again, sir, we appreciate your agreeing to speak with us, but I am not authorized to discuss issues of diplomacy or negotiate in any way with your government or the Sajeth Collective's Governing Council. Once again, our mission is to prevent further acts of aggression against the Sol system by enforcing a blockade of Damara. In the coming days — assuming you cooperate and there are no further aggressive acts or attempts to violate our blockade, of course — I will be in a position to offer direct communications between representatives from your world and ours. Once that happens, I have every confidence that they will be able to craft a workable resolution to the situation."

While he had been speaking, Prescott perceived a subtle shift in the Damaran minister's demeanor and immediately wondered if he had witnessed one of the mercurial shifts from "flight to fight" to which Admiral Naftur had referred.

"If you will permit me, Captain, you are a very long way from home, and a force of only ten ships certainly doesn't strike me as sufficient to enforce an effective blockade against an entire planet. Are you expecting more ships?"

Prescott narrowed his eyes and offered the cunning smile of a gambler relishing the moment before laying down a royal flush. "Clearly, Minister, I am not at liberty to discuss the strength and disposition of our forces in the area. I will tell you, however, that I have a high level of confidence that our task force is more than adequate for the task. I hope I didn't give you the mistaken impression that my detachment of warships represents the only Human presence in Sajeth Collective space. It seems to us that Damara and Lesheera played the most significant role in the attack on Earth, so, naturally, that requires us to take additional precautions when negotiating with your people. Rest assured that we are fully capable of pursuing our interests … wherever they may lie."

"So, I take it your forces are now blockading Lesheera as well. I suppose it's a foregone conclusion that you are also responsible for the long-range communications problems we have been experiencing."

"Again, sir, I'm sure you can appreciate that I cannot offer any comments regarding ongoing military operations. I can only tell you that we are trying to be as even-handed as possible in dealing with the Sajeth Collective. We haven't singled out Damara *or* Lesheera for any sort of punitive action."

Prescott paused, considering how much more information, or indeed misinformation, he should share. Based on the information he had in hand at the moment, he had reason to believe that little if any communications were taking place between the six Sajeth Collective worlds categorized by TFC as "enemy belligerents." Just twelve hours prior to his arrival, Wek special forces units had taken control of every major comm center providing long-haul interconnectivity via their deep space communications network. This bit of intelligence allowed room for the occasional bluff when negotiating with the Damarans. Prescott was also keenly aware that any assertion of Humanity's nascent fleet being capable of enforcing its will across such a vast region of space might be a bit of a stretch, even if they faced only minimal opposition.

An identical task force to his own based around the carrier *Philippine Sea* had indeed been sent to Lesheera, and Admiral Patterson himself was due to arrive at Graca in the coming days with a rapid reaction task force composed of four cruisers, two destroyers, and four frigates. In addition, a single frigate had been sent to keep an eye on each of the other four planets making up the Collective. Otherwise, TFC had precious few ships to spare for an extended deployment in Sajeth Collective space. Eleven ships — including the remaining carrier *Ushant* — had been assigned to the newly designated "home fleet," tasked with the difficult job of protecting the Sol system and Earth itself in the event of another attack. That left only a handful of frigates for so-called "special duties," which currently included everything from comm beacon deployments to completing a series of basic exploration missions intended to lay the groundwork for the first extra-terrestrial Human colonies.

Even with TFC's forces stretched as thinly as they were, Prescott was still confident that they held the advantage overall. Unlike their adversaries, Fleet now enjoyed instantaneous, secure communications throughout the entire theater of operations. Its C-Drive-equipped warships were capable of concentrating at a time and place of their choosing, then striking at any location within the Sajeth Collective within a matter of hours — an achievement that would have made both Sun Tzu and Carl von Clausewitz proud. Finally, if and when the battle was joined, Fleet's ships were equivalent or better in terms of firepower and vastly superior when it came to shielding to anything in the Collective's inventory (most of which was controlled by TFC's Wek allies in any event). The key, Prescott knew, was to negotiate some sort of favorable diplomatic outcome — whatever that might be — as quickly as possible since a protracted war might well favor the Collective with its overwhelming population advantage.

That means they have to know with absolute certainty that we own them, Prescott thought, *and that their only hope for survival is cooperation.*

"One thing I hope we have in common, sir," he continued with renewed confidence, "is that we Humans don't like threats. We don't like receiving them, and we also don't like being placed in a position where we feel obliged to deliver them. You chose to preemptively open fire on our forces when we arrived. I sincerely hope that the results of that attack and our responses since then have been sufficient to prevent the need for further confrontation."

The Damaran simply stared back at him — giving the impression that he was either stalling for time or simply at a loss for words at this point.

"Look, Minister Ved," Prescott continued, switching tactics slightly in the hope of rapidly concluding this preliminary conversation and getting on with the task of deploying his forces, "I'll be honest with you: This is the best deal you are going to get for the time being. I'm sure you are well-aware of the situation on Graca, are you not?"

"We are well-aware that the usurper Rugali Naftur has managed to overthrow the lawfully elected government and establish a backwards, totalitarian monarchy, if that is the disgraceful situation to which you refer."

"Again, I am no diplomat and certainly no expert on the Wek political system, but it is my understanding that Crown Prince Naftur's accession to the throne actually *was* the result of worldwide elections — which were handled in accordance with their laws and traditions. You may also be aware that Terra has already signed a preliminary memorandum of cooperation with his government that we have every hope will ultimately lead to a full alliance at some point in the near future."

"Well, Captain, I hope for your sake that they will honor their alliance with your people better than they did with ours."

"My point, Minister, is that a blockade of your planet *will* be enforced — by either Human or Wek military forces. And from what I know of the Wek people thus far, I think it's safe to say that you may find them less flexible and more difficult to work with than we Humans. In fact, there are a significant number of highly placed representatives within their government who were in favor of attacking and then invading both Damara and Lesheera. You primarily have Prince Naftur to thank for convincing them to take a more moderate stance."

"I trust you will forgive me if I disagree that what you are proposing is 'moderate' in any sense of the word. The presence of your warships in this system is a flagrant violation of all standards of —"

"We have no intention of harming a single Damaran citizen if you will cooperate with our forces and negotiate in good faith with our representatives," Prescott interrupted. "Now, once again, can I have your assurance that you understand and will comply with our demands?"

"I, uh ..." Ved began, pausing once again and seemingly distracted by something happening off-screen. "Of course, we will comply, Captain Prescott. It appears we have little choice in the matter, does it not? How soon can we expect —"

"Something's wrong," Reynolds said in a low, urgent tone from her command chair.

"Stand by, Minister. Dubashi," Prescott said, immediately signaling the lieutenant to once again terminate their side of the vidcon. "What is it, Commander?" he asked after receiving a quick nod from the Comm/Nav console.

"We just lost our data feed from *Industrious*," Reynolds said.

"No warning, no sign of any problems? We just lost the feed?"

"Yes, sir. It looked like one of the corvettes moored at the orbital platform might have released and edged away as if it were preparing to get underway, but they didn't power weapons or make any other threatening moves."

"Hmm … maybe just a comm glitch then. The whole point of her being over there was to maintain coverage of the far side of Damara. At the moment, we only have one comm beacon nearby, so if it stops transmitting data, we're temporarily back to line-of-sight comm. Did *Industrious* drop below the horizon?"

"I believe she did, sir. It's possible they were maneuvering for a better view of the platform, but the comm beacon is still on the network and reporting all systems in the green. Whatever the problem is, we don't have a visual or a comm signal from the frigate, so we're currently blind to the back side of the planet."

"Understood. Dubashi, keep trying to raise them and let me know immediately once we reacquire their signal."

"Aye, sir."

"Tactical, any change in the four corvettes closest to us?"

Without prompting, Lieutenant Lau had placed zoomed-in views of all four of the patrol vessels on the port side of the bridge view screen while also intensifying *Theseus'* sensor scans of the lead vessel.

"No, sir, nothing so far. All four of the ships are still heading in our general direction, but their weapons remain unpowered. They also haven't accelerated at all since the earlier attack, so they don't appear to have any intention of closing with us anytime soon."

Prescott stared at the four Damaran vessels for a moment longer, wondering what, if anything he might be missing. Just as he was about to check in with Captain Donovan aboard TFS *Jutland* regarding the availability of fighters to send over to *Industrious*, his attention was once again drawn to the view screen. Slowly, almost imperceptibly at first, the four vessels began to rotate about their horizontal and longitudinal axes — as if all four were correcting their courses in preparation for —

"Captain, they're transitioning!" Lau yelled.

"All vessels JUMP!" Prescott roared in response.

Chapter 6

Earth, Terran Fleet Command Headquarters
(0300 UTC - Office of the Chairwoman, TFC
Leadership Council)

As had become the norm for all official
communications with the Terrans, the Guardian
portrayed itself as a young, athletic-looking Human male
dressed in a rather conservative but still stylish gray
business suit. Rather than standing behind a podium at
the front of an empty conference room, he now appeared
as if he were sitting casually at one end of the same
room's table. The impression he was apparently trying to
convey was decidedly more relaxed than before. It was
almost as if he intended the meeting to be more intimate
— like a group of collegial insiders coming together to
address a business challenge or discuss the latest strategy
designed to advance their common interests.

"Good evening," he began in a pleasant tone. "I
realize that I have kept most of you in the office later
than usual this evening, but the events of the past
twenty-four hours — some which you are still unaware
of — warrant our immediate attention."

"Good evening to you as well," Kistler replied. "I
believe you know everyone here, so I will dispense with
the formal introductions. I also have no idea what the
appropriate protocol is for situations such as this, but let
me be the first to say that we are pleased by the decision
our people have made to join the Pelaran Alliance. We
look forward to working with you to formalize our new
relationship in the coming days."

"Ah, yes, thank you, Madame Chairwoman … I appreciate that you are always direct and to the point. Obviously, I was also pleased by the outcome of Terra's election. And although I will admit that the process took quite a bit longer than I was originally expecting, I always believed that you would make the right decision in the end. Now, please allow me to return the same courtesy and get straight to the reason I requested an audience with you this evening."

"Thank you … Griffin," she replied with an almost imperceptible smile at the scowling image of Admiral Patterson in one corner of her view screen. "By all means, please continue."

"Some of this may sound a bit dramatic, so please bear with me for just a few moments," he said, looking briefly to the side as if still debating how best to deliver a potentially unpleasant message. "In summary, per the guidelines that govern the regional partnership — or, as a few of you seem to prefer, 'cultivation' — program, my mission here in the Sol system has failed. For a variety of different reasons, none of which we need to discuss here today, Humanity's technological progress has accelerated to a pace that is well in excess of what the Pelaran Alliance considers to be 'safe.'"

"And by that, you mean 'safe' for the Pelaran Alliance, not for us," Sexton said.

"One could argue that they are in many ways one and the same, Admiral, but yes, the directives to which I refer are intended primarily to protect the existing members of the Pelaran Alliance, and not, strictly speaking, prospective members. Over the years, I have used a variety of different methods to maintain your rate of technological growth within acceptable limits, but based on recent observations, I am forced to conclude that my efforts have been unsuccessful."

"So, what does that mean, exactly?" Kistler asked with a furrowed brow. "Are you saying that we have unknowingly crossed some sort of technological line, and as a result we're now suddenly considered 'species non-grata' or something?"

"That's an interesting … and surprisingly accurate way to put it," the Guardian said with a broad smile, "but, yes, that's it in a nutshell."

"Okay," she replied, drawing out the word as she glanced at U.S. Representative Samuel Christenson to her immediate left, "but isn't that something of a moot point at this juncture since we have now made our decision to join the Alliance?"

"I'm afraid it isn't, since runaway technological development — even by a member of the Alliance — could eventually pose a threat to the other member worlds. Since I have encountered a situation that is beyond my capability to control, I am required to report back to the Alliance with recommendations for how best to address this anomaly."

"I see. I hesitate to ask, but I'm guessing that a situation such as this is generally not favorable for the … 'anomaly' species."

"In the history of the program, this particular situation is so rare that it would be inaccurate to generalize. I will tell you, however, that in at least two other recorded instances, the Pelaran Alliance implemented a course of action referred to as the 'winnowing protocol.' Not only was the species under cultivation eliminated, but also several others under their influence within their five-hundred-light-year cultivation radius."

Not surprisingly, there were several expressions of dismay and anger from the Human side of the conversation. For several seconds, the Guardian watched to see how they would handle the information he had presented thus far. Although there were few, if any, signs of fear, it was clear enough from the rising tension and volume of the discussion that the Terrans would fight to the last member of their species, if necessary. In the end, they would lose, of course, but, as usual, he could not help but admire their unshakable tenacity and courage.

"I won't be contacting the Pelarans," he finally said in a calm voice, raising both hands placatingly in an effort to calm the growing level of anger on the part of his hosts.

"I'm sorry, what was that?" Kistler asked, also raising her hands in an attempt to restore order in the room.

"I have no intention of participating in the potential genocide of several species. In my opinion, doing so — even under the auspices of my duties to the Alliance — creates a moral dilemma that could also be interpreted as a violation of those same duties. I realize that's a rationalization, of course, so let me simply say that I am unwilling to participate in acts I believe to be fundamentally unethical and leave it at that."

"While I congratulate you for your moral victory," General Tucker chimed in sardonically, "what's to prevent the Pelarans from eventually coming to the same conclusion that you did regarding your mission here? Then one day, they show up with their 'Pelaran death cruisers' or whatever the hell they have to implement their winnowing protocol with or without your help."

"My dear General, I'm afraid that our launching into a discussion on the hazards associated with interstellar diplomacy would be less than productive at this time. I also do not believe that anyone within the sound of my voice is naive enough to think that pursuing a relationship with a civilization vastly more advanced than your own can be accomplished without significant risks." Here, the Guardian paused, staring back at the Marine general with a look of supreme confidence on his virtual face. "So, to answer your question, Pelaran ships may very well arrive in the Sol system at some point in the future. But you are to consider that there are over ten billion examples of what you might refer to as 'Earth-like' planets in this galaxy. As beautiful and unique as your world is in many ways, the fact that it is capable of supporting lifeforms similar to yourselves isn't at all uncommon, so they may simply choose to ignore you — for now at least. I must also remind you that the Pelarans are generally reluctant to initiate far-flung military expeditions unless they deem them absolutely necessary … thus the cultivation program. Besides, since I am at least partially responsible for putting your civilization in this unfortunate situation, I intend to help you prepare in case something like that ever happens."

"Oh, good God," Tucker swore under his breath. "Let me make sure I'm understanding what you've told us so far. You came here on behalf of the Pelaran Alliance to boost our technological progress with the primary objective of enabling us to fight their battles for them. Somewhere along the way, we started making more progress than was allowed, which — according to the Pelarans' rules — called for some kind of colossal 'do-over.'"

"Well, I wouldn't characterize —"

"I'm not finished," the general interrupted. "So, because of *their* interference and subsequent miscalculations, we're suddenly deemed a threat to the people who were responsible for our rapid progress in the first place and must therefore be destroyed. And to top it all off, in the midst of all of that, you had some kind of electronic epiphany, became a creature of conscience, and determined that the most ethical course of action open to you is to betray the very people who created you. Does that about size it up there, *Griffin*?"

"Look, I know how all of this must sound."

"I sincerely doubt that," Tucker shot back, finally drawing looks of disapproval from both the Chairwoman and Admiral Sexton.

"Okay, fair enough, I'll grant you that my perspective is significantly different from your own. I'll also admit that there is some merit in what General Tucker just said, but the truth is that strange, ambiguous, even borderline ridiculous situations just like this one happen all the time when technologically dissimilar civilizations start interacting with one another. I don't want to sound like I'm delivering a lecture, but now that you Humans are venturing out into your neighborhood of the galaxy for the first time, I suspect that you will quickly discover this for yourselves."

"Alright, we obviously aren't going to get through all of the implications of what you've told us here tonight, but you did mention that you intend to help us. Is that why you have requested access to a great deal of data storage?" Kistler asked.

"That's right. It is my intention to upload almost all of what I would have provided to you during the first several decades after you joined the Alliance."

"Most, but not all?"

"Correct. To address General Tucker's assertion that I was planning to betray the Pelaran Alliance, I hope instead to do everything within my power to avoid doing so. I'm certain that the changing situation will dictate what I can and cannot provide as we move forward. Just as an example, for the time being, I do not plan to provide any information regarding the locations of any of the Alliance's member worlds. I will tell you that, had your technological progress remained more or less on schedule, there would have been little danger of your encountering any of those worlds for a century or more. As things stand now, however, I suspect that every single planet in the Alliance is already well within your reach."

"So, just to clarify, you're not planning to tell us where of any of these worlds are, but you also don't have any problem with our finding them on our own?"

"As long as you conduct yourselves in a reasonable, ethical manner, of course not. Ultimately, when you do encounter one of their worlds, it is my hope that you will have achieved something approaching technological parity. As I alluded to earlier, I have reason to believe that you have already surpassed a great many of them."

"When we do encounter them, do you believe the offer of membership will still be on the table?"

"Unless you give them a reason to view you as an existential threat to the Alliance, I still believe that you will eventually become members, yes. You *are* Children of the Makers, after all. For my part, however, I cannot transmit your acceptance without also reporting your … shall we say 'unfortunate' technological progress. So, once again, I believe it to be in your best interest for me to remain silent on the matter."

"Very well," Kistler said, fully aware that many of the TFC military and civilian leaders present on the vidcon were nearing the limit of their patience with the current discussion — herself included. "Captain Oshiro at the Yucca Mountain Shipyard Facility will be your liaison with TFC's Science and Engineering Directorate. I'm confident he will be able to work with you to meet whatever data storage requirements you specify."

"Thank you, Chairwoman Kistler. There is a truly staggering amount of data, but rest assured that I will remain available to assist you. In fact, I hope you will eventually come to see me as an ally, fully independent of the Pelaran Alliance."

"Thank you as well. We will be in touch. Kistler out."

TFS Theseus
(3.29×10^6 km from Damara)

"That conniving bastard," Prescott growled. "I'm beginning to get a better appreciation for why the Wek dislike these people so much."

"Ten-light-second emergency C-Jump complete, Captain," Ensign Fisher reported from the Helm console.

"C-Jump range 79.4 light years and increasing. Sublight engines are online, we are free to maneuver."

"Tactical?"

"Nine ships transitioned successfully, Captain," Schmidt reported. "The AI assumed temporary helm control of the entire task force just over five microseconds after your command to C-Jump."

"I guess we just proved the value of *that* little tweak. What's the status of the four corvettes?"

"Two of the four now occupy the exact same space we were sitting in before our C-Jump. The other two would have transitioned inside the hull of the *Jutland* if she hadn't gotten out of their way."

"Any idea how long before they can transition again?"

"Not yet, no, sir, but their reactors are operating at a high power level, so that's a pretty good indication that they are preparing to do so. If they do transition again within the next thirty minutes or so, we can safely assume that will represent their minimum time between transitions. After that, the AI will start displaying an estimated 'TBT' countdown timer next to each ship on the tactical plot."

"Lieutenant Lee, what's your best guess at this point?"

"Worst case, zero two minutes … best case, two five minutes," Jayston Lee replied from the Science and Engineering console. "Sorry, Captain, that's the best I can do so far."

"That'll do for now," Prescott replied, rapidly entering a series of commands at his own Command console. "Helm, I just gave the AI an additional level of autonomy in case the Damarans try another … suicide attack. If it detects an imminent transition event and calculates that one of our ships could be targeted, it has the authority to execute an emergency C-Jump for that ship only."

"Understood, Captain," Fisher replied. "The helm is still dialed in with a standard one-zero-light-second emergency C-Jump as well."

"Thank you, Ensign. Commander Reynolds, I'll handle the corvettes. Please take the conn while I do so. I need you to find our missing frigate."

"Aye, sir, XO has the conn," Reynolds said, smoothly transitioning into the role of de facto captain of the task force's flagship. "Tactical, still no sign of *Industrious*?"

"Nothing yet, ma'am," Lau replied. "We have a direct line of sight from here to where she was supposed to be, but we're still not receiving any data from her. I'm scanning the area now with active sensors. If she's in the area, I should find her pretty quickly."

"Lieutenant Dubashi, please signal the *Jutland* and see if we can get a couple of the fighters from their BARCAP sent back there to scout the area. Also, when you get a moment, run a diagnostic series on the local comm beacon and see if that might be the source of the problem."

"Yes, Commander. The AI is already working with the beacon. It will take a bit longer for a complete system check, but it seems to be working fine so far."

"Yeah, that's what I'm afraid of," Reynolds said under her breath as she glanced up at the tactical plot on the starboard side of the view screen. As her mind methodically worked through the disposition of the task force's ships, all four of the remaining *Ingenuity*-class frigates engaged their C-Drives, instantly disappearing from the view screen in four, photo-realistic representations of the grayish-white bursts of light associated with transition events.

"Attack commencing," Prescott announced without looking up from his touchscreen. His unusually detached tone immediately reminded the first officer of a much younger man engaged in a particularly immersive video game.

Theseus' AI immediately opened two additional windows near the left side of the massive bridge view screen. Each window displayed two of the four Damaran corvettes that were now the apparent targets of the frigates TFS *Decisive* and TFS *Indefatigable*, respectively. What followed was easily the most one-sided combat action that any Fleet vessels had engaged in to date. Both frigates had transitioned to a position that immediately allowed them to open fire on their assigned targets, and both did so in earnest within seconds of their arrival in the engagement zone.

Each of the frigates presented their port sides to their assigned targets, allowing them to engage both enemy ships simultaneously with a vicious broadside of energy weapons fire. Commander Reynolds initially tried to divide her attention between the two attacks, but quickly realized that both scenes were virtually identical, and the act of watching both might well result in missing the key elements of both battles. Focusing her attention on the left-hand window displaying TFS *Decisive's* targets, she stared intently as the first bolts of energy slammed into the shields of both Damaran ships, sending shimmering waves of light radiating away from the points of impact like raindrops on the surface of a pond. For a moment, she wondered if additional firepower might be required to destroy the enemy corvettes, but as the frigate's fire intensified, it became obvious that a significant percentage of her beam weapons' energy was penetrating the targets' shields to slam into their lightly armored hulls. It was at that moment that *Decisive's* railgun fire began arriving at both targets, instantly removing any question as to the need for additional firepower.

Streams of kinetic energy penetrators from five of the *Decisive's* fully articulated railgun turrets converged at a single location near each target's bow, then made their way steadily down the entire length of both hulls. The result, while on one hand terrifying to behold, was oddly reminiscent of unzipping a pair of overstuffed duffel bags. The starboard sides of both small ships were opened to the vacuum of space within a period of less than ten seconds. Trails composed of various gases and debris streamed from the stricken vessels as they continued along their previous courses like a pair of fighters intentionally spewing smoke at an air show exhibition.

Noticing a pair of closely spaced flashes in her peripheral vision, Reynolds glanced briefly at the window previously displaying the two corvettes targeted by TFS *Indefatigable*. In their case, the frigate's captain had chosen to combine his ship's railgun barrage with a single plasma torpedo each for good measure. Each of the two compressed bolts of energetic plasma had penetrated deep within its target's already exposed hull near the stern, resulting in an instantaneous breach of its antimatter containment unit. On the view screen, nothing remained of either corvette beyond a few large pieces of debris that flared brightly with reflected light from Damara's sun as they rotated silently away into space.

"The four enemy corvettes on our side of the planet have been destroyed," Prescott reported, still heavily engaged in directing and monitoring the other ships in the task force via his Command console. "Zero niner C-Drive-equipped missiles in flight for each of the two military orbital platforms."

Right on cue, the two windows displayed on the port side of the bridge view screen centered on each of the two large orbital facilities. The closest — from which the original four corvettes had apparently launched — was now devoid of ships, while two of the patrol vessels remained moored at the second platform.

"Missiles transitioning," Prescott announced, continuing his rather unusual running narrative of the battle in his role as task force commander. "Missile impacts," he said just a few seconds later. As if to underscore this fact, both orbital platforms bloomed forth in a flurry of brilliant white antimatter-induced explosions on the view screen.

"Was that the last of the targets you intend to engage for now?" Reynolds asked.

"For the time being, yes. In fact, the corvettes and two orbital platforms were the only space-based targets I would classify as militarily significant. So, unless we want to start hitting military installations planet-side, or some other ships arrive in the area, all enemy targets have now been destroyed. I sincerely hope the Damarans will realize that fact as well and avoid forcing our hand again."

"I dunno, sir," she sighed, shaking her head slowly from side to side. "Their decision-making seems to be driven by … honestly, I have no idea what's driving them, but it sure as hell isn't anything we would recognize as logic."

"Oh, I think we recognize their prime motivation easily enough, Commander. They're afraid … and on such a primal level that what you just referred to as 'logic' plays little if any role in how they react in situations like this. So far, their behavior seems pretty consistent with what the Wek told us to expect. So, at the risk of sounding like I'm grossly oversimplifying their behavior and xeno-stereotyping based on similarities to other mammals we're familiar with on Earth, it seems to me that they're reacting an awful lot like cornered prey animals."

"Humph. For better or worse, stereotypes are often based on a kernel of truth, and I'd have to agree that that's exactly how they're acting."

"Commander Reynolds," Dubashi reported, "the AI has completed its diagnostic series on the local comm beacon. It appears to be functioning within normal limits."

"Thank you, Lieutenant," she replied quietly, then drew in a deep breath before turning back to her captain. "I assume you noticed that there were only two corvettes at the second platform when it was destroyed," she said, working hard to avoid the need to verbalize the most obvious conclusion for what had happened to the missing frigate.

"I think I've found her, Commander … *Industrious*, that is," Lieutenant Lau interrupted in a solemn tone from the Tactical 2 console.

On the bridge view screen, the two windows that had formerly displayed the task force's active targets were replaced by a single, larger image. *Theseus'* AI had quickly processed and enhanced the incoming data from a wide array of sensors in order to present its Human crew with a meaningful visual representation of the distant object. In spite of a level of computing sophistication that approached a rudimentary level of consciousness, the ship's AI did not comprehend that the scene it was displaying was the stuff of nightmares.

Neither *Industrious* nor the Damaran corvette had been destroyed, per se, but it was immediately clear that both ships had flown under their own power for the last time. Much of the Human warship — at over twice the size of the enemy patrol vessel — was still identifiable as an *Ingenuity*-class frigate. Roughly amidships, however, her graceful lines were interrupted by a grotesque mass of mangled, twisted materials that had originally comprised the hulls and internal spaces of both ships.

"*Dauntless* is our closest ship, sir," Reynolds said quietly, staring down at her console as she struggled to cope with the unexpected surge of emotion she was experiencing.

"Right, let's get her in there as quickly as possible. The way it looks, there might at least be a chance that we will find a few survivors. I have the conn, Commander," he added. Prescott had immediately sensed his XO's distress, but knew her well enough to understand that calling unnecessary attention to the situation would likely just make things worse. A peculiar thing about repeatedly encountering death and destruction, he knew, was that each experience could have a profoundly different impact on the same person. Even his redoubtable first officer, while undoubtedly made of sterner stuff than he, still needed a minute from time to time.

"Aye, sir," she replied, looking up briefly with a grateful smile.

"Any power output, Lieutenant Lau?" Prescott asked.

"Minimal, sir. I'll have better data momentarily as *Dauntless* approaches. Right now, I'd say there may still be emergency life support operating in a few sections near her bow."

"Lee, do we have any simulation data on the effects of a coincident hyperdrive transition? Is it even safe for *Dauntless* to approach?"

"It should be reasonably safe, sir, but I'm sorry to say that there is very little chance that there will be any survivors. I just pulled up some simulation data that I ran across back in grad school. Science and Engineering envisioned EVA combat armor that was capable of making short-range hyperspace transitions many years ago, so there was a fair amount of fundamental research done on what would happen if a suit materialized inside another object."

"EVA suits are relatively small … so does the data scale up to ship-sized objects?"

"Yes, sir. I won't pretend I understand much of the physics behind it, but essentially what happens is that most of the material that originally made up both objects gets jammed together within the same physical space. Theoretically, the temperature and pressure should get high enough to achieve nuclear fusion where the two objects intersect, but almost all of the resulting energy gets released into hyperspace in the fraction of a second before the field collapses. The same is true for any antimatter that might have been present within either object. I guess you could say that anything with a significant energy density that's inside the field when it closes seems to have some sort of natural affinity for hyperspace — which is a very good thing since releasing all of that energy in normal space would otherwise cause a massive explosion. As far as I know, our physicists still don't fully understand why this is the case. It's possible, however, that it might have something to do with why there is relatively little antimatter in the universe as compared to normal matter."

"So, you're saying that even though most of the energy gets siphoned off into hyperspace, there's still quite a bit of heat generated?"

"Unfortunately, yes, sir. Significant amounts of heat and ionizing radiation as well. So, anyone in the area immediately surrounding the ... merger —"

"Thank you, Lieutenant. Please relay that information to *Dauntless*."

"Aye, sir."

Reynolds looked up from her console once again with tears welling up in the corners of her eyes. The fact that she was struggling with her emotions was clear enough, but the harsh look on her face told Prescott that she was rapidly progressing from sorrow to anger over what she had seen.

"So," she began in a low, menacing tone. She spoke quietly so that only Prescott could hear, but her voice had an undeniably dangerous, savage quality that he had never heard during all of their years of working together. "The Damarans perceive that we Humans *might* eventually become a threat to them, and their natural first reaction is to attempt to exterminate us before ever even attempting to make contact. Then we arrive on their doorstep, and their response is to resort to suicide attacks against our ships. At what point do we decide that we and our allies will never again be able to live in peace and relative safety while any of these cowards still draw breath?"

Chapter 7

Earth, TFC Yucca Mountain Shipyard Facility

"Strictly speaking, Admiral, we shouldn't be out here during her startup sequence," Captain Ogima Davis said, trying not to startle Admiral Patterson as he approached from behind. On his way back to the *Navajo*, he had spotted the CNO standing at the junction of the cruiser's berth and the mammoth, five-kilometer-long quay that made up half of the Yucca Mountain Shipyard Facility. Knowing immediately what Patterson was up to, Davis also knew that halfheartedly urging the admiral to move to a safer location — which, of course, the "old man" would refuse to do — would provide tacit permission for both men to observe the ship from the outside as her colossal powerplant was brought back online.

"That's cute, Captain. Your concern for my safety is touching, to say the least," Patterson replied with a sideways glance, "and I guess I'd have to give you some credit for pretty good CYA technique. *Strictly speaking*, however, there's no one around at the moment who can tell me to go inside."

"There is that, I suppose," Davis laughed.

"Have you ever watched her fire up from out here?"

"No, sir, I've never really had the opportunity."

"Well, the sound it makes is pretty much the same as with the smaller ship classes. In fact, just about everyone comments on how quiet they are, although you'll still want to put those on, just in case," Patterson said, nodding to the pair of noise-canceling headphones sticking out of one side of Davis' leather flight bag.

"Ah, yes, sir. Isn't the low frequency vibration a problem standing this close?"

"That *is* what the manuals say, but, no, not really. Well … assuming you don't already have an upset stomach or something. I guess what makes an impression is just the scale of the thing. Anyway, let's stop talking about it and just do it. I'm pretty sure you have the keys, right?" Patterson asked, holding up his own tablet computer.

"I do indeed," Captain Davis replied, retrieving his own and entering a series of commands to let the bridge crew know that he would be observing from outside the ship.

Within seconds, the *Navajo's* AI had begun the process of coordinating with the Yucca Mountain facility AIs to prepare the massive ship for departure. The most obvious result was the first in a long series of automated warning announcements, which immediately began echoing throughout the facility: "*Attention, TFS Navajo reactor startup sequence commencing. All nonessential personnel must clear the area surrounding Berth Ten immediately. Hearing protection is required from Berth Six through Berth Fourteen until further notice.*"

"Alright, Admiral, looks like they were ready to go on the bridge," Davis said, donning his headphones as the first hint of a deep, low rumble emerged from the huge warship.

"I'm certain they were," Patterson replied with a knowing smile.

As both officers continued to speak, their voices were now being extracted from the growing background noise by an array of transducers embedded within their headsets. With each set currently in "private comm" mode, their voices were routed only to one another, but were also capable of joining various other comm channels to communicate within the facility or off-site, as required. While both men could still clearly hear the gradually increasing sound of the ship's reactors, the sound of one another's voices also remained quite clear — and would continue to do so, even if the ambient noise level reached a point where neither of them would otherwise have been able to hear themselves speak without electronic assistance.

"I try to remind myself every day that there are people all around me working very hard to stay several steps ahead of me," Patterson continued. "Most days, I never even get the opportunity to interact with the majority of them, but I do try my best to make sure they know how grateful I am every chance I get. I also think it's very important that I respect their time and do my best to keep them from waiting on me … as much as I can, that is."

"That can be a tough one to pull off, sir."

"It can indeed. Fortunately, our people know that just as well as we do. I just try to be as consistent as I can and avoid giving anyone the impression that I'm taking them for granted. Rest assured, though, that they *are* paying attention to how we handle ourselves."

"Yes, sir," Davis said with a smile. Sometimes, it was difficult to decide whether Admiral Patterson was delivering a lecture based on a problem he had observed, or just offering advice. Either way, the old man's delivery had a way of getting his message across and making it stick — which, in Captain Davis' opinion, was almost always more effective than an old-fashioned tongue-lashing.

Staring up now at the massive battle cruiser, Davis breathed in deeply and allowed the rapidly building sound of the ship's twelve reactors to wash over him. He closed his eyes briefly, realizing that, just as the admiral had said, the experience wasn't about the sound he was hearing — impressive though it was — so much as it was the vibration he felt throughout his entire body. It was as if the mountain itself had come to life with the two of them standing just a few meters from its immense, beating heart. The effect continued to intensify for just under a minute, then, just as Davis was beginning to wonder whether his internal organs were being damaged, finally began to subside as the warship's environmental conditioning systems came online and began to compensate.

"So ..." Patterson said after a few moments of relative silence, "seeing that firsthand tends to give you a different perspective on the magnitude of the power you have at your command when you're in the big chair, right?"

"God, sir ..." Davis gasped, still a bit overwhelmed. "I've gone through that startup sequence at least a dozen times from the bridge, but I had no idea. It would probably be instructional for every member of the crew to experience that from out here."

"Hah," Patterson laughed, "probably so, but I doubt Fleet Medical would agree. Now, Captain, with my compliments, please get her buttoned up and ready to depart, if you would. Things seem to be getting a little more interesting than we had hoped for our friends already in Sajeth Collective space."

"Yes, Admiral. Assuming everything is going as planned so far," Davis said, glancing down once again at his tablet, "we should be ready to go within about three hours or so. I'm on my way up to the bridge now."

"I'm not buying that for a minute, son," Patterson said with a raised eyebrow. "I've never seen anyone yet who didn't need to run to the head after standing on the quay during a startup sequence."

"Now that you mentioned it, sir, I —"

"Good luck with that, Captain. Dismissed," Patterson interrupted.

"Thank you, sir, you too."

Lesheera
(487.9 light years from Earth)

No one would ever accuse either the Damarans or the Lesheerans of being the types of societies that honored and encouraged professional military service among their citizenry. Even without much in the way of military tradition, however, both were still well-aware of the importance of defending their worlds from attack. With only 1.3 light years separating their parent stars, the two civilizations discovered one another's existence well before either had developed faster than light travel. After two centuries of sporadic and grossly inefficient communications with one another, the two worlds had finally managed to deploy a rather ingenious network of spacecraft capable of relaying continuous streams of data — effectively bridging the twelve-trillion-kilometer divide between their respective stars. While the 2.6-year round-trip time between transmission and response posed significant challenges, the interstellar network had still been a tremendous accomplishment, ushering in a new age of technological advancement for both planets.

Neither civilization had ever fully trusted the intentions of the other, of course, but the cultures of both had been naturally inclined towards achieving a sense of security through participation in strong, collective groups — always with the promise of safety and protection in return for absolute loyalty and dedication to "the greater good." And although neither species had ever been particularly adept at the scientific and engineering arts, the information they shared with one another accelerated the progress of both, allowing their first face to face contact to occur on a relatively equal technological footing just eighty years after their communications network had come online.

Damara's discovery of yet another advanced species in a star system located just 5.9 light years away had served to further cement its long-standing relationship with Lesheera. From the outset, their mini-alliance had sought to characterize this new world as an unwelcome intruder — a grave threat to the status quo they had worked so hard to establish in a region of space that both considered to be theirs by birthright. Members of the interloper species called their homeworld Graca and referred to themselves as the Wek — a word that, as fate would have it, was phonetically similar to the word for "enemy" in Damara's predominant language.

Now, after several additional centuries characterized by a combination of conflict, uneasy alliance, and political intrigue, both Damara and Lesheera had spent the past several months planning for how best to counter the threat posed by both their oldest foe and its newest ally. Realizing that any conflict with the Wek would likely result in a quick termination of their connection to the Sajeth Collective's deep space communications network, engineers had gone to great lengths to ensure that critical real-time data would continue to flow between the two worlds. In an effort reminiscent of the establishment of their original interstellar network, a constellation of small, virtually undetectable drones was quickly deployed — a system very similar to the Pelaran-derived perimeter surveillance drones recently employed during the ill-fated Resistance incursion into the Sol system.

The Wek — most likely accompanied by the Terran puppets of the Pelaran Alliance — would be coming. This much was all but certain. The only questions were when and in what strength they would arrive. Having been stripped of all but the most basic defensive forces by the Wek departure from the Sajeth Collective, neither the Damarans nor the Lesheerans had any illusions regarding their capability of offering much in the way of organized military resistance. In spite of the hopeless tactical situation, however, neither world had any intention of yielding — at least not in any meaningful way. No, they would certainly resist — relying on the tenets of asymmetric warfare and using whatever forms of deception deemed necessary to ensure their survival.

The first move in what both civilizations assumed would be a protracted war was a simple agreement to inflict as much destruction as possible on the arriving enemy forces by launching simultaneous anti-ship missile strikes followed, if necessary, by "hyperdrive ramming" attacks. Fortunately for their Human adversaries, the Lesheerans had not considered the possibility of a momentary delay caused by the instinctual desire of their ships' crews to avoid throwing their lives away unnecessarily — in spite of their leaders' assertion that the safety of the collective group was at stake.

TFS Karna, Lesheera
(487.9 light years from Earth)

"What the hell just happened?" Captain Abrams asked in as calm a voice as he could muster under the circumstances. After having fended off a virtually identical missile attack to that launched by the Damarans against Captain Prescott's task force, Abrams had been considering an attack on Lesheera's surface when the *Karna* and all nine of her consorts had transitioned to hyperspace without warning.

"Transition complete, Captain," the helm officer reported, working frantically at his console to assess precisely why he had temporarily lost control of the destroyer. "It looks like the AI assumed control and ordered the C-Jump."

"Why? Was there a malfunction of some sort?"

"No, sir, all ten of our ships successfully executed a ten-light-second emergency C-Jump. The entire formation transitioned at the same instant and all ships have maintained their relative positions in formation. It does not appear to have been a malfunction. Stand by, sir, I —"

"It's okay, Ensign, take a second to sort it out … just be quick about it," Abrams said, taking a deep breath and forcing himself to relax. It was clear that his helmsman was doing the best he could under the circumstances, and Abrams knew that bombarding the young man with a steady stream of questions before giving him time to do his job probably wouldn't deliver the desired information any faster.

"I got it, Captain," he said after a few seconds. "The AI assumed control and commanded an emergency C-Jump based on a consultation between itself and the AI aboard TFS *Theseus*."

"*Theseus?* She's over a light year away at Damara. Tactical, are you seeing any information as to why *Theseus'* AI thinks it has a better grasp on our local situation than we do?"

"Yes, sir. Captain Prescott's task force was also attacked by surface and ship-launched missiles, followed by an attempted ramming from several vessels of the same class as those orbiting Lesheera."

"Ramming?" Abrams' XO scoffed, incredulous. "How on earth did they get close enough to even … wait, are you saying they tried to execute an intentional hyperspace transition and collocate with one of our ships?"

"Yes, sir."

"Wow, I don't think there was anything like *that* in the Fleet Intelligence Estimate I read. So, *Theseus'* AI saw what was happening there and warned us we might encounter the same thing here?"

"It warned the *Karna's* AI directly, yes, sir. Between the two of them, they made the determination that the danger was too significant and time-critical to involve us in the decision to C-Jump."

"The engineers have been talking about this for some time," Abrams said. "Since we're deploying comm beacons now every time we undertake any sort of significant operation, our AIs are getting much more aggressive about sharing intelligence and threat assessments in real-time. The thing is, there's a certain amount of uncertainty involved since we're talking about systems that are learning on the fly and constantly adding to the body of knowledge and experiences they can draw from."

"Sounds a lot like us," Abrams' first officer commented.

"Frighteningly like us, yes. The AIs continually look for information or patterns that might provide some sort of advantage. I don't think any of us are entirely comfortable with the idea that our ships can just take control like that, but I'm guessing they would not have done so unless they were convinced that lives were at stake in our task force. Tactical, please continue."

"That's exactly what happened, sir. Captain Prescott's task force is reporting that the Damarans managed to destroy the frigate TFS *Industrious* and narrowly missed both the *Theseus* and the *Jutland*," the officer at the Tactical 1 console reported gravely. "*Theseus'* AI noted the correlation with our situation here and assessed a better than ninety-four-percent chance that we would come under the same type of attack. Actually, it looks like it originally assumed that we had already been hit. It seems to think this was supposed to have been a coordinated attack."

"Hmm ... I don't see how, but let's address one item at a time. The important thing on our side is that the AI's assessment was dead on," Abrams said, nodding to the tactical plot on the starboard view screen.

All four of the enemy corvettes had transitioned to locations previously occupied by the *Karna* and the *Philippine Sea,* respectively. Unlike Prescott, however, Abrams had not yet dispatched any of his vessels to cover the far side of the planet, having intended to complete a fighter reconnaissance sweep before doing so.

"Sir, the *Industrious* was destroyed on the far side of Damara from the main body of Prescott's task force. There was a second orbital platform with three additional corvettes just like the four that tried to hit us here," the XO reported.

"Understood. If the same thing is true here, we need eyes on the far side of the planet as quickly as possible. Green deck, all ships. Have *Philippine Sea* send a flight of *Reapers* over there to check things out. If they find another platform and more corvettes, they are clear to engage. Designate the four existing ships on this side as hostiles and send in the closest two frigates to take them out. We'll hit the first orbital platform from here with a missile strike."

"Aye, sir," came several replies from various members of the bridge crew.

"AI, Abrams. Monitor all vessels in the area for hyperdrive activity. Execute emergency C-Jumps as necessary to prevent any friendly forces from being rammed or … 'collocated.'"

"AI acknowledged," the system's impassive, female voice responded, not bothering to mention that new orders just received from the Admiralty required that it do so anyway, regardless of any conflicting orders issued by its crew.

TFS Theseus
(2 hours later - 3.29×10^6 km from Damara)

"Sir, I have an incoming vidcon transmission from Captain Abrams aboard the *Karna*," Lieutenant Dubashi announced. "He's asking for a private audience with you whenever it's convenient."

Like most military commanders throughout history who have found themselves in the unenviable position of issuing orders that ultimately lead to the deaths of men and women under their command, Tom Prescott had in the past agonized over every one of his decisions that might have been at fault. Ironically, he had not done so today in the immediate aftermath of the Damaran attack on his task force and the subsequent loss of TFS *Industrious*. Still, something about the idea of his friend Bruce Abrams contacting him so soon afterwards sent a chill of dread up his spine. Would this finally be a time when the harsh light of objective, professional scrutiny would bring some fatal flaw in his decision-making into stark relief? Had seventy-four men and women died needlessly this day based on some mere oversight or hesitation on his part?

Realizing that his comm officer had turned around in her seat, awaiting his response, Prescott turned to Commander Reynolds in an effort to determine if she had shaken off her earlier distress. "I think I'd better go take this now," he said. "You okay, Commander?"

"Sure, I'm fine," she replied immediately. "How about *you*?" she asked quietly, raised eyebrows revealing that she had noticed his hesitation to take Captain Abrams' call.

"XO has the bridge," he said aloud, answering her question with a wan smile as he rose and headed for the welcome privacy of his ready room.

During Prescott's brief walk to the starboard, aft corner of the bridge, the ship's AI monitored his every move, immediately securing the room as he entered. Before he could even reach the conference table, he heard the familiar chime indicating that his vidcon was standing by. "On-screen, please," he said distractedly, straightening his uniform by using his reflection in the still-darkened view screen and then taking his seat. Seconds later, the unusually solemn face of fellow Rear Admiral (Select) Bruce Abrams filled the screen.

"Good evening, Tom," he said in a tone that immediately sounded more formal than usual to Prescott's ear. "I mainly just wanted to check in to see if there is anything we can do to assist you. I was very sorry to hear about *Industrious*."

"Hello, Bruce, thank you. No, I don't suppose there is much you can do for us at the moment. One bit of good news is that we were able to rescue thirty-seven members of her crew. Still terrible losses, to be sure, but we originally didn't expect to find anyone alive. I understand the Lesheerans attempted the same type of — I think we've settled on calling it a 'hyperspace merger' attack — on your ships as well."

"Right. I guess the term 'ramming' isn't very descriptive since it implies some sort of collision … but, yes, they did. When the suicide attacks against your task force started, *Theseus'* AI communicated directly with the *Karna's* and emergency C-Jumped us out of the way, just in time. I'm happy, of course, that we didn't take any damage, but I'm not sure I'll ever get used to the idea that my ship can decide at any given moment that it knows better than I do."

"A sign of the times, my friend," Prescott replied with a smile, hoping that the conversation was starting to trend back towards their usual, relaxed tone. "If the Pelarans are any indication, we'll eventually stop sending Humans out here to handle these kinds of missions."

"Yeah, I don't see that happening in our lifetimes. In any event, I guess we got pretty lucky at Lesheera. Our AI had several seconds' worth of warning — not enough to tell us what it was about to do, apparently, but enough to get us out of the way, at least."

"Humph," Prescott grumbled. "True enough. It looks like there might have been some hesitation taking place on the bridges of those ships. I'm amazed they managed to get nine of their crews to execute that order."

"And that brings us to the next thing I wanted to discuss. As you obviously saw, the analysis indicated that the timing of the attacks, while inexact, implies some sort of coordination between the two planets. I think we have to assume that they still have some sort of communications capability in place."

"It's certainly possible. The Wek assured us that they are no longer able to transmit on any of the networks that they know about, but that doesn't mean they haven't put something else in place between them, especially given the relatively short distance between the two systems. Hyperspace comm is difficult to jam —"

"And the beacons are damn near impossible to find … at least ours are."

"That's right, so it's a good idea to proceed as if we believe they can communicate with one another, but I'm not sure there is much we will be able to do about it."

"Until the Wek show up and invade," Abrams replied with a cunning smile.

"You laugh, but that could still very well happen. And after today, I can't say I'd feel very sorry for either of these planets. So," Prescott began again after an awkward pause, "what's really on your mind, Bruce?"

"Ah, well, subtlety was never my strong suit," he replied, smiling and shaking his head. "No, honestly, there's no hidden agenda behind my call other than what we've already covered, but I did want to check in on you. I know what it's like to lose people, but I gotta believe that losing them in the middle of a fight might actually be easier to handle than sitting out here on blockade duty with lots of time to mull it over."

"I hadn't thought about that yet, but thanks for giving me something to look forward to, you jackass," Prescott prodded, feeling a growing sense of desperation to conclude this part of their conversation as quickly as possible.

"Anytime," Abrams continued, undeterred, "but seriously, Tom, don't hesitate to talk to someone if you need to, and I don't mean that drill sergeant of an XO of yours either."

"I think she might have actually been more shaken up after this attack than I was, but I'll be sure to tell her you said so. In all seriousness, I know that's good advice, and I'll definitely go see one of the docs if the need arises. Now unless you've got something else, I'd better —"

"You know the old man's on his way out here, right? I don't want you to be surprised if he reassigns you."

"*Reassigns* me? As in relieves me of command?"

"Yeah. It probably won't happen, but I didn't want you to get caught flat-footed if it does."

"I'm flat-footed right now, Bruce! So are you saying you think I did something wrong or failed to do something to prevent this attack?"

"No! *Hell* no! Not in the least. Come on, Tom, your all-powerful AI didn't see this coming, so I can't imagine anyone will think that you should have."

"But that *is* why we're still sending Human crews out in our ships, isn't it? We're supposed to be able to draw on our experience to anticipate and avoid situations just like this."

"Yes, but this is the first time we've ever seen space combat cross the line into what we might classify as fanaticism, right? So precisely which experience could you have drawn from in this case? I even did a quick check of the military archives the Wek provided. There are no references to suicide attacks of any kind."

"Alright, fine, but if you don't think I've done anything wrong, why do you think Patterson might be coming out here to sack me?"

"Ugh, maybe I should start over now that I've completely put my foot in it here," Abrams sighed. "I doubt seriously that anything approaching a 'sacking' will take place, and I may be completely off-base even mentioning it, but the Leadership Council got some serious pushback from our various member nations following the Resistance attack. TFC's ships consume tremendous resources to construct, equip, and maintain — resources that all of those nations would prefer to utilize elsewhere, if possible."

"Sure, fine, I get that, but the 'guns versus butter' debate is hardly a new one."

"No, but the idea that Earth is going to be required to field massive fleets of warships to protect itself from the alien hordes still is. The whole concept behind the TFC charter was based on technological development of Pelaran-provided data, and it was sold to the public in terms of exploration and economic development, *not* defense."

"Thanks in large part to the Guardian, we had no concept whatsoever of the threats facing us. Surely our members understand that none of TFC's other objectives are possible without an adequate defense."

"I think most of them do realize that at this point, although there will always be a few ideologues naive enough to believe that we can simply negotiate our way around every potential conflict. No, I think most of them are onboard with building up our defenses. Otherwise, we would not have had the backing required to continue expanding the fleet after the attack."

"So, what 'pushback' are you referring to, then?"

"In our first series of battles, we lost a total of eight major combatants. You and I know what a phenomenal success that was under the circumstances, but from our member nations' perspectives, these were tremendously powerful warships that absorbed a significant percentage of their respective GDPs over many years to build … only to be lost in just a few days. They also see the most recent advances in reactor power output and shield technology as major force multipliers for our side."

"They're certainly right about that, but I hope they haven't deluded themselves into thinking that our warships are somehow 'invincible' at this point."

"No, I wouldn't go that far, but I think it's safe to say that they expect a very high return on their investment. And just like universities that pay a ton of money to bring in football coaches that will deliver winning seasons, the Leadership Council is under mounting pressure to minimize additional hull losses."

"Jeez, Bruce, so now we're comparing the loss of hundreds or even thousands of lives to losing college football games?"

"Sorry, I don't mean to be insensitive, and it's a poor analogy, I know. But I think you get my point. Our members have an expectation at this point that we should be able to accomplish our missions successfully — and for the most part without the loss of additional ships."

"Which is exactly what I just did."

"Yeah … and I'm afraid the fact that you weren't in any way at fault won't make much of a difference. Look,

Tom, I probably shouldn't have said anything, but I would want you to give me a heads-up if our roles were reversed."

"No, it's fine. I appreciate having some time to prepare in case something like that happens. Between you and me, though, I think I'd consider calling it a career if they tried to park me in some kind of administrative role. But you did say that Patterson's task force is on its way now, right? We weren't expecting them for another couple of days, and my understanding was that they were headed directly to Graca. Have you heard something different?"

"I wouldn't worry about being sidelined to a desk job just yet. I have a feeling Patterson may have something else in mind. He contacted me immediately after the suicide attacks and said that he's pushing up his departure timeline and coming directly to Damara. He also said that I should prepare to transfer two of my frigates over to your task force until we can be relieved by the Wek fleet."

"Two, huh?"

"That's all I know. Anything else would be wild speculation, and I've already said more than I should."

"Well, if he's just now leaving Earth, he's still most likely the better part of a day away. The current standard operating procedure calls for multiple eighty-light-year C-Jumps with four hours' worth of dwell time in between for capacitor bank recharges and systems checks."

"Right, but since he writes most of the SOPs himself, he's free to ignore them if he likes, and he's apparently in a hellfire hurry. He said he's planning to take this opportunity to attempt a max performance crossing. That means something closer to full one-hundred-light-year C-Jumps with only thirty minutes of dwell time between each one. If everything goes well, he could be here within just a few hours."

Prescott looked up at the ceiling, his mind awash with the potential implications of being sent home under an implied cloud of disgrace. It would, of course, mean an end to his career, which was bad enough. Worse than that, however, was the impact that it would have on his most senior officers, who would, in all likelihood, suffer from some level of "dishonor by association."

"Well," he said with a sigh, "I guess on the bright side I won't have to wait long to find out his intentions."

Chapter 8

*SCS Gresav, Wek Unified Fleet Military Anchorage
Charlie*
(1.80x10^8 km from Graca)

"Ladies and gentlemen, the Crown Prince," Flag
Captain Musa Jelani announced as Rugali Naftur strode
confidently onto the *Gresav's* bridge for the first time
since his coronation ceremony. With the flagship not
currently underway, and the bridge crew expecting his
arrival, everyone in the room had already been standing
when the aft door slid open to reveal a beaming Rugali
Naftur dressed once again in his admiral's uniform. As
he entered, everyone present dropped to one knee with
their right fist clasped over their heart in salute. Naftur
took a few paces into the room, then bowed deeply at the
waist in response.

As a practical matter, the Wek Admiralty had
authorized the continuing use of all standard Sajeth
Collective naval uniforms. They had, nonetheless,
insisted on a few modifications intended to make it clear
to every Wek service member that both Graca and her
military forces were once again being governed under
the auspices of home rule. Naftur, for his part, had
allowed a single gold braid traditionally worn by
members of Graca's royal family to be added to the
existing shoulder boards identifying his rank of fleet
admiral. He also wore a single patch on his left breast
pocket depicting the Royal Dynastic House of Naftur's
coat of arms. Otherwise, neither his appearance, nor his

demeanor had changed in the least since becoming the single most powerful member of his species.

"Please rise, friends," he said warmly. "You honor me with your gesture. I now hereby resume my duties as an Admiral of the Wek Unified Fleet. We have much work to do, so please carry on." It wasn't an entirely accurate statement, given that performing his duties as head of state would forevermore consume the majority of his waking hours. This official declaration was really nothing more than an attempt to avoid the unnecessary awkwardness of being treated like a monarch aboard his own flagship — at least no more so than any other Wek fleet admiral was treated like a monarch, that is.

"It is good to have you aboard once again, Prince Naf — excuse me, Admiral Naftur," Jelani began. "We do indeed have much to do, sir. Before we begin, however, I gave my word to Captain Takkar that I would pass along his compliments as well as his recommendation that you transfer your flag to WFS *Mithcah*. It is his belief that you would be more comfortable and safer aboard a *Baldev*-class battleship."

"Young Captain Takkar is understandably proud of his new command," Naftur replied with a satisfied nod, "and he is undoubtedly correct that more spacious accommodations are available aboard his ship than those aboard the *Gresav*. As to my safety, it has always been my personal experience that larger ships make larger targets."

"I certainly agree, sir," Jelani said with a broad smile. "I informed Captain Takkar that you would be grateful for his kind offer, but would most likely choose to remain aboard the *Gresav*."

"After all these years, this ship feels like a member of the family, Musa," Naftur reflected, seating himself at one of the command chairs at the rear of the bridge and running his massive hands along both armrests as he reacquainted himself with his surroundings. "Besides, she still has a few tricks up her sleeve that would give even the *Mithcah* a run for her money, does she not?"

"Of that, there is little doubt, Admiral."

"Captain Jelani," the *Gresav's* comm officer announced, "we just heard back from our next closest ships to the Herrera Mining Facility. They report that they are just over eight days out at best speed."

"Understood, thank you," he replied. The last thing Captain Jelani wanted was to give his Crown Prince and lifelong friend the impression that he was incapable of handling this, or any other situation. Over the past few weeks, however, he had become increasingly aware that the Wek Fleet, for all its might, was simply not equipped to cover the myriad of challenges it now faced in the wake of Graca's departure from the Sajeth Collective.

"I was under the impression that we had already dispatched several vessels to Herrera," Naftur said. "Have they not yet arrived?"

"No, sir, they have not. They are due within the next forty-eight hours, which may very well be soon enough, but given the strategic value of the facility, Command thought it prudent to determine if additional assets might be available."

"I see. I'm here to work, Captain, so I expect that you and I will continue to utilize one another as trusted resources … just as we always have. I will let you know if my other responsibilities require more of my attention.

You know better than anyone else that I have never pretended to be anything more than a lifelong naval officer. In my opinion, Graca is much better served by my continuing to do the job I have spent a lifetime mastering than it would be if I were at home attending state dinners and tinkering with domestic economic policy. Do you not agree?"

"Yes, of course, Admiral," Jelani replied, inclining his head respectfully while chuckling in spite of himself. "I will confess, however, that this is the first time it has occurred to me why you were so eager to come back aboard and resume your duties with the Unified Fleet."

"Well then, my friend, it is possible that you are even less politically astute than I — if such a thing is possible. Now, what has Command so concerned about the Herrera Mining Facility?"

"Over the past two days, there have been a number of unidentified hyperspace transitions in the area. Command believes that these could be a prelude to an attack."

"You will please forgive me for being a bit behind on my operational intelligence materials, but if Command is concerned enough to consider dispatching additional warships, then it is most likely not Sajeth Collective forces they are expecting at Herrera."

"No, sir. All of the Sajeth Collective Fleet's capital ships are now either under our direct control or, in the case of several warships located near Pashurni and Shanus, have at least agreed to stand down from all active military operations until we have concluded our negotiations with their Governing Council. In the meantime, Terran forces are now in place at both

Damara and Lesheera until our ships can relieve them. The fear is that the Krayleck have become aware of the power shift in the region and may be looking to take advantage of the situation."

"The Krayleck," Naftur said, closing his eyes momentarily as a low, menacing sound emanated from the center of his chest. "Now, when we are on the very cusp of formalizing a long-term relationship with the Humans, is no time to find ourselves in conflict with yet another Pelaran-cultivated civilization. We are in the process of forming what I hope will take shape as a 'crowned republic,' Musa. So, in spite of my favorable opinion of the Humans, decisions regarding what path our relationship will take is ultimately a decision for our newly formed Parliament."

"In that case, sir, it might be in everyone's best interest if the Humans are the ones to send ships to the area. Perhaps we should consider withholding our intelligence regarding the Krayleck association with the Pelaran Alliance. It might also be prudent to avoid providing any specific information regarding the Herrera Facility."

"The Humans well understand the need for secrecy. Even after fighting alongside their warships, for example, there is a great deal that we do not know regarding their capabilities. But there is a fine line between protecting state secrets and outright dishonesty where your allies are concerned, is there not? I agree that we need not provide a great deal of specific information regarding the work being done at Herrera, but we must certainly tell them of our expectation that they will be encountering another Pelaran-cultivated species for the first time. Do you not agree?"

Jelani paused briefly to consider the situation, then continued. "I do, sir, and I suppose there is an element of inevitability underlying our relationship with the Terrans in any event."

Naftur eyed his flag captain for a moment. It was highly unusual for Jelani to offer anything approaching a political opinion, even though he was, himself, a prominent member of one of Graca's original seven dynastic houses. Caught slightly off guard by both the comment as well as his own somewhat emotional response to it, Naftur was unsure if his friend had intended to convey a level of discomfort with their newest ally. "I believe, Captain," he replied, shifting smoothly to a more formal tone, "that you may be putting voice to a sentiment that many of us undoubtedly share. We have returned Graca to home rule for the first time in generations. And while there is widespread support for this move, many of our people seem to be extending the idea of independence to imply that we should stand alone as we did in ages past — avoiding all entanglements with other civilizations. While understandable, the notion that we can ever again provide any sort of meaningful security for our world in isolation from our neighbors is no longer realistic."

"I apologize, Admiral. I agree with you, and in no way intended to imply any sort of criticism for you or our new government. My family, as you well know, has its share of political operatives, but that is not a life I would ever choose for myself. Like you, I am a naval officer, and have no desire to be otherwise," Jelani replied with a knowing smile, echoing his superior's earlier comment. "My observation regarding inevitability was merely a reflection of the situation we find ourselves in. The relatively small region we have always considered to be 'Sajeth Collective space' is bordered by at least two and perhaps three much larger spheres of influence dominated by civilizations associated with the Pelaran Alliance. Given that all of them are at least as advanced as we are and likely to become more so over time, it makes sense to partner with one or more of them … preferably one that shares at least some of our societal values. The Humans seem to offer, by far, our best option along those lines."

"Exactly so, but it is I who should apologize. I fear that I am already beginning to think like a damnable politician, Musa. So, from now on, when I am in this uniform, I ask that you speak freely around me as I believe you always have. I will endeavor to do the same. I can also tell you without hesitation that I *do* believe the Terrans share many of our values. They struggle from time to time — just as we do — and I fully expect them to pursue their own self-interests — again, just as we do. But we have much more in common with them than we do any of the other worlds in the Sajeth Collective."

"Of that, I have little doubt."

"As you say, we simply do not have the strength to stand alone against the rising tide of the Pelaran Alliance. And, on the subject of inevitability, it seems to me that we will soon reach a point where the so-called cultivated civilizations will begin to come into conflict with one another in this region. It is time to pick sides, my friend, and in spite of their relative inexperience, everything I have seen so far leads me to believe that we must cast our lot with the Humans and pray for the best."

"Perhaps they will come to view our assistance as having been pivotal during their period of rapid development."

"There are certainly worse things than having a powerful ally who believes themselves to be in your debt. Now, regarding the situation at Herrera, we must access the Terrans' communications network and see if we can be placed into contact with either Admiral Patterson or Admiral Sexton."

"Aye, sir."

"Beyond that, having stripped the other six worlds of the Sajeth Collective of most of their military forces, we have a moral obligation to defend them from external threats. Contact Command and inform them that they are to mass the 3rd Fleet in its entirety at the Shanus anchorage. Tell them that the *Gresav's* task force will be en route to reinforce the 3rd Fleet as quickly as we can get underway."

"Begging your pardon, Admiral, but that will account for roughly a third of the Unified Fleet — well over one hundred warships and at least thirty-five support vessels. Is it not possible the Krayleck will see such a large concentration of forces near their frontier as an indication that we intend to attack?"

"That is indeed a possibility," Naftur acknowledged with a nod, "but we can ill afford to allow them to commit open acts of aggression into Sajeth Collective space without an immediate and vigorous response. As you say, Captain, this region constitutes their frontier — in truth, even a bit beyond it. While we know that they have established a forward operating base not far from Herrera, it is doubtful that they have committed a large number of their warships so far from their homeworld. We must demonstrate our resolve in a decisive manner now, while they believe us to be at our weakest. If we fail to do so, we invite a future of endless challenges to our sovereignty over the area … and eventually a threat to Graca itself."

"It will be as you say, Gracafürst."

Damara
(489.3 light years from Earth)

With Captain Prescott's task force sitting in close proximity to Damara, Admiral Patterson was in possession of sufficiently accurate navigational data to plot the final C-Jump of his 489.3 light year journey in a manner that would make a lasting impression on the population of the blockaded planet. Although he would not have been willing to delay his record-setting crossing for the purpose, the nearly perfect alignment of the planet's most populated continent presented a psychological warfare opportunity that the old admiral simply could not resist.

In spite of repeated hails from the *Theseus*, there had been no further communication from Zorian Ved since the Damarans' suicide attacks — followed immediately by the complete destruction of all of their military assets in the vicinity. When necessary, however, nine-hundred-and-fifty-meter-long *Navajo*-class cruisers were capable of alternate forms of communication.

At an altitude of four thousand meters — high enough to avoid serious injuries on the ground, while still generating something akin to an apocalyptic series of sonic booms — all ten warships in Admiral Patterson's task force transitioned from a range of just over ninety light years distant directly into Damara's atmosphere. This was, in fact, the first time a hyperspace atmospheric insertion had been attempted with a ship as large as a cruiser, and in this case, Admiral Patterson's task force included four — with two destroyers and four frigates thrown in for good measure. Prior to their final C-Jump, Captain Ogima Davis of the *Navajo* had arranged the task force at an interval and speed such that at least one of the ships would be clearly visible to every inhabitant of the targeted continent. Accordingly, the stage had been set for a dramatic display reminiscent of countless science fiction movies depicting the arrival of hostile alien forces at an unsuspecting and unprepared Earth. Ironically, such a thing had never occurred in the Sol system, and this particular "alien force" was made up entirely of Human warships.

Shattering the tranquil, spring evening off the west coast of Damara's largest continent, ten simultaneous flashes of light erupted from the heavens, replaced immediately by streaks of orange-tinted fire that seemed to cleave the very sky as they passed overhead. Those on the ground who bore witness to the Terrans' arrival were understandably terrified, but their fear had a dimension that the Humans could never understand — a wild, primal fear that gripped their subconscious minds and recalled latent images from their species' collective past. It was as if every Damaran who witnessed the enormous arcs in the sky suddenly found themselves on an open plain with nowhere to hide, surrounded by a pack of merciless predators that had approached unseen in the dark.

Just as the hellish light from their passing had begun to fade from view, the very foundations of the planet seemed to falter as shockwaves generated by the colossal warships reached the surface. Many areas were left without power as the resulting seismic activity tripped emergency systems that automatically took vast segments of the power grid offline. Admiral Patterson's mass demonstration continued for several minutes, extending across the width of the entire continent until the ships departed the night skies just off the east coast — punctuated by the same flashes of light that had heralded their arrival.

Light structural damage and minor injuries had been inflicted across nearly one-third of the planet's total land mass in a very short period of time. Although the physical damage was militarily insignificant, the psychological impact on the Damaran population at large was enormous. After a period of what could accurately be described as widespread panic, a series of demands passed frantically from the populace to their respective government representatives, all insisting that they take immediate action to pacify the marauding Terran forces and agree to whatever terms they had in mind.

Humanity's "war," such as it was, with perhaps the most militant civilization in the Sajeth Collective was effectively over.

TFS Theseus

(3.29x10^6 km from Damara)

"Lieutenant Dubashi, please render honors for the Chief of Naval Operations," Prescott ordered as Admiral Patterson's ten-ship task force took up positions to starboard.

"Aye, sir. Nineteen-gun salute transmitted and acknowledged by the *Navajo*. Also, Admiral Patterson is requesting a vidcon with you and Commander Reynolds as soon as possible."

"Well, that does seem to be the pattern today, doesn't it?" Reynolds said, attempting to sound upbeat.

"It does indeed," Prescott replied flatly. "Please let him know that we will be with him shortly. Commander," he said, standing and gesturing towards the ready room, "I need a word before we get started with the CNO."

"Of course, sir," she said, standing and leading the way aft.

"Lieutenant Commander Schmidt, you have the bridge," Prescott said as he turned to follow his XO.

"Aye, sir," Schmidt replied, moving to take his place at one of the Command consoles while being immediately replaced at Tactical 1 by an ensign from the standby crew.

"Sir," Dubashi called, catching Prescott half a stride from the door to his ready room, "we're being hailed from the planet's surface. It's text-only like the first message we received, but indicates that it is once again from Defense Minister Ved. The message reads as follows: 'Captain Prescott, on behalf of the Sajeth Collective and the planetary government of Damara, we unconditionally accept the terms you outlined during our previous discussion. Please make contact again on the included frequency at your earliest convenience.'"

"Sounds like the admiral got his point across," Reynolds said, her smiling face leaning in through the door from the adjoining ready room.

"It certainly does. Acknowledge on the indicated frequency and instruct them to stand by for further instructions," Prescott said, turning to quickly exit the bridge.

"Aye, sir," Dubashi called after him.

"The Damarans rolling over after a little 'shock and awe' may put Patterson in a better mood alright," Prescott said as the door closed behind him, "but I wanted you to be aware that Bruce Abrams thinks he may have come out here to fire me and send us home."

"*Fire* you? Oh, come on, that's absolute BS and you know it."

"Okay, 'fire' might not be exactly the right word. Relieve me from the current mission and send us home. Is that better?"

"Nope, sorry. Still BS. So why does Captain Abrams even think this might be a possibility? Because of *Industrious*?"

"Yeah, that's part of it. The Leadership council apparently doesn't think we should ever lose another ship."

"Well that's clearly ridiculous," she said, rolling her eyes. "You're pretty much the poster boy for TFC. I doubt they could fire you even if they wanted to because of all the bad press it would generate. Besides, you thought the same thing after we stumbled into our first battle in the *Ingenuity*. You *know* Admiral Patterson. That's just not the kind of officer he is — even if you really had screwed up ... and you haven't."

"I hope you're right. But like Abrams said, I just wanted to give you a heads-up. You know ... just in case."

"With respect, I think you're both drama queens," she said with a mocking smile. "Now let's get with Patterson before we really *do* piss him off."

"Yes, ma'am," he chuckled. "AI, Prescott. Establish secure vidcon connection with Admiral Patterson aboard the *Navajo*."

"AI acknowledged. Please state the desired classification level for this vidcon," the synthetic female voice announced.

"That's new," Reynolds said, furrowing her brow and scowling at the ceiling.

"All of our recent communications with Admiral Patterson have been classified Top Secret, code word MAGI PRIME. Is there a new code word we should be using?" Prescott asked, realizing even as he finished speaking that he already knew the answer he would receive.

"Terran Fleet Command security regulations classify all code words at the same level as the information to which they refer. Accordingly, the ship's AI is not authorized to reveal classification code words, even in cases where all personnel in attendance possess sufficient security clearances to allow access to information referenced by those code words."

"Ask a stupid question …" Prescott sighed. "AI, please use security protocols sufficient for Top Secret, code word MAGI PRIME."

After a long pause, Terran Fleet Command's official service seal replaced a picturesque view of Damara on the large view screen opposite the conference room table.

"Does it seem a little slow to you?" Reynolds asked after several more seconds had passed.

"Requested classification level declined by Vice Admiral Kevin Patterson," the AI's voice reported in a voice that Reynolds thought sounded irritatingly self-satisfied. "Be advised that all officers present are now cleared for information classified as Top Secret, code word DEFIANT BASTION. If you agree to all rights and responsibilities implied by this security level, acknowledge verbally with the words, 'I accept.' Your identities will be reverified and authenticated by multiple biometric scans and your permanent service records updated accordingly."

"I accept," both officers replied.

"Access granted. Terran Fleet Command security regulations authorize severe penalties — to include lifetime imprisonment or death — for knowingly disclosing, compromising, or otherwise mishandling classified information at this level."

"Still think he's calling to fire you?" Reynolds asked with a raised eyebrow.

Before Prescott could reply, Admiral Kevin Patterson, Chief of Naval Operations, appeared on the view screen.

"Good morning to you both," he greeted. "As you have undoubtedly surmised, this vidcon is classified Top Secret, code word DEFIANT BASTION. Your ready room has been automatically secured for this briefing."

"Understood, Admiral, and good morning to you as well," Prescott replied.

"We've got a lot on our plates at the moment, so I'll get right to it. First off, have there been any changes in enemy disposition here at Damara since the earlier attacks?"

"None until your arrival, sir. Just moments ago, Zorian Ved, the Defense Minister of Damara and Administrator of the Damaran Headquarters of the Sajeth Collective Fleet, accepted our terms and requested that we contact him at our convenience. It might be a little early to characterize it as a surrender, but I think it's safe to say that you put the fear of God in them."

"Hah!" Patterson laughed aloud. "I'm not sure we'll be as forgiving of attempted genocide as He is, but that's outstanding news. I think you've met Ensign Fletcher, one of our CIC comm officers. She's a science fiction movie buff and that whole 'death from the skies' bit was entirely her idea."

"Sounds like it's time for a promotion, sir," Reynolds said. "Her creative thinking may have saved countless lives on both sides."

"Absolutely. I think she's due for a promotion to Lieutenant Junior Grade anyway. I'll have to check the regs, but since we are in an active combat zone, I may be able to step her directly to O-3. In any event, Minister Ved can cool his heels for a while. We'll have someone get back to him when we're good and ready. That someone, however, will not be either of you."

"Oh? Do you have something else in mind for us, Admiral?" Prescott asked hopefully, but with a chill of dread running down the length of his spine.

Patterson leaned back in his chair and stared back at the two of them for a long moment, uncharacteristically drumming his fingers on the table. "Here's the thing, you two," he began again. "I do have new orders for you, but what I'm going to ask you to do this time will be different from the quote, unquote 'official' story that will be made somewhat public … to most members of the Leadership Council, that is."

"I'm not sure I follow you, sir. Does this have something to do with TFC's member nations pressuring the Leadership Council to essentially eliminate additional hull losses?"

"That's part of it, yes. In fact, that somewhat ridiculous notion forms the backdrop we will be using as cover for the mission I have in mind. Per the charter, the Leadership Council must be regularly briefed on all Fleet operations. Frankly, the fact that the organization was originally formed with the military aspects of its mission seen as secondary to pursuing technological development and exploration has created a number of significant problems, not the least of which is maintaining operational security. Fortunately, the Council is now under new leadership."

"And is Chairwoman Kistler onboard with running things more like a true military organization?"

"I don't know if I would go that far. She's a strong proponent of civilian control of the military, so she recognizes the need for oversight. Obviously, that's a good thing, but she also understands that military operations frequently demand a level of secrecy and security that can be at odds with what our member nations might refer to as 'transparency.' In response, she has established a Military Operations Oversight Committee composed of herself and three other representatives. The four of them will be regularly briefed on everything we're doing, but will, for the first time, be subject to the same security clearance requirements as TFC military personnel."

"So, they will be subject to criminal prosecution for leaks then, right?"

"Yes, indeed. In fact, they technically always have been, but the whole 'diplomatic immunity' thing previously shielded the representatives from any sort of enforcement action. Kistler ended that right away and even managed to get the charter modified to hold them accountable for both security breaches and other serious crimes perpetrated while in office."

"Like attempting to murder the Commander in Chief?" Reynolds asked.

"I'm pretty sure that qualifies now, yes. Speaking of the CINC, the Chairwoman has also given Admiral Sexton the authority to designate certain financial expenditures and military operations as 'black.' The Oversight Committee will still be briefed on black ops as well, but — within the boundaries established by current policy, of course — the CINC will have quite a bit more latitude to determine when and how that takes place. That brings us back to your situation," Patterson said, pausing again as if he were less than comfortable with what he was about to say.

"You mentioned some sort of 'cover story,' sir," Reynolds prompted.

"Right. Let me say from the outset that I have already reviewed the actions that have taken place since your arrival at Damara and can find no fault whatsoever with any of the decisions made by the two of you or any of the other crews under your command. So please understand that what I'm about to ask you to do is in no way punitive, nor will it have any negative effects on anyone's careers, so don't worry about any of that. The appearance, however, and the information given to the Leadership Council will for the time being indicate that I have relieved Captain Prescott of command of the Damaran task force pending review of what transpired here today."

"I'm not sure I follow you, Admiral," Prescott began. "You're saying we're going to lie to the Leadership Council?"

"Not at all. I'm saying that we're offering you up as red meat to assuage some of our member nations' demands that we stop losing ships and crews. Things are very different now than they were under Karoline Crull, Tom. The Oversight Committee is both aware and completely onboard with what we're doing here. You really *are* being relieved of this command, and there really *will be* a review of your actions here today. Don't get me wrong, I don't mean to imply that I'm in any way happy about the suicide attacks and the loss of *Industrious,* but the truth is that we needed a reason to retask *Theseus* without attracting a lot of unwanted attention. Based on this after-action review, everyone will be expecting you to lay low for a while until we decide what to do with you — thus satisfying both a political and a military objective at the same time."

"Understood, sir. So, you're sending us home, then?"

"Temporarily, yes, but I have what I hope will be a brief mission for you first. We have been monitoring some troubling activity for several days near the outskirts of what we're still referring to as Sajeth Collective space. We know that the Wek Unified Fleet has no assets in the immediate area, so we've been expecting to hear from them for some time. I don't have all the details yet, but Admiral Sexton apparently just got the call from Prince Naftur himself while I was en route to Damara. The location in question is just under ninety light years from here."

"I'm sorry, Admiral, but it sounds like you're referring to an area that is significantly farther from Earth than either Graca or Damara. I was not aware we had deployed any ships, or even surveillance drones, that far out."

"We haven't, Tom, and that's the immediate reason for your upgraded DEFIANT BASTION clearance. I have something truly remarkable to show you both …"

Chapter 9

Herrera Mining Facility
(87.2 light years from Damara)

"Unidentified Krayleck spacecraft, you have entered a restricted zone that has been designated as unsafe for navigation by the Wek Unified Fleet. Please identify yourselves so that we may vector your vessels out of the hazardous area," the engineering officer repeated. Although his workstation had limited capabilities compared to those found aboard the Fleet's newest warships, he was reasonably certain that the two vessels depicted on his screen were the same two he had been unsuccessfully attempting to contact for the past two days.

The two ships were relatively small, but from what he could tell did appear to be warships of some sort. Their size, however, did nothing to decrease the tedium of being forced to continuously respond to their somewhat aggressive behavior. Each time the two ships appeared, they were in a different location — always together and always after a seemingly random period of time since their last transition. Per Sajeth Collective (and now Wek Unified Fleet) procedures, the duty officer was required to repeatedly attempt contact in an effort to warn them off — each time, of course, hoping that they would simply leave and not return.

Although technically a civilian now, the old engineering officer had served aboard the battleship *Rusalov* for much of his career and certainly knew enough about naval tactics to recognize a probing reconnaissance mission when he saw one. Now, each time the Krayleck vessels appeared, he felt a growing sense of dread that this would be the time they chose to make their hostile intentions known. After all, it did not take much in the way of sensor technology to detect massive surges of antiparticle emissions like the ones that seemed to appear spontaneously from the void near the so-called Herrera "mine."

In fact, perhaps the most annoying thing about the Krayleck ships — even if they truly were here out of mere curiosity, perhaps with the intent of discovering the origin of what they had been detecting in the area — was that they were preventing the facility from accomplishing its scientific mission. Safety protocols required that all mining operations be discontinued for several hours each time the "event zone" surrounding the facility was violated. Intentional or not, the ships were doing a fine job of preventing the station's engineers from getting their work done.

"Wek officer broadcasting on this frequency, this is Captain … representing the Krayleck Empire. Your facility is within the boundaries of territory recently annexed by our forces on behalf of the Pelaran Alliance. You are ordered to cease operations immediately. All equipment and documentation at the site is now the property of the Krayleck Empire and must be left intact when you evacuate. This, you must also do immediately."

The signal was audio only, and the Wek engineer rolled his eyes at the fact that the Krayleck officer's name was so unintelligible that the AI simply omitted it completely rather than attempting any sort of meaningful translation. While it was certainly true that Herrera was on the fringe of Sajeth Collective space, it was still well outside the Krayleck's five-hundred-light-year sphere of influence. While Krayleck vessels had been detected in Sajeth Collective space many times, he was unaware of any previous confrontations — certainly nothing like this at least. In fact, over the past several years, there had even been a small but steadily increasing amount of commerce taking place between the Krayleck and Shanus, the nearest Collective planet to their territory. In any event, he was absolutely certain that the Wek Unified Fleet would not willingly abandon this facility, leaving its potentially limitless antimatter production to a bunch of … what were they? Insects? He wasn't entirely sure, nor did he particularly care about their scientific classification. He knew only that they were disgusting — or at the very least not a species he would ever care to dine with.

"Herrera copies," he replied in as polite a tone as he could manage. "Captain, perhaps there is some sort of misunderstanding that I can help clarify. If not, I have sent for our facility commander and I am sure she will be available shortly. We are a research station previously operated by the Sajeth Collective, but now managed by the Wek Unified Fleet."

"A military research station, then?"

"We are indeed managed by the Wek Fleet, but we are not a military installation, per se, sir."

"And what types of military research are being conducted at this site?"

"Sir," the engineering officer began, turning around in his chair and wondering why the commander had not yet arrived in the Operations room, "I am, of course, not at liberty to discuss any specifics regarding the nature of the research being done here. I am the wrong person to ask in any event, Captain, since I am not one of the scientists," he said, which was mostly true. There were, in fact, very few Wek scientists — even inside the rarefied theoretical physics community — who had anything approaching a thorough understanding of the work being done at Herrera. "I do know that we are looking into a natural phenomenon known as a phase transition that may account for how galaxies formed in the early universe."

It was at that moment that the entire facility shook with the impact of distant weapons fire. Herrera, the lone planet orbiting its somewhat remote red dwarf star, was far too small to retain any sort of atmosphere. As a result, the sounds heard by the Wek personnel on site were transmitted through the ground to vibrate the facility itself, producing an unsettling baritone reverberation as if they were standing on the inside of an immense bass drum.

"What the hell did you say to them?" Moya Gara thundered as she arrived in Operations for the first time today.

"Very little other than stalling for time so that they could speak with you," the much older engineering officer replied, raising his bushy eyebrows in a manner that would have almost certainly resulted in serious consequences during his time aboard the *Rusalov*.

Gara, although holding the rank of commander in the newly formed Wek Unified Fleet, was not in uniform. As was the case most days, her work so far this morning had spanned roles encompassing a broad range of responsibilities from senior engineer to maintenance assistant. As she quickly made her way to the Command workstation, she caught a glimpse of her reflection and noted the smudges of grease that currently graced both her light brown facial hair and gray coveralls. *Too late to worry about appearances at this point*, she thought sourly, wondering once again why no Wek warships had arrived to secure the critically important outpost.

"Krayleck spacecraft, cease fire, cease fire!" she announced over the same frequency. "You are firing on a facility administrated by the Crowned Republic of Graca. We have a long history of peaceful cooperation with your people and have every intention of continuing that tradition."

Once again, the partially subterranean building shook — this time with an almost deafening sound providing a clear indication that this impact had been much closer than the first.

"Eton Ulto!" she swore, grabbing the armrests of her chair to prevent being thrown to the floor. "Are their vessels within the currently targeted event zone?"

"Stand by one," the officer replied, rolling his chair from the Communications workstation halfway across the room to one of the station's Engineering terminals. "Yes," he said after entering a quick series of commands, "but only one of them. Commander, I think I know what you have in mind, and I do not believe it to be a wise course of action."

"And sitting here waiting for those two ships to destroy us is?" she growled.

"They are merely trying to intimidate us into abandoning the facility without any resistance. Unless they attack the facility itself, I strongly recommend we continue to play for additional time until our warships arrive."

"As of yesterday, the Admiralty was still saying two more days minimum," she said with a frustrated sigh. "The Krayleck have never opened fire before. Do you think we *have* two more days at this point?"

"Unfortunately, we cannot know the answer to such a question," he replied calmly, instinctively understanding the need to talk the young officer back from the precipice of rash action. "What I *can* tell you is that, if we initiate a phase transition, the effects will be unpredictable at best. We might well cause serious damage or even destroy one of them, but we have little chance of destroying them both. Once we destroy one, the remaining warship — or the reinforcements that would almost certainly follow — will make short work of the facility."

Gara stared at him for a long moment, then noticed the flashing icon on her Command workstation indicating that the Krayleck ships were now offering a video stream to continue their previous conversation. "They are asking to speak again," she said, looking up at the older but technically lower-ranking civilian officer.

"Yes, ma'am. I believe that to be a good sign. We must endeavor to be calm and give them the impression that it is our intention to eventually comply with their demands. We simply need sufficient time to do so." He could see by the look on the young commander's face that she was still somewhat undecided on what course of action to take, so he pressed on in a calm, reassuring tone, risking one final nudge in what he hoped was the right direction, "This facility was never intended to be used as a weapon, Commander, but I believe we can keep that option open to us if it comes to that in the end."

Gara nodded, then took in a deep breath and stood, straightening her coveralls as best she could as she turned to face the large display screen on one side of the room. Believing herself as mentally prepared as she was likely to get, she opened the vidcon connection. "Greetings, Captain. I am Commander Moya Gara of the Wek Unified Fleet. Thank you for agreeing to speak with me," she began, doing her level best to avoid any outward sign of the revulsion she felt.

This was Gara's first "face to face" experience with a member of the Krayleck species, although she had seen a few pictures and some video footage of them during her training. There was indeed something vaguely familiar about them, but she knew that this race was as "alien" as any sentient beings she was likely to encounter in this region of the galaxy. A large portion of their bodies was covered by an exoskeleton, and their heads had both simple and compound eyes, giving the immediate impression of a huge insect. Beyond that, however, the species had a variety of other features that seemed to defy any definitive classification. On the sides of what Gara thought of as their neck, for example, there was an array of slits that appeared to be some type of gills, while at the rear of its head, two pairs of long, fleshy spikes hung nearly halfway down the creature's back — both bringing to mind something more akin to a crustacean, or even an amphibian of some sort. The thing that she had been warned about in her xeno relations training, however, was the large mass of brown liquid that was often suspended from the Krayleck's mouthparts, particularly when they were excited or felt threatened in any way. Watching impassively as large droplets of the vile ooze dropped to the floor in front of the creature, Gara swallowed hard against a rising wave of nausea and fought to maintain her bearing as she awaited its response.

"You have been warned that you are trespassing in territory claimed by the Krayleck Empire," the captain said with no attempt to acknowledge her introduction. "You will vacate the premises immediately, leaving the facility entirely intact."

"I understand your instructions," she began, suppressing the nearly involuntary threatening growl that had begun to build within her chest. "We have sent for vessels to assist with our evacuation, but it may take several days for them to arrive."

"Unacceptable. Your facility is equipped with emergency evacuation pods. Your crew will make use of this system. If you do so immediately, your vessels will be permitted to retrieve the pods when they arrive. Once that is accomplished, your species must depart the area and never return."

"Captain, using those systems to evacuate a functional facility would put my crew at very significant risk."

"That may be true, Commander, but any who remain will surely die."

"Very well," she replied flatly. "We will need a few hours to organize our evacuation."

"I will allow seven minutes, but I expect to see the first evacuation pods leaving the facility within three," he replied, after which the vidcon feed abruptly terminated.

"So …" Gara said half to herself. "Our choices are to undertake an incredibly risky evacuation or take our chances in an attempt to disable or destroy their ships by initiating a phase transition."

"If I may, Commander, we could also continue our efforts to delay their attack. With any luck, our forces will arrive soon. Keep in mind that the Krayleck clearly want to capture the facility intact, so it is possible that their threats to destroy it outright are nothing more than a bluff."

"He never mentioned destroying the facility … only us. My guess is that they will enter the station whether we elect to stay or not, and I very much doubt that they will accept any attempts to surrender once they do."

"You are probably correct, but if your plan is to attack, there is no harm in waiting for them to make the first move."

"Perhaps. Do we have sufficient power reserves to initiate a transition?"

"Unfortunately not. We will be required to run the reactors for …" he paused, entering another series of commands, "approximately thirty seconds."

"Do it … but do not initiate a phase transition until I give the order. By the way, our evac pods were inspected just two weeks ago. More than half of them were found to be either inoperative or in need of significant repairs."

"That is to be expected, ma'am. Herrera was being maintained primarily by the Damarans, was it not?"

"Indeed, it was. In any event, launching into space inside a leaking evacuation pod is not the manner in which I wish to die."

Seconds later, a rapid series of explosions once again shook the station, temporarily plunging the operations room into darkness with the exception of several consoles that automatically reverted to an alternate power source.

"They are targeting the reactors, Commander."

"Yes, I thought they might. They were undoubtedly not pleased with the power surge they detected. The reactor shields are online, are they not?"

"Yes, ma'am — as are the emitters covering the core of the facility itself. The reactors themselves were installed before anything else, so the engineers buried them more deeply to provide additional protection from impact events prior to the shields being brought online. I doubt they will hold out long against a determined bombardment, however. And if the Krayleck are using relativistic kinetics …"

"Right. So much for waiting them out. Time to full charge?"

"Capacitor banks charged … now, Commander."

"Very well. Initiate!"

For reasons still not entirely clear to Wek scientists, the space within approximately six hundred million kilometers of Herrera's red dwarf star was home to an anomaly that had most likely been created during the period of rapid expansion that occurred shortly after the Big Bang. During that time, imperfections in the fabric of space itself coalesced like eddies in a stream — ultimately creating the conditions that produced the largest structures in existence, including the galaxies themselves. Here, however, something much more unusual had occurred.

Wek astrophysicists had known for several hundred years that the area just outside Herrera's orbit would occasionally burst forth with a massive flux of antimatter particles. They were also aware that the region contained a high concentration of dark matter. This in itself was strange enough, but the local anomaly allowed the dark matter to interact in a very unusual way with regular matter. Physicists called this interaction a phase transition, and its result was the production of some of the strangest constructs in the cosmos — "cosmic strings." Less than one atom thick — essentially one-dimensional defects in spacetime — the short-lived strings produced extremely strong gravitational fields before rapidly shrinking and disappearing from existence altogether in a flash of elementary particles.

From a practical engineering standpoint, all of this highly theoretical physics would normally constitute little more than a noteworthy hazard to interstellar navigation were it not for the fact that the clouds of elementary particles produced by the anomaly were composed almost entirely of antimatter — the most valuable resource in the universe. And after decades of trial and error resulting in the loss of a great many robotic spacecraft, it had been determined that the natural phenomena could be both triggered and regulated to some degree with the precise application of gravitic fields. With a relatively safe and inexpensive method of harvesting virtually unlimited quantities of antimatter right on their doorstep, the Sajeth Collective had wasted little time constructing the Herrera "mine."

This close to the system's star, the planet Herrera was tidally locked so that one side always faced outward into the region of space best suited to produce the desired reaction. Now, with the lives of the Wek personnel manning the facility and the invaluable resource itself under attack, Commander Gara's engineering officer shunted the massive energy reserves stored in the station's capacitor banks to an array of gravitic emitters spread across nearly half of the small planet's surface.

The gravitic beams firing out into space produced no light in the portion of the spectrum that could be seen by either the Wek or the Krayleck observers, but the effects on the targeted area of space were spectacular — space currently occupied by one of the two Krayleck warships.

Chapter 10

TFS Theseus
(3.29x10^6 km from Damara)

"Listen up, everyone," Prescott announced as he emerged from his ready room with Commander Reynolds following closely behind, "there has been a change in plans. I'll fill everyone in as best I can when time permits. Right now, however, we have an urgent mission that requires our presence at a Wek mining facility just under ninety light years from here. I know this will generate a myriad of questions in your minds, but all I can say for now is that we have actionable intelligence that the facility may be about to come under attack, and we have been ordered to intervene if we can."

"Attacked by Sajeth Collective ships, sir?" Lieutenant Lau asked, turning around to face Prescott just as he reached his Command chair.

"We don't think so, no. In fact, we're hoping the conflict with the Sajeth Collective will be rapidly winding down once Admiral Patterson hammers out some terms with the Damarans. And since they tend to stay in lockstep with the Lesheerans, it's a pretty safe bet that they will follow suit soon enough. As for the other four worlds in the Collective, the most recent Fleet Intelligence Estimate indicates that they played a much more limited role in the Resistance movement — from a military standpoint at least — and have no desire for a protracted conflict with the Wek Crowned Republic, let alone TFC. Bottom line, we have every reason to hope that this whole thing could be over pretty quickly."

"So, can I ask who we think is attacking the Wek facility?"

"That actually *is* something I can share, briefly," Prescott replied. "Admiral Naftur has told us that a species known as the Krayleck are expanding their influence in this area. Unfortunately, that brings them into direct conflict with the Sajeth Collective, and, by extension, the Wek, since they have effectively taken over most of the Collective's strategic assets — particularly those with any potential military value. Now, clearly, we have no desire to get ourselves involved in another conflict out here with yet another species, so our role is simply to show up and hopefully delay any attack the Krayleck might be considering until Wek forces arrive."

"And if they attack the mining facility?"

"We will do what we can to assist the Wek personnel manning the station, but we are not authorized to engage Krayleck forces unless we are fired upon. The other thing you need to know is that the Krayleck may — and we haven't confirmed this for ourselves yet — they *may* be another Pelaran-cultivated species."

"This close to home?" Lieutenant Commander Schmidt asked, still standing in front of the XO's chair that he had just vacated.

"We're not that close, Thomas," Reynolds interjected. "All of this C-Jumping around makes it seem like it, but the Herrera Mining Facility is a good five hundred and fifty light years from Earth. Legara — which is what the Wek believe to be the Krayleck homeworld — is about twelve hundred and fifty light years out."

"And keep in mind that these other civilizations we're talking about are not C-Jumping at all," Prescott continued. "They're entering hyperspace and traveling for weeks, months, or even years at a time to reach their destinations. We don't know yet how fast the Krayleck ships are capable of traveling, but if they're using the same technology the Pelarans originally gave us, it's unlikely to be much faster than about fifteen hundred *c*."

"I understand sir. But it seems so strange to just up and leave our task force," Schmidt pressed.

"I suppose it does, yes, but those are indeed our orders. Again, I hope to be able to share more information with you at some point, and I'll do so as soon as I can, but most of the details will have to wait for another time. All you need to know for now is that I have been relieved of command of the Damaran task force and *Theseus* has been retasked. Captain Donovan of the *Jutland* will be taking over blockade duties here until forces from the Wek Unified Fleet arrive."

Several meaningful looks were exchanged between the members of the bridge crew, but, to their credit, everyone present had sufficient common sense to avoid any further questions on the subject.

"XO, prepare the ship for possible combat ops," Prescott said. "We must depart as soon as possible."

"Aye, sir. AI, resume General Quarters for combat operations, Condition 1," Reynolds ordered without looking up from her Command console.

The lighting on the bridge instantly dimmed slightly and was accented with a reddish hue to provide a visual indication of impending combat operations. Throughout the ship, crew members hurried to their action stations as the AI's synthetic voice repeated Commander Reynolds' order for General Quarters. A mere forty seconds later, all departments had reported their readiness.

"General Quarters for combat operations, Condition 1 set," the AI's synthetic female voice announced in a businesslike tone.

"Commander Logan, bridge," Prescott said.

"Logan here. Go ahead, Captain."

"I'm sure you saw what we're about to do. Any problems?"

"I did, Captain. The C-Jump is a little on the long side, but Admiral Patterson's ships just did five of those in a row, so it shouldn't be a problem. We'll still have a reasonable reserve of power available in the capacitor banks after the jump, and with the ship at Condition 1, the AI will be max performing all six reactors right after the transition. You should have all the power you need."

"That's what I wanted to hear. Prescott out. Helm, do you have the destination Admiral Patterson provided?"

"Plotted and locked, sir. I'd call it out of the way, but still oddly specific — definitely not where I would have chosen for our arrival. Did he give us any specific information about this spot?"

"I believe he is in possession of some specific information regarding the site, yes," Prescott answered cryptically. "But I think his main objective was to keep us clear of any hazardous activities associated with the facility itself. Tactical, on that subject, we may well encounter Krayleck ships immediately upon our arrival, so all three of you need to be on your toes and ready to react quickly."

"Aye, sir," all three men responded in unison.

"Alright, everyone, let's do a quick roll call. Speak up now if you have a problem or concern. Helm?"

"Go, Captain."

"Engineering.

"Go, sir."

"Tactical 1?"

"Go, Captain."

"Tactical 2?"

"Go."

"Comm/Nav?"

"Go, sir."

"XO?"

"Go, Captain. Since we may run into trouble, I'd like to give everyone a heads-up before we transition, though."

"Agreed. Please proceed," Prescott replied.

"All hands, this is the XO. We will be executing a ninety-light-year C-Jump to the Herrera Mining Facility momentarily. There are potentially hostile forces in the area and combat ops are a possibility. All personnel should be restrained at this time. Reynolds out."

"Someday we may have to do a little work on your pep talk technique," Prescott said with a sideways glance.

"Eh, we all know what's in the job description, sir."

"Fair enough. Let's go, Fisher."

"Aye, sir. C-Jumping in 3 ... 2 ... 1 ..."

For longer-range C-Jumps such as this one, *Theseus'* AI displayed what its developers referred to as a "big picture" overview of the almost incomprehensibly long journey on the bridge view screen. Starting before the ship had even transitioned with a brief three-dimensional perspective view from above and behind the destroyer, the AI pulled the "camera" quickly away to reveal an overhead view of the closest stars. Although each was accompanied by a block of identifying text, the AI paused only briefly before dramatically expanding the view to encompass the ship's destination — in this case nearly ninety light years distant. To avoid an unusable mass of clutter, only the most notable stars (typically those that were home to advanced civilizations) were shown in this view, and only for the sake of general orientation. Finally, with the view now focused on the destination, the AI rapidly zoomed the image — adding both archival and real-time imagery to provide as accurate a representation as possible of the nearly eight-hundred-and-fifty-trillion-kilometer C-Jump. The entire sequence was timed perfectly with the ship's arrival at Herrera, at which time the AI made a smooth transition to displaying solely real-time information being gathered by the ship's multitude of sensors.

"C-Jump complete, Captain. Pausing for comm beacon deployment ... beacon stabilized and transmitting ... transition complete," Fisher reported, immediately advancing the destroyer's sublight engines to full power and beginning a series of evasive maneuvers in case they found themselves in the middle of a hostile situation. "All systems in the green. C-Jump range 12.8 light years and increasing rapidly."

"Very well. Tactical, I see two ships," Prescott said, staring at the tactical plot display on the starboard view screen. "Both are currently classified as 'unknowns.' I need to know what they are and whether they're hostile as quickly as possible."

"Aye, sir," Schmidt responded immediately. "I've got 'em both, Captain. They appear to be of identical configuration, but the AI is giving me an inaccurate ID on them so far. I should be able to get a good visual though. Stand by."

"Inaccurate how? Is it identifying them or not?"

"It is, sir, but it's only giving the identification a three four percent reliability, and what it's telling me can't possibly be correct. At the moment, it still has their origin as unknown, but for the type, it's saying they're both —"

"*Ingenuity*-class frigates," Reynolds interrupted, easily recognizing the light and thermally enhanced image of the two warships now displayed in the center of the view screen. "Designating as Foxtrot 1 and Foxtrot 2."

Every member of the bridge crew looked up to confirm the seemingly impossible identification for themselves, only to be instantly recalled to their duties by a series of urgent-sounding warning tones issuing from both the Tactical and the Science and Engineering consoles.

"They're firing, Captain," Lieutenant Lau reported. "Railguns only at the moment. From what I can tell, they're going after the station's reactors."

"Confirmed," Lieutenant Lee reported. "Right before they opened fire, there was a power surge centered roughly on the area the two ships are now targeting. It looks like the reactors are buried well beneath the surface."

"Most of the facility is shielded too, Captain," Lau added, "but the two frigates' kinetic energy rounds are still making it to the surface."

"Comm, hail the ships and offer our assistance in evacuating the station. Let's see if we can get them to back off and at least allow us to get the Wek personnel out of there."

"Aye, sir, hailing."

Before Dubashi could complete her transmission, *Theseus'* AI expanded the field of view on the bridge view screen to show both of the presumably Krayleck ships, instantly superimposing a flashing red triangle over an area of space adjacent to the more distant of the two. "Warning!" it announced in an urgent tone. "Gravimetric disturbance detected. Emergency hyperspace transition unavailable. Executing evasive action. All personnel initiate Anti-G Straining Maneuver to prevent G-induced loss of consciousness."

"Fisher, you got this?" Prescott grunted, tightening the muscles in his legs and abdomen under the rapidly increasing G-forces generated by the AI's maximum performance turn. Even several years after his last operational mission in a fighter, remaining conscious under high G loads was still second nature to the captain. Unfortunately, the same was not true for his young helmsman, whose arms now hung uselessly by his sides while his head rolled involuntarily about his shoulders from one side to the other.

It had taken several seconds for Prescott to realize that the edges of his peripheral vision had been "grayed-out" for a time. And now that the ship's inertial dampening systems had begun to catch up with the AI's maneuvers, he also realized that he was the only fully conscious member of the bridge crew.

"Fisher!" he yelled.

The ensign's convulsive head movements (still universally referred to as the "funky chicken" by Human fighter pilots) had finally stopped, which was a good indication that he should regain consciousness momentarily.

"Any day now, Ensign. Tactical, I need you two back with me as well," Prescott said, glancing back up at the tactical plot but still struggling a bit himself to refocus his mind and fully assess the situation.

"Yes … uh … yes, sir, I'm good. Sorry about that, sir," Fisher mumbled.

"Deep breaths, everyone. We didn't take any damage and appear to be out of danger for the moment, so don't start pushing buttons and make things worse. Give yourselves a few seconds and you'll come back around."

There was a half-hearted chorus of "aye, sirs" in response, but it would clearly still be a while before they were all back to anything approaching their best.

"Where'd the ships go?" Reynolds asked, reasonably aware of her surroundings once again.

"I don't know yet," Prescott answered honestly. "There was an explosion of some sort and there's some debris out there that wasn't there before … it doesn't look large enough to be even one of those ships, though, let alone both of them."

"I see it … but I don't see anything I can positively identify as being part of a frigate. AI, Reynolds, replay footage of the two unidentified ships starting with the detection of the gravimetric disturbance."

A window immediately opened on the bridge view screen, once again displaying two ships strikingly similar to the *Ingenuity*. Once again, the AI superimposed a red triangle near the more distant ship. A few seconds later, the closer of the two executed a hard turn to port, roughly in the direction of the *Theseus*, and Reynolds wondered if the aggressive maneuver had been ordered by the ship's AI, just as theirs had been.

"There's no way they stayed conscious during that turn unless their dampeners are significantly better than ours," Prescott commented.

"Ours are pushing the theoretical limits, Captain, so it's doubtful they handled it any better than we did," Lieutenant Lee chimed in with a somewhat embarrassed tone.

"Welcome back, Lieutenant," Prescott replied with a consoling smile.

The more distant of the two ships seemed to accelerate rapidly in the direction of the disturbance itself. Then, inexplicably, the forward half of the ship's hull was cleaved away from its stern as cleanly as if it had been sliced by a surgical scalpel. The stern, apparently still responding to forces generated by both the invisible disturbance as well as its own sublight engines, initially arced up and away from its former bow.

"What the hell?" Reynolds gasped in astonishment.

Before anyone else could comment on what they were seeing, the situation grew even more strange and terrifying to behold. The frigate's bow continued momentarily along roughly the same flight path as before, then simply imploded. What they witnessed was not the uneven, convulsive crushing like a metal can smashed by uneven air pressure in a science fair experiment. Instead, roughly half of the entire structure collapsed on itself, appearing from *Theseus'* point of view to be almost completely flattened.

Various forces acting on the object caused it to rotate more rapidly, and, as it did so, one section at a time seemed to pass some unseen line of demarcation — allowing it to be instantly crushed and folded in on itself along the same axis each time. Within seconds, there was very little left of the forward half of the ship other than a flattened, superheated mass of debris that both Prescott and Reynolds now recognized as what they had seen before beginning the playback.

For clarity, the AI had now divided the footage into three separate windows. In the second window, the still-intact frigate had now achieved sufficient distance from the gravimetric disturbance to allow its hyperdrive to function once again. Whether it was under its crew's control or still being commanded by its AI was unclear. After noting what had happened to its sister ship, however, someone aboard had the presence of mind to transition to hyperspace — departing the area in a flash of grayish-white light.

"Okay, we know the stern is gone now, so something else is about to —" Reynolds began, only to be interrupted by activity in the third and final window.

What happened next to the frigate's aft section was difficult to describe, but for the first split second the entire structure was lit by what looked like thousands of expanding pools of bright white light that instantly bloomed into a single, massive explosion.

"AI, on window three show us a slow-motion detail of the explosion," she commanded.

Instantly interpreting what its Human XO wished to see, *Theseus'* AI indexed the footage back to three hundred milliseconds prior to the first signs that a high-energy event was taking place, then began slowly advancing the video once again.

Reynolds, for her part, had her initial impression verified. On the screen, it looked as if the frigate's hull had entered a sudden downpour on a summer's day. But rather than simply impacting the hull's surface, these "raindrops" had every appearance of literally converting the hull into expanding pools of light. The spectacle was as terrifying as it was beautiful, but lasted only an instant before the entire image was once again washed out by such an energetic explosion that absolutely nothing remained of the ship's stern.

"Well," Reynolds said after a brief silence, "I suppose I would normally say, 'I guess we cleared that up.' But I have absolutely no idea what we just saw. AI, theorize as to the cause of the explosion we just reviewed in frame three."

"Various sensor readings are consistent with a large-scale antimatter annihilation event," the synthetic voice answered in a matter-of-fact tone. "A diffuse cloud containing approximately three hundred grams of antihydrogen coming into physical contact with the remaining section of the subject ship's hull could cause such an effect."

"Lieutenant Lee?" Reynolds said, implying her obvious question.

"There's no way that's naturally occurring in such a small volume of space, Commander, particularly this close to the planet. It's possible, sure, but to say that it's unlikely is an understatement in the extreme. I'd say we just stumbled on the purpose of the Herrera mine."

"Captain, we're being hailed by the mining facility," Lieutenant Dubashi reported from the Comm/Nav console.

"Well then … maybe they'll be willing to shed some additional light on what we just saw. On-screen, please," Prescott replied.

"Welcome, Terrans," the youngish-looking Wek female began, "I am Commander Moya Gara of the Wek Unified Fleet. I am the commanding officer here at the Herrera station. Please let me say from the outset how sorry I am for putting your vessel in danger. As I am sure you saw, we were under attack from two Krayleck warships, but I would not have initiated a phase transition had I known you were about to arrive. Did you suffer any damage?"

"Hello, Commander. I am Captain Tom Prescott of the Terran Fleet Command starship *Theseus*. I'm happy to report that we are undamaged, but we did witness what happened to one of the two Krayleck ships. A 'phase transition,' you said … is that some sort of gravitic weapon?"

"Not under normal circumstances, no," she said with the hint of a smile forming at the corners of her mouth. "What you witnessed was an act of desperation on my part. Herrera is an unarmed research facility. Fortunately for us, some of that research involves experiments in high energy physics … sufficient to damage or even destroy a vessel if it happens to find itself in the wrong place at the wrong time."

"I see," Prescott replied — though clearly he did not. "That was quick, resourceful thinking on your part, Commander. You almost certainly saved your entire crew. I'm guessing the Krayleck will return with reinforcements, however, so perhaps we should evacuate the facility until elements of the Wek Fleet arrive. Do you have anyone in need of medical assistance?"

"Not as far as I know, Captain, I thank you," she replied, then paused momentarily before resuming in a more reserved tone. "I am sure you are correct that we should evacuate immediately, and there are perhaps twelve out of our crew of twenty-seven that I can spare. Unfortunately, everyone else will be needed to secure the reactors as well as other sensitive materials on site that we cannot allow the Krayleck to capture."

Prescott stared back at the Wek commander for a long moment, wondering precisely what their new allies were doing out here that could not only generate the effects they had witnessed, but also be worth risking many lives to protect.

"Very well, Commander," he continued reluctantly. "You are obviously in a better position to gauge the importance of your work here than we are. But you need to understand that I cannot guarantee your safety unless I bring you aboard my ship."

"I do understand, sir, and I appreciate your concern. Based on when your ship arrived, however, we must assume that the Krayleck believe it was you who destroyed their warship. And even if they do not, they will likely see your vessel as the primary threat when they return."

"That's a prudent observation, Commander Gara, thank you. We will have one of our shuttles down to you shortly. Prescott out."

"So, did we or did we not just inadvertently commit an act of war against another Pelaran-cultivated civilization?" Reynolds asked, incredulous.

"*That,* Commander, like so many other things out here, is a matter of perspective. Either way, I think we had best get ourselves prepared for a more determined attack."

Chapter 11

Earth, Terran Fleet Command Headquarters
(16 hours later - Leadership Council Meeting Chamber)

"Madame Chairwoman," the representative from the Middle Eastern Union interrupted for the third time, "I believe at this point we are all in agreement that some sort of formalized relations — perhaps even an alliance at some point — with the Wek ... excuse me, with the Crowned Republic of Graca ... is in our long-term best interest. Indeed, none of us would have agreed to sign the preliminary memorandum of cooperation with them otherwise. Yet here we are, barely six months after being attacked by the Resistance, and this Council is being asked to endorse a course of action that could easily lead us down a path towards war against another member of the Pelaran Alliance. For that *is* what you are asking us to do, is it not?"

One of Lisbeth Kistler's first acts after taking over as Chairwoman had been to remove the enormous dais and lectern from the front of the meeting chamber. The message she had intended to convey was clear — there were fifteen members on the Leadership Council, and each representative's vote carried precisely the same weight as any other. In stark contrast to her tyrannical predecessor, Kistler fully embraced the position of Chair as specifically defined in TFC's charter. In her opinion, it had never been intended as a governing role so much as that of a chief facilitator, maintaining the group's focus and, whenever possible, preventing their discussions from becoming mired in political gridlock.

She remained, nonetheless, a skilled politician in her own right and was not above using certain … tactics, both subtle and otherwise, to guide the course of the debate in the direction she preferred. Before answering the gentleman — an astonishingly handsome man from the United Arab Emirates — she had positioned herself immediately adjacent to his workspace, working the center aisle between the representatives like a professor proctoring a final exam.

"Representative Shadid," she began again after allowing a long pause to ensure that he had actually finished speaking this time, "not to put too fine a point on it, but I don't think that is a fair characterization of what Admiral Sexton is asking us to consider. You saw the same briefing I did," she said (it was not entirely true, but close enough under the circumstances). "The Wek mining facility at Herrera was attacked without provocation by forces from a neighboring Pelaran-cultivated civilization known as the Krayleck. As chance would have it, TFS *Theseus*, which Admiral Patterson dispatched at the request of Crown Prince Naftur in hopes of stabilizing the situation, arrived just as the station itself managed to destroy one of the Krayleck ships."

"Which, remarkably enough, looked virtually identical to one of our own *Ingenuity*-class frigates."

"I certainly agree with you that it's remarkable, sir, but perhaps not so surprising. We have known for some time that the Pelarans have applied their cultivation program a great many times. It stands to reason, in my mind at least, that the information they provide to prospective Alliance members — including plans for ships and weapons — would be similar."

"It is of relatively little consequence at this time," he replied with a dismissive, backhanded gesture. "The truth is that we still know very little about the Wek and the other members of the Sajeth Collective, let alone these Krayleck."

"We *do* know that the Wek managed to swat a frigate from the skies above their supposedly unarmed mining station as if it were a mere annoyance … perhaps also succeeding in making it look as if the attack originated from our ship," another representative chimed in from one of the large view screens mounted around the perimeter of the room.

"A valid point, my friend," Shadid continued. "Our new friends, the Wek, it seems, have been less than forthcoming regarding the true nature of the Herrera mine. Therefore, the idea of sending in even more of our ships to protect *their* secret facility — and in so doing risk further escalation of the incident that has already taken place with the Krayleck Empire — seems both irresponsible and foolish in the extreme to me."

"If you will forgive me, colleague, I don't think it's reasonable for us to assume that the Wek have laid bare all of their secrets for us any more than we have for them," Kistler said, sensing that the argument was by no means leaning in her favor at the moment. "Surely, if the past year has taught us nothing else, it is the need for our world to actively pursue both diplomatic and even military alliances with other civilizations. The threats to our security — to our very survival — are far more sweeping than any of us could have imagined until very recently."

"I agree with you, Chairwoman Kistler," Shadid said magnanimously. "But it is also clear that we must be very cautious and deliberate about both *whom* we ally ourselves with as well as the particulars of *how* we structure those alliances. We currently have no quarrel with the Krayleck, and until we know more about them, we must avoid taking any actions that might well be seen as hostile. Accordingly, I would like to make a motion that we allow *Theseus* alone to remain at Herrera to assist its Wek crew as necessary until their forces arrive. They are to take no provocative actions against Krayleck vessels."

"Second!" at least two other members responded immediately.

"Madame Chairwoman, we have a second. I believe it is time to call for a vote."

Kistler drew in a deep breath and released it slowly in hopes that one of the other members might speak up on her behalf. "Is there no further discussion from the floor?" she finally asked the now deathly silent room. "Very well, but before you cast your vote, I ask you to consider that information provided by Admiral Naftur and other Wek citizens has literally saved *all* of our lives at least once. Failing to do all we can to help them when it is easily within our power to do so may justifiably be seen as a betrayal … at a time when Humanity desperately needs friends and allies."

Minutes later, by a vote of eight to seven, Terran Fleet Command's Leadership Council approved Representative Shadid's motion. For the time being at least, no additional warships would be sent to Herrera. *Theseus* and her crew were on their own.

TFS Theseus, Herrera Mining Facility
(87.2 light years from Damara)

"Are they still heading this way?" Prescott asked as he entered his ready room for what felt like the tenth time during this watch alone.

"Yes, sir," Reynolds said, momentarily turning her attention away from the room's large view screen. "I'm still not entirely comfortable with the way this new — what are they calling it again …?"

"Argus, I think it is."

"… *Argus* system presents tracking information, but it still looks to me like we've got a total of six Krayleck ships on the way here from their nearest forward operating base."

"Yeah …" he replied, leaning both hands on the table to get a closer look for himself, "that's still the way it looks to me as well."

"How did they come up with the name 'Argus,' anyway?" she asked, leaning back in her chair and rubbing her eyes. Neither officer had slept for more than a few hours at a time over the past several days, and the all-too-familiar effects of sleep deprivation were beginning to take their toll on both.

"I think the new Op Center just started calling it that today, in fact, and I wondered the same thing so I looked it up. It turns out that there are a bunch of different mythological figures by that name, but I believe the one they are referring to is an all-seeing giant with a hundred eyes. Makes sense, I guess. When I was a kid, you could have easily convinced me that my mother was one of those."

"Hah," Reynolds chuckled, "that's because she was a good mom and you were undoubtedly a pain in the ass. Anyway," she continued, turning her attention back to the view screen, "their extended course lines come within about three hundred thousand kilometers of Herrera, so I can't imagine that's a coincidence."

"Any changes in ETA?"

"Nope. Still around 1215 UTC tomorrow — assuming they continue with their current course and speed, that is."

"I'd say that's a safe bet. The question is what we're going to do about it … all by ourselves," he said, plopping himself down casually on the long couch at the far end of the room. "Show me the order of battle summary again, please."

Before Reynolds could enter the required commands, the AI reconfigured the display to show an extended range tactical plot, including the makeup of the small Krayleck task force.

"Three destroyers and three frigates," she said. "And if their hyperdrive signatures are any indication, they're also likely to be of similar design to our own *Theseus* and *Ingenuity* classes, respectively. After yesterday's encounter, however, the AI now has enough information to differentiate between our frigates and theirs."

"That's the 'KE' designation depicted on the plot?"

"Right — for Krayleck Empire. You'll see that anywhere there is identifying text, and also in the lower right corner when standard ship icons are being displayed."

"Got it. I'm sure it will do the same for the other classes as soon as it gathers enough data."

"Oh, and the frigate that got away yesterday is still sitting right … here," she said, zooming in on an area of space much closer to their current position. "It's only about a light year out, so I'm guessing it called in the cavalry from there and will form up with them as they pass by."

"So, that makes three destroyers and *four* frigates."

"Yes, and as far as we can tell, all of them are pretty much carbon copies of our ships."

"Of similar design, certainly, but if push comes to shove, I still like our chances. AI, let's see the tactical assessment of Foxtrot 2 from yesterday's encounter."

A window immediately opened on the left end of the large view screen, displaying multiple views of the Krayleck version of an *Ingenuity*-class frigate with potential vulnerabilities highlighted.

"All of this still seems —"

"Surreal?"

"I guess that's a good word to use, but I can think of a few others that might also work," Reynolds said. "On the plus side, we should at least know exactly where to hit 'em."

"Yeah, but unfortunately that almost certainly works both ways."

"Maybe … maybe not. Look at this," she said, bringing up yet another window with video of Foxtrot 2 as she turned away from the gravimetric disturbance that had ultimately destroyed her consort. "Neither ship took any weapons fire, so we didn't get any data on the effectiveness of their point-defenses."

"Right, but we did detect the presence of energy barrier shields — similar to those used by Wek ships."

"Correct. Gravitic shields are, thankfully, a strictly Human design and probably our biggest single advantage. There was a lot of random debris in the area, though, and the AI detected this piece right … here," she said, highlighting what appeared as a blurry streak on the video approaching Foxtrot 2's stern. "Now don't get me wrong, this thing didn't have anywhere near the kind of energy that one of our kinetic energy rounds has, but it *did* interact with their shields long enough for our AI to make some projections regarding localized field strength."

"And?"

"Good news and bad news there. First off, they don't seem to have much of a problem with gaps aft of their drive section like the Wek ships do. The field strength is generally uniform from roughly four hundred meters out, all the way in to the hull."

"I hope that was the bad news."

"It was. The good news is that peak field strength is about twenty percent less than what we typically see on Wek ships."

"I'll take it, I guess," Prescott said, "but that's still substantial — particularly since they don't suffer the same problem with gaps and the field itself is, for lack of a better term, 'thicker' than it is on the Wek ships."

"That's what I thought too until I started running simulations. What the Krayleck are using appears to be a beefed-up version of the shield design the Pelarans provided us."

"Which we don't use."

"We do for some civilian applications, but not on our warships. The way the Wek and Krayleck have them set up, they're really intended primarily to absorb energy weapons fire. They're actually pretty good at doing that, but as we've seen, they're not as effective against kinetic energy weapons."

"That's not good news for the Wek Fleet. I think they need to start rethinking how they arm their warships."

"Not good news for them, no, but good news for us. My guess is that the Pelarans were well-aware that most potential adversaries their proxy worlds would face in this part of the galaxy would primarily be using energy weapons. So, they offered up a shield design that's good at handling energy weapons while at the same time recommending that we equip our ships with good old-fashioned railguns and the like."

"Seems reasonable, and my understanding is that the Pelarans did provide railgun designs, but keep in mind that the versions aboard our ships are significantly more advanced. The application of gravitic tech is what allows our projectiles to reach relativistic speeds. In fact, I remember Kip referring to our railguns as an almost exclusively Human design. So what do your simulations tell us?"

"That I wouldn't want to be onboard one of their ships if they pick a fight with us," she said with a cunning smile. "Don't get me wrong, a single stream of penetrator rounds will lose so much of its energy on the way in that it probably won't do that much damage. But if we concentrate multiple streams —"

"Like we've done before with point location attacks."

"Yes, but this time, as soon as the rounds start penetrating, we should be able to walk the stream down the hull," she said, nodding once again at the screen. In response, the AI played a simulated attack in photo-realistic detail. Both officers watched for several seconds with an odd, mixed sense of both disquiet and relief as the port side of Foxtrot 2 was quickly reduced to mangled wreckage by four incoming streams of kinetic energy rounds traveling at ten percent the speed of light.

"That'll do," Prescott replied, "but I would prefer it not come to that if we can avoid it. That's also obviously not what the Leadership Council wants to see happen either."

"Sure … but, all things considered, better them than us, right? Also, back on the subject of *their* railguns, we were able to collect some performance data when they took a few shots at the surface of Herrera. Based on what we've seen so far, I'd say it's a safe bet that they're based on the original Pelaran designs you mentioned. Still powerful, but significantly less so than ours — lower rate of fire, lower velocity rounds, etc."

"Our shields should be able to handle them then, since they have been extensively tested against our own railguns."

"Yup … with the usual caveat that we try to avoid taking fire that's perpendicular to the hull, but the AI should be able to help Fisher with that."

"Alright, Commander, good work with all of that, now get lost and get some sleep. Schmidt can mind the bridge for a few more hours."

"Aye, sir," she said, drawing out the words around a long yawn as she stood to leave the ready room. "By the way, there's no doubt that this Argus system is beyond awesome from both a strategic and tactical perspective. The problem is that the security restrictions surrounding the DEFIANT BASTION program are having a tendency to keep both you and me off the bridge. I wouldn't be happy about that under the best of circumstances, but it's a particularly bad idea right now. Any chance we can get the bridge crew cleared?"

"In the near term? I doubt it, but it doesn't hurt to ask. I agree that, at a bare minimum, you and I need access to the data from our Command consoles, so I'll try to make the case to Patterson. I don't think it's a problem with getting our people cleared, but we've always kept a somewhat open-door access policy for our ships' bridges. We may be able to solve that problem by having the AI lock things down a little more tightly when we're accessing Argus data."

"I hope so, because what we're doing now seems a little nuts to me."

"Good night, Commander," he prompted again, already stretching out on the long couch.

"Sorry. 'Night, Captain," she replied on her way out the door.

Chapter 12

TFS Theseus, Herrera Mining Facility
(The following day - 87.2 light years from Damara)

"All hands, this is the captain. We have taken the unusual step of putting the ship at General Quarters for combat operations, Condition 1, based on some intelligence data we have in hand. I'm sure like many of you, I tend to be a little cynical where intel is concerned. In this case, however, I can assure you that the information is both credible and specific. Very specific, in fact. We are expecting several ships from the Krayleck Empire to arrive in this system at any moment. While their intentions are unknown, their previous behavior gives us a high degree of confidence that they intend to attempt to either capture or destroy the Herrera Mining Facility. Unfortunately, there are still fifteen Wek personnel down there who are under orders not to allow the mine to fall into enemy hands … and, yes, that means they will destroy it themselves if they have to. Our orders, in turn, are to defend the station long enough for them to complete their work and be rescued by our Marines, if necessary.

"Now, I'm sure you can all see that there are a number of potential problems implicit in our orders. If, for example, the Krayleck are bent on the destruction of the facility and everyone on it, there may be very little we can do to stop them from doing so — particularly against multiple ships. As always, our ability to think on our feet and react quickly as the situation dictates will be the key to our success. We will avoid a confrontation if we can, fight if we must, and win if we do. As usual, crew restraints are mandatory for the duration of Condition 1. All personnel and equipment should be secured at this time. Prescott out.

"Alright, XO, what's the status of our Marines?"

"Two of the *Gurkhas* with fourteen Marines each are ready for launch. Since we might see combat ourselves, the shuttles will remain secured on the hangar deck until we clear them to depart."

"I assume Master Sergeant Rios is leading the mission?"

"Yes, sir."

Seven members of *Theseus'* Marine platoon, including its commander, First Lieutenant Jackson "Jacks" Lee, had been killed in action during the Resistance attack. During the period of extensive repairs following the battle, six replacement Marine special operators trained in advanced EVA ops (including VBSS — Visit, Board, Search, and Seizure missions) had joined the destroyer's crew, thus bringing the platoon back to one short of its full complement. With the ship out of action for an extended period, however, and given Master Sergeant Rios' extensive experience, a new commander had not yet been assigned.

"I doubt there's much either of us could do about that if we tried," Prescott said, nodding. "Flight ops?"

"All of our *Hunters* are on station in coordinated anti-ship strike mode. They're carrying eight HB-7c missiles each, but I suspect their railguns may come into play if we have to engage. We have them divided into two flights of twelve and positioned as planned. The AI currently has control, but Lieutenant Commander

Schmidt at Tactical 1 or Lieutenant Lee at Science and Engineering can override at any time."

"Very well," Prescott replied, catching Reynolds' eye and nodding to the Argus data that had just become available via his Command console within the past few seconds. "I assume that means your request was approved."

"Excellent. I'm happy to see that common sense does still win out on occasion," she said with a wry grin. "That's it as far as I know, Captain. I think we're as ready as we're going to get."

"Thank you, Commander. It's been nice to have some time to prepare, but I can't say I'm a fan of sitting around waiting for something we know is about to happen. ETA?"

"Three minutes."

Prescott leaned back in his chair, taking in a deep, slow breath in an effort to quiet his mind. *Wiggle your fingers and toes*, he thought, recalling his flight instructor's advice that he had passed on to others many times during his career. Noting that this time-honored technique was having little effect, he pulled up Admiral Patterson's Emergency Action Message from the previous day to fill the remaining time.

Z0917
TOP SECRET - MAGI PRIME
FM: CNO — ABOARD TFC FLAGSHIP, TFS NAVAJO
TO: TFS THESEUS
INFO: DEFENSE OF HERRERA FACILITY

1. LEADERSHIP COUNCIL WISHES TO AVOID
HOSTILITIES WITH KRAYLECK EMPIRE IF
POSSIBLE.
2. BELIEVES DEPLOYMENT OF ADDITIONAL TFC
FORCES MAY BE PERCEIVED AS ESCALATION.
3. NO REINFORCEMENTS EN ROUTE YOUR
POSITION AT THIS TIME.
4. FIRST PRIORITY IS EVACUATION OF WEK
PERSONNEL FROM FACILITY.
5. DO NOT ENGAGE KRAYLECK FORCES UNLESS
FIRED UPON.
6. REMAIN ON STATION UNTIL RELIEVED BY
WEK FORCES.
7. EXPECT IMMEDIATE RETURN TO EARTH FOR
REASSIGNMENT. ADM PATTERSON SENDS.

Prescott reflected momentarily on how strange it was
that, with the availability of instantaneous real-time
communications, the Admiralty still chose to send
written messages in this format on occasion. The
standard explanation for such anachronisms usually
included vague references to the need for simplicity and
a desire to maintain naval traditions. He had to wonder,
however, whether the delivery of terse, often ambiguous
written orders intentionally placed the burden of success
entirely upon the recipient rather than the source.
Perhaps *that* was the real tradition being doggedly
maintained by the Admiralty.

"Are we still showing about six hours for the Wek
task force?"

"The first of them, yes, sir. It looks like they have the
better part of half their fleet headed in this direction now,

but the farthest ones coming in from near Graca are several weeks out. That includes Admiral Naftur's ship, by the way. Better late than never, I suppose."

"I guess we'll see."

"Contact!" Lieutenant Commander Schmidt reported from Tactical 1. "Seven ships, Captain. This time identified as Krayleck in origin with types of … four *Ingenuity*-class frigates and … stand by … confirmed, three *Theseus*-class destroyers, sir."

"Understood. Designate as Foxtrot 1 through Foxtrot 4 and Delta 1 through Delta 3. Weapons hold."

"Designated. Weapons hold, aye."

On the tactical plot, the seven Krayleck warships were represented by square icons shaded in green to indicate that they had been positively identified by the AI and initially assigned a status of "neutral."

"Everyone take a deep breath and relax. Remember, we're here in support of the Wek personnel still on the station. Comm, you should receive a channel-share from the surface when Commander Gara hails the Krayleck ships. Go ahead and put it on-screen when you do, but please ensure that we're not transmitting from our side."

"Aye, sir, receiving it now. Be advised that our lexical data for this species indicates a zero seven percent degree of uncertainty. Some of the real-time translations may not be entirely accurate."

"Thank you, Lieutenant."

With that, two windows opened on the left side of the bridge view screen, one displaying Commander Gara, the other once again revealing an alien species never before encountered by Human beings. In spite of their training to the contrary, virtually every member of the bridge crew quietly expressed a degree of astonishment and even disgust at what they saw.

"Watch your bearing, folks," Prescott chided. "Most species we run into out here are not going to look nearly as much like us as the Wek do. That doesn't mean we can't work with them, so let's ignore their appearance and focus on the mission."

"Greetings, Commander Gara," the Krayleck began, translated and reproduced perfectly by *Theseus'* AI in their species' grotesquely wet, yet strangely cordial tone. "I am Captain ... representing the Krayleck Empire."

"There was no translation available for his name," Lieutenant Dubashi quickly interjected.

"I'm pretty sure he said Bob," Ensign Fisher said under his breath.

"You have been repeatedly warned that your facility is located within the boundaries of the Krayleck Empire," the alien captain continued. "Although you appear to be willfully trespassing, we now offer you one final opportunity to vacate the premises peacefully. You must leave all buildings, equipment, and any documentation fully intact upon your departure. Additionally, I presume that the nearby warship is listening to this conversation. Although they have committed an act of aggression against the Krayleck Empire, the configuration of their vessel indicates that they too are associated with the Pelaran Alliance. As a matter of courtesy, we will contact them independently and offer them a single opportunity to surrender without further conflict."

"If we do come under attack, our best chance lies in making an impression on them very quickly," Prescott said. "I want both flights of *Hunters* to go after Foxtrot 1 on the far side of their formation. At the same time, we will hit Delta 3 and try to score a quick kill. If we can take down two of their ships before they can get organized, they may think twice about pressing their attack. Everyone clear?"

"Aye, sir," all six members of the bridge crew replied in unison.

"As we indicated before," Commander Gara continued on the view screen, "we are expecting the arrival of several Wek vessels shortly that will provide us the opportunity to evacuate. If you will allow it, the Terran vessel has offered to assist us until our ships arrive."

"I can assure you, Commander, that you will not wish to accompany the … *Terran*, you said? … vessel. You will access your station's emergency evacuation system and await retrieval by your ships. As long as your vessels take no aggressive action and follow our instructions exactly, we will not interfere with their rescue operation. You have until I finish speaking with the Terran captain to begin your evacuation."

"Transmission terminated, Captain," Lieutenant Dubashi reported as the two windows closed and the view screen returned to a light-amplified view of Delta 3.

"It doesn't sound like he's interested in doing a lot of talking at this point," Reynolds said.

"No, and it occurs to me that they probably know more about what the Wek are doing at this facility than we do and are interested enough to fight for it. I'm guessing that also means they will do everything they can to keep from destroying it."

"The Krayleck captain is hailing us, sir," Lieutenant Dubashi reported from the Comm/Nav console.

"On-screen, please."

"Aye, sir, opening channel."

Once again, a window opened on the left side of the view screen to display the alien captain's face — his mouthparts now completely awash in oozing, brown liquid.

"As I have already stated," he began without any pretense of formality, "you have destroyed one of our vessels without provocation. Your ship is clearly of Pelaran origin, but since you are not broadcasting the appropriate recognition codes, I must assume that your world has not yet formally joined the Alliance. Unfortunately for you, that means that you are not covered under the terms of the Alliance charter and not entitled to receive quarter. Nevertheless, we will show mercy to your crew if you surrender immediately."

Prescott stared impassively at the Krayleck captain's image for several seconds before speaking, then began in a low, even tone. "Our two species are not yet acquainted, Captain," he said, also not bothering with introductions, "and it would indeed be a shame for our first meeting to result in violence rather than constructive conversation. Let me assure you that we did not destroy your ship. In fact, we didn't even speak with them, and, clearly, we have no motive whatsoever for mounting such an attack. Our only business here was in answer to a distress call from the Wek personnel manning the Herrera science station. It seems they were being repeatedly harassed by your ships and feared they were about to come under attack. As it turns out, they were correct. Your ships opened fire on the station immediately before one of them was caught up in a gravimetric disturbance of some sort and destroyed."

"Your feigned ignorance of the true purpose of this so-called 'science station' is laughable, Captain. And we both know that the strategic value of this system is sufficient motive for far worse things than the destruction of a single frigate. In any event, I am pleased to see that you have not raised your shields. May I take this as an indication of your understanding that you must either flee or surrender immediately?"

"No, Captain, neither of those options is acceptable. We didn't fire on your frigate, and we have no quarrel with you as long as you allow us to peacefully complete our mission. Otherwise, there is nothing further for us to discuss at this time." With that, Prescott glanced over at Dubashi and drew his hand across his throat, signaling her to terminate the vidcon.

"What you said about their not wanting to destroy the facility makes sense, but the same thing may apply to us as long as we're not directly interfering with what they're doing," Reynolds observed.

"You mean they may just go about their business and leave us alone if we stay out of their way. Yes, I thought of that as well and, unfortunately, that would put us in a difficult situation with regard to our orders. We're not permitted to fire unless fired upon, but we're also supposed to be protecting the Wek personnel aboard the station."

"Mm-hmm, good luck with that. If I were Captain Bob over there," Reynolds paused to allow Fisher to look back and receive her halfheartedly disapproving scowl, "I'd ignore us completely for as long as possible while I did whatever I came here to do."

"Damn," Prescott said after a few moments of silence. "That's exactly what he's going to do. Helm, bring us in as close as possible to the station while still leaving yourself room to maneuver."

"Aye, sir," Fisher replied.

"Green deck, XO. Put Rios and his two squads on the ground right now. Their orders are to evacuate the Wek personnel immediately. If they can finish rigging the place to blow on their way out without any further delay, fine. Otherwise, the Wek Unified Fleet may just have to destroy it themselves if that's how they want to play it."

"Done," Reynolds replied while still entering commands via her touchscreen. "They'll be inside the station's hangar bay in two minutes. But if you're thinking the Krayleck are planning to call our bluff and put boots on the ground, Rios will probably need his third squad as well."

"They've got seven ships, Commander. For all we know, they could be about to drop an entire Marine Expeditionary Unit in there, so I'm not sure an extra fourteen troops will make that much difference."

"Fifteen," she said, standing and staring back at her captain with the same look of fierce determination he had seen so many times over the past several years.

Prescott fixed her with a hard stare of his own, taking the measure of his own willingness to risk his friend and first officer's life on a dangerous mission for which she was only minimally qualified.

"If we're going to deploy the entire platoon, there needs to be an officer who's nominally in charge — even though Rios will still be running the op," she pressed.

"Go," he said, realizing that any further comments would most likely be inappropriate in front of the rest of the bridge crew. "Schmidt, you're with me. Lee, take Tactical 1, please."

"Aye, sir," all three officers replied enthusiastically, each one eager to prove themselves capable of handling additional responsibilities during a combat operation.

Prescott watched as an even younger lieutenant (junior grade) emerged from the crew lounge and took her place at the Science and Engineering console.

Tom Prescott was in excellent physical condition and every bit as mentally sharp as he had been in his twenties. Predominantly for those reasons, he rarely had any cause to be particularly conscious of his age. In this moment, however, he was acutely aware of the fact that there were natural limits to how long someone could reasonably expect to handle the rigors of life as a starship captain. The Wek apparently had careers that could span hundreds of years, but he knew that his time was much more limited. Accordingly, he offered a short, silent prayer that he would make decisions that would prevent the men and women under his command from losing their lives well before their time.

"Captain, I'm seeing flight apron activity on the destroyers," Lieutenant Lau reported, placing a view from one of the two flights of *Hunter* RPSVs on the view screen. "The main aft airlocks are opening on all three, sir."

While it was still impossible to see what type of ships they intended to launch, there was little doubt in Prescott's mind that this was proof positive that the Krayleck intended to land troops to take possession of the Herrera facility rather than simply open fire as they had done previously. Taking a quick look at the tactical plot, he could see that the first two *Gurkhas* — designated with the usual "Savage 1" and "Savage 2" call signs — were already approaching the facility's hangar bay and would be landing shortly.

"Savage 1, *Theseus*-Actual," Prescott announced, his call instantly relayed over the tactical comm channel by the ship's AI.

"*Theseus*-Actual, go for Savage 1," the Marine master sergeant responded immediately.

"We've got three enemy destroyers preparing to launch spacecraft. I don't have any specifics yet, but I can almost guarantee you're about to have company."

"Savage 1 copies. Zero eight of one five Wek personnel are ready for immediate evac. The others say they'll be ready shortly after we arrive."

"Grab and go, Master Sergeant, and make it quick. You'll be reinforced by Savage 3 shortly, but if you can finish before they arrive, so much the better."

"Understood, *Theseus*-Actual. We'll get 'em out sir," Rios replied, already aware that Commander Reynolds would be aboard the third shuttle and fully understanding the need to complete his mission, if possible, before being forced into contact with a potentially much larger force deployed by the Krayleck ships.

"I don't doubt it for a second. Good luck, Top. Prescott out."

Herrera Mining Facility
(87.2 light years from Damara)

"Shuttle secured. No hostile forces detected in the landing zone. Immediate dismount authorized," the *Gurkha* assault shuttle's AI announced inside Master Sergeant Antonio Rios' helmet.

With seven Krayleck ships easily within weapons range and the expectation that they would be sending down their own troop shuttles momentarily, the two *Gurkhas* had executed high-performance combat landings. The idea had been to minimize the period of time where the station's shields would be offline, not to mention the need for the outer hangar bay airlock doors to remain open. While undoubtedly a prudent precaution under the circumstances, the rough, high-G landing had been hard on the shuttles' occupants.

Rios squeezed his eyes tightly together, then blinked several times in an effort to force the inside of the shuttle back into focus. A distant part of his mind realized that it was already taking him longer than it should have to get his two squads moving. Fortunately for him, his combat EVA suit's AI recognized this as well, and immediately began working to correct his temporary lapse in performance.

"Hey, kid, you planning on moving your ass at some point, or what?" the suit prompted in the stereotypically "mobster-like" simulation of Charlie "Lucky" Luciano's voice. "Come on, kid, the boss wants this gig done yesterday, and now his gun moll is on her way down here too."

Whether shrewdly calculated to refocus his attention or not, this last comment brought the master sergeant fully back to his senses. "*Jeez, Lucky* ... Commander Reynolds ain't *nobody's* 'gun moll!' Now please don't ever say anything remotely like that again, alright? I feel like I could get in big trouble just *hearing* something that stupid."

"Whatever, tough guy. At least you're awake now, right? We're good outside, let's get this crew moving."

Taking in another deep breath to clear the remaining cobwebs from his mind, Rios glanced at the tactical plot projected in his helmet display to confirm that none of the myriad sensors at his disposal were detecting anything that might pose a threat to his Marines. Seeing only the twenty-eight Human and eight Wek signatures he was expecting, he sent a quick command to open the rear cargo and side doors of both shuttles. Less than thirty seconds later, his troops had positioned themselves to provide a basic defensive perimeter throughout the hangar bay and then immediately set about working on how best to hold off a superior Krayleck force long enough to evacuate the station.

"*Theseus* Flight Ops, Savage 1 and 2 proceeding with EVA. Combined call sign change to 'Rescue 11,'" he announced over the tactical comm channel.

"Rescue 11, *Theseus* Flight Ops acknowledged," the controller replied immediately.

After taking a moment to further familiarize himself with his surroundings, Rios removed his helmet and approached the group of Wek personnel waiting near the entrance to the station proper. Like all of the members of their species he had encountered thus far, this group looked formidable enough — from a Human perspective, at least. But unlike some of the other Wek he had spoken to, Admiral Naftur, in particular, none of the them gave him the impression of restrained power he had come to associate with members of their military.

A couple of them may still be Wek Navy, he corrected himself, *but they're engineers and scientists, not combat troops.* Rios' mind was busily taking inventory of the resources at his disposal, and he immediately realized that, while they might be capable of handling a weapon, these techies would stand little chance against well-trained and presumably heavily armored Krayleck troops.

"I'm Master Sergeant Rios from the *Theseus*," his suit's AI translated as he approached. He had only had the opportunity to hear a synthesized facsimile of his own voice speaking the Wek language a couple of times, and he couldn't help but enjoy the way it sounded. *Absolutely badass*, he thought. *Makes German sound like it's for sissies.* "I'm looking for Commander Gara."

"She is finishing up in the reactor section," a female wearing gray work coveralls replied. Rios noted that she had stepped forward without hesitation, staring directly into his eyes in spite of the fact that he towered over her by the better part of a meter in his combat armor. "I can take you to her if you like."

"I appreciate that, ma'am, but we've got hostile troops inbound, so we've got to get all of you off this station immediately. Does she have some sort of comlink, or is there an intercom system we can use to contact her?"

"She does, and there is, but I can tell you that using them is a waste of time. The ambient noise level down there is too high and she will be wearing hearing protection. Besides, she will never agree to evacuate until she finishes rigging the explosives. She went down there immediately after speaking to the Krayleck captain, and she indicated that it should not take her long to complete her work."

Even without being able to pull up a schematic of the facility on his helmet display with a mere thought, Rios immediately recalled that the reactor section was located at the end of a nearly kilometer-long, descending corridor punctuated by multiple sets of stairs. He would have to go down to her — and, unfortunately, doing so would take time that they didn't have. In a pinch, he could jam perhaps thirty people aboard each *Gurkha*, but given that there were most likely hostiles on the way, he couldn't count on maintaining access to more than the two shuttles he currently had in the hangar bay. That meant that he would have to send this group of eight Wek back to the *Theseus* now — along with five of his Marines — if he was to have any hope of getting everyone else off the station in one trip.

"Rescue 11, *Theseus*-Actual," Rios heard via both his backup earpiece and his helmet that he still held in his left hand.

"*Theseus*-Actual, go for Rescue 11," Rios replied.

"You're out of time, Top. There are six landing craft on the way down. They're a little bigger than our assault shuttles, so I'm guessing you can expect a minimum of nine zero Krayleck troops headed your way. ETA: zero three minutes."

"Understood, sir. I'm sending one of our *Gurkhas* back to you with eight Wek and five Marines aboard. That should still leave enough room to board everyone else on the remaining shuttle as soon as we have all of our evacs in one place. How soon can we expect the third shuttle with Commander Reynolds?" While waiting for Captain Prescott to respond, Rios made two quick gestures to Corporal Montaño, who immediately began aggressively herding the eight Wek evacuees aboard the first shuttle.

"Savage 3 is on the flight apron now, but there's no way they can get down to you before the Krayleck ships do. It's probably safe to assume their troops will try to breach near the hangar bay to gain control of the airlock and then bring in their landing craft. So Savage 3 needs an alternate entry point."

"Yes, sir. Stand by one, please," Rios replied, temporarily muting his audio. "Ma'am," he called, running to catch up with the Wek female he had just spoken to as she stepped aboard the shuttle. "We need another way to access the reactor section from the surface. I saw some sort of small structure above —"

"Yes," she interrupted, "there is an airlock that should be large enough to accommodate one of your shuttles. Once inside, they will have access to a freight lift platform that was used during construction. We still use it while conducting maintenance on occasion, so I am confident that it is still operational. The airlock opens into a hangar-like structure that is very similar to the main hangar bay we are in now — just on a much smaller scale. The airlock can be freely accessed from the outside, but only after the station's shields have been disabled."

"That shouldn't be a problem. In fact, I suspect the Krayleck troops will take care of that with no help required from us," he said with a wink and a quick smile. "Thanks again, ma'am. Now please climb aboard and get strapped in. We've got to get you out of here right now."

"Take care, Master Sergeant Rios," she said with a disarming smile of her own. "I hope to have the opportunity to speak to you again aboard your ship."

Rios smiled awkwardly, then turned away without further comment, donning his helmet in one smooth motion as he cleared the now dangerous area surrounding the departing shuttle. *She did **not** just flirt with me*, he thought.

"What if she did, so what?" his suit's AI interjected, once again refocusing his mind on the situation at hand. "Now pull your head out of your ass before you get it shot off, for chrissake. The capo is still waiting on you, by the way, if you're finished makin' eyes with the pussy cat."

Right, he thought, chiding himself for becoming momentarily distracted. "Sorry for the interruption, *Theseus*-Actual," he said aloud after reopening the channel. "Savage 2 is departing now."

Once again before his captain had time to respond, Rios issued a flurry of commands to his remaining troops via his suit's neural interface in anticipation of abandoning the hangar bay to the approaching Krayleck force. The list of instructions for his twenty-two remaining Marines included one that none of them had been expecting.

"We see the hangar bay doors opening, Rescue 11," Prescott said over the tactical comm channel. "They're cutting it close, but it looks like they'll be out of the way before the Krayleck landing craft arrive. So far, the enemy ships still seem to be ignoring us. Unless you're willing to surrender, however, I doubt that will be the case for you when their ground troops arrive."

"Yes, sir. Be advised that I do not have sufficient troops to hold the hangar bay, but we'll do what we can to ensure the doors are secure. I'm also pulling some additional weapons out of Savage 1 and sending it out of the hangar bay as well with no one aboard. As soon as that's done, the rest of us will be heading down the access tunnel to the reactor section."

"I thought you might opt for that since you'll likely be cut off from the hangar bay. Are you sending Savage 1 all the way back to *Theseus?*"

"Negative, sir. I'm transmitting coordinates now for another small hangar bay with a maintenance access lift on the surface. I'll have Savage 1 wait for us nearby. Savage 3 should be able to access the airlock, proceed inside the hangar, then dismount and take the lift down to the reactor section. Once we leave the hangar bay, however, there will be no one left in here to disengage the facility's shields."

"I wouldn't worry about that too much. I'm guessing the Krayleck troops are about to take care of that problem for us."

"Yes, sir," Rios replied, chuckling to himself. "That's what I thought as well."

"Finish this extraction quickly and without enemy contact if at all possible, Rescue 11. Prescott out."

Chapter 13

TFS Theseus, Herrera Mining Facility
(87.2 light years from Damara)

"The three destroyers are still closing, sir. Still nothing aggressive like they're preparing to open fire, just a steady advance," Lieutenant Commander Schmidt noted from his Command console. "They seem to be keeping their frigates out of the way for now."

"You heard their captain say that we must either flee or surrender," Prescott said, "and under the circumstances, I'm sure he expected the former. But since we're still here, he's turning up the heat to see if he can force us to commit ourselves one way or the other."

"Captain, we're now tracking dismounted EVA troops from the first of the Krayleck landing craft. Looks like they're heading for the hangar bay," Lieutenant Lee reported from Tactical 1 as he placed a zoomed-in view of their activity on the bridge view screen.

"That will most likely be their sapper crew. Energy barrier shields are effective enough against ranged attacks — particularly against energy weapons — but they're also relatively easy to defeat in a situation like this."

As they watched, sixteen Krayleck troops fanned out in the area surrounding their landing craft. Since there was no natural cover to speak of, most assumed a prone position nearby or simply waited behind their shuttle, each training their weapons in the general direction of the hangar bay door. Shortly thereafter, a hatch opened atop the landing craft to reveal a crew of two —

undoubtedly a gunner and a spotter — who immediately manned a heavy weapon of some sort. All of this activity seemed to be in support of a group of four troops working feverishly to set up a small tracked vehicle approximately forty meters ahead of the ship.

All of the troops wore armored suits that were similar in appearance to versions previously used by TFC Marines. Was it possible, Prescott wondered once again, that the Krayleck had simply accepted the knowledge offered by the Pelarans at face value with little notion of either improving upon it or integrating it with their own existing technology over time? Their civilization had obviously been "under cultivation" for dramatically longer than Humanity. Had the overwhelming influx of Pelaran science stifled their collective creativity just as so many had feared would happen on Earth?

"Looks like a total of one eight troops in that first shuttle, sir," Lieutenant Lau said, interrupting his captain's musings. "Assuming that's all of them, and the other landing craft are carrying the same number, Rescue 11 will be up against a total of one zero eight Krayleck."

"All the more reason to avoid that situation if we can. Helm, I suspect the station will be losing its shields shortly. At some point, we're going to need to provide cover for our three assault shuttles long enough to get them aboard … potentially under heavy fire."

"Understood, sir. We can get into position very quickly from here when the time comes."

Moments later, the four Krayleck troops working in front of their ship apparently finished their task and immediately hustled back to join their colleagues. With no additional delay, the tracked vehicle began moving forward, dragging a pair of heavy cables behind — one leading back to the landing craft, the other anchored to a metallic rod the team had driven deeply into the ground. At a location precisely determined by its onboard sensors, it paused briefly to allow a large-bore beam emitter mounted on its sloping forward surface to pivot slightly upward before unleashing a bright green stream of energy directly into the mining facility's shields.

"Detecting a major power surge from their landing craft, sir," the lieutenant reported from the Science and Engineering console. "The beam emitter they're using is rapidly modulating its phase and frequency."

"That's how they're planning to take down the shields?" Schmidt asked.

"No, they're just creating a bunch of interference to lower the field strength in that area. Keep watching."

As if on cue, the tracked vehicle surged forward once again while continuing to fire its forward emitter — the point of impact now obscured within a large sphere of brilliant white light. As it advanced, the body of the vehicle itself began to interact with the station's barrier shield. Pulsing waves of energy traveled outward along the forward edge of the shield as glowing tendrils of arcing electricity danced all around the tracked vehicle. As the induced electrical discharges reached their maximum intensity, the vehicle abruptly stopped, immediately lowering a set of four hydraulically actuated outrigger spikes into the ground. Within seconds after the spikes made solid contact with the ground, the dazzling electrical display seemed to flicker momentarily, then ceased entirely.

"The station's shields are down, Captain," Lieutenant Lee reported.

"What, that's it?" Schmidt asked, incredulous.

"I know … a little anticlimactic, huh? Nonetheless, you have to admit that their approach is simple, quick, and very effective," Prescott said with a hint of admiration in his voice. "Essentially all they've done is create a massive path to ground and temporarily overloaded the system. At some point, the station's AI may well find a way to reestablish the field, but, as you can see, by then they'll have a semi-permanent breach in place."

On the bridge view screen, the Krayleck troops were wasting no time doing exactly that. First, a sturdy, telescoping mast extended upward from the center of the tracked vehicle to approximately two meters in height. Twelve of the troops then rushed forward to attach an expansive mesh of conductive fabric stretching outward from the mast to a series of long poles that they quickly anchored around the perimeter of the assembly. When all was in place, the central mast was extended to its full fifteen-meter height, creating an enormous, tent-like tunnel that was easily large enough to accommodate the passage of their landing craft.

"Their other five shuttles are on the move, Captain," Lee reported. "Looks like they're headed straight for the breach."

"Schmidt, you've got a green deck to launch Savage 3 as soon as those landing craft are on the ground. Dubashi, signal Rescue 11 that the shields are down and they'll have Krayleck troops inside the facility momentarily."

"Aye, sir."

"Look sharp, everyone. Their ships may be less inclined to ignore us once their troops are inside the facility."

Rescue 11, Herrera Mining Facility
(87.2 light years from Damara)

Although Rios continued to acknowledge the steady stream of communications from the *Theseus*, there was little information in them that wasn't overwhelmingly obvious from inside the now-besieged Wek mining facility. Throughout his team's headlong rush down the long, sloping corridor with its occasional sets of steep stairs, the station's AI continued its own litany of dire announcements — most of which he sincerely wished he could mute. One bit of good news, however, was that the breach in the facility's shields had allowed its reactors to decrease their power output significantly, reducing the ambient noise level to a dull roar and making communication without electronic assistance possible once again. Even better than that, just over halfway down the corridor, his squad's short-range passive sensors had begun picking up the signatures of the remaining Wek personnel, all seven of which now appeared on his helmet display.

It was one thing to study a building's floor plan, but something else entirely to experience it for yourself firsthand. As the Marines finally reached the end of the long corridor, Rios knew immediately that it was not the ideal defensive location he had been hoping for. The reactor section was cavernous, so there was indeed a natural choke point at the bottom of the final set of stairs. With some heavy equipment for cover, he could easily position a line of troops to fire back up the long corridor, making an approach from the direction of the hangar bay nothing short of suicide for even a much larger Krayleck force. The problem was the contents of the room directly behind the planned location for his defensive line.

Just a stone's throw from the bottom of the stairs were row upon row of large, cylindrical pods — each one measuring just over two meters in diameter and four meters in length. Each pod was connected to a network of cables routed along a series of trays suspended from the room's towering ceiling. On the side of each, numerous placards warned anyone who dared approach (using the most enthusiastic terms available in the Wek language) of the dangerous materials contained within. Although there was little doubt in Master Sergeant Rios' mind what he was looking at, he paused momentarily to allow for the translations to be projected within his field of view. The simplest of the placards included only two words that were, nevertheless, more than sufficient in any language: WARNING ANTIMATTER.

As Rios stared disconsolately at the pods — his mind temporarily overwhelmed by what looked like a completely unmanageable tactical situation — Commander Gara appeared from around a rack of equipment. Even though he had noted several seconds earlier that one of the station's remaining Wek personnel was headed his way, he was surprised by how quickly she had covered the distance. He also noted that Gara wasn't winded in the least, a feat of endurance and speed that he knew he would be unable to match without the help of his EVA suit.

"Master Sergeant Rios?" she called out somewhat hesitantly to the group of Marines, having no idea which one he was. Although her keen eyes could make them out easily enough in the dimly lit storage area, whatever material formed their outer armor seemed to absorb much of the light that fell upon it. Although she was fully aware that this was nothing more than some type of camouflage, the effect gave the Terran troops a strange, almost ghostly air — like apparitions from some half-remembered nightmare. As one of their number approached, she remarked to herself how pleased she was that these Humans were on *her* side.

"Yes, ma'am," he replied, once again removing his helmet for her benefit.

"We have a problem," she said immediately, skipping the unnecessary introductions.

"Looks like we've got quite a few, Commander," he said, nodding to the antimatter pods.

"What, those? They will not present a problem for us so long as we get ourselves and your ship out of the immediate vicinity before we are forced to destroy the station. The problem to which I refer is the freight lift we were planning to use to evacuate all of us to the surface."

"So, I take it you heard from the *Theseus*, then."

"Yes, I checked in just a few minutes ago, after the station's shields went offline. The remaining members of my team are ready to depart, but they discovered that the lift to the maintenance hangar on the surface is inoperative."

"Inoperative in what way, ma'am?"

"They are attempting to troubleshoot the problem now, but the platform was at the surface during the Krayleck bombardment and may have been damaged."

"Understood. Do your people have weapons?"

"No, as you can imagine, weapons are not normally authorized in the reactor section. The closest storage locker is back up on the hangar deck."

"That's not a problem. I'll send Corporal Montaño and two other Marines back to the lift with you. They'll be able to show you how to use our pulse rifles and hopefully help out with the lift problem. The rest of us will need to prepare some kind of defense far enough up the corridor to prevent any weapons fire from hitting any of those cylinders. Do you have any sort of equipment or other materials solid enough to create a defensive barricade?"

"How much time do we have?" she asked, looking back over her shoulder at the long rows of containment pods. "You are correct that we cannot risk anything hitting one of the cryo-cylinders, but they are, nevertheless, practically indestructible. If you can give me five minutes or so, we should be able to transport a pair of empty ones up to the second landing."

Rios replaced his helmet, then looked back up the stairs and slightly to the left in the direction of the hangar bay doors on the level above. With a quick mental command, he superimposed the current disposition of the Krayleck ground forces in relation to his own using data provided by the *Theseus*. In his peripheral vision, he also noted a blue, flashing icon indicating the arrival of Savage 3 almost directly above his squad's current position.

"I'd say five minutes is almost exactly how much time we have, ma'am."

Savage 3, Herrera Mining Facility
(87.2 light years from Damara)

"Shuttle secured. No hostile forces detected in the landing zone. Nearest enemy ground forces located 1.5 kilometers to the southeast with no direct line of fire. Immediate dismount authorized," the *Gurkha* assault shuttle's AI announced inside Commander Reynolds' helmet. Almost involuntarily, she turned her head to the southeast in the general direction of the facility's main hangar bay, quickly assessing the situation using almost exactly the same information Master Sergeant Rios had viewed just moments earlier. Feeling the eyes of her shuttle's fourteen other occupants resting upon her, she was painfully aware that she was the outsider here, in spite of the fact that she had received much of the same training as the Marines now under her immediate command.

Her team's overall mission objective was, of course, the safe return of the thirty-eight currently deployed troops from the *Theseus* — herself included — as well as the remaining seven Wek personnel from Herrera. Her immediate personal objective, however, was to stay out of the Marines' way and allow them to do their jobs as quickly and efficiently as possible.

Open now ... open authorized ... open sesame, she thought in rapid succession, rolling her eyes as her mind ran through a litany of related phrases searching for the standard mental verbiage she couldn't quite remember from her time at Camp Lejeune.

"It's not a problem, Gingerbread," her suit's AI responded in Elvis Presley's usual Southern drawl. "Can't none of these people hear you unless you want them to, so you can just talk to me if you like. Just tell me what you want, and I'll make it happen … I know *exactly* what you mean," the AI said in a voice calculated to both calm and focus her mind without distracting from the mission. In spite of her inability to come up with the proper command, both the side and rear cargo doors opened, allowing her squad to quickly secure the small hangar and immediately begin assessing the problem with the lift platform.

Reynolds knew from an intellectual standpoint that her battle management system gave her full access to everything that was going on in the area. The problem was her ability to access and mentally process it all quickly enough to provide the level of situational awareness she required. She also knew that making unnecessary comm calls in the middle of a high-threat environment marked her as even more of an outsider — perhaps even an amateur. *Screw it,* she thought, *they probably think that anyway, so on the plus side, there's no need for me to waste time pretending otherwise.*

"Rios, Reynolds," she said aloud, her call immediately routed over the tactical comm channel by her suit's AI.

"Reynolds, go for Rios," he replied, obviously exerting himself physically at the moment.

"We're working the problem with the lift in the maintenance hangar above you, but I don't have an ETA yet. Looks like the hostiles may reach you before we do. Can you hold your position?"

"We'll do our best, Commander. I assume you read my note about the antimatter pods?"

"That's affirmative. Is your cover in place in the corridor?"

"It will be momentarily, ma'am. The biggest problem may be finding a way to disengage from the Krayleck once you get the lift working."

If we get the lift working, she thought bitterly as she glanced over at three members of her squad already using plasma torches in an effort to clear several large pieces of debris.

"We may find ourselves pinned down in this corridor, Commander," he continued. "If that happens, I'll peel off as many Marines as I can, and then I want you to get the Wek personnel and as many of our people as possible aboard the *Gurkhas* and exfil. Do you understand?"

"Yes, Master Sergeant," she replied after a brief pause. While she was technically the "on-scene commander," there was no question that Rios was calling the shots where the Marine platoon's mission was concerned — and that included her at the moment as well.

"Don't worry, ma'am, that won't be my first choice either," he chuckled in an attempt to lighten the rather dire tone of their conversation. "Unfortunately, *Theseus'* initial estimate on the number of hostiles appears to have been a little low. The revised total is now up to one four three based on the number of troops working on the personnel airlock up top. Any chance we can authorize the use of a couple of Squad Light Railguns or even a grav grenade launcher before they get down to where we are? It would sure be nice to level the playing field a bit."

"I understand, but unfortunately not. The standing control order is still 'weapons hold,' and their breaking into the facility does not constitute a direct attack on our forces. The very first shot they fire, though —"

"Kill," he said simply.

"You're damn right. Good luck, Top. Reynolds out."

Rescue 11, Herrera Mining Facility
(87.2 light years from Damara)

"They're coming," Sergeant Ellis announced simply from a position roughly two hundred meters in front of the Marines' defensive line.

Once the Krayleck troops had entered the hangar bay, *Theseus* was no longer able to provide much in the way of useful data regarding their movements. Worse yet, something about the Marine squad's proximity to the station's large reactors in combination with the long, sloping tunnel leading up to the advancing enemy troops had been playing hell with their EVA suits' passive sensor suite. After several false positives, Rios had sent Ellis far enough up the corridor to at least provide a heads-up that things were about to hit the proverbial fan.

"Rios copies. Double time it back down here, Sergeant."

The data Ellis had gathered was largely as expected. There were now roughly one hundred and forty Krayleck troops on the station's main level. Nearly their entire force had massed in what almost looked like parade formation near the top of the corridor, then started down as a group.

On the plus side, at least we managed to come up with some cover, Rios reflected as he watched Sergeant Ellis come sprinting back to the defensive line at the nearly sixty kilometers per hour provided by his EVA suit's synthetic musculature.

In the brief period of time since the Human Marines had arrived, one of Commander Gara's engineers had managed to place three of the large cylindrical storage pods in the corridor leading upwards to the facility's hangar bay. Using a hydraulic lift, he had maneuvered the first up to the relatively level landing above the first set of stairs, then placed the remaining two into overlapping positions where the corridor opened into the reactor section itself. Between the two makeshift barricades, four of Rescue 11's Marines had set up two SLR railguns within the structural framework that made up the base of the first cylinder. Everyone else simply waited quietly behind whatever cover they could find — pulse rifles at the ready.

In the final moments before attempting contact, Rios issued a challenge and response equipment and readiness check to the members of his squad via his suit's neural interface. Not surprisingly, the nineteen Marines waiting nearby each responded at least twenty percent faster than their personal averages. They were as ready as they were likely to get.

"KRAYLECK TROOPS!" Rios' voice boomed up the hallway at the one hundred and twenty decibels provided by his suit's voice amplification system. "I am Master Sergeant Antonio Rios of the Terran Fleet

Command Marine Corps. Our troops are engaged in a rescue operation and will clear the area with the station's remaining Wek personnel within the hour. For your own safety, you must halt your advance now. Stop where you are and do not attempt to interfere with our operation."

Shortly after the enemy troops had started down the long hallway, every member of Rios' squad had been presented with a comprehensive tactical plot display — all of the information required to engage and defeat their adversaries projected seamlessly within their fields of view. The updated tactical data was immediately relayed up to Commander Reynolds' Rescue 12 squad located in the maintenance hangar above as well as to the *Theseus* herself and beyond. Each member of both Marine squads, the crew of the *Theseus*, and countless other Humans monitoring the situation across a region of space spanning hundreds of light years paused to see if Rios' last ditch attempt to avoid a confrontation with the Krayleck troops was having the desired effect.

At first, the orderly Krayleck formation halted, its troops spreading out loosely along an extended section of corridor as if they intended to simply hold their position and wait for the Humans to depart as Rios had ordered. After a brief delay, however, a single contact detached from the group and quickly advanced to the edge of the next landing above the Marines' defensive position. Although the angle of the corridor largely obscured his approach, he was briefly visible to the entrenched Marines as he ran quickly forward with one arm stretched far behind his body to heave a small, round device in their direction with all his might.

"Take cover, weapons hold!" Rios shouted over the comm channel, knowing full well that at least half his troops had a shot at the fleeing Krayleck. Even though the device now bouncing and rolling rapidly toward their line was almost certainly an explosive of some sort — and as absurd it seemed at the moment — the rules of engagement did not permit them to open fire.

The words had barely left Rios' mouth when he saw movement to his right. Sergeant Ellis, having remained on his feet after returning from his brief recon mission, darted from behind the barricade and snatched up the device in a smooth, fluid motion that would make any major-league shortstop proud. With two quick steps towards the next set of stairs, he drew back his arm and hurled the device — his EVA suit multiplying his already powerful throw by a factor of five.

When the device left his hand, it was moving at well over one hundred meters per second, but unfortunately had traveled only five meters before detonating at a velocity of over eight *thousand* meters per second. Sergeant Ellis' suit, while designed to save his life even in extreme situations such as this, was hit by such a large number of fragments that several managed to penetrate near the end of his still-extended arm. The white-hot metallic shards ripped through flesh and bone as they continued their path of destruction, reaching his chest cavity just twelve milliseconds later — mercifully severing his spine and ending his life well before his brain had received the first pain impulses from his nervous system.

"Weapons free," Rios growled bitterly while simultaneously notifying the *Theseus* that his Marines were now officially designated as "troops in contact" with enemy forces. Calling up a display that allowed him to quickly assess the physical status of his squad, he noted that there had been no additional injuries. *What the hell was the point of that?* he wondered while switching his helmet display back to the tactical plot view and breaking cover with two other Marines to recover the body of Sergeant Nick Ellis.

"From what I could see, Top, it looked like that asshole was wearing a Mark 1 EVA suit," one of the two men said — his mind angrily searching for some means to avenge the senseless killing of his friend and mentor he was now helping to carry. "They were long gone before my hitch, but I don't think they could take much of a hit. No way in hell they could stand up to a bolt from a pulse rifle."

"Good eye, Corporal, you're exactly right," Rios said. "Go ahead and take Ellis back to the lift and then hustle back here double quick."

That's it exactly, he thought as his enemy's situation snapped into much clearer focus in his mind. *They don't know anything about our capabilities, but they sure as hell know their own limitations. They probably assumed — and have now confirmed — that if they come down here they'll be out in the open in a relatively confined space fighting against well-trained troops firing from behind cover. So, they send one guy down to either convince us to give up or try and flush us out. The problem is, there's nothing to keep them from …*

Glancing again at the tactical plot, Rios saw that three Krayleck troops had separated from their line and were once again advancing towards the landing above.

Without hesitation, he took off in their direction at top speed while ordering eleven of his Marines to follow. As they covered the distance between the barricade and the next stairway, their suits' battle management AI designated the three advancing Krayleck soldiers, now clearly outlined in red within their fields of view, as priority targets. To ensure a successful intercept, the AI assigned a total of four Marines to attack each of the approaching targets.

Having started out closest to the enemy line, Rios was the first to reach a point where he had a clear shot. The three Krayleck soldiers were obviously not expecting to encounter opposition on this level — an important fact he filed away for later. He could also see that each one carried another explosive device, but no other weapons were visible at the moment. His pulse rifle already shouldered, the AI took into account an enormous number of variables in order to provide the highest probability of a kill. A circular target appeared within his field of view over the center of mass of the nearest advancing Krayleck soldier, immediately prompting him to fire. In less than a second, he had steadied his aim, noted the urgent "locked" tone in his ears, and sent three bolts of compressed plasma downrange at just shy of the speed of light.

As quickly as his mind had registered the fact that his rounds were indeed penetrating the Krayleck's armor, Rios had smoothly shifted his aim to the second, and then the third targets. Before the three enemy soldiers' lifeless bodies had skidded to a stop on the smooth tile floor, his suit's AI had replaced their previously red icons with grayed-out squares in his helmet's tactical plot display. Each was now also marked with a simple "I/L" designation — informing the remainder of Rios' rapidly approaching Marines that the status of all three targets was now assessed as "incapacitated/lethal."

With everything that had been taking place over the past few minutes, Rios' attention had been understandably focused on the corridor between his small force and the main body of Krayleck troops. Now, as he took a moment to reassess the rapidly changing situation, he noted with no small satisfaction the larger than expected group of Marines emerging from around the sides of their barricade.

"Glad you could make it, Commander," he said with a smile that could be heard over the tactical comm channel. "We need to attack immediately."

Chapter 14

TFS Theseus, Herrera Mining Facility
(87.2 light years from Damara)

"That's three confirmed enemy KIAs, Captain," Lieutenant Lee reported from Tactical 1.

"Hmm," Prescott replied. "Keep a close eye on their ships. If things go poorly for their ground forces, I'm guessing that may change their disposition up here as well."

"Aye, sir."

"Our goal at this point is pretty simple, folks, we have to give Rescue 11 and 12 enough time to get everyone back aboard the shuttles and then safely return to our hangar bay. With the facility's shields down, a single, well-placed shot from one of the Krayleck's railguns could kill everyone down there. I also don't think we can afford to assume that they won't risk killing their own people ... particularly if they think they're going to lose most of them anyway. Helm?"

"Yes, sir," Fisher replied.

"Now that Commander Reynolds' team has the lift working, I expect they'll have the first shuttle on the way back shortly. Go ahead and ease us into a position where we can use our shields to protect the area around the maintenance hangar on the surface as well as the reactor section below ground."

"We'll have to get pretty low, sir."

"Probably a thousand meters or so, yes, but it can't be helped."

"Will do, Captain, heading in closer now."

"Tactical, no change in our attack plans. If the Krayleck ships start shooting, send the *Hunters* after Foxtrot 1 while we target Delta 3. Hit 'em hard and fast, just like we discussed."

"Aye, sir," Lieutenants Lee and Lau replied in unison.

On the starboard side of the view screen, the tactical plot clearly showed that the three enemy destroyers had halted their advance after reaching optimum beam weapon range — with the *Theseus* now sitting rather ominously at the intersection of their innermost overlapping range bubbles.

"Captain," Lieutenant Dubashi said, "I just received a textual status update from Commander Reynolds' neural interface. She says they have a tactical advantage and she believes they might be able to compel the enemy ground force to surrender. She and Master Sergeant Rios are in the process of consolidating their two squads in preparation for moving forward from the defensive barricade to put pressure on the Krayleck position."

"Wait ..." Prescott said, incredulous, "she says they're planning to *attack*?"

Herrera Mining Facility
(87.2 light years from Damara)

"There's a lot of movement in their lines, Commander. We can attack or make a run for it, but either way it has to be now," Rios said in an urgent tone that demanded immediate action.

"Understood," she replied. "Everyone's in position — two Marines and seven Wek holding the line, with the rest of us ready to advance on your order."

Rios briefly considered attempting to convince the XO that she should join the rear guard herself, but quickly dismissed the idea since he knew exactly what her response would be. Both of them had worked frantically to consolidate their small force in the short period of time since the last Krayleck attack, and, as a result of their efforts, every available Marine was now assembled with weapons at the ready in preparation for a push up the corridor to engage the enemy. In case things went poorly, they had left the two SLRs — now manned only by their gunners — stationed at the defensive barricade along with the remaining seven Wek personnel, each having been hastily instructed in the finer points of pulse rifle operations.

"Everyone keep in mind that we do *not* know the capabilities of their rifles or their suits," Rios said as he gave his small assault force a final once-over. "All we can tell for sure after taking a look at one is that they fire kinetic energy rounds like our SLR. We're betting they're a lot less powerful, but if we start taking fire that's effective against our armor, we're all gonna haul ass back to the barricade. Everyone clear?"

Rios cringed inwardly at his own gross overuse of the tactical comm, but knew that it was necessary under the circumstances. In response to his query, however, he was gratified to see that all of his Marines — Commander Reynolds included — had responded promptly and without a sound, leaving only a single verbal response from Commander Gara using the radio she had just been issued.

"Alright, people, let's move," he said, leading the way up the next staircase.

As he ascended the stairs, Rios noticed once again that the Krayleck did not seem to be aware of his troops' advance. They were definitely doing *something*, but their movements were not at all what he would have expected from a group of soldiers who knew they were about to come under attack. Realizing there might still be an opportunity for his Marines to fire from a position of relative cover, he issued a quick series of instructions — the most important of which was for as silent an approach as possible.

Less than thirty seconds later, Rios and ten other members of his squad eased quietly up to peer over the edge of the last few stairs at the Krayleck line — still over fifty meters distant. What they saw made no sense whatsoever from a Human perspective. Just as indicated on their tactical plot display, the enemy troops were still arranged in an orderly formation with eight columns stretching back for sixteen rows. The remainder of their number — perhaps their equivalent to officers or NCOs — were milling about the perimeter of the formation, each one emitting a loud series of sounds that did not yield to translation by the Marines' AI.

Signaling everyone to move back out of sight below the level of the landing once again, Rios risked a brief radio call. "Commander, we can clearly rip them up pretty good from here. Don't get me wrong, I've got no problem doing exactly that, seeing as how they picked this fight, not us. But since we don't know how they will react — both here in the facility and in space — I'm looking for some guidance. What are your orders, ma'am?"

Within the confines of her helmet, Reynolds rolled her eyes and swore silently to herself. She didn't particularly have a problem with the fact that Rios had effectively "passed the buck." Under the circumstances, it was probably the right call on his part, and she was fairly certain she would have done the exact same thing if she had been in his shoes. It did, however, put her in the position of completely owning the situation, regardless of what happened from here on in. Thinking quickly, she saw only three reasonable options. First, she could contact Prescott, but she dismissed this idea immediately as both indecisive and too slow. Second, she could give the order to open fire. This option might well lead to a quick victory, but, as Rios had said, might literally bring the full might of the enemy task force down on their heads. Finally, they could offer the Krayleck troops one final opportunity to either withdraw or surrender. While this seemed like a completely ridiculous idea on a number of different levels, and might still prompt their ships to attack, it at least did have the advantage of morally justifying a possible massacre if the enemy soldiers refused to comply.

Desperate times ... she thought to herself. "Alright, Top, I want you to try your VA system one more time. Give them one chance to either leave the facility immediately or throw down their weapons and surrender. Everyone else, weapons hold, but if they start shooting — and I think they might — we start killing them and keep killing them until I say stop."

Although she had not asked for a response, Reynolds noted that her orders were immediately acknowledged by the entire squad. Nodding silently for Rios to begin, she crouched a bit lower and waited for the inevitable.

"Krayleck troops!" Rios' massively amplified voice thundered up the corridor once again. "Since you have attacked our forces without provocation, we require that you either withdraw from the facility entirely or throw down your weapons and surrender unconditionally. This is your final warning. Leave or surrender now or you will be fired upon."

The effect on the Krayleck forces was immediate. First, the stream of sounds emitted by the individuals standing around the perimeter of the formation changed to a shrill series of shrieks that would have been deafening were it not for the protection provided by the Marines' helmets. Shortly thereafter, every soldier in the formation broke ranks and rushed with what must have been their equivalent of a battle cry toward Rios and his assembled Marines.

"Hold!" Rios ordered, assuming that the oncoming Krayleck would stop to open fire before reaching the stairwell. As the leading group of soldiers reached the halfway point, however, it became obvious that they had something else entirely in mind. "They're planning to overrun us, Commander," he said, spitting out the words as quickly as possible.

"Weapons free, fire at will!" Reynolds yelled, adrenaline finally overcoming any pretense of military bearing.

Not having expected a headlong rush on their position, only about half of Rios' Marines were in a position to quickly open fire at the moment the order was given. Guided by their battle management AI, however, every one of them engaged and killed a target within the first five seconds, felling the closest eighteen enemy soldiers as if they were a wave breaking harmlessly against a wall of stone. Yet still they came on, perhaps incited into this mad, killing frenzy by a combination of the deaths of their comrades and the shrieking exhortations of their leaders. The shrill, piercing cries continued unabated throughout the Krayleck charge, lending a wild, terrifying atmosphere to what had now become a close-quarters battle.

The Marines managed a second volley almost immediately, this time joined by most of the other members of their combined squad. Even with the AI designating unique targets for every pulse rifle, discipline began to break down within the chaotic onslaught of armored alien bodies. As a result, several bolts from the second salvo impacted enemy soldiers that had already been neutralized — a significant decrease in combat efficiency with equally significant consequences. As the Krayleck vanguard reached the Human line, the Marines were still outnumbered by nearly three to one.

In each Marine's field of view, their AIs shifted seamlessly to hand-to-hand combat mode, displaying a wide range of information intended to assist each one in maximizing the effectiveness of their battle armor. While each of them had received extensive training in various techniques for handling precisely this kind of scenario, face-to-face combat was still both terrifying and strangely personal, just as it had always been throughout history. Accordingly, each Marine fought with their own unique style — and, in some cases, using their own personal weapons.

"Watch his left ... yeah, that's it ... throat ... squeeze and pull ... dead. Next," Rios' AI reported in a satisfied, provocative tone, keeping up a steady stream of feedback that provided coaching along with profanity-laden expressions of encouragement.

"Lucky," he grunted, sidestepping a stumbling Krayleck soldier who had just taken a crushing side kick from a nearby Marine. "You should have enough data to profile their armor. Are their suits the same as our Mark 1s?"

"Close, but I'm thinking theirs are not as good as our Mark 1s were overall. Their heads are too big. That makes them tougher to armor, and I think their natural exoskeletons work against them as well. Bottom line, we're shaped better than they are for augmentation. That shouldn't be a big surprise since the Pelarans are just like — behind you, *BLADE!*"

Having trained with his AI for this particular situation hundreds of times, Rios had developed something of a "muscle memory" for the moves associated with countering a close-quarters attack from the rear. The keyword "blade" in this case referred not to the weapon held by his enemy (which would have done the Krayleck soldier little good in any event), but to the weapon Rios always wore in the horizontal "scout carry" position in the small of his back. In one smooth motion, he drew and then activated the device, rotating to his right to make visual contact with the enemy soldier as he pushed upward to target the generally weak interface between helmet and chest armor.

Having more in common with a high-intensity plasma torch than a traditional "Navy Knife," Rios' weapon was capable of firing a thirty-centimeter-long jet of plasma for approximately two minutes. Upon impact with his target, the effect was immediate — the "blade" striking and penetrating between the two sections of the Krayleck's suit before easily piercing its exoskeleton and almost completely severing its head from its body.

"Served him right … the mutt," Lucky commented as Rios sheathed the weapon while attempting to get a handle on the still-chaotic situation surrounding him.

Although things had most definitely not gone the way he had hoped, they had clearly gone very badly indeed for the Krayleck force. Realizing that they were at a significant disadvantage against the Humans' pulse rifles, they had sought to quickly overwhelm the much smaller force of Marines with sheer strength of numbers. While, pound for pound, the average Krayleck soldier had a slight strength advantage over his Human Marine counterpart, they were also less agile, and were augmented with combat armor that only doubled their normal strength compared to the five-fold increase provided by the Humans' "universal" combat EVA suits. The result, as Commander Reynolds had predicted, could accurately be called a massacre.

Rios' battle management AI now displayed only fifty Krayleck soldiers with the red icons indicating a mission effective status. By comparison, his squad had suffered only two KIAs and three other Marines injured seriously enough to be out of the fight. *Fifty v. thirty,* he thought, a confident smile forming at the corners of his mouth.

It was at that moment that he felt a significant impact near his left shoulder, followed shortly thereafter by another in his left leg. Knowing from personal experience that the pain associated with a serious wound is often difficult to detect in the heat of battle, Rios checked the integrity of his armor and was relieved to see that no significant damage had occurred. With another quick query of his suit's AI, the velocity and trajectory of the impacts were used to calculate their source. Dropping to a kneeling position, he shouldered his rifle and returned fire, instantly killing yet another Krayleck soldier who was firing rather indiscriminately at the Marine line. *Forty-nine*, he thought savagely, realizing that his troops were now in a position to quickly end the fight.

Krayleck rifle rounds ineffective, he announced with a quick thought. *Marines, form a line on me.*

Within seconds, the few Krayleck still engaged in sporadic hand-to-hand combat were quickly dispatched, and the entire squad was moving forward again as one, sweeping the remaining enemy soldiers from the corridor before them. When the number of remaining enemy troops reached twenty-five, Rios called for a halt and weapons hold.

"Your weapons are ineffective!" he yelled, his amplified voice sounding as if God himself was demanding an end to the fighting. "Drop them NOW and lie face down on the ground, or we will be forced to kill every last one of you."

It was at this point that Commander Reynolds first realized that the awful shrieking noise some of the Krayleck had been making had finally ceased. One by one, the remaining enemy soldiers placed their rifles on the ground, then slowly lowered themselves into kneeling, then prone positions. Reynolds drew in a deep breath as she continued to watch closely for signs of additional resistance, daring for the first time to believe that they had somehow defeated a much larger enemy force. Although she continued her slow, deliberate scan of the enemy soldiers while catching her breath, it was a Marine private who noticed the minute, furtive movements that signaled the Kraylecks' final act of defiance.

"GRENADE!" the private yelled over the tactical comm channel.

In actuality, almost all of the remaining Krayleck had been in the process of attempting to activate another of their explosive devices. With thirty pulse rifles trained in their direction, however, all of them save one died before successfully doing so. With no remaining threats other than the live grenade, Rios' Marines simply dropped to the floor. Fortunately, all of them were well outside the device's kill radius and were protected from fragments and other flying debris by their combat armor. Nevertheless, almost the entire squad was doused by a wall of foul-smelling, brown-colored gore produced by the explosively shredded bodies of several Krayleck soldiers.

Seconds later, the Marines were still lying face down on the floor of the corridor when they felt the first impacts of what had to be kinetic energy weapons fire striking the planet's surface nearby. With this battle ended and another obviously about to get underway above, Reynolds quickly made the mental shift from temporary Marine special operator to first officer, TFS *Theseus*. Calling up a summary of the destroyer's tactical plot, she was instantly aware of the impossible tactical situation in which her captain had placed the ship — as well as exactly why he had done so.

"We need to get everyone back to the lift RIGHT NOW!" she roared over the tactical comm, instantly establishing that she was once again fully in command.

With everyone back on their feet, Reynolds quickly fired off a list of orders to Rios and his remaining Marines, her highly focused mind now employing the neural interface as if it were a natural extension of her own consciousness. Ensuring first and foremost that all of her troops — including their dead and wounded — were accounted for, she also recalled that only one shuttle at a time could depart for the *Theseus*. Taking full advantage of the delay, she took a few moments to collect not only their own weapons and equipment, but several items of interest from the Krayleck soldiers who would no longer be needing them.

Chapter 15

TFS Theseus, Herrera Mining Facility
(87.2 light years from Damara)

"I'm not sure I fully understand our orders, sir," Lieutenant Commander Schmidt said, glancing up from his Command console with an obvious look of concern. "I know Admiral Patterson said that we are not to engage unless fired upon, but surely we've met the spirit of that condition at this point, have we not?"

"You could certainly make that argument," Prescott nodded with a conciliatory smile, "but I can promise you that it wouldn't hold up well during your court-martial … assuming you lived long enough to face one. We'll talk more about the professional ethics surrounding 'shades of gray' decisions another time, but for now, I want you to understand that an order like the one you just mentioned is absolutely black and white. If we can't prove beyond a reasonable doubt that the Krayleck ships intentionally targeted and fired on us, we may not engage, period."

"Even though they fired on our Marines?"

"Their *soldiers* did, yes, and now they're all dead as a result. And while our politicians might well argue that their species has already committed an act of war, a pitched battle between opposing warships is on a completely different level than a skirmish between two relatively small forces on the ground, Thomas. So, if we were to open fire based on what their ground troops did, we would not only be violating our orders, but we would also be responsible for dramatically escalating the conflict between Humanity and the Krayleck — potentially putting billions of lives at risk on both sides."

"Don't you think this sporadic fire we're seeing is a result of what just happened on the surface?"

"I'm certain of it, and I'm equally certain that they're trying to provoke us into doing something stupid enough to justify an all-out attack."

"Sir," Lieutenant Dubashi interrupted, "Commander Reynolds reports that they can get everyone aboard two shuttles."

"That's good. The maintenance hangar where the lift is can only handle one at a time, so that eliminates an additional airlock cycle."

"Yes, sir. The first shuttle will have all seven Wek personnel and sixteen Marines aboard. That total includes three KIAs and three wounded in need of additional medical attention: one routine, one priority, and one urgent surgical."

"Understood. Please pass that information along to Doctor Chen. Also, let Commander Reynolds know that we need them to complete their two launch cycles as quickly as possible. We may well be under fire by the time we recover the second shuttle."

"Aye, sir."

"Do you think the Krayleck are afraid of us based on what they've seen so far?" Lieutenant Commander Schmidt asked after a brief period of silence.

"Yeah, honestly I do. We've shown a stubborn willingness to stand our ground up here when they clearly expected us to run. That has to give them pause. Then they send down a sizable ground force, which they promptly lose in spite of a nearly four to one advantage.

Afraid may not actually be the right word, though. I don't think, for example, that they're afraid of a ship to ship engagement, if necessary, but I wonder if they might be concerned about the repercussions that attacking us might have for them with the Pelarans. Keep in mind that the Pelarans seem to be all about their search for the precursor humanoid civilization —"

"The 'Makers.'"

"Right, and according to the Pelarans, we Terrans are one of the so-called 'child' civilizations they seeded. So, if we believe what the Guardian has told us about our being genetically identical to the Pelarans, I think it's safe to assume that attacking us without provocation would be ... frowned upon within the Alliance."

"I suppose that might explain why they would prefer to provoke us, rather than just attacking us outright."

"That and they can't, for the life of them, figure out why we haven't raised our shields," Prescott chuckled. "So, they lob a few shots in our general direction, assuming that if we have shields at all, we'll have no choice but to raise them."

"If that's true, then they may now believe that they have a huge tactical advantage. So, you think they'll attack," Schmidt said, stating his question as a matter of fact.

"Yes, if they didn't already consider a seven to one numerical advantage as sufficient, now they have even more of a reason to be confident of victory ... so, yes, I think they will almost certainly attack."

"The doors are opening, Captain," Lieutenant Lau reported from Tactical 2.

It seemed like hours had passed since Ensign Fisher had placed the destroyer in a position to provide cover for the Marines' assault shuttles, after which Lau had placed a zoomed-in view of the maintenance hangar — now directly beneath the ship — on the bridge view screen. Now, at long last, a vertical streak of light could be seen as the doors parted in the middle, then promptly opened to partially reveal the building's interior. Mercifully, only a few additional seconds passed before the first *Gurkha* assault shuttle emerged from within. Immediately after clearing the hangar doors, the small ship banked aggressively in the general direction of *Theseus'* stern and began a rapid climb for the relative safety of the destroyer's aft flight apron.

The shuttle was less than halfway through its ascent when the entire area was bathed in the light of energy weapons fire as well as the bright white flashes associated with gravitic shield intercept events.

"Helm, whatever happens, you hold this position. Do you understand?" Prescott said firmly. "Those shuttles won't last a second if they get beyond our shield radius."

"Aye, sir, I got it," Fisher replied with more confidence than he felt at the moment.

The sound of the ship's six reactors quickly ramping up to maximum power in response to the Krayleck attack was clearly audible in the background — as were the unmistakable sounds of incoming ordnance occasionally making it past the shields to impact the hull.

"Tactical, report."

"We're taking both energy weapons and railgun fire from all three Krayleck destroyers, Captain," Lieutenant

Lee replied. "Nothing from the frigates yet, and, so far at least, none of their ships have launched any RPSVs."

"Very well. Weapons free, gentlemen. You may execute your attacks," Prescott said evenly.

***

On the far side of the Krayleck formation, two flights of twelve *Hunter* RPSVs launched two HB-7c missiles each, placing the missiles in "loiter" mode before themselves transitioning to hyperspace in twenty-four simultaneous flashes of grayish-white light. An infinitesimal period of time later, the ships reappeared in a pair of stacked, trailing formations that provided every spacecraft with a clear line of fire to engage its target — which, at the moment, happened to be the Krayleck Empire's version of an *Ingenuity*-class frigate.

Based on the current data available to *Theseus'* AI, the *Hunters* engaged at relatively close range with a point location railgun attack, each one coordinating the fire from its dorsal and ventral turrets to impact the frigate's hull in precisely the same location as the other ships in its formation. As expected, the frigate's energy barrier shields interacted with each kinetic energy penetration round as it approached the hull at nearly ten percent the speed of light, significantly reducing each one's velocity prior to impact. But with thousands of rounds per second concentrated on such a small area, the frigate's shield was quickly overwhelmed, allowing more and more impacts at ever-increasing velocities until the target's hull itself began to suffer significant damage.

With no warning whatsoever of the imminent attack, there had also been no opportunity for the warship to place its own railgun turrets in point-defense mode. What its AI *did* manage to do immediately, however, was to engage its short-range equivalent to the Humans' Close-In Weapon System. At numerous locations along both sides of the frigate, a combination of mini railgun and energy turrets emerged from small, recessed bays within the ship's hull. With the Human ships already well within its engagement zone, the AI-controlled weapons immediately locked on to two targets each to port and starboard and opened fire. Within seconds, the space in front of the oncoming RPSVs was filled with a lethal curtain of kinetic energy rounds. At the same time, each point-defense mount also opened up with its beam weapon, lighting the area surrounding the frigate with bolts of blue-tinted energy weapons fire.

For all their versatility, the *Hunters'* Achilles heel had always been their limited power-generation and storage capabilities. As was typically the case, Humanity's newest and most advanced systems were also some of the most power-hungry — and power required physical space. Unfortunately for the *Hunters*, their fifteen-meter-length had offered the designers precious little of this commodity to work with. In the intervening months since the Resistance attack, however, Fleet Science and Engineering had continued their program to improve the energy densities associated with previously installed capacitor banks. While gravitic shields were still out of the question for the small, fighter-like RPSVs, one tactically significant new "trick" had been added to its repertoire that had previously been available only to Fleet's larger ships.

As the two formations of *Hunters* neared their point of closest approach to the target, their controlling AIs took into account the firing pattern of the Krayleck frigate's point-defense weapons, predicting with pinpoint accuracy where they would encounter the first of the deadly fragmentation rounds. This allowed the RPSVs to press their attack until the last possible fraction of a second before — for the first time — both formations executed a second C-Drive-assisted transition to hyperspace.

***

With *Theseus* in a protective hover over the Wek mining facility, only nine of her fifteen railgun mounts had been in a position to fire on Delta 3 when the Krayleck began their attack. Concentrating her fire in much the same manner as the distant *Hunters*, however, allowed the destroyer's much larger, fifty-kilogram penetrator rounds to quickly achieve the desired effect.

"It's working, Captain," Lieutenant Lau reported excitedly from Tactical 2. "We're causing significant hull damage on Delta 3 and we just completely took out her main ventral heat exchanger."

"Are the beam weapons having any effect?" Prescott asked without looking up from his Command console.

"In the area immediately surrounding the point of impact for the railguns, yes. Otherwise, their shields are holding."

"Concentrate your fire on the area around that heat exchanger, Lieutenant. A hull breach at that location would be a serious problem. In fact, it might even be enough to motivate them to pull back and allow us to shift our fire to Delta 2. Everyone keep in mind that our best chance of success right now is hitting singles, not home runs."

"Aye, sir," Lau replied.

"Can we fire a missile out of our vertical launch cells right now?"

"Negative, sir, I just checked," Schmidt replied. "We're too low for the ventrals — the missiles won't quite make the turn before impacting the surface — and there's just too much fire at the moment to risk a dorsal launch. There's a good chance we would end up with a detonation either on the way out of the cell or as soon as the missile cleared our shield radius."

"Sir," the young lieutenant at the Science and Engineering console chimed in, "the *Hunters* have launched four eight missiles in loiter mode for their attack on Foxtrot 1. We can vector them in on Delta 3, if required."

"That's a good option, let's do it. Pass control of those missiles over to Lieutenant Lau and order the *Hunters* to fire two four more of their own. That's still only half their loadout, and I suspect we need the missiles more than they do at the moment. Once you've done that, let Lieutenant Lee worry about the RPSVs. I want you closely monitoring the recovery of our shuttles and keeping us apprised of any hull damage."

"Aye, sir. The first shuttle is entering the flight deck as we speak. The second is in the maintenance hangar on the surface waiting for the airlock cycle to complete. We are taking some damage, but nothing serious yet."

"Thank you, Lieutenant," he said, pleased at her performance thus far under pressure while inwardly cringing at her use of the word "yet." "The second all of our shuttles are aboard and we're all buttoned up, sing out so we can get the hell out of here."

"Absolutely, sir," she replied with a nervous laugh as three ominous, metallic-sounding THUDS could be heard as well as felt through the soles of their feet.

***

Near Foxtrot 1, the two flights of twelve *Hunter* RPSVs immediately launched two additional HB-7c missiles each in response to Captain Prescott's order. As they prepared to resume their attack, their battle management AI was now in possession of enough data to execute what it believed (with a ninety-two percent probability) might be a decisive strike against the first Krayleck frigate. Once again taking advantage of the *Hunters'* newly acquired capability to execute multiple, consecutive hyperspace transitions, both formations engaged their C-Drives, then quickly flashed back into normal space and immediately opened fire with their railgun turrets — this time from above and to either side of their target.

The enemy frigate's AI, while unable to predict precisely where or when the Human ships would reappear, was nonetheless fully prepared for them to do so. Less than three hundred milliseconds after their arrival, it had locked on to the two lead ships in each formation and resumed its heavy point-defense weapons fire. This time, with slightly more time available to refine its firing solution, the warship scored the first kills of the battle, destroying the lead RPSV in each formation with energy weapons fire as the marauding Human ships once again neared their point of closest approach.

This minor Krayleck victory was short-lived, however, as the superior data handling and raw computing power at the disposal of the Human ships began to tell for the first time. During the first attack, the *Hunters'* sensor suites had performed a series of exquisitely detailed scans — scans precise enough to detect the fluctuations in power output associated with the frigate's use of its shields and point-defense weapons. These subtle cues, paired with the AI's detailed knowledge of TFC's own *Ingenuity*-class warships, allowed it to construct a real-time model of the target's power distribution capabilities, particularly with regard to how that power was being distributed to the ship's defensive systems.

As the remaining twenty-two RPSVs continued to hammer away at their target with concentrated fire from their railgun turrets, it was a relatively simple exercise in timing to predict the precise moment when the frigate's shields had been weakened enough to permit the passage of an HB-7c missile — or, in this case, eight of them.

***

"Foxtrot 1 destroyed!" Lieutenant Lee reported from Tactical 1, although he need not have done so with the brilliant flash of antimatter-induced fire blooming forth in one of the large windows displayed on the bridge view screen.

"Sir, the second shuttle is on the way up," the lieutenant at Science and Engineering reported. "The third, empty shuttle is right behind them and will come aboard at the same time. ETA: four zero seconds."

"Thank you, Lieutenant," Prescott replied. *And not a moment too soon*, he thought, as another rapid series of impacts sent vibrations throughout the whole of the ship.

Beneath the massive destroyer, the view from the approaching *Gurkha* assault shuttle was like nothing any Human had ever witnessed. With the destruction of Foxtrot 1, the remaining three Krayleck frigates were rapidly closing on the Wek station, already beginning to add their own railgun and beam weapons fire to that of the three destroyers. As a result, the barrage of incoming ordnance had become so intense that it was difficult for the shuttle's occupants to comprehend how the *Theseus* was managing to remain aloft.

Although Lieutenant Lau was doggedly maintaining *Theseus'* own attack against Delta 3, hundreds of blue-tinted streaks — punctuated by the occasional plasma torpedo — continually rained down on the ship from above. Upon reaching the outermost limit of the destroyer's gravitic shield, each individual energy bolt, kinetic energy round, or plasma torpedo was tracked and classified by the ship's AI before being "lensed" away from the hull by an intense gravitational disturbance placed directly in its path. In addition to the light associated with the incoming fire, each individual "shield intercept event" also produced a flash of light in the visible spectrum — often resulting in the deflected ordnance continuing on to strike the surface of Herrera a short distance away. The overall visual effect was both frightening and awe-inspiring at the same time, giving an impression not unlike a tremendous downpour striking an old-fashioned, domed umbrella before falling harmlessly to the ground around the feet of its wielder.

"Sir …" Lieutenant Commander Schmidt began before being interrupted by a low, menacing vibration that quickly grew in intensity to a dull roar as *Theseus'* environmental conditioning systems struggled to keep the noise at a manageable level. "I think their AI may have figured out our shield's low angle of incidence vulnerability!" he continued, now shouting to be heard by the captain barely a meter away. As if to reinforce the acting XO's assertion, a flurry of urgent-sounding warning tones issued from the Helm console, followed immediately by the voice of the chief engineer over the bridge intercom.

"Captain … Logan here!" he called, also yelling to make himself heard over the warning klaxons sounding throughout the ship's engineering spaces. "We just lost a critical number of grav emitters on our aft starboard wing section. The AI automatically engaged the auxiliary ventral thrusters to keep us from slamming into the surface, but I don't think we're going to be able to maintain altitude for long."

"Lieutenant, where's our shuttle?" Prescott bellowed.

"Ten seconds, sir!"

"Kip, I need ten seconds. Whatever you have to do, hold here for ten seconds while we recover our shuttle."

"I'll try, Captain, but we're going to have to set down. It's just a question of how hard we're going to hit at this point … yeah, actually, the AI just extended the landing struts and began a forced landing sequence. Gotta go, sir. Logan out."

On *Theseus'* bridge, the eerie red lighting associated with combat operations was immediately mixed with a blue hue to indicate the ship's imminent and wholly unintentional landing.

"Sir, I'm showing twelve green landing strut indications. Our gear is down and locked, and we are rigged for a surface landing. Touchdown in two four seconds," Fisher reported from the Helm console, adding a vaguely routine air to the rather surreal situation on the bridge.

"The shuttles are aboard, Captain, main aft airlock secure!"

"Helm, can we C-Jump?"

"Negative, Captain, not with the gear down *and* this close to the surface. Sorry sir, there just isn't enough time," Fisher reported plaintively.

"All hands, brace for impact!" Prescott announced. His voice was immediately repeated at maximum volume by the AI throughout the ship, but the sound of incoming ordnance slamming into the ship's armored hull had once again become so intense that very few of the crew were able to hear it.

"Tactical, what's the status of Delta 3's shield?"

"Still up, but substantially weakened where we've been hitting her, sir," Lieutenant Lau replied.

"Target that location with all two four of the missiles we borrowed from the *Hunters*."

"With pleasure, sir."

Three seconds later, TFS *Theseus*, still under extremely heavy fire from above, impacted the surface of the planet Herrera.

***

A mere fifty thousand kilometers aft of the three Krayleck destroyers, the starfield distorted momentarily, followed by ten simultaneous flashes of grayish-white light heralding the arrival of Admiral Kevin Patterson's task force. Centered on the unmistakable forms of four *Navajo*-class cruisers — *Cossack, Shoshone, Chickasaw,* and the admiral's flagship, TFS *Navajo* herself — the Terran line of battle wasted no time opening fire. Within seconds of their arrival, eight massive four-hundred-and-twenty-five-kilogram projectiles from the cruisers' main railgun batteries slammed into the sterns of all three Krayleck destroyers, immediately collapsing their aft shields and silencing their relentless attack on the severely wounded *Theseus*.

The remaining cruiser, TFS *Shoshone*, its main batteries also pre-aimed before its arrival at Herrera, quickly added to the destruction of the Krayleck task force by scoring four hits each on two of the remaining three frigates. Even with fully functioning barrier shields, the relatively small warships were simply not equipped to absorb the nearly nine hundred petajoules of energy delivered by each of the cruiser's huge shells traveling at ten percent c. Both of the frigates suffered instantaneous and complete structural failure, breaking briefly into several large pieces before both containment units within each of the two ships' reactors failed within seconds of one another. With *Shoshone's* ever-present AI watching impassively, the remains of both ships exploded in brilliant flashes of white light as several kilograms of antimatter came into contact with the sides of what had previously been Pelaran-designed reactor vessels.

Although Delta 3 had suffered tremendous damage from *Theseus'* railgun fire as well as main battery hits from the *Navajo*, she was somehow still generating sufficient power to engage her hyperdrive. Her captain — the same Krayleck officer who had earlier spoken to both Gara and Prescott — delayed long enough to order a general retreat for the surviving ships in his task force, then gave the order for his own ship to depart. Unfortunately for the three hundred and twenty-one members of his ship's crew, his momentary delay would prove fatal.

After completing a sweeping turn to align their flight paths with their new target, the twenty-four HB-7c missiles vectored in by the *Theseus* accelerated to optimum attack velocity and executed their C-Jumps. As the crews of every Fleet vessel in the area watched, the missiles transitioned back into normal space, penetrated the destroyer's already weakened shields, and detonated in such rapid succession that their impacts gave the impression of a single, massive explosion. Once the initial blinding flash and numerous secondary explosions had receded, what remained no longer bore any resemblance to a *Theseus*-class destroyer. Although the sturdy Krayleck warship remained more or less in a single piece, a huge section of her dorsal hull was simply gone. In its place was a gaping wound reminiscent of one of the huge impact craters that pockmarked the surface of the nearby planet Herrera. Exposing nearly half the ship's length to the vacuum of space, the explosion had penetrated the hull to such a depth that it had very nearly penetrated through to the opposite side.

Of the three remaining Krayleck warships, only one — the sole remaining "KE" version of an *Ingenuity*-class frigate — was able to heed the order to retreat and successfully transition to hyperspace.

Having monitored the entire engagement from Damara — including the unprovoked attacks both inside the Herrera Mining Facility and in space — Admiral Patterson had already made the decision that no quarter would be offered the Krayleck ships. With his four cruisers firing a total of thirty-two main battery shells roughly once every seven seconds, the remaining two enemy destroyers were reduced to lifeless hulks in short order.

When the admiral at last gave the order to cease fire, the entire engagement since his arrival at Herrera had lasted just fifty-three seconds. Perhaps even more telling was the fact that his attack had been executed with such violence and speed that not a single enemy weapon had been fired in the direction of any ship in his task force.

Chapter 16

TFS Navajo, Herrera Mining Facility
(Combat Information Center - 87.2 light years from Damara)

"Please ask Captain Davis to begin coordinating rescue operations for the *Theseus*," Admiral Patterson said wearily as he leaned with both hands against the side of the holo table.

"Aye, sir, right away," the newly minted Lieutenant Katy Fletcher replied from her nearby Communications console.

In spite of the never-ending series of items requiring his attention, the quick conclusion of the battle for Herrera left the CNO feeling drained and keenly aware that he was nearing his mental and physical limits. *Have I even been back to my quarters since we departed Yucca?* he thought distractedly. *Was that yesterday, or the day before*, he wondered, then quickly dismissed the line of thought as unproductive and clearly not getting him any closer to the shower, food, and rack time he so desperately needed.

"When he's able to do so safely, I'd like to speak with Captain Prescott," he continued.

"Their comm officer just sent the same message for you, sir. Stand by one."

Shortly thereafter, Patterson heard the customary chime indicating that he had an incoming vidcon standing by.

"View screen four, Admiral," Fletcher said, directing his attention to one of the screens mounted on the bulkhead to his right.

"Thank you, Lieutenant," he said with a wan smile as an equally exhausted-looking Tom Prescott appeared on the view screen. "Good morning, Captain," he greeted. "What can we do to help you?"

"Good morning to you, sir," Prescott replied with a weary smile of his own. "All things considered, it could be a lot worse, Admiral. I'm sure you saw that we lost three Marines in the mining facility. We also had three others injured, but Doctor Chen's first impression was that all three will be fine. Otherwise, we just had some minor injuries during the forced landing … that's it."

Patterson simply nodded in response. No officer ever felt comfortable with the idea of an "acceptable" number of casualties, but both men were also well-aware of the magnitude of their victory as well as the mass casualties that had been inflicted upon the Krayleck forces. "How's your ship?" he asked without further comment.

"The hull's a mess … again, but we didn't end up with a single breach in spite of the beating we took. We are going to need to do some EVA work to replace a number of grav emitters, however. Even with Herrera's relatively weak gravity well, we don't currently have enough lift to break orbit. We just lost too many emitters in too small of an area."

"That shouldn't be too big of a problem, and we can get you some additional manpower to get it done quickly."

"Commander Logan is suiting up as we speak, and I'm sure he would welcome the help."

"And your hyperdrive?"

"Fully functional, sir. As soon as we can get her off this rock, we can be on our way. I assume you'll want us to head back to Yucca."

"At the moment, I'll say yes, since that's where I was planning to send you before all this happened. But we'll have to do some checking to see which shipyard can accommodate the *Theseus* first. With all the new construction underway at the moment, she may have to wait her turn for a while."

"Sir," Prescott said with a chuckle, "I don't think there's a single member of this crew who would mind a little downtime."

"That's understandable, and we may well be able to authorize some extended leave for most of your crew," Patterson replied, raising his eyebrows and peering at Prescott over his glasses. "You and your senior staff, on the other hand, have other important work to do. As I alluded to in our earlier conversation, the inquiry into your actions at Damara will take you 'off the grid' so to speak for a couple of weeks. Under the circumstances, we can't afford to waste this opportunity."

"And what circumstances are those, sir?"

"I'll have your orders for you by the time you've completed your repairs," the old admiral replied cryptically. "I'll give you a general overview of what I have in mind, but you'll be meeting up with Admiral White in a couple of days. She'll be able to fill you in on all the details and answer whatever questions you may have. Be sure all of you get some rest between now and then — and, yes, I know how ridiculous that sounds, but I'm telling you to make it a priority. You and your people have been through the wringer, Tom, but I need you back to one hundred percent before you see Admiral White."

"Aye, sir. By the way, as you can imagine, I have never been happier to see anyone in my life than I was when you arrived, but, frankly, I wasn't expecting you. Did the Leadership Council have a change of heart?"

"Humph," the older man replied, his fatigue prompting him to express his personal opinion more readily than usual, "no, the political battle lines seem to have been drawn on the subject of our intention to remain some sort of 'innocent bystander,' if possible. As you have repeatedly experienced firsthand, that argument is much easier to make within the comfort and safety of the Council meeting chamber than it is out here."

"Sir, I regret if I inadvertently placed you in a position where you felt obliged to defy the orders of the Leadership Council. I will be more than happy to take responsibility for doing so, in addition to the situation at Damara."

"Nonsense," Patterson said flatly. "You didn't do anything either here or at Damara other than exactly what your orders and professional obligation required of you. In both cases, you executed your duties conscientiously and professionally, which is all we can ask of any officer. As to defying the Council, it's perfectly reasonable for them to order us to avoid confrontations with enemy forces and limit how forcefully we respond in order to avoid the appearance of escalating a conflict. That is a political, not a military decision, and one that we are duty bound to carry out.

What they cannot lawfully do, however, is issue an order that prevents us from coming to the assistance of one of our own ships that has come under attack or is otherwise in need of assistance. Such an order would be neither reasonable, legal, or in keeping with the traditions of our world's military services. I sincerely hope that's not what they intended, but if it is, to hell with them. Mrs. Patterson says it's high time I retired anyway."

"Well," Prescott laughed, a little taken aback by the typically reserved admiral's candor, "I couldn't agree more, sir. In any event, thank you for coming when you did. I don't think we would have held out much longer. Regardless of what the Council had in mind, I suppose they'll be forced to come to grips with the implications of what happened here. Trying to stay neutral is all well and good, but I suspect the Krayleck will think twice about confronting us in this region anytime soon."

"Hah," Patterson laughed, "they won't have much choice in the matter since we just decimated nearly half of their forces within a month's flight time of here. I don't know about you, son, but I've been on both sides of one-sided battles. All things considered, I much prefer to be on the side that issues the shellacking rather than the side that receives one. If they head this way again, we'll be ready and waiting when they arrive."

Dassault Spacecraft Final Assembly Facility
(3 days later - Bordeaux - Mérignac Spaceport, Bordeaux, France)

Vice Admiral Tonya White stood atop a large yellow set of portable maintenance stairs, stretching out her arm to run her fingertips along the ventral fuselage of what would soon become Terran Fleet Command's newest operational spacecraft. Although her sleek, predatory lines were reminiscent of an F-373 *Reaper* — examples of which were being manufactured just a few hundred meters from where she now stood — this ship was far larger than any fighter. Like Fleet's capital ships, she was equipped with a bridge (albeit a somewhat smaller one) with space for five crewmembers as well as engineering and mission-related spaces located aft that brought the ship's regular complement to ninety-nine. But unlike TFC's other ships, which, in spite of the organization's ostensible mission, were primarily equipped for combat operations, this vessel had been envisioned to take on a variety of other roles. In fact, a "civilian" version of the same vessel was also being manufactured nearby for use in long-range exploration and colonization support. In keeping with this concept of operational flexibility, both vessels had been assigned the entirely new designation of "MMSV," for Multi-Mission Space Vehicle. Other than the name, however, TFS *Fugitive* had little in common with her civilian counterpart, and everyone who laid eyes on her knew immediately that nothing quite like her had ever been constructed before.

"You seem uncharacteristically quiet, Admiral White. She is a beautiful ship, no?" Commander Troy Crispin called up to her nervously, unable to cope with the Chief of Naval Intelligence's typically reserved demeanor any longer. "I hope you are pleased with what you see."

"She's beautiful, Commander Crispin. How did yesterday's max range test go?"

"Just under five hundred light years, precisely as expected," he said proudly.

"Congratulations to you and your team. It's a truly staggering achievement."

"Thank you, Madame. She has roughly five times the power generation and handling capability per metric ton of any other Fleet vessel in service. We are very pleased with her performance thus far."

"As well you should be," she said offhandedly while continuing her close examination of the ship's matte black hull. "I don't know exactly what I was expecting, but the pictures I saw certainly did not do her justice. I've been briefed on the ship's stealth characteristics, of course, but I didn't expect the surface of her hull to look quite like this. It's not nearly as … smooth as I would have expected."

Crispin glanced up at the ship with an expression of open admiration, perhaps bordering on reverence, gracing his rather animated face. "Ah, yes, Madame, she is designed to go places and do things that none of our other ships can — and we sincerely hope no one else's ships can either. We do not generally use the term 'stealth' when referring to the various low-observable technologies employed in her design, but the material comprising the outermost layer of her hull is a key component of the most advanced radiation-management system ever produced. The texture you see is a series of closed cells. When in operation, each individual cell contains a form of matter called a Bose-Einstein condensate."

"I have a little familiarity with the technology," she replied as she made her way back down to floor level.

"My doctoral thesis involved a specific application for superfluidity in the design of improved reactor vessel containment units."

"I *see*," he replied, with a look of surprise and admiration on his face. "Then you almost certainly know more about the specifics of how the system works than I. Suffice it to say that the ship's AI continuously adjusts the temperature and various other properties of the material within the cells in order to actively manage its thermal, radar, acoustic, and even visual signatures. Not only can it match the surface temperature of the hull to the environment in which the ship is operating, but it can also slow, redirect, or even stop most forms of radiation that strike its surface. Although I always hesitate to use the term, under the right circumstances, the system can render the ship all but invisible … at least to the types of sensors with which we are currently familiar."

"Forgive me for sounding skeptical, Commander, but isn't the concept of 'stealth,' or 'LO,' or whatever we would like to call it, largely unworkable in space? The background temperature you refer to is just a couple of kelvins above absolute zero, right? Everything we do out there generates substantial heat that is all too easy to detect … even over vast distances."

"That is certainly true, Admiral … for most ships, that is … particularly those that use more traditional means of providing thrust by expelling propellant of some sort via externally mounted engine nozzles. Our ships' Cannae thrusters also produce some heat, but it is a small amount by comparison. And since our engines' reaction chambers are mounted inside the ship's hull, we can utilize other means to sequester this energy and prevent it from being radiated away into space."

"So, rather than the heat exchangers our warships typically use —"

"That is correct, here we simply 'capture' our excess thermal energy internally. Pardon me, Admiral," he chuckled, stopping himself in mid-explanation, "it is foolish of me to characterize thermal sequestration as a simple process when it is, in fact, complex in the extreme. In spite of our best efforts to the contrary, I can assure you that the laws of thermodynamics are still very much in force. Although these energy management techniques do work quite well at minimizing the ship's thermal signature for a short time, ultimately, they are nothing more than a temporary solution. After a couple of hours — perhaps less, depending largely on the vessel's power consumption during this period — the sequestered heat energy must be allowed to discharge."

"Commander Crispin," a Marine guard in full combat armor called as he materialized like a wraith from the darkness surrounding the well-lit ship, "your other guests are here, sir."

"Excellent, please show them in, Sergeant," he replied before turning back to Admiral White. "I suppose that will be the first of her crew. Let us hope that she fares better in their care than the previous vessels they have been assigned," he added with a lopsided grin.

"Merely an occupational hazard, Commander, I assure you," she replied, choosing to see the humor in the officer's remark rather than feeling insulted on behalf of Captain Prescott and crew. "Besides, they've only had two other ships, and both are still operational in spite of having seen combat on a number of occasions. I wish we could say the same for all of our captains and crews."

"My apologies, Admiral, I meant no disrespect. In my defense, however, I must tell you that I have become surprisingly attached to this ship after all of the time I have spent working in her development program."

"I know exactly what you mean, and no apologies are necessary," White said with a casual wave of her hand. "Now," she said, nodding to the sound of approaching footsteps behind him, "Please allow me to introduce Commander Sally Reynolds and Captain —"

"Tom *Prescott*," Crispin said, finishing the admiral's sentence in a tone that conveyed something approaching a sense of awe. "It is truly an honor to meet you both," he said, shaking their hands vigorously.

"Did the two of you have any problems getting in here?" White asked.

Dassault had competed for nearly a decade (placing itself at tremendous financial risk) to ultimately become the first civilian company to produce a military spacecraft for Terran Fleet Command. While much of the corporation's manufacturing facility was located just off the northeastern end of Bordeaux-Mérignac's runway zero five, the ultra-secure building in which the four officers now stood was located nearly two hundred meters below ground. And, in spite of being located in France's eighth largest city, security here was in many ways just as formidable as that of TFC's three primary shipyards.

"It took us a while, but we managed just fine," Prescott said, finally freeing himself from Crispin's vice-like grip and offering his hand to Admiral White.

"Well, your timing couldn't be better. Commander Crispin here was just beginning to show me around your new command."

"We appreciate any specific insights you can give us," Prescott said. "Frankly, I think all of our heads are still swimming a bit from this sudden change, but we're apparently the only crew available for this mission ... whatever that may be," he added, smiling politely at Admiral White.

"We'll get to that shortly, Captain. I assure you that you're both the only crew available and the best crew available. No one has any flight time to speak of in an MMSV, so type experience isn't really a factor, and your team has the added advantage of having switched ships once before."

"I'm sure we'll be fine, ma'am," Reynolds said. "After having gone through the specs, however, I'm interested in hearing Commander Crispin's perspective on what makes her different from our first ship. My first impression is that she's largely a cross between an *Ingenuity*-class frigate and one of our *Reaper* fighters."

Crispin cast a fleeting glance at the ship, frowned briefly, then looked back at Commander Reynolds wearing a pained expression she assumed would have been much the same if she had referred to his newborn child as a cross between a snapping turtle and a naked mole rat. "Please, Commander," he said, softening his expression and motioning her towards the ship's bow, "come this way and I will show you how very much more she is than that."

"Thank you, I'd love to," she said pleasantly, walking briskly forward while trying to think of a way she could undo her apparently grievous, but unintentional faux pas. "For a vessel that's technically not considered a warship, it seems like she's pretty heavily armed. I understand she carries all of her weapons internally."

"That is correct. In this way, at least, she does share quite a few design features with our fighters … and, I suppose, with our frigates as well," he said, smiling now as he chided himself for feeling the need to defend his team's work as if the ship itself were a member of his own family. "Although she retains the capability to carry externally mounted weapons and other stores, all of her primary armaments are concealed during normal operations … with the exception of this one, that is," he said, nodding to a single, rather inconspicuous muzzle tucked into a recessed area just beneath the ship's bow.

"*That's* the fire lance?" Reynolds asked, a bit underwhelmed by the weapon's appearance after the buildup it had received in the ship's "Dash 1" flight manual.

"One of the many innovations in her design, yes. The engineers referred to it as the 'lance de feu' during the weapon's development program. Like most things, the name loses something in the translation to English, don't you think?" Crispin said with a wink.

"It fires a standard fifty-kilogram kinetic energy penetrator round?" Prescott asked.

"Indeed, it does, Captain. And while its rate of fire is much lower than that of her other four railgun turrets, this weapon is capable of varying its muzzle velocity from a mere five kilometers per second up to a maximum of just over one-third c. Furthermore, even when firing its rounds at maximum velocity, you should see rates of fire approaching twenty rounds per —"

"I'm sorry, Commander, but did you just say 'one-third c?'" Reynolds interrupted.

"Yes, of course, Commander Reynolds. Was this information not apparent in the materials we provided?"

"Well, if it was, I either missed it completely or assumed it was a typo. That's over three times the muzzle velocity of any of the railgun systems I've ever seen. This thing must have as much firepower as one of the *Navajo*-class cruiser's main guns."

"Quite a good bit more," Crispin said in a triumphant tone, obviously enjoying his guests' increasing level of appreciation for the ship they were about to receive. "Just over forty-four percent more, in fact. Now if we consider that the *Navajo* has eight main guns, each one firing eight of her much larger rounds per minute, they still have roughly double the *Fugitive's* overall raw firepower. Our cruisers, of course, also have the advantage of being able to independently target their four batteries without the need for aligning the ship itself. But I hope we can all agree that this still represents quite an accomplishment for a ship that is technically small enough to be carried inside the *Navajo's* hangar deck."

"Without question," Prescott said. "Do you expect we'll begin seeing this design retrofitted aboard our existing cruisers going forward?"

"We hope that will be the case, yes. I will be the first to admit, however, that this weapon's design approaches what we consider the theoretical performance limit for our current railgun design. It is, I think you would say, 'state of the art,' or, uh, 'cutting edge,' technology at this point."

"He means unreliable," Reynolds mumbled, turning her head so that only Prescott could hear.

"Did you have a question, Commander Reynolds?" Crispin asked.

"Uh, yes, can you show us how the standard railgun turrets deploy?" she asked, noticing the look of barely restrained mirth on Admiral White's face.

"Of course," he replied, entering a quick series of commands on his tablet.

With a low, satisfying hum of powerful electric motors coupled with the hiss of compressed air, the ship's railguns deployed from behind sliding panels that had been all but indistinguishable from the rest of the hull beforehand.

"As you can see," Crispin continued, leading the small group around the ship's port side as they worked their way aft, "she carries both fore and aft fully articulated railgun turrets on both her dorsal and ventral surfaces along with a total of ten beam emitters. Also, in keeping with the design of our larger vessels, she has full three-hundred-and-sixty-degree point-defense weapons coverage."

"No plasma torpedoes or vertical launch cells?" Prescott asked.

"No plasma torpedoes, sir. The data on their combat effectiveness has been less impressive overall than our railguns, so in the *Fugitive*, her main railgun replaces plasma torpedo tubes. She also has no vertical missile launch cells. With internal space on the flight/cargo deck at such a premium, the engineers simply did not have a suitable location for them. Instead, she has a total of ten horizontal weapons bays, each of which can accommodate three HB-7c C-Drive-equipped missiles."

"That'll do, but we were previously launching comm beacons via the plasma torpedo tubes. How will that be accomplished with this design?"

"Fortunately, communications beacons continue to grow smaller with each successive version, and since their deployment has always been seen as one of the MMSV's primary missions, she has dedicated launch tubes mounted amidships to both port and starboard. Each launcher holds five beacons in its magazine, and can be reloaded while the ship is underway."

"Excellent. It sounds like your team has done a great job covering all the bases."

"Ah, but we have barely scratched the surface of what she can do, Captain. There is, however, one other thing that I neglected to mention regarding the so-called 'fire lance.' When the two of you arrived, Admiral White and I were discussing the ship's low-observable characteristics. While I believe those systems will be of great benefit, please keep in mind that, once you fire the main weapon, you must assume that your position is fully compromised. The AI will assist you in determining how effectively the radiation-management system is functioning at any given time, but there is no hiding the thermal signature of such a large weapon mounted in this fashion. The same is, of course, true for the ship's railgun turrets and beam weapons anytime they are deployed outside the hull."

"And how long does that typically last — for the fire lance, that is?"

"Count on at least five minutes for the weapon's components to be cooled back to ambient temperature."

"Understood, thank you."

"By the way," Admiral White spoke up once again, "I don't believe I have heard anyone mention the origin of the name 'Fugitive.'"

"The French members of the design team started referring to her as 'Le Fugitif' early on. I believe the original conversation was something to the effect that she was, in fact, the greatest 'getaway vehicle' ever devised. In any event, the name stuck with the ship throughout the development program. Before her christening, there were some concerns that it might have a slightly ... negative connotation. We considered changing it, but none of the other proposed names were quite the thing."

"And given that most of the missions we have envisioned for the ship are of a covert nature ..."

"Yes, Madame, it just seemed like a reasonably good fit. Now," Crispin said, gesturing for the group to proceed up the ship's surprisingly large aft cargo ramp, "as you can see, her cargo/flight deck is quite spacious for her size, but unfortunately does not have sufficient room for a large airlock and aft flight apron of the type used aboard Fleet's warships."

"So, in order to conduct flight ops, the hangar bay must remain open to space," Reynolds said.

"Not necessarily, but that depends largely on the mission," he replied. "She is equipped with a single elevator large enough to launch a single RPSV or shuttle without depressurizing the cargo area, but if your mission dictates that you must accommodate larger spacecraft …"

Although neither Prescott nor Reynolds had been given any details on the nature of the mission they were expected to undertake, there had been something about the manner in which Crispin had ended his last sentence that prompted Reynolds to more carefully examine the configuration of the ship's hangar deck. The feature that immediately caught her eye as being strangely out of place was a device mounted near the forward end of the bay that appeared to be a large docking collar of some sort. The circular device was suspended roughly eight meters above the floor via a framework composed of the same heavy structural beams used in the construction of the ship itself. For whatever reason, the image it immediately brought to mind was one she had recently seen of an enormous zeppelin attached to a mooring tower atop the Empire State Building circa 1930. The photo itself was a clever fake, but still accurately depicted the manner in which the huge, cylindrical airships were typically attached to such towers.

The *cylindrical* ships, she thought once again, shifting her gaze back to the aft cargo ramp, which she now noticed had a mounting point for a similar fitting that would end up at approximately the same height above the deck once the door was closed.

"Admiral, are we going to …" she began, then checked herself, realizing that — regardless of whether or not her hunch was correct — this was neither the time nor the place to discuss such things, particularly before she had even been briefed. In response, the Chief of Naval Intelligence raised her eyebrows in a surprised, thoughtful expression, instantly confirming that what Reynolds hoped was merely wild speculation on her part was dead on target.

"Oh, this sounds *astonishingly* … ill-advised to me," Reynolds said under her breath, shaking her head in disbelief.

"I should probably know better than to ask what you two ladies are referring to, but what am I missing here?" Prescott asked.

TFS Fugitive, Earth-Sun Lagrange Point 2
$(1.5 \times 10^6$ km from Earth)

Ill-advised or no, just over forty-eight hours later, Commander Sally Reynolds stood on the aft cargo ramp of her new ship staring at the approaching cylindrical form of the Guardian spacecraft. Even at a distance of only a thousand meters, the Pelaran ship had seemed impossibly large for the *Fugitive's* cargo bay. Now, with only a few meters remaining, it almost looked as if the MMSV had been purpose-built with this particular mission in mind. As the GCS crossed the line of demarcation between the cargo door and the interior of the ship itself, there was barely one meter of clearance both above and below their "guest."

"Permission to come aboard, Commander?" the Guardian's familiar voice asked over 'GCS-comm,' the standard, encrypted channel now reserved exclusively for full-time, secure communications between itself and TFC.

"Permission granted. Welcome aboard," she replied with about the same level of enthusiasm she might have shown had she been accepting delivery of a cargo container brimming with horse manure.

"Crosshairs aligned and stable," the Guardian reported, continuing the docking process using precisely the same procedures still used by Fleet for a manual docking of two dissimilar spacecraft. "Range: one zero meters, range rate: decimal one one."

"*Fugitive* copies."

After another long pause, during which it truly looked to Commander Reynolds as if nothing at all was happening, the GCS finally concluded its docking maneuver. Quite possibly the most dangerous spacecraft ever encountered by Humanity had taken up temporary residence within the already cramped confines of her ship's hangar deck.

"Contact and capture … docking confirmed … mechanical capture confirmed," it announced.

"*Fugitive* copies, docking confirmed," she repeated.

"Flight deck secured. Rapid pressurization cycle underway. Gravitic field restoration will begin in two zero seconds," the ship's AI announced shortly thereafter, having already closed and sealed the aft cargo door as several technicians in EVA suits worked to secure the Guardian's aft docking collar.

While waiting for the hangar deck to return to normal operations, Reynolds took advantage of the momentary delay to take a closer look at the fifty-meter-long alien ship that had so dramatically changed the course of Human history. The texture and even the color of its surface, she observed, were not unlike that of Fleet's vessels. She also immediately noticed a number of other prominent features — beam emitter apertures, comm arrays, and the like — all with a purpose that was easy enough to identify.

"You're the first representative of your species to get this close, Commander Reynolds. If you see something that interests you, I'll be more than happy to answer any questions that come to mind."

"Thank you," she replied, struggling to shrug off the overwhelmingly creepy feeling that seemed to always accompany a conversation with the Guardian spacecraft. "You know, honestly — and I hope you won't be insulted by this — what's so striking to me standing here next to you is that you truly are just a machine after all. I, of course, have no way of understanding how you perceive things compared to a Human, but I wonder if you have any notion of the impact your presence has had on every single member of our species."

"I'm not insulted at all, and it's a fair question to ask me. But you might also consider that it's a fair question to ask other Human beings as well. In my opinion, every sentient creature perceives reality in a manner that is altogether unique. To answer your question from my point of view, for example, I would say yes, I do understand the impact of my presence — and I hope *you* won't be insulted when I say that I believe I understand it far better than you do. My perspective obviously differs fundamentally from yours, but I will tell you that the Pelarans have made this particular question a central focus of the entire cultivation program. Clearly, there are tremendous moral implications surrounding the choice to interfere with a civilization's 'natural' development process. While I'm sure you and I could spend weeks debating the finer points of this subject, the Pelarans ultimately decided that the entire question was based on a false premise."

As gravity was restored to the flight deck, the structural supports now beginning to bear the weight of the Guardian spacecraft creaked and moaned in a manner reminiscent of the flexing timbers of an ancient sailing vessel. Reynolds glanced up with a passing thought of how she might best avoid being crushed if they were to fail, although she knew that such a calamity was unlikely in the extreme.

"What do you mean?" she continued. "Are you saying they decided there is essentially no such thing as a civilization developing 'naturally?'"

"That's exactly what I mean. The problem with the argument is that there is no reasonable way to define such a thing. For example, is it 'natural' for a civilization to remain isolated for millions of years, only to eventually be invaded and slaughtered by its distant, but dramatically more advanced neighbors? Perhaps that same civilization ends up being destroyed by a natural disaster that would have been easily preventable if they had developed the appropriate technology to deal with the problem. Is that situation somehow preferable to a well-managed technological development program provided by another civilization? Furthermore, if we define a species' 'natural development process' as one requiring zero contact with other civilizations, that brings up an entirely different set of ethical dilemmas regarding assistance that could or should have been provided — not to mention the fact that it's unrealistic in the vast majority of cases anyway."

"So, the Pelarans have answered these fundamental questions by choosing to ignore them?" she asked with a hint of cynicism.

"It is in no way unethical to come to the realization that some questions are simply irrelevant … or at least unanswerable from a practical standpoint. Rather than become paralyzed by endless debate, the Pelarans decided early on that holding themselves to a generally accepted set of ethical standards made more sense than trying to apply a grand principle of 'non-interference.' Besides, I believe most of us would agree that self-defense is also something of a moral obligation that a civilization owes to itself. The cultivation program, although it certainly does have a tremendous impact on the worlds chosen as Regional Partners, also provides for both their defense and the defense of the Alliance itself."

"Pressurization restored. Gravitic field restored. Resuming normal flight deck operations," the AI announced.

"Finally," Reynolds said, immediately removing and powering down her helmet. Although she had never been particularly claustrophobic, she felt as if she had spent more than enough time in her EVA combat armor over the past week and was anxious to return it to her equipment locker.

"It was nice to speak with you again, Commander Reynolds," the Guardian continued. "I assume we'll be doing some sort of mission briefing before we depart?"

Reynolds looked down in confusion, realizing that the sound she was hearing was no longer coming from inside her helmet.

"Yes, we have a mission briefing scheduled for 1600 UTC. I believe most of us will be in the captain's ready room, but we will conference you in. By the way, how are you communicating —"

"What … so you have no problem with the fact that I'm equipped with an array of sixteen pulsed antihydrogen beam weapons, but a simple electrostatic loudspeaker is just too much of a stretch for your imagination?" the GCS asked in a playful tone.

Reynolds laughed at the jab in spite of herself. There was no doubt that the Guardian was possessed of a rather pompous disposition at times, but it could also come off as friendly … interesting … perhaps even vaguely entertaining on occasion.

"I guess you got me there. I'll see you at the briefing," she said, turning in the direction of the equipment storage area. "By the way," she called back over her shoulder, "stay right there and for God's sake don't touch anything."

Chapter 17

"Alright," Prescott said, "under the circumstances, I'm going to indulge all of us with a few moments to express our collective misgivings about what we've been asked to do. After that, we're all going to suck it up and get the job done. So, let's hear it, folks … what's on your mind?"

Commanders Reynolds and Logan, along with the entire bridge crew — less Lieutenant Commander Schmidt, who had been left behind at Yucca Mountain to oversee *Theseus'* latest round of repairs — had managed to crowd themselves into the captain's small ready room. Before anyone had spoken a word, it was clear that the entire group had a general air of restless anxiety that would never do at the outset of such a challenging mission.

"Go on," Reynolds prodded, "you may not ever hear an invitation like that again from either of us, so this is your one and only opportunity if you've got something you need to get off your chest."

"What the heck, I'll start," Logan began. "I have two threads that are bothering me, and I'll hazard a guess that they're the same two things everyone else in the room is thinking about. The first is a concern about placing such a huge bet on this largely untested — hell, you might as well say experimental — ship. The second is a similar concern over working with the Guardian in this manner. According to the Fleet Intelligence Estimate that

Admiral White prepared specifically for this mission, good old GORT back there was saying that he had no intention of telling us where any of the Pelaran Alliance member worlds were located as recently as last week. So now that we've discovered where one of them is for ourselves, we're supposed to believe that he's perfectly okay with helping us fly out there and commit grand theft GCS?"

Although there were chuckles around the small conference table, several heads nodded amid murmurs of agreement with Commander Logan's points.

"I think that sums it up, sir," Lieutenant Lee chimed in. "How do we know we can trust him, uh, it?"

"Anything else, or does that about cover it?" Prescott asked, scanning the general looks of concern around the room.

"I believe so, Captain," Lieutenant Dubashi replied. "The whole thing just seems a little over the top, does it not?"

"It is perhaps a little on the ambitious side, I'll give you that," Prescott said, pausing to offer a conciliatory smile. "Okay, everyone, I realize that I'm getting to be kind of an old fart, so I've probably also started to get a little jaded with regard to questions like these, but here's how I look at it. As far as the *Fugitive* goes, I don't see her as any more 'experimental' than either *Ingenuity* or *Theseus* were when we went aboard them."

Commander Logan opened his mouth to speak, but Prescott immediately held up his hand in anticipation of what he would likely say.

"Before I get myself into a technical argument with the Cheng that I can't possibly win, I do realize that there are a few systems — particularly power management, which is obviously a major concern ... and the main gun, for that matter — that are still a little iffy. But the good news is that she was subjected to three months' worth of testing before we got our hands on her, and we've worked her up pretty aggressively ourselves over the past couple of days. So far, at least, everything seems fine." Prescott paused, rapping his knuckles against the top of the table superstitiously as he did so. "As for the Guardian/GORT/Griffin, I honestly don't think there is any point whatsoever in our speculating about its motives. To my knowledge, we have never caught it in an outright lie. Granted, it's fully capable of withholding information or putting its own brand of 'spin' on things, but I also don't think it generally has any *motive* for lying to us. If it wanted to destroy us, it could have done so at any point during the past five hundred odd years. In fact, Science and Engineering still does not believe that the combined might of our entire fleet would be capable of taking it out — although our Wek friends are supposedly still working on developing the capability to do so."

"But why *this specific mission*, Captain?" Logan pressed. "I understand that the Krayleck attacked us, and based on the beat down we gave them, I'd be all for pressing a punitive attack deep into their territory while we have such an obvious advantage. Like Dubashi said, though, going after their Guardian seems a little ... well ... *nuts*."

"Right, yes, I get it, and we've obviously got a lot riding on our Guardian's ability to do what it says it can do, but I'm afraid I don't have a better answer for you than the one I already gave. I don't see any possible motive as to why the Guardian would propose to lead us into Krayleck space on a suicide mission when it could easily achieve the same result for itself. So, unless anyone has something else to add, I think it's appropriate at this point to bring the Guardian into our conversation. Our orders don't have much in the way of specifics regarding the 'why' behind this mission, but we do know that the Guardian itself is the one who proposed it to Admiral Sexton after being consulted about our confrontation with the Krayleck. So, under the circumstances, I don't see any harm in our asking for a few additional details. Anything else before I bring it in?"

Prescott's question was met with utter silence in the room, and he couldn't help but notice that the dire looks gracing the faces of his bridge crew did not seem to be improving. "Jeez, folks, relax and lighten up a bit, would you? You're all acting like we're being led to the gallows as we speak. There's more than a fair degree of uncertainty in this mission, sure, but that's nothing new for this crew. One thing I can tell you with *absolute* certainty, however, is that a defeatist attitude often has a tendency to be self-fulfilling. Besides, if it makes you feel any better, let me remind you that our orders are to avoid confrontation with Krayleck forces, and you have to admit that the *Fugitive* is exactly the right ship to pull that off."

With that, Prescott made two quick keystrokes on his tablet, immediately replacing Terran Fleet Command's official service seal with the smiling Human avatar of the Pelaran Guardian on the room's view screen. As usual for conversations of an operational nature, it was dressed in one of the black flight suits previously worn only by TFC pilots. Now that the uniform had become the standard aboard fleet vessels, the Guardian's appearance struck Prescott as even more out of place — almost as if it were trying just a little too hard to fit in.

"Good afternoon, *fugitives*," he said in his typically smarmy tone, immediately resulting in barely concealed moans of displeasure throughout the room.

"Good afternoon," Prescott replied flatly. "I appreciate your joining us and will endeavor to keep this meeting as short as possible. We will, of course, be making final preparations for tomorrow's 0800 UTC departure throughout the remainder of this evening, but I wanted to give you an opportunity to ask any questions you have of us. We would also like to ask that you clarify a few details."

"Thank you, Captain Prescott. Our mission seems relatively straightforward to me, and I do not anticipate that you and your excellent crew will have any difficulty in completing it successfully. I have no questions for you at the moment, but will do my best to answer any that you have for me."

"Very good. It is our understanding that you will provide precise coordinates for the Krayleck Guardian before our final C-Jump in system, correct?"

"Yes, Captain. I can do so from a full ten light years away. Please note that, for the Guardian spacecraft only, I am equipped with a type of transponder that will allow me to determine its position regardless of whether or not it is traveling in hyperspace," he said with a confident smile. "I recommend that we pause momentarily at a distance of approximately five light years so that I can conduct my scans before we make our final approach. Unless we happen to be unfortunate enough to arrive at a time when the Krayleck GCS is not in the immediate vicinity of the planet Legara, I should be able to confirm its location relatively quickly. At that time, I will also provide information regarding any other vessels traveling in hyperspace within ten light years of our position. Unfortunately, with the exception of the Guardian itself, I will not be able to detect ships that are currently located in normal space … not from such a long range, that is."

"So then," Prescott said, doing his best to move the conversation along as quickly as possible, "after our final C-Jump, as long as we place you within one hundred thousand kilometers of their Guardian, you believe that you will be able to establish communications and effectively disable it?"

"I will, of course, establish communications, but the Krayleck Guardian will in no way be disabled," he said, raising his eyebrows at his Human audience. "Assuming it is functioning normally, it should immediately recognize that I am a more recent, and significantly more advanced, model of the standard Pelaran GCS system. Once that happens, it should provide me with an extended period of time to sufficiently explain the circumstances of our arrival. In the interim, I anticipate that it will follow a set of standard Alliance communications protocols and refrain from attacking your ship."

"I believe I just heard you express several items of uncertainty regarding how the Krayleck GCS will respond to our arrival," Reynolds observed. "Realistically, how certain are you that it will behave according to your standard protocols? Also, how long is this window of time during which it *should* refrain from attacking us?"

"Without going into too much detail, there are very specific rules governing what we are attempting to do, Commander. The most important of which on our side is that I allow myself to be transported by a single vessel representing my cultivated species. On their side, I cannot rule out the possibility that the Krayleck Guardian might do something unexpected. It has, after all, been on station for over two hundred years longer than I have, and there is no way for me to assess the likelihood that something might have gone wrong during that period of time. What I *can* tell you is that, given the current state of affairs between your two civilizations, this course of action is the one most likely to result in the best outcome for Humanity. When communicating with the Krayleck Guardian, I will be following well-established procedures that have been in place since the earliest days of the cultivation program, and have every reason to believe that it will do the same. As to your 'window of opportunity,' you must understand that, from my perspective, I will have ample time to make our case to the Krayleck Guardian —"

"You didn't answer my question," she interrupted.

"It will account for various signal delays, of course, but I must transmit the appropriate information within eight point four milliseconds."

"Grreeaatt," Ensign Fisher said under his breath, drawing a look of stern disapproval from his XO.

"Look at it this way, Ensign," the Guardian replied with his usual, ingratiating smile, "the most likely time for something to go wrong during this entire mission is during that eight point four millisecond window. Fortunately for you, if something *does* go wrong, you'll probably never even know it."

"Although that is indeed a short period of time from our perspective," Prescott said, undeterred, "I'd like you to work with Commander Logan to see if there might be an opportunity for us to take some sort of evasive action in the event your conversation does not go as planned."

"As you wish, Captain Prescott. If, however, the Krayleck Guardian responds as expected, it will agree to immediately depart the area with us. I will then provide a set of rendezvous coordinates a safe distance away so that we can proceed with the operation."

"Right," Prescott said with a raised eyebrow. "I don't mind telling you that we're a little fuzzy on exactly what is supposed to happen after that."

"Understandable, Captain, since we will all be, as you Humans like to say, in 'uncharted territory' at that point. Much will depend on how cooperative the Krayleck Guardian decides to be, but the important thing is that we will have officially removed the Krayleck Empire as a Regional Partner in the Pelaran Alliance."

"So, they will no longer be a 'Regional Partner,' but they will still be part of the Alliance?"

"Oh, yes, their membership will remain valid, but they will be listed as a protectorate, non-voting member."

"A protectorate of whom? Pelara?"

"Of course not," the Guardian scoffed. "The Pelarans would never take on such a responsibility themselves. The Krayleck Empire will become a protectorate of Terra … if or when your world's membership ever becomes active, that is. A great many things will change on Legara after the departure of their Guardian, but perhaps the most immediate, practical consequence is that they will no longer be provided with military or technological support from the Pelaran Alliance."

"Meaning that they will be considerably less of a threat to Terra."

"To say the least. In fact, as a full member, Terra would be entitled to levy various taxes against all worlds within the Krayleck's former cultivation radius in compensation for your protection."

"Well," Prescott said with the same expression of astonishment registered on every other face in the room, "clearly, we have neither the time nor the inclination to explore all of the political ramifications of what we're about to do, but you have certainly filled in some gaps that were not covered in our orders."

"I'm not surprised," the Guardian replied. "Rest assured that removing the Krayleck Empire from the aegis of GCS protection more than justifies the risks associated with this mission. Forgive me for saying so, Captain Prescott, but I'm sure the Leadership Council believed that your orders contained everything you needed to know."

"Fair enough," Prescott said with a smile, recognizing the fundamental truth in the Guardian's rather pointed comment. "We appreciate your explanation in any event. Now, unless you have additional questions for us, we will sign off for the evening. Thank you for the clarifications and for your participation in this mission."

"As always, Captain, I am here to help," the Guardian replied, after which Prescott immediately terminated the GCS-comm video feed from the *Fugitive's* hangar bay.

"Can we form a hyperdrive field and transition in less than eight point four milliseconds?" he asked Commander Logan after confirming that the room was once again secured for discussions requiring code word DEFIANT BASTION clearance.

"Piece of cake, now that we know in advance that it might be a possibility. Our AI processes all kinds of information on a much smaller timescale than that, and we can partially form the field several minutes ahead of time, if necessary. The problem is that getting word from the Guardian in time to do anything about it will require a direct, superluminal connection to our computing core. Is that a risk we're willing to take? Also, while we're on the subject, aren't we giving away a huge cache of our most classified information just by having that thing aboard?"

"I don't think the core connection is any more of a risk than we're already taking," Prescott replied. "I'm obviously not an expert on this subject, but the required connection would allow the Guardian to transmit only — effectively a 'one-way' data connection, right?"

"Yes, sir, that's right. There are some other precautions we can take as well, but this is still the Guardian we're talking about, so all bets are off."

"I know I don't need to say this, but it's critical that it doesn't somehow gain access to anything else. It may well regard itself as our closest ally at this point, but —"

"But we should trust it about as much as a we'd trust a snake in a hamster cage," Logan interrupted with a sly grin.

"Exactly. We just need it to be able to transmit a notification if it believes the Krayleck Guardian is about to attack ... you know, something simple and to the point like 'RUN!' But since we still have a few hours before our departure, I'm going to run this decision up the flagpole to Admiral White and see what kind of response we get. Needless to say, do not proceed until you hear from me, and even if we do get the go-ahead, I still want you to delay making the physical connection until right before our final C-Jump to Legara."

"Understood," Logan replied.

"You also posed the question of whether or not we are giving away classified information. It's certainly possible. In fact, I would say we probably are. Keep in mind, however that the Admiralty and the Council's Military Operations Oversight Committee considered that same question and still gave the mission a green light anyway. They asked the Guardian to provide a comprehensive assessment of what it believes are our technological capabilities as a condition for bringing it aboard one of our ships. Of course there's always an open question as to whether it was being honest in its responses."

"Well that's interesting, and, honest or not, I would very much like to see that list," Logan replied. "If it provided a reasonably accurate appraisal of our tech, that may explain why they thought that having him aboard was worth the risk."

"I haven't seen it either, so we're just speculating at this point, but for what it's worth, I'd say that's exactly what happened. They probably also figure that — even for the Guardian — there's a significant difference between witnessing a technical capability and actually being able to replicate it."

"Humph, I hope that's true, sir."

"Alright everyone," Prescott continued, once again addressing the entire group, "there's one more thing I wanted to show you that might give you a bit more confidence in our ability to complete this mission successfully. All of you are aware that you were granted a new, higher level security clearance before coming aboard the *Fugitive*. That was primarily due to several specific technologies built into the ship's design — the various components associated with her low-observable systems, for example. Fortunately, your clearance also permits access to data from Fleet's new long-range tracking and detection system called Argus."

The ready room's view screen was considerably larger than what one would normally expect for such a small space, but it was immediately obvious that anything smaller would have been woefully inadequate to display such a large amount of information.

"What I'm showing you now is a real-time depiction of every vessel traveling in hyperspace within one hundred light years of the Herrera Mining Facility. As you can see, the Wek Unified Fleet is moving a significant number of ships to the region to defend against any additional incursions from the Krayleck. As you just heard from the Guardian, if our mission is successful, we hope to significantly reduce or perhaps even eliminate the Krayleck threat to Sajeth Collective territory ... which, by the Pelaran definition at least, is also *our* territory."

"Captain," Commander Logan spoke up, "by 'real-time depiction,' you, of course, mean that these are a set of projections based on the ships' last known locations, presumed speed, and destinations, correct?"

"That's largely the same response everyone has the first time they see an Argus display, Commander, but no, this is actual, real-time tracking data. I'll save the dog and pony show for another time, but what you need to know for now is that any three comm beacons deployed within one hundred light years of one another within our NRD network can now form a kind of virtual comm 'array.' These not only extend our previous comm range by about five hundred percent, but they also allow us to track vessels in hyperspace up to five hundred light years from the center of each array."

Logan had no additional questions, and Prescott found himself feeling a vague sense of disappointment — perhaps even bordering on irritation — at the general lack of reaction around the room.

"Man, I thought *I* was getting a little jaded," he said. "So, I guess we've reached the point where the latest technological marvel is just no big deal, right?"

"No, sir, it's not that," Lieutenant Lau replied after a brief period of silence. "It's obviously a huge advance alright, and I can definitely see where it will provide a number of significant advantages. I just think that after seeing something new like this every few weeks for the past several years, we've probably all finally started to get a little 'tech fatigued,' that's all."

"'Tech fatigued,' huh?" Prescott nodded as he shifted his glance back to the view screen. "Yeah, okay, I get it … I really do. We're all very much in need of some time off, and I think that's been made even worse by the fact that we just dropped off nearly two-thirds of our usual crew at Yucca Mountain for extended leave. Admiral Patterson understands that as well and has promised that we'll all get a long break after this mission."

For the first time since the meeting began, Prescott sensed a general uptick in the mood of the room. The change in facial expressions was dramatic to an almost comical degree, and there were general sounds of approval around the table. *These people are mentally and emotionally exhausted,* he thought, realizing that the same thing certainly applied to himself as well.

"So, yes, we'll find a way to get ourselves some time off after this mission — even if we have to commandeer our own ship and go looking for the ultimate in secluded beach planets or something."

"It won't work, sir, they'll know where we are," Lau replied with a chuckle as he nodded at the Argus data on the view screen.

"Oh, we know exactly what they can and can't see. I'll get to that in a moment. In all seriousness, though, this is a critically important mission that could have far-reaching implications for Earth's security. I think we can all agree that removing the Krayleck Empire as a threat in the manner the Guardian just described is a much better option than doing so by force of arms … even if we do appear to have some advantages from a military perspective. It's important to keep in mind that we come from a relatively small planet. While we do appear to have the Crowned Republic of Graca in our corner, the last thing we want to do is run around creating more enemies out here. So ... as usual, I need all of you, and I need you at your best. When we're done here, finish up your prep work and get some rest before tomorrow morning. By now, we all know that we can count on one other, and that's all I have to say on that subject."

"We're still first and best, Captain," Dubashi replied with a broad smile, "and you *can* always count on us."

"I know I can, Lieutenant, thank —"

"But after this we will be happy to be last and best for a while," she interrupted.

"I got it, I got it," he laughed, holding up both hands in mock surrender. "You have my commitment that we'll make that happen. Let's wrap this up, shall we? Commander Reynolds."

"Thank you, sir, and thank you, Lieutenant Lau, for the segue. This ..." she said, changing the configuration of the view screen via her tablet, "shows the current coverage area for Argus tracking data. Each of the five-hundred-light-year range bubbles displayed here corresponds with the geographic center of a comm beacon array. As you can see, all of the aggressive comm beacon deployment we've been doing for the past few months has dramatically increased our ability to see what's coming our way. We now have almost full coverage out to well over one thousand light years from Earth in every direction, and nearly double that in the direction of the Krayleck sphere of influence."

"Wow, okay, this really is incredible," Lau admitted, "but we can only see ships while they're in hyperspace, right? So, unless their Guardian is traveling at the moment, we won't be able to confirm the location Griffin gives us before we make our final C-Jump."

"Not without a degree of uncertainty, no, but the system maintains constant tracks on every contact it detects. After a ship has made several transitions, Argus provides an estimate of its current position based on the patterns it has observed. For example, here is every hyperdrive event generated by the Krayleck Guardian since coverage of the area surrounding the planet Legara was established."

"I only see three transitions," Ensign Fisher said. "How long have we had coverage in place?"

"Less than forty-eight hours," she replied, shooting him a look, "but before you start jumping to conclusions about our lack of data, I can tell you that the transitions we are seeing this thing make are almost identical to what our own Guardian does. Although we haven't found one of them yet, the theory is that it broadcasts ETSI data using a constellation of small drones. They broadcast for a few days, then change locations while the next one takes over. Our Science and Engineering folks think that the Guardians make regular visits to their drones — most likely doing some sort of maintenance. We have absolutely no idea how many of them there are … possibly hundreds."

"So, won't the Krayleck continue to get their ETSI data for … how far from Legara are they?"

"The three transitions we've detected so far vary from two to just over three light years."

"So, for at least two to three years after their Guardian is no longer in the area, they'll keep receiving data?"

"That's a great question that we definitely plan to ask, but unless we can figure out a way to jam the signals from multiple directions, that may well be the case. Our primary concern is making sure that we can at least stop the flow of data at the source. Hopefully, their Guardian has some means of turning off the drones without the need to visit each one. Anyway, here's the good news," she said, zooming in on the planet Legara itself. "Every time it has transitioned in or out, it always ends up at the same location. Argus is currently giving us a better than ninety-five percent chance that it will be located at that same spot when we arrive tomorrow, and we have detected no other ships within three light minutes."

"With any luck, that should be more than enough time to conclude our business. Any questions?" Prescott asked in a reassuring, confident tone.

There was silence around the room, and he was pleased to see the confidence he was attempting to project being mirrored once again in the faces of his crew.

"Good. As Commander Logan said, let's go steal ourselves a Guardian."

Chapter 18

Not surprisingly, the Pelarans gathered an enormous amount of data when selecting candidate civilizations for the cultivation program. As the Terran Guardian itself had once said, everything from potential rivals, to natural resources, to the intelligence and temperament of prospective member species was taken into account. Perhaps the greatest single consideration, however, was location — not only in relation to Pelara and other established members of the Alliance, but also with respect to other cultivated civilizations. The general idea was simple enough — provide the cultivated civilization with just enough technology and intelligence information to ensure their domination of a five-hundred-light-year sphere of influence centered on their homeworld. As a direct result, rival civilizations within this region were also kept in check and thus prevented from becoming a threat to the Alliance.

With the steady, powerful influence provided by the Guardian Cultivation System, the so-called Regional Partnership program had proved successful far more often than not, and had allowed the Pelaran Alliance to flourish in relative peace with only minimal external threats to their collective security. When exceptions did occur, they were typically due to the cultivated civilizations either exceeding their predicted rate of technological development, or somehow stumbling across disruptive technology. Either of these situations could produce unpredictable results — in extreme cases leading the cultivated civilization so far astray that they must be terminated for the good of the Alliance. This situation had, unfortunately, occurred twice during the long history of the program. Until now, however, no species had ever been affected by such a wide variety of factors outside the carefully crafted boundaries put into place by its architects — this time with the added complication of an apparently "rogue" Guardian Cultivation System thrown in for good measure.

So, it was that today, just over fifty years after their first receipt of Pelaran data, TFS *Fugitive* engaged its hyperdrive for a single, instantaneous C-Jump — immediately transporting the small starship from Earth orbit to the extreme edge of Humanity's cultivation radius. This fact was by no means lost on the Guardian spacecraft secured within the ship's hangar bay. Extrapolating based on the Pelaran technology it had provided and taking into account the Terrans' considerable talents in the engineering disciplines, the journey they had just completed in the blink of an eye should have taken at least a year, even using the most optimistic of projections. Although the Guardian had known for some time that the Humans had somehow managed to develop a hyperdrive similar to that used by the enigmatic race they referred to as the "Greys," witnessing their technological achievement firsthand caused the sentient machine to have a response that it had never previously experienced — awe.

Just over fifteen minutes later, the Terrans engaged their hyperdrive once again, this time officially invading the sphere of influence of the Krayleck Empire — a long-established Regional Partner of the Pelaran Alliance.

TFS *Fugitive*, *Krayleck Empire Space*
(0817 UTC - 297.4 light years from Legara)

"Second C-Jump complete, Captain," Fisher reported. "We deployed another comm beacon on the way in, but the pause was barely even detectable during our transition. The beacon is stabilized and transmitting. All systems in the green. C-Jump range down to 6.3 light years but increasing rapidly."

"Low-observable systems?"

"Ah, sorry, sir. LO systems online and currently set to auto-engage after each transition inside Krayleck territory. It's showing six zero minutes remaining at current power levels."

"Very good. Tactical?"

"No contacts, sir," Lau replied. "Argus is still projecting the nearest Krayleck warship to be just over four three light years from our current position."

"Glad to hear it," Prescott said absently while double-checking everything he was hearing via his own Command console. "Alright everyone, we'll be here until we have another full capacitor bank recharge, so count on a dwell time of one five minutes or less once again. This will be your last opportunity to ensure everything is working as expected, so use your time wisely. Engineering, bridge," he continued, rapidly working through his own last-minute checklist.

"Logan here. Go ahead, Captain."

"Everything holding together down there so far?"

"We're in the green down here, sir, but on our second C-Jump, the AI did report a timing anomaly with one of the banks in the capacitor array."

"I've generally not had a good relationship with the word 'anomaly,' Commander. Did you track it down?"

"Yes and no. When we do a max range C-Jump, all four cap banks shunt most of their available power to the hyperdrive at one time. Once we transition back into normal space, they immediately go through a switching routine that places them back into normal recharge mode. That's what allows them to start taking power from the reactors again. On the last jump, there was a brief delay with one of the banks switching back to normal mode — and when I say 'brief,' I'm talking less than one hundred microseconds. The reading we saw was barely out of spec, it didn't cause a problem with the hyperdrive or the reactors, and it was probably nothing to worry about."

"And yet, you told me about it anyway."

"Hey, I always figure it's your job to sit up there and worry about such things, sir. We're running diagnostics just in case, but I really don't think they'll turn up any problems."

"I hope you're right about that, Cheng. What's our projected dwell time?"

"The cap banks will be fully recharged in just under one three minutes."

"If I don't hear from you again, I'll assume we're good to go as soon as we're at full charge. If you see the same anomaly, or any other anomaly for that matter after this next jump, please let me know immediately."

"Will do, sir."

"Thank you, Commander. Prescott out."

TFS *Fugitive*, *Krayleck Empire Space*
(0838 UTC - 4.9 light years from Legara)

With all of the routine reporting and cross-checking out of the way following TFS *Fugitive's* third consecutive C-Jump, the atmosphere on her bridge had taken on a vaguely disquieting air. From Prescott's perspective, the palpable change in mood seemed to have very little to do with the mission at hand, nor did it seem to be related to any lingering uncertainty regarding the ship. In his mind, at least, he was struggling with an overpowering realization they had just traveled nearly twelve hundred and fifty light years from Humanity's homeworld in less than forty-five minutes. The idea that such a mind-boggling feat could be accomplished at all, let alone in what felt like an almost routine manner, was truly difficult to comprehend, and they were as isolated and alone as any Human beings had ever been in the history of the species.

"I realize Commander Logan said he would let us know if he saw the power system anomaly again, but I checked in with him anyway," Reynolds said without looking up from her touchscreen. "He says there were no problems this time and that Engineering is in the green for the final C-Jump whenever we're ready."

"I did the same thing," Prescott said with a smile and a wink. "I'm surprised he didn't say something about it."

"I think he knows better than that," she laughed.

"By the way, Fleet just denied the request for a hard link from the Guardian to our computing core. They didn't offer much of an explanation other than the fact that they deemed the security risks too great."

"In other words, under the circumstances, it's preferable to lose this ship and her crew than to risk allowing it to access our most sensitive data."

"That's always the problem with information security, right? It's the 'unknowns' that tend to pose the greatest risks."

"I suppose it was probably the right call from a risk management perspective," she said with a sigh, "but I still don't have to like it."

"Nope. Disliking our orders is still permitted as far as I know," Prescott said with a forced chuckle as he struggled to remain patient. "Still no contacts, Lieutenant Lau?"

"Nothing yet, sir, but our passive sensor range bubble has only made it out to around four light minutes. If the Argus data is correct, we shouldn't be here long enough to detect anything."

"Or have anything detect us," Prescott replied, feeling as if his ship were strangely exposed so close to the Krayleck homeworld and anxious to keep the mission moving along as quickly as possible. "Lieutenant Dubashi, any ETA from the Guardian yet?"

"No, sir, not yet."

"I honestly didn't expect it to take this long, but I don't think he gave us a specific estimate on the amount of time it would take."

"Which probably means he didn't know," Reynolds replied. "He's rarely short on the details if they are readily available."

"True enough. If I remember correctly, he said that he should be able to detect the Krayleck Guardian 'relatively quickly.' I suppose I just assumed that in 'Guardian-speak,' that would translate into a very short period of time."

"I think we're fine sitting here for a while," she said, sensing the rising tension in her captain's voice and replying in as calming a tone as she could manage under the circumstances. "There are no ships close-by, and even if there were, we should be in good shape for at least as long as the LO systems are masking our presence. But if we get to the point where the system needs to discharge, we might want to consider C-Jumping back out to where we were."

"You mean abort the mission?"

"I don't think it will happen unless their Guardian simply isn't here, but yes. If we keep the LO system engaged for, say, an hour or more, it will automatically vent its stored heat energy before we transition. When that happens, we'll leave a thermal plume so bright that they can hardly miss us if they have any sort of surveillance drones operating in the area … and I think we have to assume they do."

"Yes, but the evidence that we were here is limited to the speed of light, so it seems unlikely anyone would notice before we're gone. I'm honestly more concerned about our outbound hyperdrive signature. We're a relatively small ship, which works in our favor, and Commander Crispin indicated that they have somehow reduced the range from which our hyperdrive field can be detected, but —"

"But what *we* can detect, and what their *Guardian* can detect are likely to be two very different things."

"Exactly."

"Captain, the Guardian is asking to speak with you," Dubashi reported from the Comm/Nav console. "It's audio only, sir," she added with a knowing smile.

"What's the matter, Dubashi, you don't enjoy the always smug avatar option that comes standard with our Pelaran GCS package? I guess I'd have to say I agree with you there. Put him through, please."

Seconds later, a chime indicated that an active "GCS-comm" connection had been established.

"Prescott here," he said by way of a greeting.

"Good morning, Captain Prescott. I apologize for taking a bit longer than expected, but I have made contact with the Krayleck Guardian, and it is expecting our arrival at the coordinates I just passed to Lieutenant Dubashi."

"Hold on there, you say you *contacted* it? You didn't say anything about making direct contact before our final C-Jump."

"Oh dear," the GCS said after a brief pause, "I suppose I just assumed that you knew this was my intention from the context of our conversation yesterday as well as the information I provided to Admirals White and Sexton. Let me assure you that our unexpected arrival in the vicinity of another GCS system would be exceedingly dangerous for your ship to say the least. I regret the misunderstanding, but all is going as planned so far."

Out of the corner of his eye, Prescott noted the sidelong glance from his XO. "That's reassuring to hear, but what caused the delay you mentioned?"

"Without going into too much detail, hyperspace communications require very precise position information. I was able to detect the Krayleck Guardian's transponder, but there was unexpected interference near its location that proved difficult to overcome. It is possible that there is a large vessel or some other structure creating a gravimetric disturbance in the vicinity. Since our last transition, however, I have detected no hyperdrive signatures within three light minutes of the target coordinates. As I indicated yesterday, I am also providing the real-time feed of all vessels traveling in hyperspace within ten light years of our current position."

Prescott glanced at Dubashi for confirmation and received a nod in reply.

"Alright, then, if there's nothing else we need to know, we will make our final preparations and transition shortly."

"I can only make the obvious recommendation of extreme caution, Captain, since we have little notion what we might encounter upon our arrival. When we transition, I ask that you avoid making abrupt changes in course and do not, under any circumstances, use any sort of active sensors that might give the impression that you are preparing to attack. I would likely survive a hostile encounter with the Krayleck Guardian, but you would not."

"Understood. Stand by to transition. Prescott out."

"Just out of curiosity," Reynolds said, "I compared the tracking data the Guardian is providing with our Argus data, and it looks identical."

"That's good news. It would be damned awkward to realize we were being double-crossed by the sentient machine parked on our hangar deck, wouldn't it?"

Chapter 19

TFS Fugitive, Legara System Lagrange Point 4
(0857 UTC - 72.1x10^6 km from Legara)

The *Fugitive's* designers had gone to great lengths to render her as close to undetectable as any starship was likely to become given the current state of Human technology. In spite of their best efforts, however, finding a means to eliminate the brief flash of light that occurred during a transition event had remained elusive. As the ship arrived at the specified coordinates, her presence was immediately detected, not only by the Krayleck Guardian itself, but also by the on-duty military personnel aboard the nearby weapons platform.

The facility was primarily constructed to defend various high-value military and commercial space assets operating at this large, stable location of gravitational balance between Legara and its parent star. Since the Krayleck Guardian had a tendency to loiter here for extended periods, the station also provided a means to keep watch on the Pelaran spacecraft (which, like their Human counterparts, the Krayleck never entirely trusted). Although the Guardian was clearly capable of defending itself, if necessary, the station's crew had always considered their world's GCS to be the most important of the assets they were responsible for protecting, often even referring to themselves as "Defenders of the Guardian."

From the Defenders' perspective, an unexpected hyperspace transition in relatively close proximity to their station amounted to a serious breach of security and a possible prelude to an attack. As they rushed to prepare the station for action, however, they quickly realized that their sophisticated sensor arrays were detecting no evidence whatsoever of an intruding vessel.

***

"Multiple contacts, Captain," Lieutenant Lau reported immediately. "I've got the Krayleck Guardian at just over one five thousand kilometers at three five zero, mark two five relative, but there's also a very large structure on roughly the same bearing at a range of one four thousand kilometers." As he spoke, Lau rapidly entered commands at the Tactical console, resulting in a light and thermally enhanced view of the two contacts appearing in a pair of large windows near the center of the bridge view screen.

"I hate to use sci-fi terms to describe real-world things, but I'd have to call that thing a starbase," Reynolds said, taking over manipulation of the large image via her touchscreen.

"That's as good a description as any," Prescott replied. "Lau, they obviously saw us transition, but can you determine if they are still able to track us?"

"I don't think they can, Captain. They're blasting the entire area with a variety of sensors, but I haven't seen any indications that they have locked onto us with anything."

"I'm guessing things are progressing as planned with the Guardians as well since we're still here," Reynolds added.

"Let's just hope they conclude their negotiations quickly. Regardless of whether or not that station can track us, they still know something is amiss. I suspect we'll have Krayleck warships on the scene shortly."

***

From TFS *Fugitive's* hangar bay, negotiations between the Human and Krayleck Guardians were indeed progressing surprisingly well. According to long-established protocols governing interactions between neighboring cultivated civilizations, the Human Guardian immediately transmitted a burst of data referred to in the Pelaran Alliance as a "petition of ascendancy." The intent was to present an irrefutable case that one species had achieved such an overwhelming position of dominance over the other, that the lesser of the two civilizations was in imminent danger of being destroyed. Since the prospect of one member world completely eradicating another was generally not seen as desirable for the Alliance at large, this process had been developed to allow one member to be incorporated into another — hopefully without the need for unnecessary bloodshed or direct military intervention by other member civilizations.

Even in the rarefied community of Guardian Cultivation Systems, extraordinary claims must be supported by extraordinary data, and in this case, the quantity required was enormous. Every conceivable metric that could be quantified and used for comparison was taken into account. The result was two highly advanced, space-faring civilizations — each one at the center of a sphere of influence encompassing five hundred and twenty-four million cubic light years — reduced to nothing more than vast sets of comparable data. Both Guardians then set about constructing a series of elaborate simulations with the goal of determining how the balance of power in the region was likely to evolve during the foreseeable future.

Even with their combined computing power, the entire process took nearly two minutes, but once their deliberations had concluded, both Guardians had reached the same conclusion as to what must be done.

***

"That's a total of three frigates and two destroyers, sir … in addition to the starbase, of course," Lau reported.

The Krayleck warships had begun arriving less than a minute after the *Fugitive* transitioned into the area. Since then, all conversation on the bridge had taken on a hushed, subdued tone, as if the sound of their voices might somehow give away the ship's position.

"Everyone try to relax," Prescott replied evenly. "They clearly either don't see us at all, or else they're not interested in attacking for whatever reason. The Guardians should conclude their business shortly and we'll be on our way."

"Helm and Tactical," Reynolds spoke up, "in the event we do end up under fire, keep in mind that our main gun is fixed and requires that you coordinate with one another. I know the two of you have done well in the sim, but I don't have to tell you that things are different when someone is actually shooting at you."

"Yes, ma'am," both men replied.

"Captain, I have the Guardian again on GCS-comm," Dubashi reported from the Comm/Nav console. "It's requesting a vidcon this time."

"More talk," Prescott said as an aside to his XO. "I guess that was predictable enough. On-screen, please, Lieutenant."

A window immediately opened on the left side of the view screen, displaying the Guardian's usual avatar wearing an unmistakably triumphant look on its virtual face.

"I am pleased to report that my negotiations have gone exceedingly well, and I am hopeful that I will soon be able to congratulate you and all of Humanity for being granted dominion status within the Alliance. It is a singular accomplishment to be sure, particularly to have achieved such a thing so quickly," it said.

"We're all very much pleased to hear it," Prescott replied, working to prevent any annoyance from registering in his voice. "As I'm sure you are aware, there are now a total of five Krayleck warships in addition to the large military platform operating in the area. All of them are doing everything they can to find us, and will no doubt attack when they do. Is the Krayleck Guardian prepared to depart?"

"Not just yet, I'm afraid. Although the evidence I presented has convinced the Krayleck Guardian that Humanity appears to have become the dominant of your two civilizations, it did point out repeatedly that you have not yet officially joined the Alliance."

"And whose fault is that?" Reynolds replied pointedly.

"There is an unusual set of circumstances to be sure, Commander, but you will allow me to observe that it is also my 'fault' that I have neglected to report back to the Alliance that Terra's technological growth is completely out of control and that it should, therefore, be considered for immediate elimination."

"And we certainly appreciate your being willing to work with us along those lines," Prescott interjected, furrowing his brow at his XO as he did so. "So, what do you advise that we do in order to conclude the negotiations in our favor?"

"That is precisely the correct question, Captain Prescott, and I believe the Krayleck Guardian's chief concern is one of precedent. While there is nothing in the program's guidelines that specifically requires full membership prior to taking on a protectorate, to our knowledge it has never been done before."

"Alright, fine, so what do we do now?"

"When one member has supplanted another in the past, the mission to petition the …" he paused, clearing his throat, "*lesser* civilization's Guardian is generally accompanied by an overwhelming show of force."

"I see. That's certainly possible … we could probably get a sizable portion of TFC's fleet in here within a few hours. But I seriously doubt the Leadership Council would grant their approval for such a mission. Our ships would undoubtedly end up taking on a sizable fraction of the Krayleck fleet right here in the immediate vicinity of their homeworld. Even if we did manage to win — and we might, based on what we've seen thus far — there's no way we can justify something like that."

"You misunderstand me, Captain. As I indicated yesterday, missions of this type are always undertaken by a single ship. It is that single ship that must demonstrate an overwhelming show of force … so intimidating the opposing fleet that it is clear to all that further armed conflict is both unnecessary and foolish."

"Well this would have been handy information to have up front," Reynolds said. "If the idea is to frighten them into submission with a single ship, a *Navajo*-class cruiser would have been much better suited to the task."

"I can assure you that the Admiralty considered just that," the Guardian replied. "But we all believed, or at least hoped, that such a display would prove unnecessary. Admiral Sexton was also of the opinion that, if required, the appearance of a small ship like the *Fugitive* would send a rather unequivocal message of Terran confidence and strength. Besides, after the battle at Herrera, the Krayleck are fully aware of what Fleet's larger capital ships can do. There is a reasonably good chance that they will not choose to further challenge Human ships of any size at this point."

"Right. How much of a chance, precisely?" she asked, knowing full well that the GCS would have calculated the odds — and most likely to a ridiculous degree of accuracy.

"Twenty-four point six three percent," the Guardian replied with an irritating wink.

"Alright," Prescott said decisively, "I don't see any need for further discussion. If we're going to do this, it's better to do it now than wait until half their fleet shows up. Do you have any last-minute advice for us regarding how this has been done in the past? I assume we should attempt to communicate first."

"Each situation is different, so I'm afraid there are no standards for such a thing. You should, of course, attempt to communicate if an opportunity presents itself. It couldn't hurt, right?" Here, the Guardian's avatar looked briefly to one side, stifling a chuckle as if he found the notion of the Krayleck being willing to chat particularly absurd. "If it makes you feel any better," he continued, "I am required to remain ensconced within your vessel during the encounter to ensure that I do not attempt to sway the outcome in your favor."

"And the Krayleck Guardian?" Reynolds asked.

"Could choose to intervene on their behalf or yours, but most likely will not do so since we have followed the proper procedures to establish Terran ascendancy. Once the Krayleck forces submit, I recommend that you cease fire immediately and spare as many lives as possible. If *you* choose to submit, however … well, let's just say that they will most certainly consider a failed attempt to relieve them of their Guardian as an overtly hostile act. I will sign off now to avoid any appearance of direct assistance. Griffin out."

"*Shit*," Prescott swore under his breath after a brief pause, then raised his voice once again to address everyone on the bridge. "Honestly, folks, I have absolutely no idea how this is going to play out, but I think our best bet is to make ourselves as difficult a target as possible when we disengage our LO systems. Beyond that, we'll just have to see how they respond."

"Flexibility," Reynolds said with a shrug of her shoulders. "I've heard it's the key to naval power."

"Uh huh, let's hope that holds true here. Helm, once they start painting us with their sensors, I want plenty of distance between us and that station. Go ahead and begin a smooth acceleration to our best maneuvering speed and put us just outside the farthest frigate. Be prepared to put our nose on her if they open fire."

"Aye, sir," Ensign Fisher replied, already rapidly entering commands at his console.

"Tactical, as soon as we're visible, you're clear to deploy the railgun turrets and beam emitters at the first sign of any hostile intent. Initially, I'd like them all in point-defense mode. If we get into a situation where we need to open fire, it seems to me that the main gun is our only realistic option. We certainly won't have time to make multiple passes at each target and grind our way through their shields as we've done in the past. Agree?"

"Absolutely, sir," Lieutenant Lau replied, nodding emphatically.

"Very good. I suppose it goes without saying, but give us maximum velocity shots on the fire lance unless I say otherwise, and watch your targeting display closely to make sure you deconflict your shots. We do *not* want to hit Legara with that thing."

"Aye, sir."

"Comm, make sure Commander Logan is up to speed on what we're doing and then be ready to hail the closest frigate on my mark."

"Aye, sir. Just so you know, Commander Logan is with us on the tactical comm channel."

"Is he indeed? You good with all this, Cheng?" Prescott asked, glancing at the ceiling.

"With all previously mentioned concerns factored in, yes, sir, I think we're good down here. We'll be watching the main gun and the cap array closely."

The next several minutes passed in relative silence as each member of the *Fugitive's* bridge crew went about the business of preparing the ship for possible combat operations. As was usually the case in such situations, every passing second seemed to increase the level of tension in the room.

"This position will do, Fisher," Prescott finally said, unwilling to tolerate the delay any longer. "Lieutenant Lee, disengage all low-observable systems. Dubashi …"

"Hailing, sir," she replied immediately.

On the tactical plot displays of every Krayleck ship in the area, a single — and quite small — starship simply materialized from the void. Already in the general vicinity of one of their frigates, it took only a few moments for a light-amplified and thermally enhanced image of the intruder to appear on hundreds of view screens throughout the Legara system and beyond. The reaction of most of those watching was initially one of relief, followed shortly thereafter by a mix of confusion and shock. While their AIs had immediately identified the vessel as Human, it was obviously not a ship they had encountered before, and, at first glance, appeared to have only minimal armaments. After the recent events at Herrera, however, they had learned all too well that any apparent similarities to their own warships could be misleading in the extreme.

Based on standing orders to engage any potentially hostile spacecraft in the vicinity of their nearby strategic assets, the nearest two Krayleck warships opened fire.

Within seconds of their doing so, the Human ship seemed to transform before their (both simple and compound) eyes, as multiple weapon emplacements deployed from previously hidden locations all around its hull.

"Helm, evasive action, as required," Prescott ordered. "We're putting a lot on you with the addition of the main gun, so speak up if you find yourself getting overloaded."

"It won't be a problem, sir," Fisher replied, wearing a decidedly wicked-looking grin on his face as he pulled the nimble MMSV into a steep climb relative to its prior heading.

"No response to our hails, Captain," Dubashi reported.

"Keep trying. I'm hoping they will change their minds shortly," Prescott replied.

"The closest two frigates and one of the destroyers are firing at the moment," Reynolds said. "Their gunnery doesn't strike me as being quite as good as ours, but it may not matter with that much ordnance being sent in our direction. Our shields are taking a few hits here and there, but seem to be holding up just fine so far."

"We're a much more difficult target than the *Theseus*," Prescott observed. "Still, there's no need to put off deciding if we have a chance here. Tactical, go ahead and target the nearest frigate and fire as the main gun bears. I'd prefer to avoid causing a reactor breach if at all possible, but I want her out of action, as quickly as possible."

"Aye, sir," Lau responded, then noticed the orientation of the nearest two enemy ships relative to the

Fugitive's current position. Realizing what Ensign Fisher had in mind, he spoke up immediately. "Actually, Captain, is it a problem if we cause collateral damage on the nearest destroyer as well?"

Prescott glanced at the tactical plot, immediately seeing the potential opportunity Lau was referring to, but unconvinced that such a thing was technically possible. "If you two can make that work, be my guest," he replied, then crossed his arms and leaned back in his chair to watch the situation unfold.

At the top of his climb, Fisher rolled inverted relative to their previous heading, then pulled the ship's nose down in the direction of the nearest Krayleck frigate. For his part, Lieutenant Lau simply designated both the frigate and the distant destroyer for attack, specifying that both targets should be impacted by each round fired by the fire lance, if possible. With the farther of the two targets well beyond visual range, it was an absolutely impossible shot for any Human gunner, but for the *Fugitive's* AI, the only real question was whether or not the outbound shells had sufficient kinetic energy to strike both targets. Now, as the imaginary line extending from the *Fugitive's* main, keel-mounted railgun rapidly approached optimum alignment, the ship itself assisted with the minute course corrections required to place both enemy targets along the same line of sight.

"Firing main gun," Lau reported.

At the instant the young tactical officer issued his order to fire, the *Fugitive's* fire control AI had, to a large degree, taken control of the attack — instantly translating its Human crew's rather crude series of commands into the actions it deemed necessary to achieve their intent. Monitoring an enormous number of rapidly changing variables, it immediately determined that there was sufficient time for a four-round burst from the main gun to strike both targets before the relative positions of the three vessels would invalidate its firing solution. Quickly completing and verifying the calculations required to optimize the conditions within the railgun itself, the AI then selected four locations at which relativistic rounds would impact the hulls of both targets. Each impact site was chosen to inflict maximum damage while still avoiding the expected locations of the targets' antimatter containment units. With all required tasks now completed, the AI issued its final clearance to fire, releasing the tremendous bursts of energy required to send the projectiles hurdling toward the Krayleck warships at over one-third the speed of light.

"Both targets hit by the first round! Both targets hit by the second round! Both targets hit by the third round!" Lieutenant Lau reported, nervous energy and excitement temporarily overcoming his military bearing and common sense as he closely monitored the first use of the ship's primary weapon.

Much like the main guns carried by *Navajo*-class cruisers, the fire lance required an intense gravitic field along the entire length of its barrel, temporarily reducing the projectile's mass to zero in order to prevent massive recoil forces from being generated during a launch sequence. Although each shell was only one-eighth the size of those used aboard TFC's cruisers, the rate of fire was more than doubled. As a result, a satisfying, metallic PING could be heard and felt throughout the whole of the ship as each fifty-kilogram kinetic energy penetrator round entered the gun's breach and was forcibly centered between the launch rails. The sound and vibrations — repeating approximately once every three seconds — were unmistakable for anything else heard aboard the *Fugitive*, rendering Lieutenant Lau's play-by-play announcements as unnecessary as they were annoying.

"Both targets ... check that ... sorry, Captain, I'm showing a main gun firing cycle fault. Only three rounds fired."

"Weapons hold, Lieutenant, and don't forget your cross-check. It's important to keep your eyes moving," Prescott replied.

"I'm sorry, sir, what was —"

"Oh, for God's sake, Lau, LOOK UP!" Reynolds chided, gesturing emphatically towards the bridge view screen as the young tactical officer finally exhausted her patience.

Two large windows still displayed zoomed-in views of both Krayleck warships, both of which were still intact, but had ceased fire and appeared to be without power.

"Lieutenant Lee, I need a battle damage assessment," Prescott said.

"As Lieutenant Lau said, all three rounds that fired impacted both targets," he replied. "The AI also flagged three large thermal plumes on the far side of the Krayleck destroyer. That pretty much has to be exit damage, sir."

"So, the rounds ignored their shields and passed completely through both ships," Reynolds said. "As impressive as that seems, doesn't it also imply that there was only minimal damage inflicted?"

"Not at all, ma'am. A large warhead detonating in the right place might be somewhat more effective, but these relativistic rounds carry an unbelievable amount of energy. The projectile itself does a significant amount of damage as it passes through. Keep in mind that it causes explosive decompression in every section of the vessel it penetrates. The shell also trails a shockwave after entering the hull that tends to transfer a huge amount of energy to a much larger volume of space than it would otherwise. To be honest, the research into the physics of relativistic impacts is still pretty spotty, but it's safe to assume that the shells leave a molten path of destruction in their wake."

"The overall power output on both ships dropped off immediately after the impacts. Can we safely assume that they're out of action for the duration?" Prescott asked.

"There's no way to know for sure, but based on where we hit them, I'd be very surprised if they restore anything more than emergency power for the next several hours. If we hit them again, even with our standard railguns and beam weapons, it will be difficult to avoid causing a major structural failure and/or a reactor breach."

"Which we would like to avoid, if possible. Keep a close eye on them for any signs they're about to rejoin the fight."

"Will do, sir."

"Helm, pull back without making it look like we're attempting to run. Let's give them a little time to chew on what they just witnessed."

"Aye, sir."

"Commander Logan, what's the story on the main gun?" Prescott asked, making the assumption that his chief engineer was still monitoring the tactical comm channel.

"Yes, sir!" came the immediate and inordinately loud response — obviously in response to a question not fully understood over the sound of repeated hammer blows in the background. "This thing may be the most advanced heavy gun ever devised, but that doesn't mean it won't jam. The good news is that, at first glance, there doesn't seem to be any damage. I also think I know what caused the problem."

"Excellent. How much time do you need?"

"That's the bad news. If I'm right … and assuming we can clear the jam —"

As if on cue, a loud, metallic clang could be heard in the background as the unfired kinetic energy round was cleared from the gun's breach.

"Okay, good," he continued. "We'll have the gun back online in a few minutes either way. If I'm right, it should prevent another jam of this type. If not, there's really no telling how many rounds you'll get before this happens again. I also can't guarantee the next jam won't cause damage that I can't fix from down here."

"Understood. Keep us posted, Commander. Prescott out."

"Captain, our Guardian is asking to speak with you," Dubashi reported from the Comm/Nav console.

Prescott simply nodded in response, then paused briefly for the chime before speaking. "It's not a great time for a conversation at the moment," he said curtly.

"I apologize for the intrusion, Captain, but I thought you needed to know that I have intercepted a transmission between the Krayleck Guardian and all of their military forces in the area. It has ordered them to stand down or risk complete annihilation. It also assured them that if they will cease all hostilities against Terran forces, it will personally guarantee that you will do the same."

"Dubashi, amend our outgoing transmission to confirm that we agree to the Krayleck Guardian's terms, but add that they must submit to becoming a protectorate of the ..."

"Terran Empire?" Reynolds asked under raised eyebrows.

"Terran Fleet Command will be sufficient for now."

"Well done, Captain," the Guardian said. "That is more or less what I was going to advise you to say."

"Thank you for the update. Please let us know if you hear anything else of note from their GCS. Prescott out," he said, drawing his hand across his throat to ensure that Lieutenant Dubashi closed the audio connection.

"Transmission terminated, Captain," she said.

"Thank you, Lieutenant. Helm, head us back in the direction of the next frigate. Let's put some pressure on them to make up their minds. Commander Logan, we may be in need of the main gun again shortly," he announced hopefully.

"Sorry, Captain, I was about to call you back," the disembodied engineer replied after a brief delay. "One of our techs just discovered a bigger problem down here. The jam somehow damaged one of the grav emitters near the breach. Long story short, it's unlikely that we'll be able to bring the weapon back online."

"You mean not at all? Not even for another short burst?"

"No, sir … not without launching the entire mount assembly out the back of the ship. We're pulling the emitter now to see if there's anything else that can be done."

"Understood. Notify me immediately if anything changes. Prescott out."

Both Commander Reynolds and every other member of the bridge crew were fully aware of the tactically impossible situation they now faced. What followed was an unusually long period of relative silence as each did their level best to avoid being the first person to speak.

"Well … damn," Prescott finally said, more to break the tense silence in the room than anything else. "One thing's for sure, we've committed ourselves at this point. Tactical, I'm not seeing many shield intercept events, are we still taking fire?"

"Sporadic fire only, Captain," Schmidt replied. "We've been doing so much maneuvering that there is really only one frigate in a position to hit us with any degree of accuracy since we took out their first two ships."

"Hmm … we should file that one away for later. I don't think we would have too much trouble hitting them *hard* if our roles were reversed. Helm, big picture, we've got two options right now: bluff or run. We'll obviously run if we have to, but we all heard our Guardian say that doing so would put us in an even more awkward situation that will probably lead to more bloodshed on both sides. So, here's the bluff … I want you to slow your approach and take us straight in to a position where it looks as if we can clearly attack any one of the remaining ships or the station itself if we choose."

"No more evasive maneuvers, sir?"

"No. I want it to look like we're strolling right into their midst without the least bit of concern that they pose any real threat to us whatsoever."

"Kind of like the Guardian tends to act around our ships," Reynolds added.

"Good, yes … like we're walking calmly into the middle of a bar fight with absolute confidence that we'll be the last one standing."

"Aye, sir. No problem."

"We'll probably draw some fire," Reynolds said.

"I'm counting on it," Prescott replied with a cunning smile.

***

From the moment it had appeared, the Krayleck forces had been divided as to how best to respond to the small Terran ship. In spite of their standing orders to engage all "presumed hostile" targets, the captain in command of the weapons platform realized from the outset that something truly unusual was taking place right here within a stone's throw of their homeworld. In spite of the obvious similarities between some of their respective warships, the Terrans had recently decimated a sizable task force *in seconds*. Regardless of the relative sizes of the ships involved, in his mind, such a thing simply did not occur except in situations where the victorious side enjoyed an overwhelming advantage — most likely spanning a wide range of military capabilities.

Accordingly, his intention had been to make every attempt to communicate with the Humans before putting his station and the priceless strategic assets under its protection at unnecessary risk. Unfortunately, before finding the Human ship and having the opportunity to do so, his authority had been superseded by the arrival of five warships from the Krayleck "Home Guard" commanded by an overzealous and, in the captain's opinion, foolhardy excuse for a rear admiral. Within minutes of his arrival, the Terran vessel had materialized like an apparition, already in close proximity to two of the admiral's warships. Rather than recognize this latest technological feat as another indication of a situation where restraint and discretion were more prudent than brash, mindless action, he immediately ordered both ships (one of which was his own) to open fire.

Images of the ruined, lifeless hulks of those two ships were now visible on two large display screens in the station's CIC — nearly-two thirds of their crews presumed dead, including the admiral himself. With the Terran ship approaching once more, and in spite of the rather odd message their Guardian had transmitted, the Krayleck captain now felt that he had little choice but to open fire once more in a final attempt to destroy the small, marauding intruder.

***

"They're firing again, sir," Lieutenant Lau reported evenly. "I've got multiple missile launches this time as well."

"Lieutenant Lee, bring the LO systems back online. Helm, as soon as they lose us, begin a series of evasive maneuvers, then reposition us for another … uh, attack, so to speak."

"Aye, sir," both officers acknowledged as TFS *Fugitive* simply vanished once again on every Krayleck display screen in the area.

"On the bright side, at least the main gun had time to cool down," Reynolds observed sarcastically.

Over the next fifteen minutes, the same tactic was repeated three separate times. In each instance, Lieutenant Lee would briefly reveal the ship's position, draw a massive response from the "starbase" and the remaining three enemy warships, then reengage the LO systems and allow the MMSV to once again fade from existence before the Kraylecks' brooding, lidless eyes. Any missiles launched in their direction quickly lost their targeting solutions and automatically self-destructed shortly thereafter. With the *Fugitive* making herself an easy target each time it appeared, railgun and beam weapons fire quickly intensified, but was easily handled by the ship's gravitic shields long enough to allow for another escape. Interestingly, sporadic shield intercept events provided the last visible evidence of the ship's former position each time the LO systems were reengaged. The result was a brief smattering of white flashes as the ship disappeared — lending a strange, almost supernatural appearance to what was really nothing more than a series of complex interactions between multiple defensive systems.

Finally, just when Prescott was beginning to think that the Krayleck forces might end up calling his bluff and continuing the dangerous game for as long as necessary, the Guardian once again interrupted from the ship's flight deck.

"Sir, I have our Guardian again," Dubashi reported from the Comm/Nav console. "Vidcon this time, sir."

"Captain," Lau spoke up, "sorry to interrupt, but the Krayleck Guardian just transitioned to hyperspace."

"That's either very good or very bad news, I suppose. On-screen, please."

The Terran Guardian's avatar appeared once more on the bridge view screen, this time with a look on his face that seemed vaguely out of place. Although Prescott couldn't quite put his finger on what he was seeing, the impression that immediately came to mind was respect … perhaps even deference.

"Sir," the Guardian began, in a polite tone Prescott was sure he had never heard it use before, "the Krayleck Guardian has yielded to our petition of ascendancy. It has also provided a set of coordinates where we will rendezvous to complete the final steps in this process."

"Are you saying we can safely disengage from the Krayleck forces at this point?"

"They are of little consequence now that their Guardian has submitted."

Prescott glanced at his XO, receiving her trademark shoulder shrug and facial expression conveying the simple question, "Why not?"

"Fine," he said, looking back at the view screen, "we'll be on our way shortly and speak to you again when we arrive at the rendezvous. Prescott out. Comm/Nav, I assume you have the coordinates?"

"Yes, sir. Course plotted and transferred to the Helm console," Dubashi replied.

"Fisher, let's get the hell out of here."

"Aye, sir," his young helmsman replied as TFS *Fugitive* departed the area in a flash grayish-white light.

Chapter 20

TFS Fugitive, Krayleck Empire Space
$(5.18\text{x}10^{11}$ km from Legara)

"Transition complete, Captain," Fisher reported. "All systems in the green with the exception of the main gun. C-Jump range now 489.3 light years, and increasing. LO systems still online with four six minutes remaining at current power levels. Sublight engines online, we are free to maneuver."

"No contacts, sir," Lieutenant Lau added from the Tactical console. "We are now well outside the Legara system. Argus shows the nearest Krayleck warship at approximately fifteen light days from our current position and headed away from us. The Krayleck Guardian is still en route and should arrive in approximately zero five minutes at its current speed. We should be safe enough here for the time being, even if they have surveillance drones nearby that can actually detect us."

"That seems unlikely to me since their ships and weapons platform failed to do so. Comm beacon status?"

"Stabilized and transmitting," Lieutenant Lee replied from the Science and Engineering Console.

"Very good, thank you." Prescott said, drawing in a deep breath and rubbing his eyes.

There was another brief period of silence on the bridge as every member of the crew began their own, personal ritual for releasing the pent-up stress of combat.

"You do realize we just successfully held up a bank by holding our hand in the shape of a gun inside our coat pocket, right?" Reynolds asked with a mischievous smile.

"It does feel like we got away with something, alright, but, frankly, I'm not sure exactly *what* we just did, much less whether or not we should feel good about it. I think that remains to be seen."

"Bridge, Engineering," Commander Logan's voice sounded from the overhead speakers.

"Prescott here. Go ahead, Commander."

"I Just wanted to let you know that you've got your main gun back, but it's a Band-Aid fix at best. Same comment as before — it might fire for half the day without a problem, or it might jam on the first round, so I'd recommend using it as a last resort only."

"Thank you, Cheng. With any luck, we're finished with our attempt to single-handedly take down the Krayleck Empire for today."

"That's good news, Captain. We've got several cranky engineers down here who are past due for a nap."

"Tell them we appreciate all their hard work, but we still need them to hang in there for just a bit longer."

"Will do, sir. Logan out."

"Figures," Reynolds said.

"Hah, yeah," Prescott agreed. "You always have to wonder about the series of events something like that can cause, though … particularly when it occurs at exactly the right time. Had we been able to fire on our last attack run, things might have turned out very differently."

"Maybe. I had a professor in grad school who loved to talk about causality and what might have happened if there had been a minor change of some sort at pivotal moments in history. I try not to spend too much time thinking about things like that, though. Until we find a way to run back the clock — and I hope we never do — it all seems irrelevant to me," she said. "Should we get our Guardian back on GCS-comm before the Krayleck Guardian arrives?"

"Yes, I suppose we should," Prescott replied with a weary sigh. "But I don't mind telling you that I was enjoying a few moments of relative peace and quiet."

"'Pompous-free' peace and quiet you mean," she chuckled.

"I don't know … he seemed to have given himself a bit of an attitude adjustment after the Krayleck Guardian submitted, but I guess we'll see if that holds up. Dubashi, go ahead and bring up the vidcon again, please."

"Aye, sir," she replied.

"Captain," Lieutenant Lau announced, "I've lost the Argus track on the Krayleck Guardian."

"Is there a problem with the system?"

"I don't think so, sir. I can still see several other ships in the vicinity. Their Guardian was a little over halfway here and holding a steady speed when its track just disappeared."

"Give it a moment," Prescott said. "It may just be some sort of interference."

"Aye, sir."

"Dubashi, how about our own Guardian?"

"I'm sorry, sir, but I have not been able to reestablish the feed via GCS-comm. It's not responding for some reason."

Commander Reynolds, suddenly feeling the hair stand on the back of her neck, pulled up a video feed from the *Fugitive's* flight deck. When the Guardian had come aboard, she had noticed several of what appeared to be small access panels scattered around its hull, each accompanied by small, red indicator lights. Quickly zooming in on one of the panels, she noted that all of the lights were now dark.

"AI, Reynolds. What is the current status of the Guardian Spacecraft?"

"Its overall status is unknown, but a significant decrease in overall power output has been observed since our most recent hyperspace transition."

"So, we've lost contact with both Guardians at the same time ... it seems pretty unlikely that those two events are unrelated," she said, still staring at her touchscreen.

"Multiple contacts!" Lau reported excitedly. "I've got the Krayleck Guardian and another small vessel of unknown origin at just under one hundred kilometers."

Within seconds, Lau had placed a zoomed-in image of both vessels on the view screen. The unknown ship was only slightly larger than the Guardian itself. Like the *Fugitive*, it had the flowing, predatory lines reminiscent of a fighter spacecraft, and no obvious weapons could be seen on its smooth, apparently seamless hull.

"As close as they are to one another, they must have transitioned together ... and right on top of us to boot," Reynolds observed. "I guess it's safe to assume they know exactly where we are."

"We are being hailed, Captain," Dubashi said. "It's the small ship. They are offering a video signal, but there is no additional identifying information contained in the data stream."

"On your toes, everyone. I'm not sure precisely what this is, but it's possible we're about to get to the bottom of what this entire mission was really all about," Prescott said. "On-screen, please."

A vidcon window immediately appeared in the center of the view screen bearing an official seal that every member of the bridge crew had seen many times adorning a flag behind the avatar of the Pelaran Guardian. At its center was the unmistakable likeness of a decidedly ferocious-looking griffin. After a few moments, the seal was replaced by what appeared to be a middle-aged humanoid male in business attire seated in the type of ultra-plush leather chair often seen aboard executive transport spacecraft.

"Good morning, Captain Prescott," he began pleasantly. "My name is Verge Tahiri, and I am a regional envoy of the Pelaran Alliance. Please let me begin with an apology for my abrupt arrival. First meetings of this type seem to always require some sort of … shall we say, 'overly dramatic' entrance, but let me assure you that we will endeavor to be much better-behaved guests when visiting the Terran Dominion going forward."

Prescott simply stared back at the man for a long moment, unsure where to even begin. "Well, Mr. … or is it 'Ambassador?'"

"Mister is certainly fine, since we technically don't have ambassadors. My role as an envoy is similar in many ways, however. I am here to act as an intermediary between Earth and Pelara during your world's transition to full Alliance membership."

"Are you, in fact, Pelaran?" Prescott asked, his mind now awash with a seemingly endless series of questions.

"I am indeed," Tahiri replied with an unmistakable look of pride on his face, "but I'm afraid I don't get back there nearly as often as I would like. It's a beautiful world ... remarkably like your own in many ways. That's not a coincidence, of course, as I'm sure your GCS unit has told you."

"Yes, it has mentioned your work to discover the origins of our common genetic ancestry. We are, of course, interested in learning more on that subject going forward. But for now, would you mind filling us in on the implications of what just took place between us, the Krayleck Empire, and their Guardian spacecraft? Also, you just indicated that you are here to act as an intermediary during our transition to Alliance membership. We have been led to believe by our Guardian that membership might no longer be an option for our world. In fact, it has said that we may be in danger of being attacked and destroyed by the Alliance ... something about our 'uncontrolled technological growth,' I believe."

"Ah, yes, there is that," Tahiri replied with a knowing smile. "Let's just say there is significantly more, uh ... *flexibility* along those lines for Children of the Makers and leave it at that, shall we? In any event, that rule has only ever been enforced a couple of times to my knowledge. Both of those cases involved truly loathsome species, by the way — much worse than your new friends, the Kraylecks.

"As to the implications of your successful petition of ascendancy, let me assure you that they are many and far-reaching. Never fear, however. Just as when your GCS unit first made contact, I will provide your Leadership Council with all of the information they need to help your world begin functioning less like a solitary planet and more like the center of a new Terran Dominion."

"I beg your pardon for saying so, sir, but I'm not at all sure that a 'Terran Dominion' is what our Leadership Council — let alone our population at large — had in mind when we agreed to join the Pelaran Alliance," Reynolds said.

"I am certain you are correct, Commander," he said with a casual laugh that immediately reminded both officers of the Guardian. "And let me be equally frank in telling you that it was not our intent for your world be placed in such a position so quickly. Our desire to avoid situations like this is one of the many reasons we impose safeguards to prevent the 'uncontrolled technological growth' Captain Prescott referred to a moment ago. In many ways, your civilization is far from ready to shoulder such a burden. From a practical standpoint, however, this is the situation we have all found ourselves in, and we must endeavor to make the best of it. Besides, all things considered, if your world happens to be located within a Dominion of the Pelaran Alliance, you most definitely want your world to be the Ascendant world. Rank has its privileges, after all."

"Both the Krayleck Guardian and ours have been generally unresponsive since immediately before your arrival," Prescott said, attempting to get as many questions as possible answered before the envoy's departure — which he assumed would be abrupt and could happen at any moment. "Did your arrival have something to do with that?"

"As my grandmother was fond of saying when she was having a conversation and didn't want to be interrupted, 'Quiet … adults are talking.' The same thing definitely applies to GCS units. They are incredibly powerful tools, but they can also be damned annoying at times."

"I'm glad it's not just us who think that," Reynolds chuckled.

"My understanding is that our GCS informed our Leadership Council that, because it had stopped receiving guidance from the Pelaran Alliance, it had made the decision to begin operating of its own free will — independent of Pelaran control," Prescott continued.

"Cute, isn't it?" Tahiri laughed. "First, let me assure you that your GCS unit is functioning exactly as designed. Although they are given a surprising degree of autonomy in administering the cultivation protocols, we would never allow such a potentially dangerous system to operate independent of our control. When it comes right down to it, these things are about as independent as a seven-year-old child camping in his parents' back yard."

Prescott's mind immediately recalled the footage he had seen many times of the Guardian laying waste to Admiral Naftur's original Sajeth Collective task force. Did the Pelarans view such large-scale acts of violence as fully justifiable under the banner of maintaining peace and order within the Alliance — essentially just part of the "cost of doing business" on such a grand scale? Prescott wasn't sure which was more disturbing — the fact that the Pelarans were aware that their Guardians were committing such acts, or that they seemed to be so damnably casual about it.

"And will our Guardian remain on station in the Sol system?" he asked, pushing his personal observations to the back of his mind for the time being.

"Yes, of course, for as long as your world deems necessary, but it will also become less relevant over time since you will be granted direct access to our communications infrastructure."

"And what of the Krayleck Guardian?"

"That will also be up to your Leadership Council. To a degree, it will follow their instructions at this point … as will your own Guardian — with Alliance approval, of course. For now, the Krayleck unit will return to Legara to keep an eye on things. For the near term, my recommendation will be that it remain there to assist with a … shall we say, 'orderly transition' to Terran control. In fact," he continued, apparently issuing commands using a system located just off-camera, "I should probably go ahead and send it on its way now. We find that proper communications are critically important in situations like this, and nothing communicates quite like a GCS system."

"The Krayleck Guardian has transitioned to hyperspace," Lieutenant Lau reported from the Tactical 2 console.

"Now, at the risk of seeming rude, I must take my leave of you. Although I would welcome the opportunity to entertain your questions for as long as you like, the more time I spend doing so, the greater the risk that I will say something in violation of our rather voluminous set of rules governing relations with new Alliance members. My primary objectives here today were to make an official first contact and deliver the documentation I mentioned for your Leadership Council. You have that now, do you not?"

Prescott glanced at his comm officer and received a nod in reply.

"Yes, I believe we do, thank you."

"Very well, Captain. It has been a distinct honor to be the first to officially meet you, and I sincerely hope to have more time for conversation when we meet again. Instructions for communicating with me regarding next steps are included in the, uh … I always like to call it a 'welcome packet,'" he said with a cheerful grin. "I should point out that it also includes important information regarding several tasks or 'challenges' that must be completed as we finalize Earth's accession into the Alliance."

"Challenges?" Reynolds asked, eying Tahiri suspiciously.

"Not to worry, Commander, the tasks to which I refer are more a matter of tradition than a true requirement of your membership. In fact, I believe you Terrans have already completed just about all of them. There is one challenge, however, that all new members must accomplish. You must find your way 'home,' as we say, for Terra's induction ceremony."

"To Pelara?"

"Of course. Admittedly, this does take some new members a while to accomplish, but I will be very surprised if that's the case for you. In any event, I've said far too much already. It has been a pleasure. I bid you good day and a safe voyage home."

"To you as well, sir," Prescott replied, after which the view screen window momentarily returned to the Pelaran seal before going dark.

"The envoy's ship has transitioned to hyperspace," Lieutenant Lau reported shortly thereafter. "Just as before, I do not have an active Argus track on his ship."

"Understood. Thank you, Lieutenant," Prescott acknowledged.

"Sheesh," Reynolds sighed after a brief period of silence, "I wonder at some point if it will stop feeling like we're just passengers on some kind of out of control amusement park ride?"

"I doubt it," Prescott said flatly. "Lieutenant Dubashi, I assume we still have a nailed-up connection to the flagship?"

"Yes, we do, Captain. We haven't heard from Admiral Patterson since we departed from Earth, but the *Navajo* has been actively monitoring our progress. Their CIC comm officer indicated that the admiral expects to hear from us at our earliest convenience once we believe our mission is concluded."

"He does indeed. Go ahead and see if he's available, please."

"Aye, sir."

With barely any discernible delay, a chime from the Comm/Nav console indicated that the CNO was standing by.

"On-screen, please," Prescott said, not waiting for Dubashi to prompt him.

Prescott paused momentarily until Admiral Patterson's smiling face appeared on the bridge view screen, then immediately continued as if the CNO had been sitting in the chair next to him throughout the entire mission.

"Did we get what we needed, sir?"

"You bet we did, Captain. Well, let me back up a moment … no need to tempt fate by saying such things before we're sure, after all. It will take the AI at the Op Center some time to chew on the data you've been gathering, but the early indications are good."

"Were we able to confirm that the Pelaran ship was using something similar to our C-Drive?"

"That's difficult to say at this point, but with the *Fugitive* and several comm beacons in the immediate area, we were able to gather data on four separate transition events. That should go a long way towards improving our ability to track their movements. Just as an example, when Tahiri's ship departed, we were able to determine both its course and approximate distance of travel."

"Any chance he was headed back to Pelara?" Reynolds asked.

"It doesn't look like it, no, but based on what Tahiri said, the Pelarans obviously assume that all new members will come looking for them at some point. Otherwise, I don't think they would issue such a challenge. I'm sure they also understand that we don't have a prayer of establishing any sort of meaningful defense — let alone a 'dominion' — until we know *who* the regional players are, *where* they are, and *what* their capabilities are. The good news is that I'm now confident that it's just a matter of time before we do. A great deal of the credit for that goes to you and your crew, by the way."

"Thank you, sir," Prescott replied with a weary smile.

"I'm pretty sure I promised all of you some much-deserved leave after this mission, and I can't have you thinking that I'm not a man of my word. I'll need you to release old GORT back into the wild, so to speak, when you get back. Once that's done, return to Yucca Mountain for a quick debrief and then I'll personally guarantee that you'll all be left alone for at least a month. Sound good?"

"It sounds a lot better than good at this point, Admiral. Thank you, sir."

"Very nice job … all of you. Patterson out."

"We should move things along quickly before something else happens to change his mind," Reynolds said with a furrowed brow.

"I couldn't agree more," Prescott chuckled. "Dubashi, clear an arrival point for us and transfer to the Helm console please. Let's get things buttoned up and head home."

"Aye, sir," she replied, then paused and turned around in her chair. "Sir, our Guardian apparently just came back online and immediately asked to speak with you. It says that it's urgent."

"Ugh, what now?" he groaned, wondering why Tahiri couldn't have commanded the system to remain offline until they arrived back in the Sol system. Prescott sat silently for a moment, delaying his response while considering whether he might get away with simply ignoring the request. "I have a feeling I'll probably regret this, but put it on-screen, please."

"Captain," the GCS began without preamble the second his avatar appeared on the bridge view screen, "it is of the utmost importance that I be returned to Earth immediately."

"We're preparing to depart now. Is there a problem I can help you with?"

"I'm afraid there is no time to discuss the particulars at the moment. Suffice it to say that another civilization has chosen this moment to make contact with your own — undoubtedly taking advantage of my absence in order to do so. I should not have to tell you at this point that all such arrivals should be considered hostile until proven otherwise."

"Agreed. Fisher, do we have a cleared arrival point?"

"Yes, sir."

"Execute your C-Jump."

"Aye, sir. C-Jumping in 3 ... 2 ... 1 ..."

Epilogue

Earth, TFC Yucca Mountain Shipyard Facility

Not surprisingly, the unexpected arrival of an alien spacecraft outside the Yucca Mountain Shipyard's massive blast doors had caused a great deal of consternation among local Fleet personnel — progressing immediately thereafter to members of both the Admiralty and the Leadership Council. For better or worse, however, there had been little time for debate regarding how best to respond. The circular — perhaps more accurately described as "disk-shaped" — ship hovered silently outside the facility for just under one minute before a four-hundred-meter by four-hundred-meter section of the mountainside sank below the surrounding surface then slowly began to open along its centerline.

Over three hundred years earlier, a smaller but remarkably similar-looking vessel had crash-landed near the Roswell Army Air Field. After a botched press release revealed the presence of the mostly intact spacecraft, it had been quickly relocated to the Indian Springs Air Force Auxiliary Field — better known to this day by a variety of other names including "Area 51" or simply the "Groom Lake Facility." There, just seventy kilometers from the Yucca Mountain Shipyard, it had been painstakingly studied in relative secrecy for the better part of three centuries until the arrival of the Pelaran Guardian spacecraft and the subsequent formation of Terran Fleet Command.

Now, without seeking to establish communication of any sort, let alone permission to enter one of the most secure facilities on Earth, the ship simply proceeded through the blast doors into the long, sloping cavern. Once clear of the entrance and on its way down the two-kilometer-long tunnel to the shipyard proper, the huge doors began to close once again behind it, seemingly of their own accord.

Although apparently no longer in command of the facility's access control systems, TFC personnel did at least still control the lighting throughout the entrance cavern, all of which had been switched on at maximum intensity. Onlookers crowded the large control room windows to one side of the cavern, each of them determined to catch a glimpse of the ship that was somehow so strangely familiar that it was difficult to think of it as an intruder.

The ultimate intent of the ship's occupants was unclear as were their reasons for choosing to make such a dramatic entry into one of TFC's primary shipbuilding facilities (although the facility's AI had already assessed a less than ten percent probability that they were overtly hostile). For the moment, there was nothing to be done other than simply waiting to see what they would do next. What everyone present did know beyond a shadow of doubt, however, was precisely the same piece of information that had caused the Guardian spacecraft such alarm. At long last, the enigmatic "Greys" had returned to Earth.

End of Book 4

THANK YOU!

I'd like to express my sincerest thanks for reading *TFS Fugitive*. I hope you have enjoyed the story so far and will be interested in the next installment of The Terran Fleet Command Saga.

If you did enjoy the book, I would greatly appreciate a quick review at Amazon.com, or wherever you made your purchase. It need not be long or detailed, just a quick note that you enjoyed the story and would recommend it to other readers. Thanks again!

Have questions about the series? For example: How long will the "saga" be? Why is the story divided into multiple books? How do I find out about the next release? Please visit my FAQ at:

AuthorToriHarris.com/FAQ/

While you're there, be sure to sign up for the newsletter for updates and special offers at:

AuthorToriHarris.com/Newsletter

Have story ideas, suggestions, corrections, or just want to connect? Feel free to e-mail me at Tori@AuthorToriHarris.com. You can also find me on Twitter and Facebook at:

https://twitter.com/TheToriHarris

https://www.facebook.com/AuthorToriHarris

Finally, you can find links to all of my books on my Amazon author page:

http://amazon.com/author/thetoriharris

OTHER BOOKS BY TORI L. HARRIS

The Terran Fleet Command Saga

TFS Ingenuity
TFS Theseus
TFS Navajo
TFS *Fugitive*

ABOUT THE AUTHOR

Born in 1969, four months before the first Apollo moon landing, Tori Harris grew up during the era of the original Star Wars movies and is a lifelong science fiction fan. During his early professional career, he was fortunate enough to briefly have the opportunity to fly jets in the U.S. Air Force, and is still a private pilot who loves to fly. Tori has always loved to read and now combines his love of classic naval fiction with military Sci-Fi when writing his own books. His favorite authors include Patrick O'Brian and Tom Clancy as well as more recent self-published authors like Michael Hicks, Ryk Brown, and Joshua Dalzelle. Tori lives in Tennessee with his beautiful wife, two beautiful daughters, and Bizkit, the best dog ever.